# TO STOP NATHAN BRAZIL OR NOT
# TO STOP NATHAN BRAZIL—
# THAT WAS THE QUESTION!

But a solid majority, it appeared, did not give a damn about the rest of the universe, didn't care about anything but its own survival and was all for a fight. That was to be expected, Ortega knew. When a nation was faced with a choice between abstract principle or complete self-interest, it took self-interest every time.

A discussion followed.

Finally it came down to a vote.
   713 voting:
      431 to stop Brazil
      184 to try some kind of deal
       98 abstaining or, in essence, voting to do
          nothing

The tally was remarkably close to the guesstimate Ortega had made on his map during the debates.

"So the motion's carried."

"IT'S WAR!"

Also by Jack L. Chalker
*Published by Ballantine Books:*

# Twilight

## AT THE

# Well of Souls:

## THE LEGACY OF NATHAN BRAZIL
Volume 5 of
THE SAGA OF THE WELL WORLD

## Jack L. Chalker

**A Del Rey Book**

BALLANTINE BOOKS • NEW YORK

A Del Rey Book
Published by Ballantine Books

Library of Congress Catalog Card Number: 80-66176

ISBN 0-345-28368-6

Manufactured in the United States of America

First Edition: October 1980
Second Printing: October 1980

Cover art by Darrell K. Sweet

This one, believe it or not, is for the National Park Service, for having such wonderful places as Stehekin, Washington, where the Well World was born, and such nice folks as those rangers at Chiricahua National Monument, without whom I might never have been seen or heard from again.

# CONTENTS

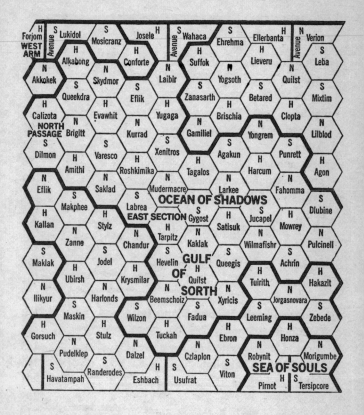

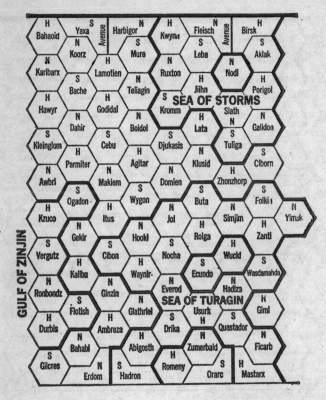

H – Highly technological
S – Semitechnological
N – Nontechnological

# THE WELL WORLD
## Section of Southern Hemisphere

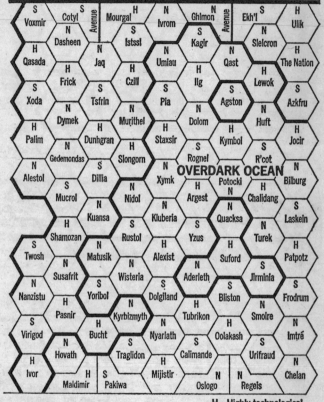

The Well World map, Section of Southern Hemisphere. Hexagonal regions labeled:

Voxmir, Cotyl, Avenue, Mourgal, Ivrom, Ghlmon, Avenue, Ekh'l, Ulik, Dasheen, Istssl, Kagir, Slelcron, Qasada, Jaq, Umiau, Qast, The Nation, Frick, Czill, Ilg, Lewok, Xoda, Tsfrin, Pia, Agston, Azkfru, Dymek, Murithel, Dolom, Huft, Palim, Dunhgran, Staxsir, Kymbol, Jocir, Gedemondas, Slongorn, Rognel, R'cot, Alestol, Dillia, Xymk, **OVERDARK OCEAN**, Potocki, Bilburg, Mucrol, Nidol, Argest, Chalidang, Kuansa, Kluberia, Quacksa, Laskein, Shamozan, Rustol, Yzus, Turek, Twosh, Matusik, Alexist, Suford, Patpotz, Susafrit, Wisteria, Aderleth, Jirminia, Nanzistu, Yoribol, Dolgiland, Bliston, Frodrum, Pasnir, Kyrbizmyth, Tubrikon, Smoire, Virigod, Bucht, Nyarlath, Oolakash, Imtré, Hovath, Traglidon, Calimande, Urifraud, Ivor, Maldimir, Pakiwa, Mijistir, Oslogo, Regeis, Chelan

H—Highly technological
S—Semitechnological
N—Nontechnological

# South Zone, the Well World

"A MORVATH SQUAD REPORTS IT DEFINITELY JUST killed Nathan Brazil," the Czillian said wearily, limbs drooping and pumpkinlike head somehow conveying a note of exhaustion as well.

Serge Ortega sighed. "How many does that make today?"

"Twenty-seven," the plant-creature responded. "And it's early yet."

Relaxing, Ortega sat back on his great serpentine tail and shook his head. "You have to admire the genius of it, though. He *knew* the Well World Council would never dare let him back in. So he gets surgeons back in the Com to remake a bunch of people roughly his size and build and sends them through. Got to admire it. Got to admire the guts of the people who let such a thing be done to them, too—unless they're damned naïve or just damned fools."

The Czillian's vineline tentacles formed a very human shrug. "No matter. What does it get him? We just kill every one that comes through, anyway—and we *know* he has to come through looking pretty much the way our photos say he looks. Even if he should get by in some kind of disguise, we *know* he has to show up in Ambreza—and that hex is an armed camp with wall-to-wall watchers. How could one of known appearance, naked, shorn of disguise, ever hope to elude them?"

"You don't know Brazil," Ortega responded. "I do. Now, stop thinking like a computer for a moment and start thinking like a pirate. Nate's a nasty, clever pirate—almost equal to me in the way he thinks. Smart, Grumma. Real smart. He understands us, the way we

1

think, the way we react to things—look how easily he
figured he'd need all this window dressing to sneak
in. Now, he certainly realizes that we would expect
him and lay a snare. If *you* guessed that far in advance of putting this plan into action, and *you* knew
the limitations, when would *you* arrive in the Well
World?"

The Czillian considered that one a moment. "I cannot say. Wait, perhaps, until we're so sick and tired of
killing imitations that we stop?"

Ortega shook his head firmly from side to side.
"Never. Too risky. Communication between the Well
World and the rest of the universe is strictly one way.
He'd have no way of knowing when we reached that
point—or if we'd ever reach it. Uh uh. Not like Nate
to take that kind of a risk when the operation's so important."

"When, then?" The Czillian was curious. Coming
from a hex whose social system resembled a great university, the creature was well versed in the most esoteric knowledge, but its life had been a sheltered one
and this sort of devious thinking was beyond its experience.

"I keep wondering about the others, the first
through," Ortega told Grumma. "Okay, so you send
your key people in first so they get through. That
makes sense. If we'd known something was up on this
scale ahead of time, we'd have stopped the plan right
there. And the Chang girl—why did she actually stop
in here to see me? Old times' sake? She has more reason to kill me than anything else—and she's one of my
kind, too. No idle curiosity, either. The risk was too
great that I'd smell a rat. Uh uh. Why come in, introduce herself, then tell me there was this great plot in
the works and that Brazil was coming back?"

The Czillian was patient but only to a point. "All
right. Why?"

Ortega smiled admiringly. "It came to me only this
morning, and I could ram my head against a wall for
not catching on sooner. She did it for several reasons.
First, she sounded me out on how I'd feel about all
this and got a measure of what power I might still

have here. Second, she guaranteed that this sort of operation—a hunt for Brazil—would take place."

"But that would doom Brazil," the Czillian pointed out.

The sickly grin widened. *"Not if Nathan Brazil was already here,* ahead of them all. We'd waste so much time hunting for him, we'd never look for him in Ambreza until it was too late. Want to bet?"

"Do you have any proof of this?" the Czillian asked skeptically.

"It's the old shell game," the snake-man continued, partially ignoring the question. "You take three shells, put a pebble under one, then shuffle them in such a way that you misdirect the sucker. He *thinks* he sees the shell with the pebble move to the right, but that's illusion. The pebble's stayed in the middle. That's what happened this time. First the pebble—Brazil—slipped in, then we were left staring at the shuffling of empty shells."

"But do you have any proof?" the Czillian persisted.

Bushy eyebrows rose. "Proof? Of course. Once I realized that I'd been had, it was simple." Ortega reached across his *U*-shaped desk and his lower right hand pushed a combination of buttons on a small control panel. A screen on the far wall flickered to life, showing a still of the great Well Gate chamber through which entered all who fell into the teleportation gates of the long-dead Markovians. Cameras had been set up in there for as long as any could remember so that no one would enter without being seen and given his introduction and orientation to the Well World.

Images flickered across the screen; strange shapes from twenty or more different worlds, their only commonality their carbon-based structure. Non-carbon-based life automatically went to the North Zone.

"We're going backward," Ortega told his associate. "Backward from the point at which Chang and her friends came through."

"How far back in time are we now?" the plant-creature asked, while examining the image of a spindly structure seeming without head, tail, or limbs.

"Three weeks. I went back further than that. There! There's the one I was looking for!" One of Ortega's six arms shot out and stabbed a button, freezing the picture. "That, my friend, is Nathan Brazil," he said flatly."

The Czillian stared. The figure on the screen was small and lithe, but it was by no means the sort of creature Grumma knew Brazil to be. A humanoid torso of deep blue ended in hairy, goatlike legs; the satyr's face peered through dark-blue hair and a full beard: two small horns protruded atop the head.

"That is not a Type 41," the Czillian noted. "That is a 341—an Agitar."

Ortega chuckled. "No it's not. Oh, true, it *looks* like one, but it's supposed to. A fine make-up job, if I do say so, but Nate probably called in the best costumers in the business on it. The disguise is so perfect it'd fool the Agitarian ambassador here, I'm sure —provided Nate didn't have to demonstrate his electric-shock ability. He counted on nothing but coming in, meeting with the duty officer, receiving the standard briefing, and then being shoved through the Well. Very clever. We'd never even notice. We get two or three of his type every century. Very clever. Insidious."

"Then why are you so sure he isn't just a 341 Entry?" the plant-creature persisted.

"He made a slip," Ortega responded. "One lousy slip. A slip I would never catch until too late—that nobody would catch here in Zone. Deliberate, I think. At least there was no way around it. He didn't know the language of the . . . Saugril, I think they call themselves out in the universe. That race and the Com never met, so he couldn't know it."

"You mean in the preliminary interview he spoke something else?" the Czillian pressed, amazed. "And that's what gave him away? But, then, why wouldn't it have betrayed him at the time?"

Ortega chuckled. "How do you and I converse? I'm speaking Ulik, a tongue your rather odd vegetable sound generator couldn't approach. By the same token, your speech is the wrong set of frequencies for me to even hear. Yet we talk normally like this and are understood."

"Ah!" the Czillian's strange pumpkin head came up, its perpetual look of amazement only adding to its body language of understanding. "The translators! Of course! Basically they are telepathic projectors."

The snake-man nodded. "Sure. And for purely diplomatic reasons, we all wear them in Zone. All of us. The master communications system here is only a larger, more sophisticated external version so we can understand the Entries without an operation. He knew it'd take whatever he spoke and translate it into our own languages as if he were speaking ours."

"But isn't that dangerous? Didn't he risk running into a former 341 Entry?"

"Pretty slim, you'd admit," he responded. "And, besides, most races have a number of languages— and things change even more with time and distance. No, he slipped because of the language he used and the fact that I was one of the very few people on the Well World who might recognize it. I have to tell you I needed computer help to defeat my own translator mechanisms."

"And the language?"

Ortega smiled. "It is ancient Hebrew. We had a couple of rabbis come through, and the language is in the data-center computers. It's Hebrew all right—a Type 41 language and one he knows well. Oh, the man is so damnably clever!"

The Czillian shook its head slightly in wonderment. "He is quite an actor," it noted. "Who was the duty officer who processed him?"

Ortega spat. *"Me,* damn his hide. *Me!"*

"This means that Brazil arrived before his agents," the Czillian pointed out needlessly. "He was through Ambreza before we even knew anything was amiss. He could be anywhere by now. Anywhere!"

Ortega shook his head slowly from side to side. "No, not anywhere. Ten to one he moved from Ambreza into Glathriel as quickly as possible. He knows the territory well. I think he is the Markovian who designed that particular race. They're still pretty

primitive, but that would give him an advantage. Get
some dye to make himself a little darker, like the
people of Glathriel, some native dress, and he'd fit
right in. Lie low until his people could help him out.
He'd be conspicuous on the move, remember. He'll
need help, native help—or native-looking help anyway. That's our only ace in the hole. Our only one.
He couldn't prepare much in advance. Once in, he'd
have to hide and wait."

"He seems perfectly capable of hiding out indefinitely," the Czillian noted with unmasked apprecia-
tion.

"Hiding out, yes," the Ulik agreed. "But he can't
hide out. Not indefinitely. Sooner or later he's going
to have to come out of his hidy-hole and move. At
the very least he's got something like eight hexes to
traverse—well over three thousand kilometers. And
we can be sure he'll take anything but the direct
route. The only thing he has in his favor now is that
we have no idea to which Avenue he's going, or
when, or how."

"The only thing," Grumma repeated sarcastically.

"Once he starts to move, he's playing my game,"
the snake-man continued, oblivious to the other's
tone. "Only trouble is, he knows that as well as I do
—and he's been a step ahead of us all the way."

"What do we do in the meantime, though?"

"We put people on all the key agents, the ones
who came through first. Mavra Chang in particular
—she's the best he's got, possibly the most dangerous
woman I've ever known. And she thinks like him.
Beyond that, I think we must convene an emergency
session of the council—North as well as South."

The Czillian appeared surprised. "Is the North
necessary?"

"It is. It's their fight, too, remember. And consider
this. I have reports of a large number of Entries
winding up as Northerners."

"But that's impossible!"

"Uh uh. We have only 780 hexes here in the
South, all in careful balance. The population's maintained, stablilized by the Well so it never exceeds the

available resources. It's overloaded already. We're doubling the population, you realize that? And there's no end to them! So the Well's kicked in its emergency system—it's started filling in Northern Hexes as well to distribute the flood tide. And that means Brazil now has loads of Northern followers as well."

"But he can't get past North Zone," the Czillian pointed out. "You know the Well Gates don't work that way."

"I only know that centuries ago a whole shitload of Southerners, Chang included, went North. We can't afford to overlook anything. It'd be just like the son of a bitch to come back to Zone, go to North Zone, then into an Avenue from the other side. Who'd expect it?"

"I'll set the Council session up," the plant-creature responded meekly. "Anything else?"

"Yeah. As quickly as possible, I want reports on Chang and the other two who came in with her. I want to know what they are, where they are, and what they are doing now. Let's move!"

The Czillian left hurriedly, and the door to the Ulik Embassy at South Zone hissed closed. Serge Ortega leaned back wearily on his massive, coiled serpentine tail and sighed, then turned silent, his six arms folded contemplatively. He rocked back and forth, slowly, as if meditating, although actually he was deep in thought. The silence was absolute.

And then, quite suddenly, it was broken by the sound of someone clearing its throat.

Ortega jumped and whirled, shocked by the sound, then stopped, staring wide-eyed at the intruder, who was lounging quite comfortably on a cotlike couch.

The alien was a Type 41—a human, just as Ortega had once been, but that had been so long ago he had almost forgotten what it was like. Lanky, dark-complected, with a lean, heavily boned triangular face, he was dressed in a plaid work shirt, heavy slacks, and well-worn boots. For a moment Ortega thought it must be Brazil, and a thrill shot through him. But, no, he told himself, Brazil could disguise himself in a number of ways, but he couldn't add fifty or more centimeters, at least not so convincingly.

"Who the hell are you, and how did you get in here?" Ortega asked the newcomer.

The man shifted around and put his arms behind his head, looking comfortable and slightly amused by all this. "Just call me Gypsy," he replied lightly. "Everybody does. Mind if I smoke?"

His insolent manner irritated Ortega, but curiosity overwhelmed all other emotions. "No, go ahead."

Gypsy reached in a shirt pocket and removed a long, thin, Com-style cigarette frm a pack, then a small silver lighter, and lit up. Curls of blue-gray smoke rose into the air as he puffed to make sure it was lit.

"Thanks," he responded, putting the lighter away and resuming his comfortable posture. "Filthy habit, I admit, but handy. What with the Ambreza monopoly on tobacco here, they're better than gold."  •

A coldness crept up and down Ortega's spine. "You have to have heard that at a briefing, probably one by Brazil," he guessed. "The humans here don't look much like you. You have just arrived here. I'm surprised they didn't shoot you."

Gypsy chuckled. "They didn't shoot me because I didn't just arrive at all. I've been here for weeks, in fact. As to how I got here, I came through the Zone Gate."

"Now I know you're lying," the Ulik accused. "The Ambreza wouldn't let *any* Type 41 through the Gate right now."

"I didn't use the Ambreza gate," Gypsy responded cooly. "I used . . . ah, shall we say, a different gate. I'd rather not say which one right now."

The chills were back, although Ortega couldn't say why he believed this man. "That's impossible," he retorted. "The Well doesn't work that way."

"I know it doesn't," the newcomer responded, unperturbed. "If you say so."

"Maybe you had better explain yourself," the ambassador said warily.

Gypsy laughed. "No, I don't think so. Not right now, anyway. But I found your conversation with the Czillian fascinating. You took a lot longer to catch on than we'd figured, you know."

That was the most irritating comment so far, mostly because Ortega had to agree with Gypsy. He didn't like being suckered. He liked to be, and usually was, in control.

"Anyway," Gypsy continued, "I'm here to talk to you. Just talk. As an ambassador, you might say, from the newcomers."

"From Brazil, you mean."

"Him, too," Gypsy admitted. "Mostly you got it doped out right now and we want to know what you're gonna do next."

Suspicion creeped into Ortega. "You're not another Markovian, like Brazil?" he suggested. "I kind of figured if there was one, there were more."

Gypsy laughed. "No, not another Markovian. I'm not even as old as you are, Ortega. And Brazil—well, I'm not sure what he is, but I don't think he's a Markovian."

"He claims to be God," Ortega pointed out.

Gypsy laughed again. "Well, maybe he is. I don't know. And you know what? I don't really give a damn. All I know, all *anybody* knows, is that he's the only guy around who knows how to work the Well of Souls. That's all that really matters, isn't it? Not who or what he is, or you are, or I am. But, no, that's wrong. What you are counts a little, I think. That's why I'm here."

Ortega's bushy eyebrows rose. "Why?"

"Why don't you let 'em get in there, Ortega? Make it easy on them. You know he ain't gonna do anything to louse up your little empire here. He doesn't give a damn."

"You know I couldn't, even if I wanted to," the Ulik responded. "I don't run this world, no matter what you may think. Self-interest runs the world here, just like everywhere else. He's trying to get into the Well to switch it off, make repairs. Too many nervous governments here to allow that."

"But the Well World's on a separate machine," Gypsy pointed out. "His turning off the big machine won't really do anything here. They all should know that much, anyway."

Ortega shrugged all six arms. "They only know what I know and they only believe a fraction of that. We have only Brazil's word on that sort of thing. And if we take him at his word, then this new universe he's going to create will need seeds, new Markovian seeds like the last time. This planet was built to provide those seeds. If we take him at his word on how the system works, he'll depopulate the Well World in that reseeding. The Well governments face extinction, Mister Gypsy, or whoever you are. No getting around that!"

"Not if you help," the man came back. "You and I know that the natives are already murdering hordes of newcomers in many hexes. There are proposals simply to kill everything that comes in through the Well Gate. You gotta stop that, Ortega. One way or another. Don't you understand? These newcomers *are* the seeds!"

The Ulik's jaw dropped in amazement. "Of course! That makes sense! I don't know what's wrong with me these days. Senility, I guess. But—just saying so won't make the plan acceptable. They're scared, mister. Scared little people. They won't take chances."

"But you can stall, do what you can. Your influence is still pretty strong here. You know it and I know it. You got blackmail on most of those little men. We need time, Ortega. We need you to help us get that time."

Serge Ortega leaned back and sighed once again. "So what's your plan?"

Gypsy chuckled dryly. "Oh, no. We trust you just about as far as you trust us. One thing at a time. But you know your part—if you'll do it. There's no real cost to you, I promise you. You have Brazil's word on that and you know that's good."

"I'll do what I can," the snake-man responded, apparently sincere.

Gypsy got up, stamped out his cigarette on the shiny

floor, and looked around at the large office. "Tell me, Ortega, how do you stand it—being trapped in here all the time, year after year, for so long? I think I'd go nuts and kill myself."

A wan smile came to Ortega's face. "Sometimes I think of that. It's easy, you know, for me. All I have to do is go to the Zone Gate and go home. I'm over two thousand years old, you know. Too old. But the spell that keeps me alive traps me here. You should know that." His voice dropped to a dreamy whisper and he seemed to be gazing at not his visitor or the wall but something beyond the wall, something only he could see. "To feel wind again, and rain, and see the stars one last time. Oh, by God! Do I dream of that!"

"Why not do it, then? At least, do it after this is all over."

The Ulik snorted. "You don't really realize my trap, do you? I'm a Catholic, Gypsy. Not a good one, perhaps, but a Catholic nonetheless. And stepping back there—it would be suicide. I can't bring myself to do it, you see. I just can't kill myself."

Gypsy shook his head in silent wonder. "We make our own hells, don't we?" he murmured, almost too softly to be heard. "We make 'em and we live in 'em. But what kind of hell could be worse than this one?" He looked squarely at Ortega and said, louder, "You'll hear from Brazil himself shortly, and I'll keep in touch." And with that he walked over to the office door, which opened for him, and stepped through. It closed behind him, leaving only the butt on the floor and the smell of stale cigarette smoke as signs he had ever been there.

The Ulik wasted no time. He rammed an intercom button home. "Attention! Apprehend a Type 41 just leaving the Ulik Embassy." He gave Gypsy's dress.

There was silence on the other end for a moment, then the guard outside, working to handle the hordes of incoming people more than as a police force, responded, puzzled, "But, sir, I've been just outside your door the past hour. Nobody's come out. Not a soul since that Czillian, anyway. And definitely no Type 41."

"But that's impossible!" Ortega roared, then switched off and looked over at the floor. The crushed butt, to his great relief, was still there.

The intercom buzzed and he answered it curtly.

"Ambassador Udril here," came a translator-colored voice.

"Go ahead," Ortega told the Czillian ambassador.

"On that information you wanted on those three Entries. The one, Marquoz, is a Hazakit and is, well, it's hard to believe after only a few weeks . . ."

"Yes?"

"Well, Ambassador, he appears to be the new head of the Hazakit secret police."

Ortega almost choked. "And the others?"

"Well, the woman, Yua, appears to be enlisting fellow Awbri into some sort of military force with surprising ease. And as for Mavra Chang . . ."

"Well?" Ortega prompted, feeling increasingly out of control.

"She seems to have appeared as a Dillian, enlisted some local help, and, well, vanished."

"Vanished! Where? How?"

"A few days ago she and a small party of Dillians went into the mountains of Gedemondas. Nobody's heard anything from them since."

# Hakazit

IT WAS A HARSH LAND. THE PLANET FOR WHICH IT was a laboratory model must have been something hellish indeed, Marquoz thought. The terrain was a burned, ugly, hard-packed desert with jagged, fierce-looking volcanic outcrops. Occasionally earth tremors would start slides and the very rare but horribly violent storms sometimes turned dry, dusty gullies into deadly torrents which carved great gashes in the landscape.

With almost no water on top, and the ocean to the north salt water only, the people were where the fresh water was—underground, on the bedrock at the water table, in huge caverns carved by millennia of erosion on the basic limestone and marble beneath. There had been predators, too; terrible, fierce beasts with skin like solid rock and endless appetites for Hakazit flesh.

And so, of course, the Hakazit were built for combat and for defense. Like granite itself, their fierce, demonic faces were tough skin over extremely thick bone, their features fixed in a furious and chilling expression, broad mouths opening to reveal massive canines capable of rending the flesh of their wild natural enemies. Their eyes were skull-like sockets that glowed blazing red in the darkness. It was not a traditional method of seeing, not eyes in the sense he had always known them, yet to his brain they served the same way, giving up long range for extreme-depth perception and, perhaps (he could never be sure) altering the color sense quite a bit to emphasize contrasts. Bony plates formed over each socket like horns. The great, muscular steel-gray body was humanoid, a mass of sinew with arms capable of uprooting medium-sized trees and snapping them in two. The five-fingered hands ended in lethal, steellike talons also designed for ripping and tearing flesh, and the thick legs ended in reptillian feet that could grasp, claw, propel that heavy body over almost any obstacle. Trailing behind was a long tail of the same steely gray ending in two huge, sharp bones like spikes, which could be wielded by the prehensile tail as additional weapons. The body itself was so well armored, so tough and thick, that arrows bounced off its hide, and even a conventional bullet would do only minor damage. Control of the nervous system was absolute and automatic with the Hakazit; pain centers, for example, could be disabled in a localized area at will.

It was, thought the former small dinosaurlike creature, the most formidable living weapon he had ever seen. The males stood over three meters tall with a nine-meter tail; females were smaller and weaker: only two and a half meters, on the average, and just able to crush a large rock in their bare hands.

But now he, as one of them, was being taken down to a great cavern city, a prisoner, it seemed, of the local authorities. The city itself was impressive, a fairyland of colorful lights and moving walkways, scaled to the size of the behemoths who lived there. A high-tech civilization to boot, he noted, amazed. No handicaps, like some of the hexes on the Well World where only technology up to steam was allowed or where nothing that didn't work by mechanical energy was possible. Yes, the world the Markovians had in mind for the Hazakit race had to be one real hell.

Everybody seemed to wear a leather or cloth pullover with some rank or insignia on it. He couldn't interpret them, or the signs, or the codes, but it looked quite stratified, almost as if everybody was in the army. Here was a crisp, disciplined place where everybody seemed to be on some kind of desperate business with no time to dawdle or socialize. No trained eye was necessary to see that some of the creatures were there to keep an eye on the other creatures. One group, in particular, wearing leather jerkins with targetlike designs on them, wore side arms of an unfamiliar sort. Marquoz had no doubt that *those* pistols could penetrate to the vital parts of a Hakazit.

His escort, Commander Zhart, delighted in showing off Harmony City, as it was called. He pointed out the Fountain of Democracy, the People's Congress, the Avenue of Peace and Freedom, and so forth. Marquoz just nodded and looked over the place. It somehow seemed all too familiar to him, an echo of every dictatorship he had ever been in. Coming from a world that didn't even have a central government yet hadn't had a major war in thousands of years, this was something of a contrast. Yet he had spent long years in the "human" Com, where dictatorship was the rule and things didn't appear to be all that different.

They finally headed for a giant, palatial structure built into the side of the cavern and dominating it and the city skyline. The seat of government, he guessed, probably for the whole hex. Finally he could stand it no longer. "Where's the enemy?" he asked Zhart.

The other stopped and turned, looking slightly puzzled. "What do you mean?" he asked, not suspiciously but just befuddled.

Marquoz waved a massive arm back in the general direction of the city. "All this. The militarization of the population, the fierceness of the race. All this points to a really nasty enemy. I just wanted to know who or what."

"There's no enemy," Zhart responded, sounding slightly wistful. "No enemy at all. Used to be—long, long ago, maybe thousands of years. You can visit the Museum of Hakazit Culture sometime and see the dioramas and displays about it. But there's nothing much now. None of the surrounding hexes could live in the radiations of the day, and they're not up to tackling us even if there was a reason." He shrugged as they continued walking to the palace.

That was it, of course, Marquoz realized. A warrior people created for a nightmare planet that they had conquered here, thereby proving that they could make it out there in the real universe. But that had been during the Markovian experiment, who knew how many millions of years ago, gone now, done now, leaving the descendants bred for battle but with nothing left to fight.

It would create a strange, stagnant culture, he decided. He understood now what sort of entertainment probably went on at the People's Stadium, for example. So a rigid sort of dictatorship would be necessary to control a population made up of such muscular death machines—although he wondered how any regime could sustain itself for long if the people truly got pissed off at it. Maybe they were so accustomed to the situation they never considered the alternatives, he speculated to himself. Or maybe, deep down, they knew there was only one way to keep the place from breaking down into carnage and savagery—as it ultimately would, inevitably, anyway. This dictatorship was just buying time, but it was the best justification for a dictatorship he could remember.

The palace proved to have surprisingly few people in it. He had been conditioned by the Com to expect a huge bureaucracy, but only three officials were in evidence in the entry hall, and he had the impression that two of them were waiting to see somebody or other. Commander Zhart introduced him to the one who seemed to belong there and bid him good luck and farewell.

The official looked him over somewhat critically. "You are an Entry?" he asked at last.

Marquoz nodded. "Yes. Newly arrived in your fair land."

The official ignored the flattery. "What were you before?"

"A Chugach," Marquoz told him. "That would mean very little here."

"More than you think," the other responded. "Although we're both speaking Hakazit, I wear a translator surgically implanted in my brain. It translated your own term into a more familiar one. There's a bit of telepathy or something involved, although it'd be easier if you were wearing one, too. I got a picture of what your people were like and I recognize them. Here on the Well World they are called the Ghlmonese."

"Ghlmonese," Marquoz repeated, fascinated. His racial ancestors . . . Somehow that had never occurred to him. He decided he would like to visit there someday, if he could.

"You told Commander Zhart that you worked mostly on alien worlds in your old life," the official continued. "Glathrielites and Dillians mainly. Naked apes and centaurs. Very unlike your own kind. You said you were a spy?"

Startled, Marquoz realized suddenly that somehow he had been bugged since being discovered on the surface by a military patrol. This explained Zhart's chumminess in contrast to the coldness the others showed—but it didn't really matter. What mattered was that he should have anticipated this and had not. He hoped he wasn't becoming old and senile.

"A spy, yes," he admitted, realizing, too, that this individual was some sort of psychologist, possibly for the inevitable secret police. "You understand that my people were discovered by the others. They were an aggressive, warlike lot with a strong sense of cultural superiority that matched their real technological superiority. We hadn't developed space travel, and most of our weaponry was museum vintage, even to us, except in sport. They had a big interworld council, of course, but we were entitled to only one seat and one vote as a one-world culture—hardly a position of influence. They needed somebody out there, traveling around, observing trends, attitudes, threats, and possibilities, and reporting same. A lot of somebodies, really, but I was the only one to really succeed at it."

The psychologist was interested. "Why you? And why were you successful when the others of your kind were not?"

Marquoz shrugged. "I'm not sure. In terms of getting in the right positions, well, the dominant races have psychological quirks that make them either de-

stroy lesser races, absorb lesser races, or, in some odd
and perverse tendency, to bend over backward to show
that they don't consider your race lesser even if they
actually do. I've always had some sort of knack for
being where trouble is, even on my home world. If
there was a big storm, or a fire, or some equally major
event, I somehow usually wound up being there. Call
it some kind of perverse precognition, I don't know
what. I happened to be in a position to overhear plans
for a minor but nasty rebellion and took the opportunity to report it. The Com Police crushed the rebellion, of course, and I became some sort of minor
celebrity to them. From there it was easy to worm my
way into the Com Police itself, not only because I delivered the goods, so to speak, but also because, as a
Chugach, I would be a symbol of their liberalism.
There are some mighty guilty consciences there, I suspect. That helped immeasurably. And the deeper
entrenched I became, the easier it was to pick up
everything, from trade to forbidden technological information, and pass it along to my own people."

The psychologist looked disturbed. "Do you think
your being reborn as a Hakazit means that we are in
for some particularly bad trouble?"

This race's mouth wasn't built for expression so
Marquoz's sardonic smile wasn't evident to the other.
"Oh, yes, I'd say so. I'd say that a catastrophe of major proportions is going to hit not only Hakazit but the
whole of the Well World any minute now. I'm afraid
I'm part of the cause this time, though. You see, I'm
here on a mission." He tried to sound really conspira-
torial.

"A mission?" the psychologist echoed, looking more
and more disturbed.

Marquoz nodded gravely. "Yes. You see, I'm here
to save the universe in the name of truth and purity
and justice."

They kept him waiting for quite some time and he
became very bored. There weren't many people to talk
to, and those who did come in or out were hardly the
talkative type. He knew that somewhere in this build-

ing they were arguing, discussing, deciding his fate, and that he could do little about it, at least until they made their own moves. He wished terribly that he had a cigar. The Well World was supposed to change you, even make you comfortable in your new form—and it had. A rebirth is only a rebirth, he reflected glumly, but a good cigar is a smoke.

He tried a few of his old dance moves but soon discovered that those, too, were gone for good. Ballet ill-befitted armored tanks.

Finally someone came—not the same one, he decided, who had interviewed him. He was finding it easier to tell individuals apart now, more so as he went along, although he knew that non-Hakazit might have a problem in that direction.

"Thank you for waiting," the newcomer said pleasantly, as if he had anywhere else to go. "The Supreme Lord will see you now. Follow me."

He started and almost repeated the title aloud. The supreme lord? Well, no use getting your hopes up too far, Marquoz, he reminded himself. Around here that might be the term for chief palace janitor. These folks looked like they loved titles.

It was soon apparent, though, that this was a personage of considerable rank. Not only the smartly uniformed guards along the hall attested to this, but also the hidden traps, emplacements, and other nastiness that only his trained eye could make out signified rank and importance. Finally he entered a pair of huge, ornate steel doors and found himself in a barren hall. He looked around warily. Yes, television sensors, definitely, and a lot more—but no people. The steel grid he could barely make out under the flooring probably meant the possibilities of instant electrocution should he not meet with the unseen onlooker's approval. He studied that great set of doors now sliding shut behind him. Some kind of detection system there, too, he noted. Probably x-ray, flouroscope, metal detector—the whole works. One thing beyond the power of this Supreme Lord was dead certain: Whoever and whatever he was, he was scared to death.

Finally he heard a click, as if a speaker had opened,

and an electronically colored voice instructed, "You will go to the center of the room, under the large chandelier, and stay very still." The voice held no menace, just a little suspicion. He did as instructed, and was told to move his tail a little this way or that, shift a bit here or there, until he was wondering if he was posing for a magazine layout. Finally the voice said, "That's excellent. Now remain perfectly still. You will not be harmed."

Suddenly he was engulfed in a series of colored beams, some of which felt oddly hot and irritating. That lasted only a few seconds, but it was damned uncomfortable. Even after they were cut off, he tingled uncomfortably.

"Now proceed to the door and enter the audience chamber," the voice instructed. He looked around, realizing for the first time that an entire wall was silently sliding away. He shrugged and walked into the smaller chamber, which was spartanly furnished with a few tables, some glasses, and little else. The wall slid shut behind him, and he glanced back at it for a moment. Guards, booby traps, steel doors, wired rooms, sliding walls—what else?

What else proved to be a flickering in the air opposite him and the rapid fade-in of a figure much like himself, differing mainly in the fact that this newcomer wore a scarlet tunic and cape trimmed in expensive-looking exotic furs. The Supreme Lord, he knew, appearing as some sort of hologram. What kind of paranoia would sterilize somebody against germs when he was only going to meet a projection?

The Supreme Lord looked him over critically. "Well, I can tell you really are an Entry," the Hakazit leader snorted. "None of the bowing and scraping or inbred social gestures."

"For a solidograph?" Marquoz retorted.

The other laughed. "One of my predecessors had people salute his photograph, which was everywhere," he responded. "He didn't last long, needless to say."

Marquoz studied the image, thinking furiously. "So that's why you take all these precautions? Everybody's out to bump you off?"

The Supreme Lord roared with laughter. "Now I know you are an Entry!" he laughed. "Such a question! Tell me, how did you come to that conclusion?"

"Most dictators fear assassination," the Com worlder noted. "It's not unusual, since they hold power by everybody else's fear of them."

The Supreme Lord stopped laughing and looked at the newcomer with interest. "So you know that this is, in fact, a dictatorship? You're not very much like any Entry I've ever heard of before. No, 'Where am I? What am I doing here?' and all that. That's what's so interesting about you, Marquoz."

The Entry looked around the room. "Is that why so many security precautions? Because you think there's something funny about me?"

"Well, no, not really. Not entirely, anyway," the Supreme Lord replied. "Ah, you call Hakazit a dictatorship. In the purest sense of that term I suppose it is. I flip the intercom, dictate an order, and it is unquestioningly carried out no matter how stupid. And yet—well, Hakazit is also the most democratic nation on the Well World."

Marquoz's head snapped up. "Huh? How's that?"

"I am fifty-seven years old," the dictator told him. "Fifty-seven. And do you know how many Supreme Lords there have been in my lifetime? Sixty-seven! And at least one ruled for almost four years. The record according to recent history is nine years, three months, sixteen days, five hours, forty-one minutes. In a history that goes back over a thousand years!"

Marquoz sighed. "It figures," he muttered. "And that's despite all this protective stuff, this gimmickry, the best electronics you can devise. I suppose for every charm there's a countercharm."

"Exactly," the Supreme Lord agreed. "Right now there are hundreds of officers trying to figure out how to get to me. One will, one of these days, and then they'll add me to the books."

"I'm surprised you don't know who they are and have them taken care of," the Entry noted practically. "I know *I* would."

The ruler sniggered derisively. "Marquoz, you fail

to appreciate the problem. *Every* Hakazit is doing it. Schoolchildren do it for fun or abstract exercise. Storekeepers, bartenders, you name it. Everybody. You can't get rid of everybody—then you would have nobody to take dictation."

"It's a problem, all right," Marquoz admitted. "It's a wonder you'd want this job—or that anybody else would want it under those conditions."

The Supreme Lord looked puzzled. "But what is the purpose of life if it isn't to become Supreme Lord? It's the only thing people have to *live* for!"

That stopped the newcomer for a moment as he digested the idea. A warrior race with no wars. What's the result of conquest? The ability to order everybody about, to do anything you wanted, to have anything you wanted. The ultimate fantasy. And that position was here, open, available to *anyone,* regardless of rank, sex, social position, or authority, who could knock off the reigning leader. It was as crazy an idea as he had ever heard, as nutty a social system as he had ever thought about—and it made absolute, logical sense. That was the trouble. It made sense.

He changed the subject. "Well, one thing has got me curious. Why did you say you had only a thousand years of recorded history? Surely this land and this race are a lot older than that."

"True," the other agreed. "But, you see, combat is built into us. We're the most aggressive race on the Well World, and we're surrounded by hexes designed to make it impossible to conquer or even reasonably fight them. Radiations lethal only to us, poisons lethal only to us, and the like. We hire some of the people out as mercenaries, guards—even pirates—that kind of thing, to others, but the system has us boxed in. We're too rational to fight to extinction or maybe fight a war when there's absolutely nothing to be gained, since we can't hold what we gain. So, naturally, after a while the system—any system—we create to hold things together here collapses. Civil war, anarchy, a return to barbarism when all the restraints are off. Civilization gets destroyed and has to rebuild again. Our people say any social system lasts an average of two thousand years, so we're in the middle of a period now. You have no idea how ferocious these social breakdowns can be. And neither do we. After all, they're so bad that almost nothing survives from the previous age except crumbling ruins and a few relics."

Marquoz nodded. He appreciated what these creatures would be like in an all-out war with no quarter given or asked and surrender unthinkable. It was a wonder that any of them were left, he thought. But, no, as long as a single male and female were left, the Well would gradually replenish the stock, or so he understood the system. That thought was unsettling, though. Such devastation as the Supreme Lord intimated implied that those wars were literally wars of self-genocide; it was probably only the ones away from hex and home that returned to rebuild. The dead end, he thought glumly. The left overs from the Markovian dream in the eternal replay of the rise and fall of civilization. It was pretty damned depressing.

"I can understand Your Lordship's interest in me," he said carefully. "Here I show up in the middle of nowhere, an Entry or an exile, either one the same, but without any of the psychological problems or wonder of what you're used to. You figure I'm the one to get you—right?"

The Supreme Lord shrugged slightly. "Are you?"

Marquoz sighed. "No . . . no, Your Lordship, absolutely not. The last thing I want is your job. That may be hard to believe under these conditions, but you're a very clever man or you wouldn't be where you are. I'm sure your lie detectors are telling you now that I'm being sincere."

The other gave him a look of grudging admiration. "Clever one, aren't you? But a psychopath would register the same."

"Your Lordship, use those truth detectors now and believe what I say. Inside of a few weeks, if it hasn't started already, you're going to be flooded with Entries, and none of them are going to be typical. And I don't mean ten, twenty, a hundred. I mean enough so that they'll quickly double your population. *Double* it!"

The hollow burning red eyes of the projection shifted to a point outside the image, as if checking on something—a chart recorder, most likely, Marquoz guessed.

"Hakazit couldn't support them," the Supreme Lord said in a thin, worried tone. "We would have to kill them."

"They won't be that easy to kill," Marquoz cautioned. "And, besides, they won't be here to eat you out of house and home. They'll be here to do a job and fulfill a set function." Quickly he explained about Brazil, about the Well of Souls, about how it was damaged and had to be repaired.

"What are you offering?" the Supreme Lord asked warily.

"A battle. A full be-damned war! A war that could be fought by proxies trained by your people or by a combination of the two. An outlet for all this aggression, an outlet for all this pent-up civilization. And, of course, on the right side should Brazil gain the Well. And he *will* get there. Bet on it. Whether I die, whether Hakazit joins my side or opposes us, no matter what, he'll win. And once he's inside he might be able to help this situation you've got here. Think about it on a different level, too. This outlet, this release, will be enormously popular. You have a people who love war and have none. Now they'll have one, and a set of purposes and objectives for it. It could be the safety valve you lack, put off collapse for many thousands of years—perhaps long enough to work out, this time, a more permanent system. And you'll be a hero, too, for giving it to them. How long have you been Supreme Lord?"

The leader was thinking it over. "Huh? Oh, a little over three years."

"Wouldn't you like to hold on and maybe break that fellow's old record? Hell, even if the yen doesn't fade with the war, think about this: your biggest threats are going to be in the forefront of planning and leadership in this thing—not only too occupied to have a serious go at you, but up front, where you can see who's really got a chance."

"The people . . . they'll have to be pre-prepared for this, you realize," the Hakazit leader muttered. "It'll have to be carefully planned, carefully orchestrated."

Marquoz nodded. "That's why I was sent here, specifically here, to Hakazit," he told the other, realizing the truth himself, now, for the first time. "Uh, tell me, you have a secret police, of course."

"A very good one," the Supreme Lord confirmed proudly.

"Uh huh. And how does one get to head that service?"

The leader looked a bit sheepish. "Well . . . you know . . ."

"Oh," Marquoz managed. "Your Secret Police chief, he doesn't have this place bugged, too, does he?"

The Supreme Lord looked shocked. "Of course not! Only *I* control this. The proof is that I'm still here."

That seemed reasonable to Marquoz. "Hmmm . . . this chieftan, is he a nice fellow as people go? Loving wife and kiddies?"

"General Yutz? Ha!" the dictator chuckled. "He's a rotten son of a bitch, the rottenest I've ever seen. Strangled his last wife and his oldest son because he thought they were plotting against him."

"I'm so *very* glad to hear that," Marquoz responded sincerely. "Otherwise I'd have guilt feelings when I knocked him off."

The leader looked surprised. "Knocked him off? Easier said than done, my friend."

The newcomer chuckled dryly. "Oh, come on, Your Lordship. If *you* couldn't kill him any time you felt like it, he'd have your job by now. His death should be simple to arrange."

The Supreme Lord of Hakazit looked at Marquoz as if for the first time, shaking his head slowly in undisguised admiration and fascination. "You know, Marquoz," he said after a while, "I think this might be the beginning of a beautiful friendship."

"Could be, Your Lordship," Marquoz responded, managing a slight smile on his stiff, fierce face. "Could be indeed. I'd much rather work with you than overthrow you. It makes *my* job so much nicer."

So much nicer, he thought to himself, and so much easier. Much easier than the alternate plan, which would have been to overthrow the whole damned system.

"Let's do it," the Supreme Lord said at last.

# Awbri

THE LAND OF AWBRI WAS A STRANGE JUNGLE RAIN-
forest, thick with huge trees growing out of a dense
swamp, rising thousands, perhaps tens of thousands, of
meters into the air. The atmosphere was heavy and
humid; little droplets seemed forever suspended in the
air and there was nothing, really, but water, water,
water. . . . Water from waterfalls spilling down the
trees and over broad leaves in a series of cascades,
going down, ever down, into the forest floor below.
And yet there was little sunlight; the great trees
blocked it somewhere, up there, in the omnipresent
gray clouds themselves, perhaps even above those
clouds. The people of Awbri, if they knew, did not
seem to care.

And below, far, far below, was the Floor, the base
of the forest and the destination of those cascades.
Down there, it was said, was a horrible swamp with
quicksand and quagmire the rule and in which lived
terrible, voracious mud and swamp creatures, creatures both animal and parasitic plant—and even carnivorous plant—that fought one another in a continual
battle and devoured all that came near. None could
climb, however, and even the parasites seemed
stopped as they grew upward, halted by secretions
from the great trees. The insects were mostly symbi-
otic, or, if parasitic, were so on animals and not the
trees. Of insects there seemed an infinite number,
some of which could penetrate and draw life-giving
blood even from the bodies of the Awbrians, but that,
too, was fair: in addition to the fruits of the trees and
the vegetables from the vines that clung to great limbs,
the Awbrians ate enormous quantities of those insects.

27

The Awbrians themselves lived only in the trees, from about the hundred-meter level to the clouds at about the fifteen-hundred-meter level. They had comic-looking short duck bills that were somewhat flexible, mounted on thin, flat heads whose long supporting necks joined lithe, almost infinitely supple rodentlike bodies. Their four limbs all terminated in identical monkeylike hands, each with opposable thumb; there was no difference between hand and foot, which, with the Awbrian's infinitely flexible backbone and limbs, were used as either as the situation warranted. Except for their bare gray palms and long, flat, almost rigid, kitelike tails, their bodies were covered in thick fur whose oils repelled water. All limbs were connected by fur-covered membranes, and their bones were hollow, allowing them considerable birdlike buoyancy in the air, something they needed because, with arms and legs outstretched and using the tail as a rudder, these creatures could fly between the treetops and glide for long distances, agilely darting around limbs, leaves, and other obstructions. Unlike birds, they were ultimately victims of gravity, more gliders than powered flyers. Yet by sensing the air currents and speeds and distances, they could, like a glider, remain aloft a long, long time.

Such was the physical world into which Yua, former high priestess of Olympus, had been reborn through the Well of Souls. The cultural world had been, for her, the greater shock.

As with her own people, there were many more females born here than males, perhaps ten or more to one. But here the men ruled supreme, whereas in her old world they had functioned merely as pampered courtesans. She had sought out the leadership of this land when she first awakened here and had been directed, finally, to the local council, which had its headquarters in a great tree that seemed set apart from the rest. So far, she had been treated with discourtesy, even downright rudeness, and had little liking for her new people, a feeling that grew even more ominous when she discovered she was to be assigned to a family of low rank. She was pragmatic; she accepted their rule for now because she could do nothing else about it, and because the alternative was to be drugged or lobotomized into acceptance and submission.

Awbri had no central government. It was made up of clans, each of which was an extended family all living and working together. Each tree could support between a dozen and twenty or so Awbrians; clans spread to adjoining trees and their relative power and social ranking was based on the number of people in the clan and, by extension, the number of trees it inhabited and controlled. Within each clan, which ranged from as few as a hundred to more than five thousand, male rank was a combination of age, birth, and tests of strength and endurance. Female rank depended more on age and relationship to the chief male of the clan than on anything else, although the highest-ranking female was always well below the lowest-ranking male.

A young Awbrian female came for her in the morning. She was Dhutu of Tokar, she told the newcomer, and she was here to help Yua get to her new home and to help her in adjusting.

Dhutu was friendly, at least, and helped her with the fine points of flying, although the more Yua did it the easier it became. She seemed instinctively to know distances and to "feel" and "see" the sluggish air. Still, lacking complete confidence in her ability as yet, she grabbed trees and took things in short stages. Dhutu was amused but patient, and it was during such stops that Yua learned more of the culture of Awbri.

The men, it seemed, spent most of their time in combat-type sports and rivalries, although they also regulated commerce and trade, swapping whatever their clans produced for whatever they needed. They decided what would be grown on the limbs and in the mulch-lined hollows of branches; they decided just about everything, in fact. Only males received any sort of education. She found Dhutu's ignorance almost appalling. The female considered reading and writing things of magic; books and letters were mysterious symbols that "talked" only to males. She had no idea what lay over the next grove beyond her own local neighborhood, let alone the fact that she was on a planet—or even what a planet was. She knew there were other races, of course; hexes were too small to conceal that fact. But she knew nothing about them, for they were all monsters and could be understood only by clan chiefs. And anyhow, she had no curiosity.

The women, it turned out, provided the labor. They not only bore and raised the young, they farmed the limbs, harvested the vines and fruits, created the special mulches for better yields, and were also the craftsmen and manufacturers. Working in wood was elaborate work here, since it was incredible and ornate, yet it had to be done without killing the tree. They built and maintained highly detailed homes inside the trees and created the intricate woodwork, the distinctive furniture, objets d'art, and household equipment, such as vases. They also made strange musical instruments for elaborate compositions—written by men, of course—and the tools and weapons for their own work and for the men's sport.

They reached a tree—*her* tree, Dhutu told her— and landed on a lower limb. "This is a new tree," she was told, "that is, it was acquired in a trade with the Mogid clan, who needed additional fruit production. We had extra fruit trees off near their border, they had some spare life trees near by, and we needed new space. It has caused us great excitement, for such a thing has not happened before in any of our memories. We are only now starting to develop the tree properly, work in which you will share." She said it with such enthusiasm that Yua supposed that she was expected to feel thrilled or something at that.

They entered a large cavity and descended a ladder to a lower floor that was more developed. The trees were huge; she guessed that the tree must be thirty or more meters in diameter, with its own life system in its outer area. The trees seemed naturally hollow, so there was little damage done by living inside them, but what was done inside was something impressive indeed.

The new level was in the process of being transformed. Females busily worked hand-sanding areas, using planes and small tools to refashion and reshape the interior into something that looked more manufactured than grown, yet with such thought that it used the contours of the tree and the tree's various natural wooden supports to good benefit. Shaping, sanding, polishing, and finishing were all being done in different areas. Artisans also worked carving elaborate designs into the wood. It was obvious that the thick flooring was also mostly natural, but it had been finished so slickly that it was now completely level, shined, and polished like finished wood on furniture.

Dhutu stopped and called out, "My sisters! Meet our new sister, Yua, who will join us!" The others halted their work, turned, nodded to her in friendly fashion, then went back to work. "Come on, let's get you settled in," the Awbrian continued, and went to a neatly concealed trap door, opened it, and climbed down. Yua followed. There seemed nothing else to do.

Lower levels were finished and appeared all the more impressive. What was most fascinating, she thought, was the way in which some sort of luminous sheen had been carefully applied all around, allowing the light from very tiny glass-covered lamps to illuminate those huge rooms. The living tree was moist enough that the small oil lamps provided almost no threat of fire, but a huge blaze, like the kind that would be required to illuminate the room in normal circumstances, would have been far too dangerous even if there had been some outlet for the smoke.

On one level they did not stop at all, and it was blocked by high curtains from floor to ceiling from view. "The men's quarters," Dhutu explained, and they continued. The next level was living quarters for a number of older Awbrian females, the supervisors of this world. "All are past their Time," Dhutu whispered enigmatically. "Respect must be shown them at all times."

Yua was taken to one ancient Awbrian, who was reclining on a soft, huge pillow, somewhat catlike in manner. Yua needed no guide to know that this one was old indeed; her bill was blotched with odd marks of age, and her fur seemed mottled not only with

white but with mange. Her hands were wrinkled and
withered, and she was so thin she looked almost skeletal; her skin, already loose because of the membranes, seemed to hang baggy and limp all about her,
from face to tail.

"Revered grandmother," Dhutu said, bowing slightly,
"this is the one we have been told to expect."

The ancient female peered myopically at the Entry.
Finally she said in a cracked, withered voice, "You
are one who was once some other creature?"

Deciding that it was better at this stage not to anger
the leadership, particularly the lower-echelon leadership, Yua nodded but said nothing.

The elder seemed satisfied. "You won't like it here,"
she said abruptly.

Yua decided that called for a comment. "It is not
what I am used to," she admitted. "I admire the trees
and the work, but not some of the ways I have been
told you have here."

The elder nodded. "What work did you do—before?" she asked.

"I was a speaker, a traveler, a . . . a religious
leader," Yua replied, groping for the right words in
this new tongue.

"I suppose you could hold a book so it would talk
to you?"

Yua nodded. "I could—but in my old tongues, of
course."

The elder Awbrian sighed. "You won't like it here
at all," she repeated with emphasis, then fell silent for
a time so long that Yua felt awkward and feared the
old one had fallen asleep. But Dhutu still stood there
respectfully, and so she thought she might as well do
likewise.

Finally the old female opened her eyes again and
looked right at Yua. "Better you had been a carpen-
ter, or farmer, or artisan," she croaked. "You have no
skills of use here, so you are fit only for the most bor-
ing, repetitive, unskilled work. It will drive you mad.
You will try to show your cleverness, and if there is
one thing men will not allow, it is that in women. You
will be a threat, and threats must be dealt with. Even-

tually they will send you to a Healer and then you will think no more."

Yua considered this. "You don't sound very dumb or ignorant yourself," she noted.

The old one's bill curved in the Awbrian version of a smile. "But I am a survivor," she said proudly. "Growing up in this society I found ways to be clever and to learn but never to betray that fact. It is something born of a lifetime's experience, and you have not the lifetime to learn it. It is called subtlety, I believe. And to what end? To spend my last days on a cushion inhaling drugged vapors and dreaming of what a waste it all has been?"

If Dhutu was shocked by all this, she showed no sign. In fact, she barely moved at all.

"I should think," Yua almost whispered, "that there is more here to this society than meets the eye of a newcomer—or a man."

Again that smile. "Yes, that is so. Within the clans are the guilds, and within the guilds are things that— help. A hidden school, you might say. I tell you this only because it will be more obvious to you than to the men, and you will get along better if you make no obvious betrayals, to ask no wrong questions. You understand the men's rule here is absolute. You are property, not a person at all. They may do anything with you they wish, and you have no rights or say in the matter. As a result, all that we do is at great risk, yet it is necessary. We have the same brains and talents as they, yet we cannot show it. We must work far in the background, so that our own ideas are thought of as men's ideas, not ours. It is the way we progress, and it is the only way possible."

"But why?" Yua wanted to know. "Why is it so? This system looks ripe for revolution." She struggled with the last concept, which had no equivalent in the Awbrian language. The word came out something like "changing the way things work," but it made the point.

The elder sighed. "My child, you do not yet know or understand. When your first Time is done you will understand that this way is the only way. Now go. I release you from work until your first Time and clan induction. After that, things will be clearer to you. After that you may want to kill yourself." Her eyes narrowed. "And remember, if there is any chance that you might, even accidentally, betray what you now know, you will have an even easier, and more sudden, out."

With that threat the interview was over. The old woman settled back, took up a small box filled with some fine white powder and form-fitted to her bill, inhaled deeply, and seemed to sink into some kind of pleasant oblivion. Dhutu gestured and they went out, down to the next level.

The women stayed in spartan quarters on several levels, divided according to guild—carpentry, farming, artisan, etc.—with the bottom-most level left for those without guild or classification. It looked much like the others, a barren hall with straw pillows for sleeping, an ingenious plumbing system where outer waterfalls were tapped and brought through the thick trunk and then back out again, and toilet facilities, open to all, flushed in the same manner by the force of a trickle of running water in a trough. But unlike the trough for washing, bathing, and the like, the toilet outlet went to an area below the lowest level, where a natural system filtered it out. The fecal matter of the Awbrians helped nourish the tree, so it was a clever system, but it made the level just above one nasty stinking place —and that, of course, was the level for unskilled and non-guild workers, her level.

"You'll get used to the stench," Dhutu assured her. "After a while here you don't even notice it any more. We all started in a level like this. Most of your sisters will be very young and not yet apprenticed to guilds —or very, very stupid. You understand."

Yua nodded less than enthusiastically. "Dhutu, there's something I'm still puzzled about. This thing about my 'Time.' At first I misunderstood you, thinking you were talking about time in general. But you're not. The ancient one above referred to it. What does it mean?"

Dhutu hesitated a moment. "Best you experience it.

It is hard to describe. It is just your Time, that's all. You'll see. Then you will not need it explained."

That wasn't satisfactory, but despite all her pressing, that was all she was going to get.

The next few days passed slowly, but she was allowed some freedom to see the kind of work that went on in making a life tree ready and was given some introduction to the type of life they lived here. The different kinds of trees for different purposes interested her. Only some of the trees were life trees, huge with hollow interiors able to support colonies of Awbrians; some grew specific fruits; others offered nothing on their own but had flat branches with depressions in them in which the mulch, mixed from chewed bark, straw, insects, and lots of other stuff and molded together by saliva from glands only the females possessed, was deposited and then the mess seeded expertly, fertilized, and tended lovingly until a crop of some kind of vegetable or even straw was raised.

She grew more puzzled, too, at Obie's grand design. Something, she felt certain, had gone wrong. She was to organize and lead an army, or as much of one as possible, rallying others along the way to her cause, finally linking up in some place called Glathriel with forces raised by Marquoz and Mavra Chang, wherever and whatever they were now. But even if she knew where that was, and where she was, the Awbrian system made it all but impossible for her to do what was required. And she couldn't really see what sort of skills the Awbrians possessed, anyway. Perhaps she had become the wrong thing, she feared. Or, possibly, Obie *did* need the Awbrians for some reason, some balance of forces—there was the omnivorous character and the flying, for example—perhaps he forgot in his encoding of her to specify sex. Perhaps she should have been an Awbri male. It would make more sense.

Time was running out, too. In a very short while the flood of people into the Well World would begin —if it hadn't already. The Well World's population was due to double, even in Awbri. In some cases the system would break down completely. Perhaps, she thought hopefully, when Olympian Entries outnumber

the Awbrian population the revolution would come
automatically and she would then be in a position to
rally and lead them. Perhaps. She could only hope
and wait, impatiently.

Several times she thought of escape, but that seemed
a dead end. She alone would not rally anything; each
hex was like a separate alien planet anyway, and she
had no idea where on the world she was.

But it was maddening all the same, made even
more so by this totally degrading existence.

A week after she arrived she started having odd
feelings, strange dreams she couldn't quite relate to
any reality, and hot and cold flushes. She was afraid
she had become ill, but the others assured her what
she was experiencing was normal, natural. She was
approaching her Time.

And, one morning, she awoke to it in full. She felt
an enormous ache, an absolute need to be satisfied,
like a drug addict too long without her drug. It was a
craving beyond reason, beyond belief. Her entire body
ached with longing and she could not think at all,
couldn't get control of herself. Her entire being
wanted, needed, desired only one thing, and nothing
else would matter until she got it. The elders knew,
too, and made the arrangements, and soon she was
up on the upper-level quarters, in the quarters of the
males, and they in turn gave her what she wanted,
needed, craved. She had no idea how many of them
there were, nor how long it took, nor, afterward, could
she even remember anything of the experience except
the tremendous, ultimate pleasures it brought and the
fact that she would have done anything, anything at
all, for them.

Later she learned it had lasted for two days and
nights—about average, they told her. And it recurred
about every six weeks except during pregnancy—the
hormones pregnancy triggered made an individual
docile and somewhat dreamy, increasing more so as
term neared.

She felt even more degraded, not merely from the
experience but because of her own uncontrollable pas-

sions. She had had sex before, as an Olympian, but it had been nothing like this. Nothing. This was in and of itself a drug, a feeling so pleasurably intense and so total that the memory remained as a pleasing ache and her mind kept anticipating her next Time even as her intellect feared and abhorred it.

And this, she realized, was the trap. This is what they meant, why there had been no revolution nor was there a likelihood of one, and why the men were so secure in their position. The women could rebel, all right—and the men would simply wait for the Time to bring the rebels crawling, begging, so much in heat they'd probably kill their best friend if that friend tried to stop them. Here was a cruel biological control on this society, and an absolute one. The female reproductive system, it seemed, was very chintzy with its eggs, and even with this system pregnancy was usual only once in every two or three years. Conditions, both for male and female, had to be absolutely perfect to produce young.

About the only positive thing was that all the women now called her "sister" and she received far better treatment from everyone in the clan, even from the very few males she ran across. She was one of them now.

All this made her reflect once more on the ancient matriarch's comments and warnings. Something had definitely gone wrong with Obie's plans and now she was trapped, totally trapped. Even escape was now out of the question, since the Time was open-ended and continued until release was found, and there was only one way to get that.

That night, totally down, facing assignment the next day combing through the dung accumulation and gathering enough for certain kinds of fertilizer, she slept, finally, fitfully, and she dreamed. She was aware that she was dreaming, yet it seemed so real. She was an Olympian again and she was bathed in a strange, shimmering purple glow. There was a presence there with her, she sensed. All around, all-encompassing.

"Obie?" her dream self called out.

"I'm here, Yua," came the familiar tenor of the great computer.

"But you're dead!" she protested. "I'm dreaming all this!"

"Well, yes, I must be dead or at least badly damaged," the computer admitted. "Otherwise we wouldn't be having this little chat. Obviously my fears were realized—the union with Brazil badly damaged or destroyed me and, therefore, the job must be done the hard way. Too bad. If he just hadn't been so obstinate I could have beamed him down to the Well World at an Avenue and we wouldn't have had these problems." He paused. "Well, who am I kidding? With the rip in space-time I was too screwed up to do the job anyway. It doesn't matter. It only matters that, if we're talking like this, you must be in Awbri and past your first Time."

She started in surprise. "You know about that? But —what am I saying? This is a dream. Wish-fulfillment, nothing more. I'm not really talking to you."

"You're right on most counts but wrong on that last one," the computer responded. "Yes, this is a dream. You're asleep somewhere in the bottom of a tree in Awbri right now. And, yes, I'm not really here or near by. Even if I could get there, I doubt that I would have the power to overcome that nullified space and that tremendous short circuit of Markovian energy. But we *are* having this conversation—already had it, in fact. When you went through me for the last time, all of this was planted by me deep in your subconscious to pop up at the proper moment. Only after you'd gone into heat for the first time could it come out. You had to know what you were up against."

"I don't really believe this," she told herself and the ghostly computer. "I'm just fantasizing what I desperately want to happen."

"Well, fantasize this, then," Obie came back. "Right now you're seeing a map of your area of the Well World, and you see where you are in relation to Glathriel. Also in your mind at this point is a briefing on the lifeforms and such of the hexes in between.

And, here, I'll give you a complete political-topographic map of Awbri as well. You'll need it before long."

And it was true. There it all was, in glowing detail, so much a part of her mind now that she doubted she could ever forget it. She began to feel a glimmer of hope that, perhaps, her dream might be real.

"But what good does all this do me, Obie?" she asked, still defeated. "If you had made me a male, I might have done something, but this!"

Obie chuckled. "Sorry. I thought you of all people would be a bit stronger than that. Think about it. The women have the numerical superiority, for one thing, and just as many brains as the men. Maybe more. And, of course, they have the biggest stake in a change. The men would fight you, probably kill you outright. They have a nice, neat, packaged little world that exists for their own pleasure and enjoyment. They are opposed to all change—more conservative types you cannot possibly imagine. Almost all creativity and progress in Awbri come really from the women, nurtured secretly and then sort of put into the minds of a young male here and there. A composition whistled while you work, an idea for a simple spring-loaded mechanism instilled in a young male while still at his mother's knee that, later, he miraculously 'invents' and really thinks he did. You name it. Without the women the place would have stagnated into unthinking animalism, nothing more. But when push comes to shove and the Awbrians have to choose sides between joining the forces of Brazil or stopping him at all costs, the men of Awbri will be right there with the stop-at-all-costs faction. They have to be. He could upset their little applecart, their nice little world."

She was beginning to understand. "But not the women."

"Exactly! They have the most stake in change. Never was a place more ripe for, or deserving of, revolution. Tell me, do you think the women would revolt if they could?"

She thought a moment, remembering particularly the ancient female's comments on lost opportunities.

"Not all of them, of course—but the leadership, certainly. The ones with an ounce or more of brains."

"The ones who count," Obie noted. "The rest will follow like sheep whoever wins and cheer that side. Now, what's stopping them? What's kept a revolution from happening?"

"The Time," she responded quickly. "When you go into desperate heat every six weeks, there's not much you can do."

"Uh huh," the computer agreed. "And so what do we have to introduce to produce a revolution the way we want it—on schedule, on time, just waiting for the load of new Entries?"

"You'd have to kill off all the males," she responded, then stopped. "No. That wouldn't work. That would only put us all in unending heat."

"What you need," Obie continued, "is something that will keep the Time from coming. You need the one thing a race that reproduces so slowly it still has females in heat would never consider, not even the most intellectual of them. You need a birth-control device—or, rather, a birth-control chemical, something that would fool your body into thinking it wasn't the Time."

The thought excited her. "Yes! Of course!" Then she hesitated, considering the idea. "But there are two problems there. One is the psychological addiction to the experience. Obie, it's unbelievable! The direct pleasure center of the brain is stimulated. I don't know if anyone who has had the experience could bring herself to deny it again."

"Not even you?" the computer shot back.

She considered it. "Of course *I* could, but I could see becoming so addicted I couldn't stop. Most of the women in Awbri have been through this so many times it would be impossible. And, of course, there'd be the other problem—that with a race reproducing this slowly, there would be some hesitancy in giving women this out, even by the female leaders. They wouldn't want to wipe out their race."

"True on both counts," the computer admitted. "Now, I chose Awbri for a number of reasons. One is geography—you can get where you're needed quickly. Another is mobility combined with agility. Don't underestimate the potential of your race as fighters, and their ability to fly is combined with a toughness and flexibility not found in birdlike species. Unlike the bird, you are not fragile. A lot of protection is built in. And the final reason is that the choice of Awbri converts a certain enemy into an ally. In order to do this I had to analyze the Awbrian biochemistry and the biome of the hex and see if what I wanted was possible. If it were not, you wouldn't be there."

"There is a way out, then!" She was excited now, the dream becoming more real than her true situation —lying, asleep, on a straw pallet above a dung-heap on the Well World.

"Yes. Indeed. If there weren't, this conversation would have been wasted and, frankly, you would be somewhere and something else." Obie had a nervous pause right now. "Um, that's assuming you *are* in Awbri and I didn't foul up. Oh, my. If that's the case, tell me what you are and I'll switch to a different set of messages that might not be of as much help but should do something, anyway."

"I'm in Awbri," she assured him. "Otherwise, how could we have had the earlier conversations?"

"My dear, you fail to understand that this conversation, for me, never even happened at all. It's a stimulus-response thing, with your own mind filling in the gaps from my multitudinous leads. Well, anyway, let me continue. First of all," Obie said, "there is a potion created out of seven different plants that will cause what would medically be a hormonal breakdown, but won't actually impair you and will free you of the Time. The potion is easy to make and should be terrible to drink but such sacrifices for a revolution are necessary." With that, into her mind came a complete set of ingredients, where to get them and how to mix them properly. Some heat was required, she noted, and she didn't like where two of them came from.

"Those are Floor fungi!" she objected. "Obie, do you know how dangerous that Floor *is?*"

"No," the computer responded. "Do you? But, so what? A little risk is required. Now, to continue, I should warn you of several side effects. One is that the stuff is physically addictive. But I wouldn't worry too much about that—a little goes a long way, as you can see from the recipe. Take a dose every day for a full six-week cycle, then, when Time should come and doesn't, you'll know it's effective. The effect on the women who take it should be electric. After that, a dose every five to seven days will keep it that way. Fortunately, you needn't keep a calender; your body will crave the stuff when necessary—and an increased dosage is not required after the initial period. You'll need a supply to travel with, but I'm including the complete chemical formulae for each ingredient. Nothing's so odd or rare in biochemical terms that a high-tech hex couldn't whip up a batch, maybe even in pill form, in a matter of weeks. Make that requirement known as soon as you link up, even just for communications purposes, with the others. And, finally, I should warn you that the drug will cause a physical attraction between women. I shouldn't think this would bother you, considering Olympus, and I doubt if it will be a major problem with the Awbrians. It'll stimulate, in a much milder way, those pleasure centers and make breaking the psychological habit easier."

"But will the ancients go for it?" she asked, still not convinced. "I mean, we're spelling the end of their race."

"Not at all," Obie responded. "First of all, they will be in control of who ultimately gets the drug, and there's that extra power they'll love. Second, the Well regulates population. Centuries ago they had a war—one in which I had a part—and a large number of races were decimated. All that happened was that the survivors bred like flies until the numbers were back to normal again. The same will happen here. Those who do *not* get the formula will get pregnant a lot faster, and there will be a lot more multiple births.

The Awbrian female is designed to give forth a litter of six. That's why there are six nipples. On a planetary scale and in a horribly hostile environment, they would need it so even a few survive. Here they would crowd out your small hex, so births are rare and hard. The grandmothers all know this. They remember what it was like in times of famine, flood, whatever."

She considered this. "But what of the men? They aren't going to stand idly by while all this goes on. Surely they'll try to stamp it out."

"Hm . . . you overestimate them," the computer responded. "They have done so little over the years they couldn't take a bath without help from women. Who prepares all their food? Women. Add this to the food of key people—the ugly-looking brew should be disguisable somehow, I'd think."

She had another thought. "Obie, what will the potion do to the men? Anything?"

"It's double duty," he informed her. "Only some of the ingredients are needed to produce the effect on the females. The others . . . ? Well, let's put it this way. Suppose the tables were turned. Suppose for a number of weeks they couldn't do with you and then for a few days they couldn't do without you? I'd think that one or two cycles of that and you'd have the men eating out of your hand."

"Some of the matriarchs will think that's enough," she pointed out. "They might use it only on the men."

"I can't do everything," he retorted. "You have to do some, you know. Part of it is political, of course. Besides, you don't *need* the current population. You only need the Entries that will be coming in. There should be a suitable compromise. No reason Awbri should fight our war—although if they want to help they're welcome. That part is up to you."

That sounded reasonable. There was only one other question, but it loomed big in her mind. "Obie, tell me, what happens if we run out of the stuff despite all precautions? On the trail, I mean. What would withdrawal be like?"

"Unpleasant," he said gravely. "It would be increasingly physically painful, bordering on the excruciating. You see, the substance *replaces* hormones produced naturally by the body. The body, in reaction, stops producing them. Withdrawal would cause some breakdown, since it occurs faster than the body can recover and replace not only the hormones but the cellular enzymes replaced as a by-product of the drug. Eventually, after a few days, it would break and the body would overreact once more. The Time would then come with full force, but, this time, for a long, long time. Depending on the body, constitution, and the like, it might take weeks. In a few cases it might never go away. So there is a risk."

She shivered, and a part of her mind wondered how you could shiver in a dream like that. But that was a terrifying thought—all the more so to one who had gone through it—to be in that kind of heat forever!

"That's all," Obie told her cheerfully. "If I can be of any help to you in the future, I might pop up like this. I've placed a number of contingency positions and possible solutions in your brain just in case, so we may meet again. But let's hope we do not, for, if we do, it will mean something has gone terribly wrong."

Yua awoke with a start and looked around. The others were still there, snoring away. It was not yet morning. How long, she wondered, had the whole dream lasted? Not very long, most likely—if, in fact, it had taken any time at all. She sank back down on her straw mat and tried to relax. She would have a busy day tomorrow, she'd need her sleep. In the early part, she would work in a compost heap; later on, she would see an old woman about overthrowing the underpinnings of her society . . .

# Dillia

IT WAS THE START OF SPRING IN DILLIA, THE BEST time of year. The air was warm, the sun bright and cheerful, although there were a few cool breezes from the direction of the high mountains to the west that felt, sometimes, like gentle silk caresses.

Mavra Chang had stood still for a long time, staring at the reflection in the waters of the stream, one with the birds, small river animals, wind and nearby waterfall sound, one with her own thoughts. It was not her reflection, of course, but she hadn't expected that after going through the Well—and, yet, she knew it *was* her reflection, not only as she now was but as she could have been, would have been, had not events in her life taken such a strange turn so long ago. Not the tiny, slightly built Oriental woman the back-alley surgeons had changed her into, disguising her from her enemies but also erasing all connections with her early childhood and ancestry, but, instead, the way it might have been had her native world not fallen into the hands of the dictatorial technocracy that was the Com in those early days.

Oriental. That word had lost its meaning many thousands of years before, when mankind spread out to the stars from Old Earth. A third of mankind perhaps more, had been of one race and they had gone in search of the land Old Earth no longer could give them and the space in which to breathe and live and grow beyond teeming, packed cities and communal farms. Almost everyone looked a little Oriental after a while, and that had been something of a leveler; those purely of the other races of man were very few and far between and tended to stand out in any crowd.

Brazil, of course, and the small, scattered, but hearty
band of Jews on many worlds, and the other odd ones
bound together for racial survival like the gypsies.
Very few and very rare.

Her face now was an exotic face, a sexy face, not
one reflecting the racial mix usual on human planets.
Amost none there had pure golden-blond hair, except
by coloring it, nor deep, icy-blue eyes except with
lenses. Without blemish, her skin, too, was very pale,
although she knew it would darken with the sun, and
her breasts were large, much larger than they had
been before, and perfectly formed. They moved when
she moved, and she was somewhat conscious of the
fact.

She was not, of course, human; only the face and
torso were that, memories of might-have-been. The
human part blended into the equine form perfectly
matched to the human body, also covered in shorter
hair of golden blond with a tail that was almost white.

Obie had made her a centaur twice now, although
she was aware, in the back of her mind, that this time
it was for keeps. She had stood there, thinking after a
while, trying to understand the computer's point. Finally her gaze was drawn from her reflection in the
pool upward toward the nearby mountains, cold-
looking and purple, wrapped in clouds and capped by
snowy peaks that would be a long while melting. That
was not Dillia, she knew, but Gedemondas, mysterious
Gedemondas, which only she remembered—and even
that memory had now been dimmed by centuries of
experience and life. A strange, mystic, mountain race
that had enormous powers yet kept, hermitlike, completely to itself in its mountain rookeries and in its
volcanic steam-heated caverns far beneath the placid
surface. Their thought processes were—well, nonhuman, really, was the term, she supposed, when the
rest of the Southern hemisphere, at least the parts she
had seen, tended to think along more familiar paths,
no matter how bizarre their form and life style. The
Gedemondans had known her and been interested in
her once. Perhaps again?

She turned and walked away from the stream and

waterfall, down the path toward the small village she knew was there, conscious of the fact that she was traveling down the same route that her grandfather had so very long ago, and with the same ultimate destination in mind: the Well of Souls computer itself. Her grandparents had gone there with Brazil, although not really by their own plan.

The village sat at the source of a great glacial lake, far removed from the mainstream of Dillian life. It had remained relatively small, still something of a wilderness community, despite the passing centuries —mostly because the population of the hex was kept relatively stable. There was no overpopulation on the Well World, and therefore none of the pressures that would long ago have forced this area to develop. Nor were there resources here worth despoiling the land; this was a semitech hex, nothing more than steam power allowed, and the deposits of seemingly inexhaustible coal and crude oil were far to the south.

What resources there were here were of greater import to the local population. Fish spawned here throughout the myriad streams that fed the lake, creating a bountiful and carefully managed industry that fed, in more than one way, the food, fertilizer, and special-oils industries elsewhere—Downlake, as the rest of the hex was known to these people. That, and the bountiful game of the Uplake forests, were the resources that counted up here.

Still, she saw, things had changed quite a bit from the last time she had been here. The village *was* larger; there seemed to be more cabins in and between the forest groves, and things seemed a bit more modern. Torches had been replaced by gas lamps, apparently fed from a huge natural-gas canister, near the lake itself, that had connectors for marine refilling. There also seemed to be a large number of small boats moored in neat rows around the small harbor; almost a marina, she thought. The buildings, too, looked newer, not merely the log cabin style of earlier times but some prefabricated units as well. Change was slow to come to places on the Well World, yet change was inevitable everywhere. Still, it disappointed her in a way. Some of the personality seemed to have gone.

Her nakedness didn't bother her; with the coming of warm weather most of the centaurs went without clothing, and only her pale complexion really set her apart from the more weathered bodies moving about.

She sought out the office of the local constable, the only real government they had up here. No sense in going around ignorant and alone when these people had always been a friendly bunch.

She couldn't read the signs, of course, but only one small building, a prefab, had official-looking seals on both sides of the door, seals that could only be the Great Seal of the hex. That meant officialdom, and unless they had really changed, that meant who she was looking for.

Things *had* changed, but it didn't matter. The town, it seemed, had become incorporated, mostly to keep the tourists under control, and this was city hall. A mighty small city hall it was, too; if all four officials the mayor, treasurer, clerk, and constable had decided to be in at the same time, there would have been no room even for furnishings. But, the clerk assured her, that never happened. Things changed, but not all that much. The three others were all on the lake, fishing.

The clerk, a sharp-nosed, businesslike woman with mottled gray-and-white body hair, proved pleasant enough. "My name is Hovna," she told Mavra. "Somehow, when we heard there were a bunch of Entries from your part of space, we expected at least one of you to show up here."

Mavra's eyebrows rose in surprise. "Oh?"

The clerk shrugged. "Four times in our history people from your area have come in, and all four times at least one has wound up here. Must be some kind of affinity."

That interested her. "Are there any others here now?"

"Oh, no," the woman laughed. "Last one was hundreds of years ago, before any of our times. I think you're the first Entry in my records, in fact, from any-where."

That will change shortly, Mavra thought sourly. She would have to alert the authorities here so that some sort of temporary accommodations that wouldn't screw up this pretty and peaceful place could be made for the newcomers. For now she just said, "Well, I'm pleased to be here. My grandfather was once one of you, back in the old days."

The clerk frowned. "Grandfather? I don't remember . . . Anyway, how could that be? Once here, you're *here*."

"Not if you go out through the Well of Souls," Mavra replied.

The clerk, obviously confused, just shrugged and said, "Before my time."

Mavra didn't press the matter. "For now, I only need a few days to get my bearings and such. I'm afraid I'm not your typical Entry—I have some work I was sent here to do."

Her statement was even more puzzling. "Work?" The clerk gave a sideways look that indicated she thought the newcomer was more than a little mentally unbalanced. Still, there was an official register for such cases that declared her a citizen and the like and gave her certain legal rights, which weren't much —but it was a pretty loose government, anyway. Only her first name was taken; the Dillians used only one name and never saw much necessity for two. Fortunately, her name, Mavra, was composed of syllables common to the Dillian tongue and needed no alteration.

"There's a guest lodge at the head of the lake," the clerk told her, scribbling something on a piece of official stationery. "You take this over to them and they'll give you a room until you can get settled. It's still early in the season, so there'll be rooms. You can eat there as well, if you like." Again a second note. "And take this to the smith down the street. You'll need shoes in this country anyway. Beyond that it'll be up to you to find your place here. Lots of things to do if you like this part of the country, or go Downlake for more civilized and paved-over type work." She said the last disdainfully. There were city people and country people, and she made no attempt at concealing which she was.

Mavra looked at the two sheets. "I'm sure this will be fine," she assured the clerk. "Um . . . I can't read them, you know. Which one's which?"

The clerk looked apologetic, then drew a little inverted horseshoe on one. Mavra nodded, thanked her, and left.

She felt hungry, but decided to look around the town before going up to the lodge. Shoes . . . Funny, she hadn't thought of that, she told herself. The Rhone, the centaurs of her old sector, had developed rather sophisticated protections that didn't require them—but shoes might be a good idea here. She headed for the smith's.

This was rather like having a broken bone and having to go to a doctor, she decided. The fact that it wasn't supposed to hurt and would be over quickly didn't diminish the anxiety that came from the thought that the huge, burly, chestnut-colored centaur, who looked as if he could bend steel bars like noodles, was going to drive a bunch of nails into the bottom of her feet.

When she entered the smithy, the smith, a friendly man named Torgix, eyed her appreciatively as any man might, grinned like a schoolboy through a thick beard, and hurried over to her. He took the paper with the horseshoe mark, glanced at it, and told her where to stand.

"Just relax, beautiful," he roared in a voice that fit his physique, "and I'll have it done in a jiffy."

It was pretty nerve-racking to see him measure her hooves, then bend red-hot steel to the proper shape with an artisan's quick skill, and she couldn't bear to watch as he drove the special nails through the small holes in the shoes and then into her hooves. It was true that she felt no real pain, except, perhaps, a residual muscle ache from the force of the blows— truly the man had no idea of his own strength—but the psychic pain was intense. Glad when he was finished, she walked about hesitantly, feeling the extra weight and the odd balance the horseshoes gave her.

"You'll get used to them," he assured her. "In a couple of days you'll forget what it felt like not to wear 'em—and your feet will thank you in the days and months to come. The alloy is good; there'll be no rust or warping, although the nails, naturally, come loose over time. If you have any problems, any smith can do simple repairs. Anything else I can do for you?"

She shook her head. "Nothing, thanks. But I could use a drink, I think." She hesitated. "But that takes money or some kind of payment, doesn't it?"

"I wouldn't worry about it," he chuckled. "You're the most beautiful woman in these here parts, I'll tell you, and you got the moves, too, beggin' your pardon, if you know what I mean. You won't have no trouble gettin' a drink. You was a woman—before?"

She nodded.

"Then you know what I means," he said knowingly, and winked.

She smiled slightly. Yes, she knew exactly what he meant.


The culture she remembered from her last time through Dillia had been communal. If there had been any money, it hadn't been used here, in the village Uplake. Again things had changed, although not to the complicated degrees found elsewhere even on the Well World. You had a number—*she* had a number, on those notes—and that gave you an account, kept by the clerk in the village where you were registered. It wasn't a very definite kind of thing—the units were sloppy and not even named—and the only thing required was to do some sort of productive work known to the community to keep your account open. There was no trouble going to a store or seller's stall and just getting what you needed—as long as you worked and produced.

She wondered how far an Entry's account stretched

before it ran dry. A little, anyway, she decided. There hadn't really been a time limit—although, of course, the clerk hadn't explained the system nor read her out her number, either. Best to be wary with folk from alien cultures who might abuse a charge account, she decided. But she *was* beautiful, and she did, unconsciously, have the moves, as the blacksmith had said, and the system was easily explained to her.

She had gotten sloppy and lazy, she decided. Bars had always been her element; she grew up in and around them, worked them and worked in them. She had always been what others thought of as cute, which had worked to good advantage, but she was now the center of attention and she was rusty at handling it. Obie had been a close friend, a companion, the closest thinking being to her for a long, long time, and she missed him terribly. But he had also been a drug, she was now realizing, a magic genie that could give you anything you wanted or needed at the snap of a finger. The old tough, totally self-reliant Mavra Chang had been lost somewhere along the line. It had been an insidious kind of thing, not missed until needed, and now she realized the disadvantage she was at.

She had been a total world unto herself for the early part of her life, and fiercely proud of it. She had clawed her way to the top by her own wits and abilities—not without a helping hand here and there, but that was true of everyone in the universe, she knew. She had changed, though. Magic wands do that to you.

She found the men and women in the bar mostly loud, boisterous, and very boorish. That had always been the case, of course, but she had always been able to tolerate such behavior and to fake fitting in to get what she wanted. Doing so was increasingly difficult now; the routine social acting seemed somehow impossible, the pawing and passes hard to ignore and easy to cause irritation. She left as quickly as she could and walked up to the lodge, a huge wooden building of logs with a wide porch fronting on the marina and lake.

It was a pretty place inside; the entire first floor was

open, except for the huge log ceiling bracing beams, and there was a fireplace at each end and one in the center with an exhaust vent rising up to the roof. The rooms split off in two-story wings from the back of the main social hall, small and basic but what was needed. Dillians slept standing up, although they liked to be braced for sheer relaxation, and there was an area with two padded rails for that; also a sink with running spring water, a pitcher, and some linen for just washing up. The common latrine was down the hall, just a bunch of stalls you backed into. Nothing fancy, but it would do.

Between the two wings was the dining area, posted with signs she couldn't read but which were easily translated by a friendly staffer as serving times by room number. The basically vegetarian Dillians prepared their plants in a thousand different and delicious ways, both hot and cold, and always highly seasoned, but no one would ever starve in this forest land, no matter what. In a pinch, all Dillians could eat just about any plant matter, including grass and leaves, although the taste often left something to be desired.

She stayed a few days like this, mostly wandering the back trails, staring at the mountains, and trying to find that old self she needed now so much. At one time she had been proud of isolation, reveling in being totally alone and on her own. She still thought she did, but she could not shake the feeling of intense isolation from these simple folks. Part of the difference, she told herself, was that, now, she was working for someone else's ends—but, no, she had always taken commissions from others and always delivered. Still, it had been *her* plan, *her* preparation. Even with Obie she had the sense of being independent, doing what she wanted, the way she wanted it. Not now, though.

What had changed in her, she wondered. Was it the same with people as with this hex, this village? Subtle changes as you grew older, all changing you beyond recognition? Had she changed so much that she no longer had the tools to do a job?

That, of course, was it. Tools were more than fancy

equipment; they were also mental. Extreme self-confidence was a must, but also the social tools to get what you wanted from anybody you needed. That was what her life with Obie had robbed her of: the instinct for making people and events bend to her will. She hadn't needed it; Obie was the ultimate persuader. She had lost the ability, somewhere, and she couldn't seem to discover where. Take Marquoz—he still had it, had always had it. The Chugach was firmly in charge not only of himself but of those around him, the way she used to be. And Gypsy—whoever, wherever he was—he, too, had it. Where did they get it? They weren't born with it, certainly. It was something you acquired as you grew—something *some* acquired. And how did you lose it? By not using it constantly, as Marquoz and Gypsy had always used it.

She was, she thought, like the big frontier fighter who had fought and clawed his way to the top, then wound up in a huge mansion with all that he desired at his beck and call. Take that away after many years and he would be lost. His skills would be rusty, out of date, or, worse, atrophied from long years of disuse.

Atrophied. That bothered her. The wild catlike animal she had been had become tame, domesticated, fat, and lazy. Now that it was thrown again into the wild, its pampered self found that wilderness an alien place, no longer its element at all.

There was no getting around that fact, although she hated to admit it even to her innermost self. She not only needed other people, she needed people she could depend upon, even trust with her life. Perhaps if she had had more time, or were more in control of events and able to alter the plan or the schedule to suit her, she might have reclaimed more of her old abilities, reverted to the wild whence she had come. But she could not, and time was running out even now. Events beyond her control would soon force actions and reactions of which she had foreknowledge—her best weapon—but could not change.

She walked along the riverbank in the late afternoon thinking about this when a curious, harelike animal leaped into view. Its gigantic ears and exag-

gerated buckteeth gave it an almost comical, cartoon-
ish quality that was offset by one look at those
powerful legs. It was also more than 150 centimeters
high, even without the ears—a formidable size indeed
—although the species was harmless. It stared at
her, more in curiosity than in fear, and she stared
back. Somewhere in the corners of her mind a notion
stirred and forced itself to the fore. There was something decidedly odd about the animal, something she
couldn't quite place but which seemed somehow important.

In a moment she realized that the animal was
brown from the face down to its shorter forelegs, but
beyond that the hair slowly was replaced by snow-
white fur. Looking closer, she could see signs of occasional white fringes even in the light brown.

She had seen such creatures before, but they had
been mostly white or mostly brown. Now, suddenly,
she knew why. White was its winter coloration, making it almost invisible against the snow. Now, with
spring here and every day getting a bit warmer than
the last, the animal was turning brown, a better protective color for the now blossoming forest. Slowly
the white was being pushed out, with the seasonal
change—and that meant that, for one of two times a
year, the beast was unable to rely on its camouflage
for any sort of protection. Now, during early spring as
it would be later in fall, it was a target. Hunting parties were coming Uplake now; she had seen them, and
cursed herself for not putting the facts together.

Hunting was a major industry for Dillians; the
natives used the furs and skins for a variety of things
and sold the meat to adjoining hexes. Hunting parties
—professionals, mostly—meant tough people who
knew their way around. But the hunting wasn't done
in Dillia—that was possible only in Uplake, and Uplake's wildlife was reserved for Uplake's permanent
residents in order to conserve it. No, Dillian hunting
was done in Gedemondas, on the high trails.

She decided that her best place was back in town
after all, this time looking for a way into Gedemondas. What she needed from Dillia could be ar-

ranged for later; Gedemondas was more critical, particularly since there might not be time enough later to do anything.

Early attempts at linking up with an expedition resulted in failure. Although the hunting parties were composed of females as well as males, the Dillians having few sexual distinctions when there was a job to do, she was too soft, too pretty for them to take seriously. It was a frustrating experience for her. All her life she had been not merely small but tiny, and had never been taken seriously then, either—until it was too late. But now, to be scorned because she was too attractive, that was an unkind blow. Not that the hunters, particularly the huge, strutting males, weren't interested in her—they just weren't interested from the business standpoint.

She felt as if she were going back to her beginnings, when, poor and trapped on a backward frontier world, she had gained money, influence, and eventually a way out by renting her body and other services. But things were different now; Dillia had some similarities, but not that way out—not now and not here. And she had nothing else, not even a thick coat for the wintry cold of the hunting grounds, nor any real weapons skills. Oh, she knew a laser pistol and its related cousins inside and out, but this was a semitech hex, where nothing beyond combustion weapons would work; and the hunting ground, Gedemondas, was a nontech hex, where killing was accomplished with bows and arrows and similar weapons, weapons that required a constant honing of skills, of which she had almost none, particularly in this new and larger body.

She was becoming discouraged, and some attempts with both bow and crossbow hadn't given her any more of a lift. She was lousy with them.

Still she continued to meet, greet, and talk to the parties still coming in, now in a rush to make sure they would still be able to stake out some unclaimed hunting territory. They were all at the bar, and one man, the leader of a party, was gustily downing huge mugs of ale and telling the locals about Gedemondas. Most

had never been there and never would go there; it was
a mysterious and dangerous place even for those who
knew it well, and what common sense didn't prevent,
superstition did. Despite the fact that Dillian young
could discuss hexes and creatures halfway around the
Well World, nobody knew much about their next-door
neighbors. They maintained no embassy at Zone, and
histories said nothing about them. Geographies generally described them as shy, but nasty, savages glimpsed
only from distances. Dillia did not have permission to
hunt in Gedemondas, but there had never been an ob-
jection. All these made the hex an eerie, forbidding
place of legend.

The hunter, whose name was Asam, was a big burly
Dillian in early middle age but aging extremely well.
His tanned lean, muscular figure was matched by a
craggy, handsome face that looked as if it had seen the
misery of the world; yet, somehow, there was a kind-
ness there, perhaps accented by his unusual deep-green
eyes. His beard, flecked with white, was perfectly
trimmed and he was, overall, rugged but well-groomed.
His voice matched his looks: thick, low, rich, melodic,
and extremely masculine.

"It's always winter up there," he was saying between
long pulls on a two-liter-plus mug of ale. "Aye, a warm
summer's day could freeze yer hair solid. We hav'ta
take extra care, rubbin' each other down regular so
the sweat don't turn into little iceballs. And y'do sweat,
make no mistake. Some of them old trails are almost
straight up, and yer' carryin' a heavy pack. Sometimes
you lose the trail completely—hav'ta go out onto the
snow and ice, which is double bad this time o' year,
for snow melts from the ground up and the sun do
beat down, it does. So y'get hidden crevasses that can
swallow a party whole and never leave a trace, and
nasty slicks and soft spots, and snow bridges, where it
looks like solid ground but there's nothin' underneath
ya but air when ya try it."

His accent was peculiar; it translated to her brain as
something out of a children's pirate epic, colorful and
unique. She wondered how much of it was put on for
the show of attention, or whether, as with some others

she had known, he had put on the act so often that he
had become the character he liked to play.

His audience was mostly young, of course, and they
peppered him with questions. Mavra eased over to one
of them and whispered, "Who *is* he, anyway?"

The youngster looked shocked. "Why, that's Asam
—the Colonel himself!" came the awed reply.

She didn't remember anything about rank in Dillia.
"I'm sorry, I'm new here," she told the awe-struck
youth. "Can you tell me about him? Why is he called
the Colonel?"

"Why, he's been completely around the world!" her
informant breathed. "He's served more'n fifty hexes at
one time or another. Doin' all sorts of stuff—smugglin',
explorin', courier—you name it!"

A soldier of fortune, she thought, surprised. A
Dillian soldier of fortune, an adventurer, an anything-
for-a-price risk-taker—she knew the type. To have
gotten this old he had to be damned good even if half
the stories told about him probably weren't true. If in
fact he had been around the Well World, he was one
of the very few who ever had. That alone said something about him—and was the kind of accomplishment
to make a legend right there, thus probably true.

"And the Colonel part?" she pressed.

"Aw, he's been every kind'a rank and stuff you can
think of in a lotta armies. When he got the plague
serum from Czill to Morguhn against all the Dhabi attempts to stop him, why, they made him an honorary
Colonel there. Dunno why, but he stuck with that. It's
what most everybody calls him."

She nodded and turned again to the powerful and
legendary center of attention, who was off on a tan-
gent, telling some tale of fighting frost-giants in a far-
off hex long ago.

"If he's that kind of man, what's he doing here?
Just hunting?" she asked the youth after a while.

An older man edged over, hearing her question.
"Pardon, miss, but it's his obsession. Imagine being all
over the world here and doing all he's done and have
Gedemondas right next door—he was born here, Uplake. It's a puzzle for him. Off and on he's sworn to

capture a Gedemondan and find out what makes 'em tick before he dies."

Her eyebrows arched and a slight smile played across her face. "Oh, he has, has he?" she muttered under her breath. She stood there for a while, until the story was done, then pressed a question through the throng to him. "Have you ever seen a Gedemondan?" she called out.

He smiled and took another swig, eyes playing appreciatively over her form. "Yes, m'beauty, many times," he replied. "A couple of times some of the creatures actually tried to do me in, pushing avalanches on me. Other times, I seen them at a distance, off across a valley or makin' them strange sounds echoin' off the snow-cliffs."

She doubted the Gedemondans had ever wanted to do him in. If they had, he would be dead now, she knew.

She had Asam on the right track now, and finally he looked around and asked, "Anybody else here seen a Gedemondan? If so, I wanta know about it."

There it was. "I have," she called out. "I've seen a whole lot of them. I've been in one of their cities and I've talked to them."

Asam almost choked on his ale. *"Cities? Talked* to them?" he echoed, then leaned toward the bartender. "Who is that girl, anyway?" he asked in a low rumble out of the side of his mouth.

The bartender looked over at her, following the gaze of the rest of the patrons, also staring at her, mostly wondering if the insanity was contagious.

"A recent Entry," the bartender whispered back. "Only been here a few days. A little batty if you ask me."

Asam turned those strange green eyes again in her direction. "What's yer name, honey?"

"Mavra," she told him. "Mavra Chang."

To her surprise, he just nodded to himself. "Ortega's Mavra?"

"Not exactly," she shot back, somewhat irritated at being thought of that way. "We don't have much mutual love, you know."

Asam laughed heartily. "Well, girl, looks like you'n me we got a lot to talk about." He drained the last of the mug. "Sorry, folks, business first!" he announced, and made his way outside.

The structure, like most, was open to the street on one side, but even then it was a problem for the two of them to make it outside. Still, the youngsters followed in what looked like a slow-motion stampede, Mavra thought with a chuckle.

Asam was using a hunter's cabin, the kind of place built for working transients, and it was to that log structure, one with walls and a door that shut, that they went.

Finally assured of some privacy, he sighed, relaxed a bit, and took out a pipe. "You don't mind if I light up, do you?" he asked in a calm, casual tone that retained some of the accent though not nearly as much as he had put on in the bar.

"Go ahead," she invited. "You're the first smoker I've seen on this whole world."

"Just need the right contacts," he replied. "Stuff's damned expensive, and the only varieties worth a damn are grown in just a couple of far-off hexes. We Dillians are crazy about the stuff—I dunno, maybe it's the biochemistry. But only a few of us can afford it."

"Watch it," she said playfully. "Your education's showing."

He laughed. "Oh, well, we hav'ta do somethin' 'bout that, don't we? Yer can't let yer act slip, right?"

She returned the laugh. She was beginning to like the Colonel—he was her kind.

"So," he said after a few moments, "tell me about Gedemondas."

"I was there," she told him. "A long, long time ago, it's true. I may look like a youngster but I'm a spry thousand-year-old. If you know Ortega well enough to recognize my name, you know the basic story."

He nodded. "I know the basics from the history tapes. I do a lot of work for him, off and on, and we got to know each other real well."

She was suddenly suspicious. "You're not working for him now, are you?"

He laughed again. "No, I'm not. But I'll be honest with you; he *did* get in touch with me. Me and a lot of others, I suspect. Asked me to be on the lookout for you and the others and let him know."

"And have you?"

He shook his head. "Nope. Not going to, either. Let's face it, there's no profit in it. And I'm pretty well doing what I want to do these days. Besides, I didn't know until a few minutes ago you were in Dillia, let alone as a Dillian. Bet he'll know as soon as word goes Downlake, though. It was kind of a general all-points, you know. Before I decide much of anything, I want to know just what the hell's up. And, most of all, I want to know about Gedemondas."

They weren't kidding about his fixation, she realized. But that was all to the good.

"First of all," she began, "do you know who Nathan Brazil is?"

He chuckled. "That's sort of a joke on the Well World, you know. A supernatural creature, a myth, a legend, whatever."

She nodded. "It's not a myth or legend anymore," she told him. "He's coming again to the Well World. He has to get into the Well of Souls." Briefly, she outlined the basic history to date, the rip in space, the damage to the Well World and consequently to all reality, the fact that Brazil was going to the Well to, in essence, turn it off, fix it, then start it up again.

He listened intently, green eyes reflecting the flickering gaslight almost like a cat's. He didn't interrupt, although he did occasionally grunt or nod. She did not elaborate on the plan or the problems; that would come much later, after it was clear which side Asam was on.

He was ahead of her. "I can see a big battle," he said after she had finished. "If he shuts it off, it all ceases to exist and it wipes the memory or whatever it has clean. Don't look surprised; just because Dilla's a semitech hex doesn't mean we don't know or use other folks' machines. Just not here. A little cooperation. There's more of that than you realize. There was once a plague and the people couldn't stop it—no

technology. But a far-off hex with labs and computers
went to work on it, created a serum, and made enough
for me to take over four thousand kilometers to the
people who needed it but couldn't make it or even
isolate it. We saved a lot of folks' lives and I got my
title."

"Why that one?" she asked him. "Out of all you've
gathered?"

There was a faint smile and a faraway look in his
eyes. "The only one I ever got for *saving* lives," he
responded softly. Then he snapped out of his reverie
and returned to business.

"You and I know the rules," he pointed out. "If
he's going to rebuild the universe, then he's going to
need live models. Us. Don't sound like I have any per-
centage on your side—nor would anybody else on this
world of ours."

"He won't destroy the Well World," she assured
him. "In a little while our army's going to pour
through the Well. Probably already is. Huge numbers.
They'll be the fighting force for him, and they'll also
be the prototypes for his new universe. Not you."

"And you?" he came back. "Where will you be if
he does this?"

She smiled grimly. "I wish I knew. One thing at a
time. I'm not certain if I'll survive to that point—and
if I do, I'll face the situation when it comes.
Gedemondas, for one. I have to go there. I have to
talk to them, explain the situation, see which way they
will go."

He nodded. "I'll accept that answer. And the per-
centage?"

She realized he was talking about himself. "And
after? Well, it would be nice to be on Brazil's side if
he reaches the Well, wouldn't it? At least, I'd rather
be on his side if he gets in than one of his enemies."

He considered that. "One thing at a time. Gedemondas will do for now. You think they'll talk to you?"

"I think so," she replied. "They did before, anyway. And I'm the only one who was there who they
allowed to remember exactly what happened, to remember them at all."

"Um. Wouldn't do much good if we went in there and I came out never remembering a thing, would it?"

She shrugged. "No guarantees. I'm surprised you believe me now. Nobody else did."

"Ortega did," he told her. "He couldn't afford not to check it out completely. There were just enough tiny inconsistencies in the others' stories to cast doubt, and he had no sign of that in you. He concluded you were telling the truth. Matter of fact, he once held your account out to me as bait for a job. Knew I couldn't resist."

"I need to go there," she told him flatly. "I need to go there soon. I have other things to do. But I don't know the hex, don't know the trails, don't have any guide, or credit for provisions or anything. I need your help—badly. And I'm your best shot at meeting the Gedemondans."

He nodded agreement to that last statement. "All right, I'll get whatever you need. You're welcome to come with us."

She sighed. Mission partially accomplished. "How many are you?"

"Five, counting you. All Dillians." He put on a mock leer. "All male except for you. That bother you?"

"I can take care of myself," she responded flatly.

He grinned and nodded approvingly. "I bet you can, too."

# Embassy of Ulik, South Zone

"THE GRAND COUNCIL, SOUTH, IS CONVENED." ORtega declared solemnly from his office, but it was ritual only. It meant that all the embassies at Zone were now connected together in an elaborate communications net. The creatures who breathed water, the ones that breathed one or another mixture of air, and some who didn't really breathe at all could now converse. Not all the hexes of the Southern hemisphere of the Well World were represented; and some, like Gedemondas, never sent anyone and their offices were empty. A fairly large number of councillors, like Ortega, were Entries—people who were originally from other places and races in the vast universe and had blundered into Markovian gates. They made good council members; such people were usually more adept at handling new Entries, having gone through the experience personally.

"This meeting was called at my request because I believe it is imperative we all understand what is going on and decide on a common policy of dealing with it," Ortega went on. Briefly he explained the situation as he understood it, holding nothing back.

Finally, he got down to the real business. "We have several options here," he told them. "The first is to do nothing. This will result in a temporary doubling of the Well World's population, a severe strain on resources—but only for a short time. Unimpeded, Brazil would go to the Well, do what he has to do, then reduce the population by the same factor as he increased it in his overall restocking process. This would result in inconvenience, yes, but not anything we couldn't handle."

"If he used the newcomers only to do that restocking," someone noted. "If he uses all of us, it's the end. Or if he isn't choosy whether there are newcomers or natives, for that matter."

Ortega nodded in reflex toward the speaker, although there were no television circuits. "That, of course, is precisely it. I know Brazil. I know he's a man of his word. But, in all fairness, he's going to be doing something all by himself that the Markovians did as a race—and that's not the way the system was designed. We don't know if he has that kind of control or confidence. He will be doing it for the first time and can't really know, either. He's a Markovian for sure—I've seen him in his natural form. But if we trust his own story—and though I'll take his word of honor on things, I would never believe any of his stories without proof—he himself says he was a technician on Hex 41. A technician but not the creator. Now, the fact that he also claims to be God, the Prime Mover, the supreme creator of the universe, should give you some idea as to just what to believe."

"I'd tend to believe it," said another alien voice. The circuits were such that the first to punch the talk bar blocked the others so only one could speak at a time. Otherwise there would be another Babel.

"That he's God?" Ortega was shocked.

"No, of course not," the ambassador responded. "That's just the point, you see. His self-claims are of the most grandiose sort. He claims to be God, or thinks he is. Someone who claims that would claim almost reflexively that he was the creator of a hex and not a mere technician if he felt compelled to make something up. He didn't, therefore I'll go along with the idea that he was lower down. That bothers me even more, of course. We have computers here in Ramagin that are quite sophisticated. If one needed minor repair, then I'd trust a technician. But if one needed programming from the word go and there wasn't any copy of the original program to feed in, I'd want an expert. Brazil didn't program anything, not even Hex 41—so how can we trust him to know what he's doing on something like the Well, something so complex that no mind I know can conceive of it?"

Ortega cut off further comment. "Good point. I see a number of you wish to speak, but if you'll permit me, I'll go on so that we won't be in this meeting for the next three weeks. Time presses."

He paused, allowing the little lights to wink out as they accepted his ruling, at least temporarily. Satisfied, he continued. "Now, our second option is to contact Brazil and try to make a deal with him. If he manages to get to the Well and he's mad at us, we may have precipitated a self-fulfilling prophecy. If he has to fight to get there, he's going to be damned mad at all of us and in a position to get even. We have to consider this. If he *can* do the job, he might use only the newcomers if he gets there easily, or he might just use *us* if we fight him all the way, harm his people, that sort of thing."

"*Could* we make a deal with him?" someone else asked.

"Probably," Ortega responded. "We could get his word—which has been good in the past. But we couldn't *enforce* the bargain. The last time he was here a bunch of us tried to do that, you know. We got into the Well, but it was as incomprehensible to us then as it is now. Worse, he was in Markovian form and fully capable of doing damned near anything just by some sort of mental contact with the great computer."

"Would *you* trust him?" somebody put in.

Ortega considered the question. "I would. But I wouldn't necessarily trust him to be able to keep his promise, for reasons we just went into. Working the Well on a few individuals is one thing; fixing and then working the entire computer on the whole damned universe is something else. He's a cocky little bastard—I'm sure *he* thinks he could do it. But I'm not sure I do."

For a moment no lights showed as the others thought about what Ortega said. Then everyone tried to speak at once and again he had to cut them off.

"The third alternative, the one Brazil anticipates,

is that we will oppose him—keep him from reaching the Well at all costs. His agents are already here, organizing the newcomers and playing on the national self-interests of a number of vulnerable hexes that might on their own support him. His army is coming through now, ready to rally to those organizers. If we try and stop him, we have to face several ugly facts. First, we can capture him, imprison him, do all sorts of nasty things to him, but we *cannot* kill him. The Well won't permit it, no matter how hard we try. Something always happens to give him an out. Therefore, we are talking about virtually perpetual imprisonment. Second, we're talking about a hell of a fight. We're not sure just where he is, and he hasn't surfaced as yet. That last is probably all to the good, since we know he's a Type 41, we know his general physical description, and we'd know sooner or later. He'd be spotted, and if he were in a vulnerable spot, say on the ocean, he'd be open to immediate capture. We have to assume he's somewhere in and around Glathriel or Ambreza, even though we've searched in vain for him there. He's not dumb enough not to have prepared an almost foolproof hiding place. So, we have to wait for him to move. He'll wait for his army or armies to spring him, give him the muscle to move northward. That means a multinational, multiracial set of armies must be established and set in strategic places, ready to oppose them at every turn. Since he picks the route, we'll be at even more of a logistical disadvantage than they, but we'll have sheer numbers and the lay of the land." He paused for a moment, then added, "And, third, of course, by so doing we'll be condemning ourselves to being, eventually, the only life forms in all of creation."

Again the board was blank, the speaker was silent for a very long time, followed by everyone trying to speak at once. They talked for hours; they argued, they wrangled, they tried to find other ways out of it. Ortega let them go on, taping the whole thing and also making notes on a map of the Well World when the speakers could be identified as to their own leanings. It was an interesting score. Of the seven hundred or

so hexes represented, about a third were either potentially ineffective—the ones whose natives couldn't
leave their home hexes such as the plant creatures
who had little or no mobility, that kind of thing—
or indecisive. A few times he caught hints that some
of the hexes might align themselves with Brazil's forces
if chance came their way, and it was obvious in which
hexes Brazil agents had been at work. Marquoz clearly
had the Hakazit sewn up, for example. The Dillians,
on the whole not very combative people, were taking
no governmental position—they had very little government anyway—and letting their people decide for
themselves.

But a solid majority, it appeared, did not give a
damn about the rest of the universe, didn't care about
anything but their own necks, and were all for a fight.
That was to be expected, he knew. When a nation was
faced with a choice between abstract principle or complete self-interest, it took self-interest every time.

They would fight—or enough of them would, anyway. He couldn't stop it, and only when talk turned to
pogroms against the newcomers did he step in once
more. "I wouldn't recommend any mass wiping-out
of these Entries!" he cautioned fiercely. "Consider:
you must allow for the very real possibility that, in
spite of all our best efforts, Brazil will get to the Well.
Any race that has wiped out its surplus at that point
will be, of necessity, faced with total annihilation.
You can't afford to kill them! Consider your people's
lives, your own lives! *After* Brazil is in our hands,
then you can do as you wish. But only then."

"But all the Entries are on his side!" somebody
wailed, echoing a lot of the sentiment. "You're saying
we have to take a treasonous army into our midst,
one that would kill us!"

"That's where he's got us," Ortega admitted. "But,
remember, you don't have to give them much, if any,
freedom. Control them as best you can. My guess is
most will bolt for prearranged rendezvous as soon as
they can—if you let them. Don't let them. Reduce his
army and control it inside your own borders. It's up
to you to play it smart—and subtle."

He knew that they would not all take his advice, but most would. Self-interest again. They had to hedge their bets. Many innocents would be slaughtered, of that he had no doubt, but most would hesitate, most would pause. He hoped so.

Finally it came down to a vote. Of the 713 hexes represented, 431 voted to stop Brazil, 184 to try some kind of deal, and 98 abstained or, in essence, voted to do nothing. The tally was remarkably close to the guesstimate Ortega had made on his map during the debates.

"So the motion is carried. It's war," he told them at last. "All right. As we have no power to compel the dissenters to support the majority position, I must make several moves at this time. First, I must ask any who wish to change their votes to so signify to me, reminding those in the minority that there will be some bad feeling toward those hexes not joining in this effort, bad feeling that could translate into a lot of forms from trade sanctions and boycotts to a rather callous disregard for a neutral or opposing hex that happens to get in the way of a fight." It wasn't an idle threat or an attempt at coercion; he felt it had to be said because he knew it to be true. Win or lose, nations that committed heavily to a fight and lost their own lives and resources in the process would not be kindly disposed toward those who sat it out.

Interestingly, three of the abstainers and two of the make-a-deal faction moved to the war column, and two voting originally for war dropped off the voting board. The outcome was a net gain, but surprising.

He nodded absently. "All right, then. The Well is to be divided into military zones, each under an overall commander. Each participating hex will mobilize and choose its own commander, but all of them will be subject to an overall sector commander, who will be from outside the sector and therefore of a race not related to any of the troops under its command. War is not something we are used to—our enemy will be more accustomed to it. Yet, it can be waged, and successfully. Logistics defeated the first Well War, but that was for conquest and involved no cooperation among hexes in the way of objectives. The second War of the Well was fought for limited objectives, to reach a certain point before opposing armies could. Again, there wasn't the cooperation we now have among the many hexes. And we are moving in *response* to another army. In this case things are on our side—the enemy is moving toward an objective, and all we must do is stop them from attaining that objective. The disadvantages are theirs, although they will pick the route of march."

There was a lot more discussion, followed by general agreement to the plan. All would make nominations for sector commanders and submit them to Ortega, who would use the most sophisticated computers in the high-tech hexes to pick the best one for each position.

"I will also notify the North and send a transcript for their council to consider," he told them. "Brazil is tricky—and travel to the North *is* possible, although with great difficulty. It would be just like him to cause all hell to break loose down here while he popped up there—where, if this volume of Entries keeps up, the Well will also be putting newcomers—and make for an Avenue from that side."

Though as yet unheard of, it was already becoming apparent that the Well of Souls, the great computer heart of the world, was actually putting some carbon-based Entries into those eerie, non-carbon-based hexes up North. Such a thing shouldn't happen, but the Well was acting in sheer self-defense. It had to distribute the unprecedented volume of newcomers as evenly as possible over the whole world to make certain it had the resources to manage them. Brazil had counted on that—he needed double the population of all 1560 hexes, not just in the South.

And as for himself . . . Ortega rocked back on his giant serpent's tail and folded all six of his arms in contemplation. Ulik, of course, would go with the majority. He had voted that way, the way he knew his own people would vote. The word would go off to them shortly by courier while he stayed here, stuck in this luxury prison.

That's what this was, he decided. Prison. It wasn't the first time he had thought about that concept. Brazil would be trapped in such a prison, probably one of the unused embassies. It annoyed him that they were voting to try doing to Brazil what had been done to him.

Trouble was, of course, that he had done it to himself. Committed himself to this cold, sterile prison rather than face death. Pushing toy armies around tables, putting pins in maps, that would be his battle, his campaign, his war. It might as well have been a billion light-years away, he thought. And yet, to go out there meant death, sure, certain, probably quick death.

He recalled the ancient legend of his original people, the legend of Faust. And when the demon Mephistopheles had been ordered back to Hell, he had replied, "Why, this is Hell, nor am I out of it."

Ortega looked around his comfortable office.

Why, this is Hell, he echoed the ancient line in his mind for the millionth time, nor am I out of it.

No wonder Brazil was batty. Nobody, he thought, understands that man more than me. He wished he could talk to the strange little man now.

He wished he could talk to somebody.

Why, this is Hell. . . .

# Dahbi

THE GREAT HALL OF HOLY ANCESTORS STOOD EMPTY;
barren stone carved out of solid granite far beneath
the surface, without ornamentation, without light, yet
a perfect cubical space some two hundred meters in
any direction. Silent, tomblike, it waited.

Suddenly a portion of one wall glowed eerily, and
something, a presence, came through into the chamber. It glowed with its own eerie white phosphores-
cence, a pale, smoky thing like a piece of ghostly satin
rippling in an unfelt wind, its only features two jet-
black ovals at the top of its rounded "head" that must
be some kind of eyes.

And yet it seemed to have mass, and some weight,
for once through the seemingly solid rock wall it ad-
hered to the side, then slowly made its way down to
the floor of the place, always in contact with the wall's
edge. An observer might think it was floating, yet
closer examination would show that it did need contact for movement, and was neither as ghostly nor as
insubstantial as it first appeared.

Now other forms oozed in from different points in
the four walls and also through the ceiling and up
through the floor. All converged at the center of the
Great Hall. Twelve in number, they looked identical:
glowing white shapes each the same roughly two meters in height, all looking like people dressed in some
kind of sheet—rounded head with two eye-holes, then
the shape tapering down, seeming to bulge a little at
the middle, then fanning out to a wide, flat base.

No words nor glances were exchanged. They stood
there, waiting, waiting for something—or someone.

Suddenly from one of the walls came still another

like themselves, yet not quite like them, either. It seemed larger, more formidable, and, in some inexplicable way, more ancient.

"Peace be unto the brotherhood!" proclaimed the newcomer, standing in front of the others and now raising what seemed to be insectlike forelegs, sucker-tipped and etched along the leg with wicked-looking spikes. The appendages were invisible when folded.

The others slowly raised their own and chanted, "And to you, most revered and holy leader."

The one who was so obviously in charge now underwent a slight change. The ghostly head moved slowly back, the "eyes" moving with it, revealing a head and a face, a vicious, ugly face, with bright multifaceted eyes that seemed to generate their own light, flanked by a sharp proboscis under which extended menacing mandibles.

"You all have been briefed on the situation?" It wasn't really a question. Anyone who hadn't would have to execute the staff that should have kept the leader informed.

"As you are aware, then, I instructed us to vote with the majority," the leader continued. "Our somewhat unique abilities should make us invaluable in a fight. And yet I am unhappy, for I do not like things left to the fates. Our ancestors would demand more of us."

They didn't comment, keeping their heads tucked in reverently. It *was* partly reverence, partly respect—and partly that even they, the twelve who ruled their land as an absolute theocracy, were terrified of Gunit Sangh.

Anyone in Dahbi could enter the priesthood; those with a lot of brains and guts could rise far inside the hierarchy, too. But to reach the top, the pinnacle, you had to have more. In a land ruled by ancestor worship, old age commanded the greatest respect. And in a land where only the smartest, the most ruthless, the most totally amoral could reach the top of the order, the oldest of that hierarchy was not only the leader, but also the nastiest bastard the race had yet produced.

"Hear my commands," intoned Gunit Sangh. "First, we shall prepare a force under the overall Zone council command. We will contribute whatever is asked, in equal measure, from each prefecture. Choose your people well. I want the most expendable, to be sure, but also I want people who can take orders, who can fight—and kill."

The twelve gave a silent nod in unison.

"However, this is not sufficient," Sangh continued. "Suppose the battle occurs far from Dahbi? This would leave us as helpless pawns, known to be fighting this Brazil creature yet unable to do anything to influence the outcome. That is intolerable. Zilchet, you have a report on the Entries in our land?"

One of the twelve stirred, and the vicious insectlike head rose. "I have, Your Holiness. We have received approximately three hundred so far. I say "approximately" only because one seems to pop up almost every hour."

"And you have interrogated the newcomers?"

"I have, Your Holiness. Our psychologists find them a truly alien mentality—which is to be expected, of course, but not quite to this extent. They seem to have all been females of the Type 41 category—the same as Brazil. They are part of a religious cult of some kind that believes Brazil to be God—not *a* god but *the* God—and will do whatever he wills. In other words, fanatics on a holy mission."

"They wish to proceed away from Dahbi?"

A slight nod. "They do, Your Holiness. They are quickly learning their new bodies and adjusting with astonishing rapidity to new forms and abilities."

"It is to be expected," Gunit Sangh noted. "Whoever planned this operation knew the Well World before they ever got here. They have been thoroughly briefed. They *knew* they were going to become different forms with different abilities and were told to explore their new forms and adjust quickly. They are not here as ignorant children to live a new life; they are here as preprepared soldiers. You see what I mean, my brothers. We could lose this thing."

They seemed to shimmer a bit at this idea. It was disturbing to them, as it was to Gunit Sangh.

"You have them under restraint?"

Zilchet sounded slightly miffed at the question. "Of course, Your Holiness. Any who appear are brought as quickly as possible to a central receiving facility, where they are carefully interrogated and then restrained, awaiting Your Holiness's decision."

"My decision is to let them go," the leader told them.

This astonished them, and there was much agitated rippling of their ghostly white forms.

"Tell me, are they of the same race? The same world?"

Zilchet had barely recovered from his shock. "Yes, Your Holiness. The same. Remarkable uniformity, in fact, if I do say so myself."

"Do they appear to know each other personally—as from before?"

"No, it is not evident. At least I have seen no indication of such. Not that it might not happen, but if you are talking about a population of a billion or more, as we surmise, it would be pure chance."

Gunit Sangh seemed pleased at this. "And is your understanding complete enough to allow, say, three hundred Entries to go where they will—and four hundred Entries to arrive there? In close company all the while?"

"Four—" Zilchet seemed confused, slightly hesitant. Then, all at once, he got the idea. "Oh, I *see*." He considered it. "Superficially, at any rate. I would prefer not to have them travel as a group. A chance encounter, yes, but not moment-to-moment. No. There are too many tiny details. You could slip so very easily and never know. But we *could* send three hundred, then another hundred a day or so behind them, following. Conditioning so many would be out of the question, too, but we could condition a few, say six or seven real Entries. They would lead the group and would see nothing awry in our own party. *That* we could easily manage, and it should work."

"Then we do it that way," the leader ordered. "We need some of our own people on their side. We won't be the only ones, either, of course. The biggest weakness his side has is that it can't possibly know the true nature of everyone in its armies, nor their loyalties. They must know this. But most will be there as spies, nothing more. Ours will have a different task."

"And what is this?" Zilchet was so involved he forgot he wasn't supposed to prompt the leader.

Gunit Sangh gave him an icy stare as a reminder, but otherwise let it go. This was far too important to execute the wretch now. But he would remember the lapse. . . .

"Of all the different Entries, only a few are not of this soldier type. These are his commanders, of course. A number of them. Information from the central command Ortega is establishing tells me, though, that at least one of these has more than utilitarian meaning to Brazil. This is the woman Mavra Chang, now a Dillian. He regards her as something of a sibling with that curious bond lesser races have for such. I want our people there to behave just like good soldiers, to fight in Brazil's forces, take orders, do all that they would be expected to do. But if it looks as if Brazil will attain his goal, if it looks like his side will win, I have a special task for them."

"Holiness?"

"No one can control Brazil directly once he is inside to the Well. But if we hold this Mavra Chang, secretly, *outside* the Well, while I or one of us enters with him, that is just as good."

"But what if, once inside, he merely wills himself to find her and free her?" Zilchet asked dubiously.

"I seriously doubt whether any mind, even a Markovian, could pick out an individual on the Well World without knowing her location, captors, or status. I think Brazil could easily create a race, but not change a mind unless he knew all the particulars. At any rate, the odds favor our taking this action. We really have nothing to lose."

Zilchet was still worried, and his rippling showed it.

Gunit Sangh glared at him. "Well? What is it?"

"I was just wondering how many other races have exactly the same idea," the other responded.

"Probably several," the leader admitted. "She will be a major target, have no doubt—and, because of that, most assuredly well protected. We must see that we are the ones who get her—if the military action fails, of course. If not, it is an academic exercise. But we will not fail. Our ancestors have shown us the true course, and they will not let us fail."

They bowed again in prayer, and, although they wouldn't have realized it, they sounded more than a little like religious fanatics themselves.

# Gedemondas

IT QUICKLY GREW NOT ONLY COLD BUT STEEP AS WELL; the blue-white mountains that made such a beautiful and romantic scene from Dillia were, very quickly, a different and alien land. Only a few kilometers in, the trees diminished to practically nothing and the forest gave way to barren tundra, covered only with hardy grass, moss, and lichen. Even this didn't last long; within another three or four kilometers the land, going ever upward, became flecked with wet, dirty snow; waterfalls, mostly small, were wherever there was any sort of rocky outcrop or drop, and rivulets were everywhere. Roughly two degrees-centigrade was being lost for each five hundred meters upward they went—and the trails were always up.

Mavra began to appreciate the centaur's body more as they went on. It certainly had more strength for such climbing and trail work, and it could carry an extremely heavy load of supplies, if properly balanced, on the equine midsection. She wore a loose-fitting jacket first, but as they went on, she switched to a heavier, minklike fur jacket, fur stocking cap and heavy, leathery gloves that were fur-lined. While the equine part of the Dillian was well insulated by thin but dense hair and layers of fat that trapped the cold and kept in the heat, the more human parts were only slightly tougher than her former skin and needed a great deal of protection.

Colonel Asam, unlike her, was a deep brown that tended to hold the sun more, and he continued to dress loose and comfortable, seemingly oblivious to the cold. Even when the going became heavy and she found her massive lungs pounding, he kept up an almost constant dialogue, telling of many of his adventures and the people and lands he'd seen. She let him talk, partly because he seemed to enjoy it— though his associates looked fairly bored, having probably heard all this before—and also because he was a fascinating man. Occasionally he would ask her to compare notes on something, or tell some similar episode in her own past, and it was some time before she realized that, very subtly, he was trying to get a lot more information on her. For whom, she wondered? Himself? Some employer? Asam was very much as she had been, as her husband had been so long ago: an adventurer, a freebooter whose word was good but who would be loyal to any commission he undertook. She decided it was best if he did most of the talking.

"That business about the plague," she prompted him. "What was that about?"

He smiled, appreciating a fresh audience. "Well, lass, that was twenty year or more ago, I guess. There was these two hexes, Morguhn and Dahbi, next to each other, and Morguhn was a rich agricultural land that raised all sorts of livestock and fruits and vegetables—tons of it—and exported it for stuff they needed, mostly manufactured goods. They're a semi-tech, like Dillia, and that gave 'em the power they needed for irrigation and all that other stuff. Their food and skins, over the years, bein' so superior to most else in those parts, Morghun become a kind o' big market everybody went to. Hell, most of the other hexes didn't even bother much with agriculture and such any more—didn't have to. The high-techs in particular, now, they go in for all that fancy stuff. Most of 'em, no matter what the culture, can't see a piece of good pasture without dreamin' of pavin' it over for something. So they made the fine special alloys for the Morghun machines and lots of other stuff the best machines could do best—synthetic fertilizers, prefab farm buildings, like that. Not to mention good holidays for the farmers when they wanted. It all worked out."

"And Dahbi?" she asked, interested.

"A race of bastards," he told her. "All of 'em. Scum of the earth. There's some like that on this world, though thankfully not very many. Theocracy based on ancestor worship. Very brutal, very repressive. Ritual cannibals, for example—the standard method of execution. They get eaten in a religious service by the congregation—alive, that is. They think that, that way, they're eatin' the soul and so the fellow won't be around as an ancestral spirit. Kinda like big grasshoppers, I guess that'd be closest—albino grasshoppers, all white. But they ain't like you and me and most of the races you meet. Somethin' crazy in their make-up—they go right through walls."

She stared at him. "You're kidding!"

"Nope. Not a door in the whole damned hex. They just kinda ooze through the cracks, you might say, and walk down the walls on the other side.

"Well, anyway, a religion's not a religion if it's that strict that long. Hexes ain't that big—sooner or later, particularly if you trade, your people start seein' that other folks don't have to be as miserable as you and they start givin' the folks ideas. They're nontech, so for the comforts of manufactured goods they got to trade. Mostly minerals. When you can go through rock, it kinda makes you a natural miner. They even hire out work teams, through the religion, o'course, to mine other places, explore for wells, that kinda thing. Now, what can that cult offer 'em? Promise 'em a better afterlife? Good for a while, but when the folks around you are livin' better than your religion's afterlife, well, you start to wonder. A lot of Dahbi started to wonder, and you can't kill the whole population. The leaders are smart—nasty, but smart. For their own survival, they decided to produce—and that meant opening up adjoinin' hexes, like Morguhn, to Dahbi settlement, domination, and control."

"But I thought that was impossible," she responded. "I mean, walking through walls or not, you really can't expect a nontech hex to defeat a high-tech or even a semi- in a war."

"True enough," Asam agreed. "And the Dahbi knew it, though they're great close-up fighters. Got slashin' blades on their long legs and nasty chewing pincers. No, what their leader, an ultimate son of a bitch if there ever was one named Gunit Sangh, came up with was a deal with a high-tech Northern hex that didn't even understand what the hell things were like in lands like ours. They synthesized a bug, a bacterium, whatever, that laid the Morghunites flat. It was just the start, understand. Eventually the Dahbi planned to rush in with some kind o' miracle cure mixed with religious mumbo-jumbo and 'save' the remaining part of the Morghunite population. By then, o'course, the Dahbi would've been in there in force and runnin' things."

"And you stopped this?"

He nodded proudly. "Well, sorta. See, nobody knew the Dahbi were behind it. Diseases break out all the time in one hex or another, and the damned creatures had acted up to this pretty much like any concerned neighbor—friendly, helpful, you know. And since no bugs from one hex can affect another race, well, there was no danger to them. The Morghunite ambassador, who was down with it himself and close to death, appealed to the Zone council for help, and got Czill, a high-tech hex that has walkin' plants and does mostly research—like a big university, sorta—interested. They isolated the bugger, and once they had, and established it was artificial, they worked out a counter. Trouble was, there was no Morghunite able to even get to the Zone Gate and able to pick it up, so a couple of neighboring hexes volunteered to handle the job. Things happened, the shipments never arrived. It was clear that somebody was stoppin' 'em."

"And how did you enter into it?" she asked, getting more involved in this Well World intrigue.

"I was in Dhutu, not far from there, and Ortega got in touch with me, explained the problem. The Dhutu ain't very mobile—they kinda crawl slow, take all day to cross the room, but they're tremendously strong. No trouble gettin' the serums in, but then I rounded up a crew and we started off for a four-thousand-kilometer trip to Morguhn. It was a hairy trip, I'll tell you."

Of the dozen in his party, only four had survived the trip. Dahbi had hired mercenaries to waylay them

and when his party fought them off, had come themselves, oozing out of the ground or rock when you decided to take a rest, quietly slitting throats and fading
back into the solid rock once more.

"Then how did you finally beat them off?" she
pressed.

He laughed. "Accident, really. One came up out of
a rock face when I wasn't lookin' and almost
had me 'fore I saw it out of the corner of my eye. I
was away from my weapons, the only thing I had in
my hand was a big bucket of water from a stream I
was bringin' back for rubdown purposes. Well, I
whirled around and flung the bucket at the bastard,
missed him, hit the rock above his head, and the water
sloshed out and some of it hit the Dahbi. It was weird,
you know? It was like he suddenly became solid flesh,
like us, where the water hit him. With no warnin'. The
part that got wet seemed to go real smooth, then
dropped to the ground. He screamed holy terror and
what was left of him went back into the rock."

"But—water?" she responded with disbelief. "I
mean, they must have a lot of water in their own hex,
and certainly in the mines."

He shrugged. "I dunno. I think maybe they can be
solid, like you or me, or somethin' else, like when they
ooze through rocks. Maybe they rearrange their—
what'dya callit, molecular structure, I guess. They can
be one or the other, but not both. When they're solid,
their reaction to water's just like ours—and I know
they drink." He grinned. "They even bleed—yellow,
but they bleed. When they go into that other state,
the water that's in 'em—in their cells—changes to that
new form, too. But when it does, a heavy concentration of liquid makes whatever it hits turn back solid
and they come apart. I guess it has to be a real splash,
too, since even rocks got water. Well, after that, we
just took buckets with us and got a bunch of 'em. Got
to Morghun, and what could the Dahbi say? Publicly,
they thanked us for doin' a wonderful job savin' their
*dear* friends. Privately, them and we knew who it was
started it. So did everybody else—but you couldn't
prove nothin'. They covered their tracks too well.

They lost, let it lie. But old Gunit Sangh, he put a curse on me and I got back home fast. Haven't gone near there much since, I admit. Not as long as Sangh's still alive."

"You think he still hates you, after all this time?" she asked him.

"Oh, yes. Now more than ever. Blood feud. His boys have tried me lots o' times in the past twenty years. Lots o' times. He's given up recently, I think, but that don't mean he's forgot. If he got the chance, he'd slit my throat and eat me. And if *I* got the chance, I'd damned sure carve him up in little pieces. I doubt if either of us will ever get the chance, though. Who knows?"

The wind was kicking up; clouds had come in, partly obscuring the sun, and the temperature had quickly dropped several degrees. They were into the lower snowfields now, where the temperature was at freezing or slightly below, and with the wind, the effect was *far* below.

"There's a shelter not far up the trail," he told them all. "If there's no other party already there, we'll stay the night there. It's gettin' pretty late and the wind's rising something fierce."

Throughout the major trails of Gedemondas Dillians had built an entire network of these shelters for their hunting parties. If the local inhabitants objected, they hadn't made it known nor molested them.

The cabin, a huge log affair with chimney on the back, looked peaceful enough. Inside, if previous users hadn't depleted the supplies, would be bales of grain, cooking pots and utensils, and even a few cords of wood, stocked regularly by Dillian service patrols.

"No smoke," Asam noted. "Looks like we're in luck." Still, he frowned, and when she started to go forward he stopped her. She glanced around and saw that the others in the party had spread out on the flat-sculpted, snow-covered outcrop and were slowly reaching for their bows.

"What's the matter?" she whispered, more puzzled than nervous.

He gestured with his head. "Over there. About

three or four meters beyond the cabin, right at the edge."

She stared in the indicated direction. Something dark there, she thought. No, not dark— It was hard to see in the cloudy, late-afternoon light, particularly through snow goggles she'd donned almost immediately upon their reaching the snow area, for her blue eyes provided little natural protection against snow blindness.

Cautiously, she lifted up the goggles to get a better look. Red—crimson, a red strain in the snow, very near—no, actually at the edge. And the marks of something having been dragged.

"It could be an accident," she said softly. "Or the remains of some hunter's kill."

"It *could*," he agreed, but now his bow was cocked. "Can you handle a weapon? I forgot to ask."

"About the only thing I might be decent with would be a sword," she sighed, a little disconsolate at the idea.

"Why not?" he shrugged, and reached back into his pack. He pulled out a scabbard—not a puny, plain sort of thing but a monstrous scabbard covered with strange, ornate designs. It was clearly a broadsword of some kind, the hilt solid, firm, and yet also ornately sculpted with the shapes of creatures she couldn't guess the true form of. He handed it to her. "Everything comes in handy sooner or later," was his only explanation.

She strapped it around her waist, the place where the humanoid part of her met the equine, and pulled out the blade. It had good balance and feel to it and seemed so perfect she found she could cut a swath with one hand. But for serious business, like skull-cracking, two hands would be best.

"Colonel?" Jodl, one of the aides, whispered. Asam nodded, and the other centaur crept slowly forward, crossbow at the ready, eyes on the cabin door itself.

All had shed their packs; in a fight, baggage would unbalance them. The advance man was light and cautious, but made no attempt at concealment. He was, after all, over two and a half meters tall and more than three long and weighed in around seven hundred kilograms, hardly the sort of being who could make a surreptitious entry.

"Who do you think it is?" she whispered to Asam. "One of your old enemies?"

He shrugged, never taking his eyes off the door. A second man started out, keeping distance and interval. They were going to approach the cabin from all sides and make sure that only one would be attacked first —if attacker there were. "Could be anybody," he told her softly. "Hired assassins, freebooters, criminals, Dillian or foreign. Hard to say."

It startled her slightly to consider Dillians as criminals or killers. They were a rough but likable and levelheaded lot. But there must be some bad ones, she realized. There always are.

They were fanned out now on all sides of the cabin, keeping at least ten meters from the cabin door. They didn't worry too much about any other place of attack; the rocky ledge gave them a measure of protection from above, the far trail was fairly clear to the eye, and the cabin sat on the edge of a sheer cliff. Thinking of the Dahbi, she considered their disregard of the cliff area a mistake. If this world had creatures that could pop up through solid rock, they had dozens that could cling to the sides of sheer cliffs or, perhaps camouflage themselves into near invisibility. Some of the latter had once almost done her in in the distant past in far-off Glathriel.

The point man had reached the area in question on the far side of the cabin. She stayed in back of the men's semicircle, feeling helpless and a little irritated that she was not up to this kind of thing. And, for all her own great mass, she was still smaller, yet no more maneuverable, than the males.

Still, she held the rear guard, sword at the ready, and pulled her goggles back down. Her eyes were already beginning to hurt slightly.

"Colonel!" the point man called, his voice echoing slightly off the walls near and far. "Party of three. Hunters. Our people. Pretty messed up. They cut 'em up and then tossed 'em over the cliff. They're forty, fifty meters down when the slope smooths out." He didn't attempt to whisper the word. If the killers were still around, they most certainly knew just where they were by now.

Asam considered, then turned back to Mavra. "Could it have been Gedemondans who did this?"

She shook her head violently. "Not a chance. If they want you dead, they just point a finger and you curl up and die."

"Didn't think so," the Colonel muttered, and turned back to the cabin. "All right, boys, let's go visitin'."

They converged, very slowly and carefully, on the cabin until the closest was only a few meters from the front door. It was Mavra who saw that, for the first time, they were twenty or thirty meters out in the open from the rock shelf above. Something was up there, a shadow, a discontinuity . . .

*"Asam!"* she screamed. "Above and behind you!"

At that moment the attackers leaped off their high perches and fell toward them. There were more than a dozen of them, some armed with pikes, some with crossbows, others with swords.

They were bats—no, apes, of some kind, with bat's wings—or— Whatever they were, they were small, agile, they could fly, had blazing eyes and sharp teeth, and wore some kind of dull coppery uniform.

But they were not flying down; rather, they made a controlled plunge, like skydivers, but with some maneuverability, and they were uttering singularly alien screeches that sounded like high-pitched bagpipes trying to yodel.

Two with crossbows loosed their bolts while still falling, but they missed their target and plowed into the snow; Jodl and one other who were at an angle to the fall whirled and raised their crossbows. From a firm standing position, they didn't miss. The force of the Dillian bolts was so strong that the two struck almost seemed suddenly to fly backward, then hit the wall and start forward again, limp.

By the time this happened, though, the others were upon them, two leaping directly on Asam. They were small but extremely powerful; one fell right for his head and torso, the other for his hindquarters. The

Colonel reared and twisted, flinging the one off his behind, then, dropping his own bow, he grabbed the other creature by its wicked, extended claws and heaved him against the rock wall with tremendous force.

Before Mavra knew what was happening, one was coming right at her. She waited, then thrust herself outward, both hands on the sword hilt.

The thing impaled itself on the sword and spurted thick red blood, but it was not dead; somehow, awful hate in its distorted, terribly ugly face, its right arm raised the sharp spear in its hand while its body weight on the broadsword forced Mavra down with it to the ground. She had only a split-second to decide what to do. Falling, off-balance, there was only one thing she *could* do: she accelerated the fall and rolled; the spear came at her, tearing through her thick fur coat, and she felt a stabbing pain in her left side.

Too mad to pay any attention to it, she got up with as much speed as possible and saw that the thing, still impaled on the sword, twitched and gibbered. A wave of utter fury swept over her and she reared up on her hind legs and came down, forelegs with their heavy steel shoes crashing into the thing again and again and again.

Meanwhile, the rest of the creatures were down and slashing now. They were effective; two of the centaurs were down, bolts or spears in them, but Asam still stood, a bloody but superficial wound on his equine body's left side. Rearing, turning, charging, all the time yelling at the top of his lungs, he charged the things again and again. One of the creatures managed a roll and tried to take off into the air, throwing a spear at the raging Colonel. It struck, but all he did was flinch, cry out, more in fury than in pain. He reached around, pulled the spear out of his side, and threw it at the now airborne attacker. The spear struck the thing, and it paused for a moment, then fell like a rock over the side of the cliff.

Mavra whirled, oblivious to the pain, and charged into the midst of the fight. Suddenly leathery wings seemed to strike her in the face, then there was a mas-

sive shock, so hard it felt as if her brain were re-
verberating inside her skull, and then there was
darkness. She never even felt herself fall.

She felt as if she were drowning in a sea of thick
liquid, unable to get her bearings, unable to see anything but the swirling wet mass that was all around her.
She tried to struggle against it, tried to fight its over-
whelming, engulfing motion, but it was impossible.
There was pain, dull throbs and sharp stabbing sensations about which she could do nothing, and it was
alternatingly suffocatingly hot then icy cold. She
thrashed out at the swirling, liquid mass, tried to beat
it off.

There seemed to be others in the mass as well;
strange shapes and faces that would occasionally focus
and then fly away. Some were horrible, gargoylelike
creatures that swooped in and out but out of her reach,
jabbering and mocking her; others were more familiar,
yet no less threatening: giant, catlike creatures with
glowing eyes; tiny, mulelike beasts whose eyes showed
agony; phantom minotaurs, great scorpions, phantoms
out of her past.

In the midst of all this activity, there stalked a
small, frail-looking figure, his back to her, oblivious to
all the horrors. She reached out for him, tried to call
to him, but the liquid that she seemed suspended in
prevented that, though he seemed oblivious to it.

Finally she managed some sort of scream, a scream
of terrified helplessness. He *must* hear! He must! He
must! She concentrated all she could muster on the
walking figure.

He stopped, seemed to hear, and slowly turned. It
was the face of Nathan Brazil she saw, and he stared
back, looking more bored than sympathetic.

"Brazil! You-must-help-me!" she gasped, reaching
out a hand to his.

He smiled, took out a coin and flipped it to her.
"Glad to be of service," he responded lightly. "Any
old time. Got to go now. I'm God, you know. Too
many things to do. . . ."

He turned from her and walked into the mists, not

heeding her anguished cries, then faded into the swirling, milky whirlpool and was lost from view.

She was alone, alone again with the liquid and the horrors that floated by her, mocking her, striking out at her.

Alone.

"Help me!" she screamed at nobody in particular. "Will no one help me now?"

Figures appeared, kind-looking human figures. A handsome, middle-aged man and a stunningly beautiful woman. They stretched out their arms to her, beckoned her to come to them, to run to their protection. She started for them, but suddenly a great dark shadow came out of the whirlpool and intervened between the pair and her. A great, angelic shape in white robes, it smiled at her even as it put out its own outstretched arms.

She hesitated, then started to approach, but the kindly figure began to undergo a terrible metamorphosis, changing from its human perfection into some sort of hideous, ugly frog-creature that gibbered and drooled and turned from her to devour her parents far in the distance, laughing as it did so.

She felt herself falling, down, down, into some sort of pit still awash in that liquid that now had the foulness of decaying garbage.

She struggled even more against the noxious odor, reached out for something to grab onto, but no one was there, no one at all. She was sinking, sinking further into the filth and slime, and the terrible creatures still floated around laughing, mocking, joking, and jabbing.

A tough-looking pasty-yellow face with hair nearly white appeared at the edge, smiled at her, and offered a hand. But the hand decayed as Mavra touched it, became a skeletal thing. The infection finally consuming the old woman, and when that happened she felt herself sinking even more into the bottom layers of slime. She felt more and more alone, more and more like she was going to remain forever in this bottomless pit of torment and corruption.

Now another face appeared, a kind face, a face

that was representative of all the races of Old Earth, a handsome face that said it wanted to help. He reached out his own hand and took hold of her, pulling her up, up from the muck and the mire, and for a moment she thought she was free. She could see air ahead, and stars, millions of twinkling, blinking lights spread everywhere before her.

There was a sound, a loud explosion somewhere near her, and as she looked again in horror, her savior's face seemed to be coming apart, exploding grotesquely, and the grip slipped.

*"Gimball!"* she screamed. *"No! No! My husband . . ."*

But he was gone, and she was alone again, sinking again in the filth, never free of the swirling liquid, and it seemed to her as if the gibbering creatures were enjoying it all the more now.

Black shapes moved in, bound her, sliced her up into pieces of herself, made her a deformed, helpless monster. Still she struggled against them, fought the dark forces pushing her deeper and deeper in the muck. Another, misshapen, mutilated like herself, approached as the creatures swirling around started to close in on her, to choke her off. A gargoyle raised a spear and thrust it at her, hate in its eyes, but the other moved quickly, took the spear, and vanished, too, into the corruption.

A purplish light broke through the muck, and she heard Obie's voice, calling to her, and she reached the light. "I'm your magic genie," he told her. "Where in the universe do you want to go?"

"Everywhere!" she cried, and, in fast, flashing scenes she did. Yet, there was something wrong, very wrong. Every place they went had more of the foul corruption she thought she had escaped. Every place had more and more, all stinking, rotting, garbage.

The purple glow faded, and standing there, once more, was Nathan Brazil. He shrugged and gave her a crooked smile. "Well, what did you expect?" he asked her. "After all, I created the damn place in my own image."

And there was just the swirling, engulfing liquid

and the stench and corruption, the chills and burning
sensations, the pain, and nothing else. Nothing. Nothing.

Alone. She was alone. Alone forever in the
muck . . . She hated that muck, she hated that stench,
and, most of all, she hated a universe teeming with life
in which she could be so utterly, so completely alone.
If this was the way the universe was, it was better destroyed, she thought fiercely. Clear the muck, throw
out the garbage, clean and cleanse, cleanse . . . But so
empty now, so alone, so very alone . . .

Yet somehow she was not alone, not now, not at
this point. She had the impression of someone hugging
her, transferring warmth and caring to her, someone
whispering gently to her, telling her it was all right,
that someone else was there. She anxiously fought to
open her eyes, to see who or what it might be, and
finally managed, but the world wouldn't focus. A figure, just a figure, no more, no less. A figure, bending
down, concerned, worried. A weathered, tough, handsome face whose eyes showed some ancient wisdom
and gentleness he might try to hide but could not.

Suddenly she felt terribly tired, terribly worn, and
she sunk back, not into the coma, not into the muck,
but into a deep, dreamless sleep.

She awoke, blearily looked around, and tried to
move. She was in some kind of harness and couldn't
quite get free.

There was a crackling fire in the fireplace. Two of
the party were in sleeping stalls like herself, suspended
by elaborate but obviously jury-rigged harnesses made
of belts, straps, strips of fur, anything available.

Two other centaurs moved around, one stoking the
fire and checking a pot of what was probably melted
snow, the other standing at a small table and looking
over some papers. Neither looked in the best of health
themselves; the one at the fire, a mass of professional-
looking bandages and deep scars, was favoring his
right foreleg; the other, at the table, was Colonel
Asam, whose humanoid torso was covered with puffy

bruises. He, too, had a number of slick surgical bandages on various parts of his body.

"Asam?" she called out, sounding weak even to herself. "Asam, what happened?"

Both men turned, and the Colonel approached her quickly, a smile on his face. One of his eyes was swollen almost shut and his face was so bruised and puffy it shocked her, but he smiled, reached down to a pouch, and took out a cigar. "Well, well! Welcome back to the land o' the almost-living," he cracked.

She smiled. "What—who were those things?"

"Tilki. Pretty far from home, too. Bloody bastards. If this hadn't been a nontech hex, they'd have had us sure. Them high-tech bastards usually are pretty lousy with close-up weapons."

"Bandits?" she guessed.

He shook his head. "No. They had uniforms. Army. A neat little ambush team."

"They were . . . assassins, then?" she asked cautiously, still thinking of Asam's tale of a blood feud.

"Assassins, yes," he agreed, "but not for me. We got 'em all—I think, anyway. Unless they had some they held back who took off when we got the upper hand. Doubt it, though. One or two more would've finished us."

"Not for you? But—"

"I've got a translator, remember," he told her. "I understood their jabberin'. No question in my mind it was you they was after. Heard your name a coupl've times. They mighta gotten you, too, if there'd been fewer of us, or if they hadn't been screwed up by the earlier group of hunters. They picked their spot well —this would be the logical first night's camp, and, flying, they could reach it without havin' to go over the tall peaks. Trouble was, when they got here they found the hunters already there. They knew you wasn't with 'em. I don't think they had too clear an idea of your looks, but the others were all men and they knew you was a woman. Only a guess, you understand—no witnesses left. I'd say they probably drew out the hunters, who had no reason to fear and would be just damned curious at meetin' Tilki up here, of all places. My guess the bastards took 'em so quick they never even knew what hit 'em."

She considered this. "You said they were Army. Why me?"

He grinned. "You told me a lot about what was goin' on right now. I'd say the Zone Council's decided on war, sifted through their records to find who the key ringleaders on the other side would be, and are out to wipe out Brazil's generals before they start. They might also be nervous about Gedemondas. Unknown quantity, you know. If you can't get to 'em, they're outta the fight."

She nodded and looked around. "The others . . . ?"

His expression became grim. "We're it. The survivors. Malk and Zorn, there, they're gonna need better medical care than we can give 'em. In a way we were lucky they hit us here, instead of just inside Dilla—infection's much less of a problem. We're battling only the bugs we brought with us."

"How are you ever going to get them to a hospital?" she wondered, feeling sorry for them.

"A group of hunters came through yesterday. They'll carry the news to Uplake and get help. I think they can stand it here another day or two until help arrives. We're not really into the bad country yet, so they ought to be able to get 'em down without much trouble."

"I see. Well, I— Did you say a group of hunters came through *yesterday?*"

He smiled and nodded. "You been out three days. We thought we were gonna lose you. Most of your wounds aren't really bad, nothin' serious. It was the concussion that almost did you in. Bastard came in and hit you with a sapper."

"A . . . a what?"

"Sapper. Stiff skin laced around lead shot. Damn thing can crack your skull. Don't think it did, though —but you got a hell of a bump. Sent you into shock."

"Why . . . why am I trussed up like this?"

"We'll get you unhooked if you feel up to it." He reached over and started undoing some of the knots. "Like some of the large animals of the world that are

our distant cousins, we breathe back of our under-
bellies. If you're down on your side for more than a
couple hours, your own weight will press down on
the lungs and suffocate you. We had to get you up and
keep you up—not easy, I'll tell you. The two of us
ain't in the best shape, either, but we're a lot better
off."

"I . . . I saw you take a spear . . ." she began.

He chuckled. "Oh, it takes a lot more'n that to get
me. Didn't hit anything vital and only hurts when I
laugh. We're just lucky they moved so fast from their
home hex they didn't have a chance to really look
things up properly. All their tips were poisoned with
what I guess they consider a horrible deadly toxin.
Tannic acid. Maybe the next time we meet those
bastards we ought to dump a pot o' tea on each of
'em!"

She laughed, and when she did she felt all the
wounds and bruises and sores she had accumulated.
There were a lot of them, and over a large area, but
she had had as bad or worse before and it hadn't
bothered her for long. Uncomfortable, yes, but little
else.

Freed from the harness, she stood alone and tried
walking out of the stall. Immediately she felt dizzy and
wobbly, and had to hold on. "Guess I'm still a little
weak," she muttered to herself.

"Take it easy," he cautioned. "That's a nasty crack
on the head. Ease into normal activity."

She tried it again, more cautiously, and found that
as long as she was holding onto something it was all
right. He went up to her and let her lean on him, and
together they made it out into the main room.

"Feel like you could eat something?" he asked her.
"You really should."

She looked over at the bales of strawlike material
at the far side of the cabin. She didn't really feel like
eating, but decided he knew best.

The stuff tasted awful, but she found herself unable
to stop once she started. Asam chuckled and told her
to go ahead. "You don't realize just how much food
we Dillians need a day. Eatin' regular like we do, that

is. When you take it in at one gulp after a few days
off, it can seem pretty piggy."

Piggy wasn't the word for it, she decided when she
was finished. She went through most of a bale, a little
at a time, and each bale weighed close to twenty kilos.

Later she did feel better, and managed to find a
small mirror. She had double black eyes and felt like
she had bitten the inside of her mouth half through, but
otherwise the damage didn't appear all that bad. The
wounds on her equine back and side were painful and
there was some internal bruising, but there didn't
seem to be serious damage and she felt she could
live with them.

Asam, too, was as tough as his reputation. After
seeing him in action, she decided she wouldn't doubt
any of his stories and legends again, and she said as
much.

He grinned. "You did pretty fair yourself, you
know. I don't know too many folks, man or woman,
could hold their own like that." He looked at her and
the grin faded, but only a bit. "You know, you asked
me once whose side I was on. After this, you don't
have to ask any more. You understand? And not just
me. Those fools did half the work for you. They
slaughtered innocent Dillians in cold blood, Dillians
with no politics, no positions, just good, ordinary people. I know my people, Mavra. They'll want to get
even." He paused and smiled broadly once again.
"And as for me, I've gotten to know you and see you
in a number of different situations. I'd be proud to
serve with you, any time."

She smiled, took his hand, and squeezed it. She felt
like hugging the old adventurer, but they were both
too bruised for that. Still, she thought back to that
dream, that bastard child of her innermost mind that
had been raised by the sapper. She wished she was as
certain of her side and her cause as he now seemed
to be.

"So what do we do now?" he asked her. "I wouldn't
stay here much longer, if you feel like moving. There's
always the chance that they had somebody as observer,
or maybe agents in Dillia will carry the news. Either

way, they hit us again here as soon as they can mount another force. I've been uncomfortable with the idea for the past couple of days. How do you feel?"

"Lousy," she replied glumly. "Still, what are the options?" She looked at the cabin, which had become such a hospital ward.

"We can wait for the rescue party. They should be here in the next few hours if luck holds. Remember, they had nobody to send without leavin' Uplake without its one good healer. Probably a good, strong team came in on today's boat or on a special and they're on their way even now. They'd need supporting equipment, anyway, which would slow them down."

Going back. She wanted to go back, back to the peaceful village with its ale and companionship and gentle waterfalls.

"If anybody wants to make a try at us, that'll be the time to do it," she pointed out. "And any observer will have a pretty good description of me now."

"The only alternative is for us to press on," he pointed out. "And neither of us is strong enough to carry a full load or force-march. In a few days, yes, but not now. You're still pretty rocky, and the trail gets pretty hairy from here on."

She went over to the table Asam had been standing at when she had come out of it. Spread out was a chart of Gedemondas, a topographic map with trails, shelters, and cabins marked. It was easy to find where they were now, the first cabin above the snow line. She studied the map, and he came over and looked over her shoulder.

"What're you lookin' for?" he asked.

"A collapsed volcano," she replied. "A huge crater of some kind, high up, surrounded by high mountains."

"Most of Gedemondas is volcanic," he noted. "Active, too, a lot of 'em. Not very dangerous, for the most part—you could outrun a lava flow if you had to. Some of the big ones puff a lot, though."

She nodded. "The Gedemondans live in volcanic chambers and use interconnecting lava tubes to get around beneath the surface. The network is fantastic and complex. They also use the volcanic steam for heat and primitive power—even though this is a non-tech hex, they have natural, rather than machine-generated, steam combustion. It's comfortably warm in there, too."

He raised his eyebrows in surprise. "Steam power? And what do they use it for?"

"I have no idea," she told him honestly. "We heard what could have been the turning of gears and levers for some great machine, and we got the idea that there were lots of things going on there we never knew about, but we saw only what they showed us—and I was in a worse position than most to be observant. I think all the entrances are farther in, though, in the high country."

"On some of the old and little-used trails, maybe?"

She shook her head negatively. "Uh uh. It doesn't matter where—might as well be comfortable. We just need to be higher. . . ." Her voice trailed off as she continued to look at the map, settling on an odd set of concentric rings, like tree rings, and an open area in the middle. "In *that* direction," she told him, pointing to it. "I know they have openings into that crater from their main complex."

He looked at the spot. "Or did have, centuries ago," he half-muttered, worriedly.

"We go there. Easy stages. You game?"

He grinned. "You know I am. But, like it or not, I think we ought to leave tomorrow morning, not right now. We need the extra rest and healing"—she knew he referred to her—"and we ought to make sure these folks get back—at least wait for the rescue party."

She didn't really want to, but her head was throbbing and she felt very weak and tired. "All right, Asam. In the morning."

Although the trail was firm and well-marked, it was not easy going for either of them. The wind cut into them, and even the reduced packs seemed to shift onto every cut and bruise. Asam, as befitted his character in more ways than one, grimaced occasionally but never complained, nor did she. Still, dark thoughts pervaded their climb, mostly her own self-doubts about what she was doing. Was she, in fact, on the right side? Not that she should be on the Well's side, but why should she be on *any* side?

She knew the answer to that, of course. Brazil had refused to fix the Well unless she was there, unless she specifically ordered it. She wondered who would give the order if she were killed in this crazy battle of wits. Maybe nobody. Maybe he would just go into the Well, put himself back in the regular universe in whatever place he liked, and sit back and wait for eventual destruction. The responsibility was hers, not his. He had as much as said so.

Well, she hadn't asked for that responsibility, she told herself, and didn't want it. It wasn't fair. Nothing in her whole damned life had ever been fair, but at least she had been the mistress of it. Now they had even taken that away from her.

There were doubts, too, about her part in it all. She was to establish herself in her hex and wait for instructions. That had been all they had told her—that and the fact that the Entries would eventually rally around her, form up into a multiracial fighting force, one of several that would, on signal, converge on a single spot and combine into a mighty army, perhaps the greatest the Well World had ever seen: an army fed and supplied by other hexes as it marched, by other Entries and diplomatic friends who would, it was presumed, be there always with whatever was needed. It sounded pretty damned chancy.

And yet, if Asam were right, Dillia would follow her. Right now they would follow—not all, of course, but enough for a substantial force. That was all she had been asked to do. Why was she in Gedemondas? A hunch? Or was it, she wondered, her subconscious self's desire to throw enough of a joker into the deck that she could, as usual, be more in command?

Another night, another cabin. They felt better, slept better, as the journey wore on, and out of the comradeship of the first day's battle had grown a true affinity.

That, too, worried her. He was Asam, a great man

and good friend, it was true. But he was Asam, a Dillian centaur born on the Well World who, because of that, would never leave it. She was Dillian only superficially; inside she was still the same Mavra Chang, still the same woman of a very different race and, beyond that, a very different time and culture. At the end of this was the unknown and unknowable. Perhaps Brazil knew, but where was he?

And so she rejected Asam's affection, kindly but firmly. She saw that it hurt him and because of that it hurt her, too. But anything else just wasn't fair, not to him, not to her.

On the fourth day out, they were close to exhaustion. The going had been very rough on the icy slopes where melt never happened, and the peaks had few and difficult passes. Neither of them, she knew, could take much more of this. They got into the cabin, a much smaller affair than the usual since this was a relay point to other valleys and not a base camp. As dark closed in, they settled down with a good fire going, and both were so damned tired they hardly said a word to each other. A stillness fell with the night, a stillness so absolute it seemed unnatural, unbroken even by word. There was nothing but the crackling fire and their own slow breathing as they slipped into sleep.

She dozed fitfully, for she was so tired she was having trouble sleeping, and so the crunching sound, as if some heavy, large animal were trudging through the snow, only half-registered on her. Was it truly something, or was it dream? Or was it, perhaps, an echo of her hopes? She didn't know, and felt too far gone to give it much thought.

The door opened, creakily, noisily, but neither of them stirred. In Gedemondas, you stirred if they wanted you to stir.

The Gedemondan stood upright, like a human or ape, but at almost three meters it almost touched the ceiling. Its face was doglike, with a long, thin snout and a black button nose, but its eyes were very much like a human's or Dillian's eyes, large and a misty, pale blue. It was covered in snow-white, almost brilliant-white fur, fairly woolly, like a sheep's, and two earflaps dangled down on either side of its head.

The Gedemondan gave the sleepers little attention at first, going over to the packs and looking casually through them. It came upon Asam's cigars, pulled one out, and looked it over carefully, as if trying to figure out what it was. It ran a thin, pink tongue over the wrapper, cocked its head as if in contemplation, then shrugged slightly and stuck the cigar in an invisible marsupiallike pouch just above its crotch.

Finally it seemed satisfied, then noticed the map of Gedemondas. It unrolled the map and looked at it for a few moments, and from deep inside it came an odd sort of rapid clicking sound that might have been chuckling. Using its odd, flexible three-finger-and-thumb hands, it rolled the chart back up and replaced it. At rest, the hands formed an almost rounded pad that hardly looked like hands at all.

It turned now and went to the rear, where the stalls were, and looked briefly at Asam, slumbering peacefully. Then it moved to the next, where Mavra slept, deeply, now, as if drugged.

The two pads went first to her head, where they seemed to stroke it. A hand uncoiled and gently moved the long blond hair so that the ugly-looking bump on her head was clear and exposed. Hoping it would drain and subside on its own, Dillian Healers hadn't bandaged it.

The hand formed again into a pad, and from the odd-looking hairy pinkish palm came a sticky-looking secretion. The Gedemondan, holding back the hair with its other hand, applied the pad with the secretion like a compress on the swelling.

Now, for the first time, it seemed to realize the bruises were bruises and the bandages covered other wounds. Carefully it removed the bandages and looked at the wounds. It had some difficulty getting to her hindquarters, and at one point actually pulled her gently out of the stall, but neither she nor Asam awakened.

A second Gedemondan entered now and looked at the two sleepers, then nodded to the first who was with Mavra. It seemed to sense immediately that the two were injured and went to work on Asam, whose injuries, deeper and nastier than he had led Mavra or the others to believe, were consequently much more painful.

In the course of their mysterious treatment, the second Gedemondan made a slight grumbling sound and pointed to Asam's throat. The first nodded, then gestured back at Mavra and shook his own head negatively. The meaning was clear. Asam had a translator; they could talk to him, but not to Mavra, and not to these two. It was clearly Mavra they wished to speak with.

They had a problem, they understood. They needed a language specialist, and there was not one here. They needed to take these two elsewhere, but wondered how far they could be moved. But they were in a public cabin on a public trail in hunting season. Neither wanted to wait it out here, risking discovery.

Both mulled it over. The debate had been entirely silent, not even telepathic. They had simply known the words that needed to be said, the facts that needed pointing out, and with an occasional gesture an entire conversation had been boiled down to almost nothing at all.

One made a decision and went over to Asam, still asleep, and started making noises at him, noises like the yipping of some small dog. Still held by whatever power these two used and therefore still hypnotically asleep, Asam spoke.

"Mavra Chang, hear us."

"I hear you," she replied as if drugged, eyes still closed, breathing evenly, and as she said it Asam repeated it.

The Gedemondan nodded to itself, seeming satisfied. The other understood intuitively its feelings: it wasn't perfect, but you made do with what you had at the time.

"The Well is damaged," the Gedemondan said through Asam. "We know it. We felt it as it happened. It is a machine, but it is also in many ways like a living organism. It is in agony. We gave you medical help, and this was easy to do. The Well, too, needs this help, but it cannot help itself. This, too, we understand. We will help you to do this, for our own vision is cloudy, our own minds affected, for we are attuned to the Well." It paused. "Speak to us now."

"Brazil seeks to fix the Well," she told them. "The nations combine to stop him. There will be war. Any and all help is desperately needed."

"We understand the plan," the Gedemondan told her. "We have had our share of Entries, too, but, unlike most other hexes, the Entries are of little help to you. They are us physically, certainly, but our powers are through training, study, intensive concentration from even before birth, even selective breeding for certain things. These are not things one can learn overnight, only over a lifetime. Speak now."

"Your powers are needed by us, though," she told them. "Desperately needed."

"We understand. Now you must understand that we are only messengers here. We learned of your presence only when we sensed the violence of the attack upon you. The two of us were closest to you and we hurried as best we could. But we are not the ones you need, nor the ones to decide. We may only take the data from you and pass it back to wiser heads. Speak now."

"Then we must go with you to where those who can help are," she told them.

"It is not possible," the Gedemondan told her. "There is not enough time. A meeting is being called. It is necessary for you to attend. Speak now."

"I know of no such meeting," she responded. "Who has called it, and for what purpose?"

"Your own people have called it, to plan greater strategy. It is to be in the place called Zone, in the place reserved for us for which we have no need. Speak now."

"The Gedemondan Embassy?" she murmured, managing some surprise even in her state of light hypnosis. "Then I must get to a Zone Gate."

"Your Zone Gate is far from here," the Gedemondan told her. "You must go to it as quickly as possible.

After the meeting we might be ready to contact you again. Speak now."

"Your own Zone Gate would be closer," she pointed out. "We should be taken there."

The creature stared at her a moment, seemingly thunderstruck. It was obvious that this had never occurred to the great white thing; their Zone Gate had never been used in recent memory and so was irrelevant to them.

"You could use our Gate?" it asked.

Even through the thin fog they had placed upon her, Mavra sensed the creature's amazement and felt some satisfaction. Deep down, even if buried in her subconscious and not readily available, would be the new knowledge that Gedemondans were neither all-knowing nor all-powerful.

The first Gedemondan stalked over to Asam's pack and withdrew the map once again, unrolled it, and looked at it carefully, then nodded to his companion. She was right. Their Gate was much closer, particularly through the tunnels of Gedemondas only the natives knew.

The decision was made then and there. The two were put under much more deeply and called out. They were helped into their heavy cold-weather clothing, but the packs were ignored. Then, slowly, deliberately, the two Gedemondans walked out the door and the two spellbound aliens followed meekly.

Hours had passed as they went deeper into Gedemondas. Then a rocky wall had parted, and they had entered the warm interior tunnels of the strange, unknown hex, and now they walked in its mazes, hour after hour, without pause or complaint. The two were more securely bound than if they'd been tied with ropes and had guns to their heads. They knew absolutely nothing of the journey, of the passing through many busy arteries and through centers of Gedemondan activity. More than once their keepers changed, but they continued onward.

Finally, they reached an old dust-ladened hallway that clearly hadn't been entered in a very long time.

Just off a main tunnel, it didn't go far before widening into a smooth chamber. The evidence was such that the single Gedemondan and the two centaurs were the first in known history to be there. At the far end of the chamber was a hexagonal shape of deepest, impenetrable black. It seemed unnatural there, out of phase somehow with the reality of the rock walls and floor.

Mavra Chang awoke, and, seeing the Gedemondan ahead of her and the looming dark shape in back of them, she smiled. She had no memory of how they had gotten there, nor of any of the previous conversation, but she knew she had gotten through. More interestingly, the hurt was gone. She felt clear-headed and without any pain for the first time since the battle, although she also felt ravenously hungry. She glanced over at Asam and realized immediately that he was in some sort of artificial sleep.

"My apologies for not being able to provide food," the Gedemondan said in a clear, pleasant voice. "I'm afraid all this was put together at the last minute, so to speak."

She realized with a start that he was not wearing a translator and was somehow synthesizing a normal tone in a throat that couldn't possibly handle those sounds or shape the words. She wondered how he did it. More interesting yet, he was not speaking Dillian but rather the far more sophisticated and complex language of the Com.

"Yes, it's Com speech," he admitted, seeming to read her mind. "We are getting a pretty large number of Entries from there right now for reasons we both understand, and a number of us have taken up studying the speech. I hope it's all right."

"Yes, perfect," she replied, noting that she was speaking Dillian. She tried to concentrate on her old tongue.

"Don't bother," the Gedemondan told her. "It's too much of a strain. You talk Dillian, I'll talk Com, and if there are any concepts your old language can handle better, I'll understand." He looked around. "Sorry for the housekeeping, too, but we don't use this very much. I suppose we will have to clean it out, though. Your Entries are no good to us, but they and some volunteers from our side will be necessary if we are to reintroduce our species into the universe." He paused and looked almost wistful. "We aren't there now, you know. We died out on the last try."

She nodded. "That's one reason I thought of you."

"We're well aware of what you thought. Perhaps better than you. And, yes, we'll help, certainly. We would have in any case, even if you had not come— but that unwarranted attack within our borders, that is intolerable. It will not happen again."

She looked at Asam, noting his bandages were off but there was little sign of old injury. Even his face had regained much of its original look and color. Her hand instinctively went to the back of her head, where she could feel a slight tenderness, nothing else.

"Thank you for whatever medical help you gave," she said sincerely, then glanced over at Asam. "You know, he has dreamed his whole life of just meeting and talking with you. It's a shame you can't bring yourself to wake him up, at least for a moment."

The Gedemondan shrugged. "Against the rules, really. Wiping a mind is a lot harder than this, and is for the same purpose. The fact is, you'll have to get to Zone as quickly as possible anyway—your people are meeting shortly, using our own empty embassy there. We haven't completed our analysis of your information and ours to decide what ways we can help as yet. You understand that, while we have great powers, we are actually pretty vulnerable, nocturnal, and hardly inconspicuous. These things have to be weighed. In these mountains we're invulnerable, but out there, in the rest of the world, we're not nearly as effective. I seriously doubt if any Gedemondan could wage the type of fight you think of. We'll decide and be in touch shortly, wherever you are. The only thing I can promise is that we will do what we can to aid you."

"That's all I wanted," she replied earnestly. "And I thank you for it."

The Gedemondan just stood there a moment, looking

at her with a puzzled expression and slightly cocked head. "You are troubled. You are in pain," he said, concerned.

She shook her head slowly. "No. I feel fine. Nervous about the future, yes, but nothing more than that."

The Gedemondan gestured at the still-sleeping Asam. "He is in love with you, you know that."

She sighed. "I suspected as much."

"And yet you reject him. Why?"

She was puzzled, too. But she didn't like the Gedemondan's sudden change in direction toward the more personal. It was none of this creature's business.

"You feel an equal attraction to him," the Gedemondan said flatly. "I can sense this."

"It's . . . it's a little complicated to go into now," she responded, trying to get him away from the topic.

"You are wrong," the creature told her. "You think of him as you would an alien creature, but he is not. He is of your own kind."

"He is a Dillian," she noted, growing more irritated.

"You are a Dillian, too," the Gedemondan responded. "No matter what you once might have been, you are a Dillian now. If you die on this world, you die a Dillian. If you live on this world, you live as a Dillian. You can not alter that. Even if you were to undergo the Well of Souls in the recreation, you would still be what you are now. You are this, now and forever." He reached out the padlike hands, took her head in them, and held it, gently, for a moment.

"Ah," he said. "Apprehension. Insecurity. Again you are wrong. If you should die tomorrow, there is still today. If you or he should die at any time, that would not negate the time you spend together. You still mourn your husband's death, he a thousand years dead. Why?"

She felt held, compelled to look at the Gedemondan's eyes, compelled to answer.

"I loved him very much."

He nodded. "And did you love him because he died?"

"Of course not!" She wished all this was over.

"You see. You mourned him because of the good

life you had together. It is only *life* that has meaning, not death, O foolish child. Here, I will render what aid I can."

There was a sudden cloud over her mind. She felt something, some energy, something alien, yet warm, kind, not at all threatening there. It was no hypnosis or mind control, merely some sort of reinforcement of what the Gedemondan was saying.

The huge white creature went over to a wall near the gate itself and rubbed off a lot of dust, so much that his arm started turning gray. To her surprise, it was a polished surface, glasslike yet seemingly natural.

"It is solid obsidian," he told her. "Smoothed and finely polished in the earliest days of this hex. There, now, look into it and tell me what you see."

Curious, and slightly amused by what seemed like dime-store psychiatry, she walked to it and looked. She saw herself, perfectly reflected in the mirrorlike surface.

"I am suppressing certain neural circuits in your brain," he told her. "Nothing to do with thought or judgment, but sedating, shall we say, those extraneous matters that always color our thinking. It's a simple thing, but useful. I doubt if we here could get along without the ability to do it to ourselves when need be. We can teach it to you easily, as it is simply conscious control of something the mind does anyway, but with less success in many cases."

There were no more nightmares, no more lurking monsters in the shadows of her mind. For some reason she felt freer, clearer-headed than she could ever remember before. It seemed odd that suppressing something in the mind could make it crisper, somehow cleaner.

She looked again at her reflection and thought, almost curiously, That's me. Face, breast, long, flowing blond hair, down to the golden-haired equine body that seemed perfectly shaped, perfectly suited to the rest, matched, a part of the whole. She had always, somehow, thought of centaurs, Rhone or Dillian, as simply humans with a horse stuck on the back. Now she saw

that wasn't true at all; she was a distinct, logical creature now, one which, in many ways, was far superior
to the form in which she had been born. And, she
realized, the Gedemondan had been right. The person
she remembered wasn't really her, not any more. It
had never really *been* her. Its physical shape and
form, so deliberately assembled so long ago, had been
no more authentic than this form she now wore.

And what was form, anyway? Just something that
made things harder or easier, depending on how you
looked. Inside, where it counted, behind the eyes of
those she had felt strongly about, that was truth. All
her life, she realized, still looking at the sleek form
reflected in the obsidian, she'd been living for the future or mourning the past. Seven years, seven short
years so long ago were the only bright, shining jewel.
Not because of her accomplishments—she had had
them aplenty, and she was proud of them—but because of living, real joy of living.

She turned to the Gedemondan. "Yes, I would like
to learn that someday. I think you have a lot to teach
the rest of us. Maybe that would be your perfect role."

He nodded. "It will be considered."

She paused a moment more. "I think we're ready
to go now," she told him at last. She went up to him
and hugged him, and if he could have smiled, he certainly would have. Finally she said, "Your people
seem so much wiser, so much more advanced than
any I have known. I wish more could learn what
you know."

The Gedemondan shrugged. "Perhaps. But, remember, Gedemondans and Dillians both went out
into the universe at the same time. Your race survived, grew, built, and expanded. Ours died out."

He gestured at Asam, who walked to and through
the blackness of the Zone Gate. She turned and followed him.

The Gedemondan stood there a moment, then
walked over and studied his own figure in the clear
obsidian. It was a perfect surface and an exact reflection, and it worried him a great deal that there
seemed to be an indefinable flaw in it.

# The Gedemondan Embassy, Zone

THEY WALKED DOWN THE CORRIDOR, FIGHTING MOBS of people, trying to find the correct spot. The masses of humanity were unbelievable, not just to Asam, who hadn't really visualized what was going on, but also to Mavra. Reality had the abstract beat all to hell.

Much larger than the humans making their way along the corridor, they pretty much had to push their way past. She looked at them as if they were an unknown species. How small and puny and weak they look, she thought.

For their part, the Entries, not yet processed through the Well, stared in mixed wonder and apprehension at the huge centaurs, which were at one and the same time familiar, from their experience with the Rhone, and yet alien as well.

At a particularly tight squeeze Mavra stopped suddenly. Asam looked at her and shouted over the din, "What's the matter?"

"Just thought I might be missing a bet," she yelled back. She concentrated hard, trying to get the simple thought into a form this mob could understand. Oddly, she still thought in Com speech; but now what she thought went through some sort of filter in her brain and came out in Dillian. The reverse was true when she heard Dillian spoken, although, as the Gedemondan had shown, she could understand Com speech as well. Thus she could make out the words of this babble but had to concentrate hard to get over the automatic translation. Still, the effect was that she finally started thinking in the native language and she tried to force her mouth to say the Com, rather than Dillian, words.

"I am Mavra Chang!" she shouted. "Remember me?"

Some of the women nearest her heard it, and started repeating the name, which caught on down the line. She started to push on through, every once in a while shouting "Mavra Chang," the same in both languages. Although her pronounciation was heavily accented, and slightly garbled, they seemed to be getting the message.

It might have been a mistake, and in a lot of cases made it harder to move, for the humans, hearing the name, shouted questions or simply wanted to touch her, confirm her reality. Still, they reached their destination and the hex-shaped door opened to admit them, then closed behind, completely shutting out the din. The sudden silence was almost deafening.

Asam breathed a sigh of relief. "Umph! Gonna be hell gettin' in and outta here, you know. You sure you did the right thing back there?"

"I wish I could do it for all of them," she responded without hesitation. "It would make things easier if everybody knew I was a Dillian, knew where to look for me. Still, that little bit will travel up and down the mob and maybe some word will get around."

"Maybe," he said dubiously. "And it can't do a lot of harm, I suppose. After all, we *know* the enemy knows where to look."

They looked around the area, which was totally barren, just smooth walls with rounded corners, a smooth floor and nothing else whatsoever.

Asam looked back at the door. "I thought that only opened when willed by a member of the race the embassy was for," he noted. "That's how *ours* works."

"I think we're expected," she told him.

"The Gedemondans?" He looked at her accusingly. "Damn it, I still don't understand how we got here. From goin' to sleep dead tired back in that cabin I don't remember nothin' until we come outta the Zone Gate. Damn it, that wasn't fair, Mavra!"

She shrugged. "What could I do? *They* control *you*, not the other way around. To be truthful, until we were at their gate I don't remember very much, either. Sort of a hazy, dreamy thing. They have some really remarkable mental powers, Asam. I know we were both pumped for information, but I remember talking with one of them."

He grumbled a bit under his breath and sighed. "So you didn't get anything firm, huh? That's why we're here at this abandoned embassy?"

She shook her head. "No, it wasn't the Gedemondans. Somebody else called a meeting and they knew about it—how I don't know. Somebody picked this one because they knew it was empty."

He looked around glumly. "Don't look like the party's started as yet."

"Then we wait," she responded. She went over to him, put an arm around his humanoid waist, and squeezed. "There are some very pleasant ways to kill time, you know, and this is a *big* empty place."

He looked surprised, but pleased.

Marquoz had very little trouble getting through the mob despite his enormous size. With his red eyes glowing in a demonic skull atop massive muscles, vicious talons, and a spiked armored tail, people fell all over themselves getting out of his way, even the Well World guards who were herding the people through.

He relished the feeling of power it gave him; the Hakazit were large and formidable indeed. Before, humans had considered him cute or exotic, like an unusual pet, and he had had to breathe fire to get his way with them. Now they were literally terrified of him, and he loved it.

The door opened when he reached it—a nice touch, he reflected—and he walked into the bare office.

"Oops! Excuse me!" he muttered and stopped dead. "Looks like I'm interrupting something."

The two Dillians stopped and turned, startled but not looking in the least embarrassed.

The female relaxed, flexed her body and shook her head a bit to get herself back together, then turned and stared at him.

Marquoz, deciding there was little else to do, stared back. Finally he said, "I could go for a good cigar about now."

"So could I," agreed Asam, "but for different reasons. I'm afraid I lost mine back in Gedemondas somewhere."

"You think you got problems," the Hakazit grumbled. "The way this damned body's built I can't really suck in any more. Suffer."

The attitude and tone fascinated her with its familiarity. "Marquoz?" she ventured. "Is it really you, Marquoz?"

"At your service, my lady," he responded, bending a knee a little.

"It's Mavra, Marquoz. Mavra Chang."

He chuckled. "Well, well, well. You haven't changed much since I saw you last. Changed color, but that's about it."

Asam looked at her in amazement. "You were a Dillian, before?"

"For a while," she told him. "Not naturally. Long story." She turned back to Marquoz. "This is Asam. A native—on our side."

"On your side, anyway, not to mention back," the Hakazit responded. "Well, at least I feel like I got the right message. Who issued the invitations?"

"Your guess is as good as mine," she told him. "I got mine delivered secondhand by the Gedemondans. You?"

"Messenger. Dropped it off at the embassy for transmission back home. They didn't indicate much else except the ambassador said it was a Type 41 who delivered it. I figured that was Brazil."

"Could be. I hope so," she said without much feeling.

"I have to say you look very well for somebody who's dead, though," the Hakazit remarked.

Both the centaurs' heads snapped up. "What?"

"I mean it," he told them. "Reports all over a patrol of some little nasties jumped you and cut you up into little pieces."

"They tried," Asam responded. "It'll take more than that to finish either one of us, though."

"I can believe it," Marquoz said approvingly. "Well, that's a load off my mind anyway."

"Wait a minute, Marquoz, how'd you get that report? And since when would an ambassador deliver personal messages to you?" Mavra asked.

The huge gray war machine shrugged slightly. "They're scared to death of the Hakazit Secret Police —and I'm the head of it. They only *thought* they had a secret police until I took over. My trips to some of those Com worlds were not in vain. Hell, I'm the first SP chief with guts enough to go out in public."

She shook her head in wonder and muttered, almost under her breath, "I'm not going to ask. I'm *not* going to ask."

"That explains why we can talk," Asam chipped in, rescuing her. "You have a translator."

He nodded. "First thing I had done after assuming control. I gather Mavra doesn't?" When you had one of the little crystalline devices produced by a northern hex implanted surgically inside you, it was sometimes hard to tell that others didn't unless you looked closely and listened even better.

She nodded. "I'm going to need one, though. And soon."

"Have it done in Dillia," he cautioned. "These things should be put in by people who know your native brain and nervous system. Tell 'em to charge it to the government of Hakazit."

Asam laughed. "I'll arrange for it. I was gonna pay for it myself, but thanks for savin' me the money." As the supply was drastically limited, the devices cost more than most except high officials could ever afford, and the operations even more.

Marquoz shrugged. "Always glad to spend anybody's money but my own." He sounded like he meant it.

They were about to continue when the door slid open again and in walked a strange, small gray-furred creature. The newcomer stopped at the sight of Marquoz and looked around uncertainly.

"Give us your name and we'll tell you if you're in the right place," Mavra told it.

The creature stood up, revealing massive folds of skin connecting all its limbs, and rested slightly on its fanned tail. Its rodentlike face looked uncertainly at them and it chattered something that sounded like clucking and clicking far back in the throat to Mavra.

The other two seemed to understand immediately, and Marquoz responded with, "Well, well, well . . . Welcome to the club, Yua."

"No translator, either," Mavra pointed out to the other two.

Marquoz just sighed and said, "Another drain on the Hakazit treasury, then. Oh, well, it's going to complicate any kind of summit meeting, though."

"Looks like the gang's all here," said a voice behind them. They started and turned. There, in a corner of the room with no entrance or exit and which they all could have sworn had been vacant, stood . . .

"Gypsy!" Marquoz bellowed, and moved toward him.

Gypsy put up his hands. "Easy, Marquoz! You could break my back just saying hello!"

The great battle lizard roared with laughter but hesitated to come closer. Finally he said, "I kind of thought you hadn't made the trip. You didn't show up at the other end."

Gypsy shrugged. "I'm here, and that's all that counts. And I called this meeting, along with a lot of other meetings." He paused, seeing their surprise. "You didn't think you were *it,* did you? Lots of stuff to get under way. But you're all vital, particularly now that you've survived your initial entry and gotten established." He grinned at Marquoz. "You most of all. One of these days you're going to have to explain to me how you did it. Not now, though," he added hastily, seeing that Marquoz was just itching to tell them all.

"You've changed as much as we," Mavra noted. "Oh, you look the same while we don't, but your whole manner, your attitude has changed. Even your speech has cleared up. I assume that's Com speech you're using?"

He nodded, then took out and lit a cigarette. Since that particular variation of tobacco was unknown on the Well World, more than one of them wondered where he kept getting them.

"Make yourselves comfortable and I'll come to the point right away," the mystery man said, pointing to the floor. "You Dillians and Marquoz can look down on me. I'm gonna sit." And, with that, he sat, legs folded under him, on the floor and idly flicked an ash.

"First of all," he continued as they drew nearer, "we're meeting here in the Gedemondan embassy simply because it was one that Ortega had never paid much attention to. He bugged it anyway—don't ask me how—but a couple of good hired techs from Shamozan and I went over and blanked them. I'm satisfied the place is secure, even though the Shammies are with the other side. I had some of *our* people check it afterward, just to make sure."

"What's this all about, Gypsy?" Marquoz pressed. "I always knew there was something funny about you, but I rather expected you'd sit this one out like you always do. You never liked a fight."

He nodded. "That's true, but this is different. I really don't want to explain a lot right now. I'm more effective this way. But you must believe me when I say that I'm in this not only because I oan do certain things, like act as a middleman, that others can't, but also because I have a personal stake in it all. It'd be easy for all of us if you or Brazil could manage some of the things I can, but you can't and that's that. And I can't teach them to you. Wouldn't if I wanted to. That, too, we'll let pass for now. Right now, the important thing is that I'm the only messenger who can get behind enemy lines, get to you wherever you are, and also get to Brazil."

"Brazil!" It was Yua who made the exclamation at the name. She had no translator and her vocal equipment wasn't right, but they knew what she meant.

Gypsy nodded. "Yes, he got in. As Ortega has figured out, too late. We did it by the simplest con you could think of. We put him through ahead of all of you. He's been here more than a month."

"But that's impossible!" Mavra exclaimed. "He *personally* flew us to Serachnus for our trip here. He saw us off! Wished us well! *You* were there—don't you remember?"

He grinned. "I'm sorry, we *had* to trick you. The truth is, he wasn't there. *I* played both parts. And, yes, I know you saw us both together. It's a knack, I admit, but a con all the same. Making you see what I want you to see. It's a trick a lot of Well World races know, as Colonel Asam will agree."

"I've seen it. After all, I've just been held in a hypnotic state against my will for several days." Asam was still grumpy about that.

Gypsy nodded. "It's a variation of the way I always used to walk into and out of places, guards or no. Not 100 percent, though—I had Obie's help in creating a solid-looking and solid-seeming me."

Mavra's mouth formed a slight oval. "I'm beginning to catch on now. Obie used to have a lot of little tricks up his sleeve. He did a split, didn't he, when you went into the machine? A simulacrum based on your pattern emerged and we thought it was you. You, on the other hand, he shot someplace else, probably Olympus."

"Something like that," he agreed. "Brazil left even before the final staff meetings. I took his place, masquerading as him. Almost made a bad blunder dropping you off on that God-forsaken rock, too. I kept wanting a cigarette—and Brazil smoked cigars."

"But why not tell us?" Yua asked, feeling a little like she had been considered untrustworthy.

Gypsy sighed. "We didn't know what kind of reception you'd get here. We didn't even know if Brazil had made it. But if he *had* made it—and he did— then you could have been subjected to all sorts of hypnos, mind probes, anything like that. We needed to buy all the time we could, and that meant counting on you to believe Brazil had not yet appeared and to convey that to anybody who asked. It worked."

"And when you—that other you—stepped into the

Well Gate it simply ceased to exist," Mavra said thoughtfully. It was becoming clear now. Such creatures, not built around a living being, could not be sustained, which was why the Well World had been built in the first place, and why living prototypes were needed for the re-creation. It didn't explain how Gypsy, looking like Brazil, had gotten here without being killed, nor why he now looked like his old self. She was about to press that point when he short-circuited it.

"Brazil is ready to move," he told them. "He is well hidden, I assure you, but once he's on the move he's fair game—and Ortega and the rest know that. He's a little impatient where he is—it's damned uncomfortable, frankly. We have trusted people in position and all is prepared. Now, I provided the diversion that allowed him to get this far. It's up to you to play the same game the rest of the way."

He reached inside his vest and pulled out an old and crumpled map. It was a close-up of an area of the Southern hemisphere. They looked down at it while he pointed at one particular hex. "This is Glathriel. The savages there are the prototypes for what I and all of you, except Asam, were before the Well —and I still am. Now, Marquoz, you'll move first since Hakazit's to the southwest and you have the easiest way through. It's not gonna be easy, but except for the Ambrezans, you shouldn't have a big fight, and they're not the type to see their neat little world destroyed. You'll gain allies as you move. Then you go up the isthmus—Ginzin's the only nasty climate there. We'll get word that you're through. Then *your* force, Mavra, heading due west, intercepts and joins Marquoz and yours, Yua, will prepare the way until the main force catches up to you. You'll head toward the Verion-Ellerbanta Avenue and get further instructions when you're in that neighborhood."

Marquoz looked at him. "I assume we have certain diplomatic contacts with our brothers under the skin? We won't be in a continuous fight?"

"I doubt it," Gypsy replied. "Probably none at all until you link except a few stubborn and token pockets. Once you start to move for an Avenue, though, they'll throw everything they've got in the way. It'll be hairy then, but we'll have some surprises in store."

"Still, they'll pick the time and place," Asam noted. "They don't care about us—they want Brazil. Even if Brazil escapes, he'll be an alien in a totally foreign landscape where everybody's got a wanted poster with his picture on it."

"That's a fair statement," Gypsy admitted.

"But not the true one," Mavra said knowingly. "I think I have this figured out. Brazil won't be there. With everybody chasing us, he'll be heading somewhere else."

Gypsy smiled enigmatically. "Could be," he said agreeably.

"Then you won't fool Ortega," she maintained. "He'll see through it ten minutes after we pull it."

"You're probably right," he agreed. "But we'll put logical bait in the way, bait he can't afford to ignore. If, in fact, Brazil is picked up and seen with your forces—specifically, with you, the people in this room —there won't be any question. Ortega knows how the Well works. He's seen enough phony Brazils come through recently he'd probably tell the real one here in Zone to go jump in a lake. But that's *before* anybody goes through the Well. The system says that only Brazil will still look like Brazil at the other end. Nobody else could—and the medical techniques we used on the Com aren't known here. Why should they be? No need."

"How will you manage two Brazils?" Yua wanted to know.

"Watch closely," Gypsy said with a grin, and closed his eyes. For a moment nothing happened; then, suddenly his body seemed to shimmer and blur, and to shrink slightly. Slowly, ever so slowly, Gypsy became the physical image of Nathan Brazil.

"You never told me you could do that," Marquoz grumbled. "Hell, it would have saved me a lot of shit."

The image of Nathan Brazil, now very solid and very real on the floor, gave him a Gypsy grin. "There's a lot of things I didn't tell you, old friend." He looked at each of them. "Well? Think it'll work?"

Except for Asam, who had never seen Brazil, they all gaped at the figure. It was Brazil, perfectly, exactly, to a hair. Even the voice and inflection were correct.

"It'll work," Mavra told him. "You could convince me, and I saw it." But, deep down, it disturbed her a great deal. Obie hadn't given him the ability to do this, despite Gypsy's claims. Obie may have known Gypsy had the ability and planned accordingly, but giving Gypsy the talent would be beyond even Obie. To become somebody else, to appear and disappear at will, one had to go through the dish. There was only one possible explanation.

"Hypnosis will fool a living observer," she noted, "But never a camera."

"It's not hypnosis," said the Brazil who was not Brazil. "It's for real. It'll photograph, even—pleasant thought!—stand an autopsy. I am, cell for cell, the spitting image of Brazil. And as long as you all treat me as if I were Brazil, and as long as I can remember to act Brazil-ish at all times, it'll work. They'll come after us like bees after honey."

Yua stared at him a moment. "You are more powerful than Brazil," she said flatly. "How is that possible?"

Gypsy chuckled uneasily. "I wish that were true. In a sense, I *am* more powerful. But only as regards me. I couldn't change any of you into anything at all, couldn't hypnotize you, force you to do anything you didn't want except by nagging or talking you to death, anything like that. And, no, Yua, I have abilities Brazil does not have in his present form. So do you all, if you think about it. But that's all it is. A con, really. Just another scam. Just remember this: I can be killed just as easily as any of you. I expect to die in this. Maybe we all will. But not Brazil. He *can't* die. The Well won't let him." He paused for a moment, considering his words, almost as if trying to decide whether or not to say anything at all. Finally, he said, "Look, this is just guesswork, but I think Brazil wants to die. I think he's planning on it."

"You just said he couldn't," Marquoz pointed out.

"Not here. Not now. But in there, inside the Well itself, he *can* die. He's a guardian. He's had a rough job, too. He's had to stick around for maybe billions of years, watching everybody else grow old and die, experiencing all that can be experienced, and I bet he's bored to death. The records said that the last time he was on the Well World he didn't know he had ever been here before. He didn't remember. He'd blocked it out of his mind completely, mostly as a compensation, I guess the psychmen would say. He wanted to forget and he forgot. It took the Well World to completely unblock him, and I think he's been trying to forget again ever since."

"I'm not sure I couldn't take that," Mavra murmured aloud. "After all, I'm not bored after a thousand years."

"You may get the chance," Gypsy warned her. "Or one of the others of you. I think he intends, once he goes in there and does what has to be done, to pick somebody else, train them to do it, then die. I'd almost bet on it."

Breaking the long silence following that statement, Yua said, "I don't believe it. He couldn't. He is the Lord God."

Gypsy shrugged. "Don't believe it, then. But I think you know there's a grain of truth in it, even from an amateur psych like me. You've all researched him, met him, talked to him. I've also got a pretty good idea who he's chosen as his replacement."

Mavra caught his eye and nodded almost imperceptibly. She remembered that Brazil refused to take the responsibility for turning off the machine for repairs and thereby condemning all those trillions to oblivion. He had insisted that *she* give the order to him, and, therefore, take that responsibility. She was seeing it, more and more, as the passing of a torch. But did she *really* want it?

She saw she was going to have a lot of sleepless nights over that one—if, that is, she lived to get that far.

# Embassy of Ulik, South Zone

SERGE ORTEGA WAS FURIOUS AND FRUSTRATED AT one and the same time, and that made him something like a fearsome madman.

"First," he screamed at the intercom, "first this idiotic attempt on Mavra Chang. Fools! Worse than fools! Sloppy! You turned a hex that was inclined to stay entirely out of this into one of theirs, and in the process managed to injure and get mad at us the closest thing to a national hero they've got! And now—this! A summit meeting of the enemy commanders right here, not a thousand meters from me, right here in South Zone. And by all that's holy, we don't know a thing! And why? Because they hire some from our own side to blank out communications! Our own side! Free enterprise . . . bullshit!"

No reply was allowed, nor did they expect the opportunity. In fact, most of the embassies hooked in had turned their own intercoms down to a very tiny roar until he was spent, and it took a long time for him to be spent. In the back of his mind, Ortega knew this, too. But it made him feel better, and that was all it was ever intended to do.

Finally he said in a normal tone, "You can all come back now. We have to do some serious work."

It took another twenty minutes for all of them to be notified that they could dare turn up the volume and turn back to business once again.

For longer than any Well Worlder could remember Serge Ortega had been its imprisoned tyrant. Not that he actually ruled; none could do that. But he had been an old man, near death from natural causes, when he discovered the arcane fact that there was at least one race, and a southern one at that, with the power to extend his life. It wasn't any great scientific leap, or unique minerals; nothing like that.

It was magic.

There was magic on the Well World. Not a lot, and it was pretty scattered around, but it was there in some races. The entire world was a laboratory, a set of experiments used by ancient Markovians to prove out their races before establishing them out there, in the universe. But when your largest social lab is 614.4 kilometers at its widest point near the equator, compensations must be allowed for. Not merely the technological handicaps, either, but often more. Magic. The ability to do something no other race could do, apparently out of nothingness. Of course, what was magic to the other races was magic only because they didn't know how to do it or simply couldn't. All it meant was that these races could draw those powers from the great machine that kept everything working, the Well itself. The mumbo-jumbo, if it existed, came later.

And one race had a spell that could sustain him indefinitely, keep him from aging. It was relatively easy to get them to do it; he had spies all over the Well World and he had all the embassies thoroughly bugged. He knew where everybody's bodies were buried, and if they had no skeletons in their closets, he was perfectly capable of creating them to order and to need. But there were limits to magic, too.

This magic worked only in the home hex of the spell-caster. Not all magic was like this—some worked anywhere. Not this, though. And since the hex was not only a water hex but a deepwater hex, he could hardly move there even as alien-in-residence. The spell was against aging, not drowning.

The only other place such things would work would be here, in Zone, and so that's where he remained. His home hex of Ulik didn't mind; as they saw it, they benefited two ways. Their ambassador was the most powerful and crooked (but not corrupt—there is a big difference) politician on the Well World. As such, Ulik benefited greatly from the fear and respect

Ortega generated. And, of course, they never had to worry about such a powerful personage as Ortega ever coming home to muck up the local works. He could not leave. That would break the spell, and he was very old.

And so they let him rant and rave, and let him tell them what to do the few times some crisis or another came up. And they hated him for it. He knew it, but really didn't give a damn.

"Now, then, Ambassadors, now that we've had our little prologue," he continued sweetly when he knew by his broad and long experience that they were back, "let's take a *rational* look at this. You have now seen what unilateral action does; it gives the enemy more converts and more power. Even had the attempt on Chang succeeded, the involvement of the Colonel alone would have been enough to guarantee their emnity—and never mind the murders of those innocents. What's worse, the Colonel has done an awful lot of favors and undertaken an awful lot of work for many of us. Some of you, firmly voting with us not long ago, are now wavering toward neutrality, and we've all seen what that road means. Others of you are undertaking pretty vicious pogroms against Entries, despite our agreement not to do so. Well, it's your neck. But if you agree to a common policy and then violate it, well, what chance do we have on the battlefield? Make up your minds which way you will go. You are either our friends, which means you agree to work as part of a coordinated whole and abide by its policies and decisions, or you are our enemies. Is there anyone who wishes to change over to the enemy list? Speak now. We will not overlook breaches in the future."

Nobody spoke.

After waiting as long as he thought reasonable, Ortega sighed and resumed. "Very well, then. The killing stops. Now. Think of them as hostages, but not as hunter's quarry. Not now, anyway."

"All pretty well for you to say," an acid-sounding voice responded. "We have no room for such newcomers, and no way to treat them other than as fertilizer. Should we ship them to you?"

The Ulik thought it over. "Why not? There are a number of hexes with open expanses, even some where the entire surface isn't used. These would make pretty good camps, which could be managed by very few guards. Mix up the species and they'll be a mishmash of alien creatures who can't even talk to one another. How about the ambassador from Kronfushun? Kent Lucas, you there?"

"I'm here," a voice responded, sounding none too thrilled. Kronfushuns were creatures of extreme Arctic cold, odd, whirling disks that skipped across the frozen ice and could not live in temperatures approaching zero.

"Kent, you're an Entry from the Com, as I know. You're best to handle this. Can you put together a committee—Entries at or near our level, if possible—to see to that?"

"I'll give it a try," Lucas responded, still sounding none too enthusiastic.

Ortega couldn't blame him, but nonetheless felt that a recent Com Entry would tend to be far more sympathetic to saving lives, particularly the lives of their old race.

"On the military front, we've organized into wet and dry military zones across the whole hemisphere," he told them. "Mobilization is proceeding fairly well, particularly in the critical areas—the routes away from Glathriel, where we're sure the enemy will head first. You water hexes and boating cultures are particularly important now. If Brazil tries to run by sea, we really don't have anything like a navy to stop him, and there's no time to build one. But if we know he's on a ship, and where that ship is, we can certainly arrange to sink it without problems, then pick Brazil off the inevitable iceberg that will be conveniently floating by near him, even if it's in a tropical hex. Things will turn our way shortly, the staff meeting means they're getting ready to move. When we see *where* they move, after converging on Ambreza-

Glathriel, their logical first move, it'll be all our way after that."

"You really believe that?" somebody asked.

"I do," he responded firmly. "And you'd better, too."

"He outsmarted us to get here," somebody else noted. "What makes you think he won't pull any more fast ones?"

"He very well might," Ortega admitted. "I have no idea. That's what we have to watch out for. Remember, though, we'll have people undercover with their forces as well. Once their plan starts, it'll become clear what they're doing."

It was mostly a pep talk, and after he said his piece he let them rant and rave and worry at each other while *he* tuned *them* out. Somehow, he thought grumpily, it doesn't really seem to matter any more.

He reached down and pulled out a sheet of crumpled paper from a desk drawer, smoothed it out, and read it again. It had been put on his desk not long ago, while he had stepped out to the bathroom. There were no signs that anybody had entered or left the office, but there it had been. He looked at it again and again, as if it were some impossible ghost from the past—which, in a sense, it was. It was written in Com language, in a clear hand, with what looked like a quill or fountain pen.

Dear Serge,

Sorry to have missed you on the way in, but you'll understand why I didn't stop to chat. I wanted to get this off to you first to stop all the unnecessary killings of those Nathan Brazil copies. I'm in. You don't have to do that any more. As you might have been told, I'm not doing this by choice, either. Frankly, the only real appeal all this has is that it promises some fun, a little change from the ordinary—but you'd understand that, wouldn't you?

I don't understand you, I'll admit that. It seems to me that what you want to do to me by force you have done to yourself—put yourself in a velvet prison. That isn't the old Serge I used to tear up bars on dozens of worlds with. Not even the old S.O.B. who took me for a sucker the last time I was here. If you want *out* of that prison, then come and join me if you can. Contrary to what you believe, the spell won't suddenly turn you into a thousand-year-old wizened corpse. You'll just pick up where you left off. So if you want to be in on the big finish, just come on out at the right time. If you make it into the Well with me, I can even fix your problems. You have my word on it.

You doubted my story about being God when most people swallowed it whole. We're two of a kind, you and me. We understand each other. But whether I'm God or not, I know how to work these damned machines. *That* you know, so you know I can make good. Think it over. Even if you've changed so much we don't meet again, well, it's always a pleasure to match wits with you. But if you go against me this time, I'm going to whip you so bad that that long tail of yours will tie itself into knots of its own accord.

My best, regardless. This is going to be fun, isn't it? Like old times . . . And in that spirit, I am, as always,

Nathan Brazil

He held it there, staring at it over and over, then finally reached into his desk again, came out with a box, some matches, and a small ceramic tray. Striking a match, he lit the letter and held it until he had to drop it, flaming brightly, into the tray. Soon it was completely consumed. Only some small bits of ash still with traces of writing remained, and they were easily crushed into powder.

*Had* he changed, really? he asked himself—and not for the first time, although this situation, and in particular that letter, had made him ask it with more intensity and urgency.

Yes, he decided. He had changed—before the Well World. Decades as a smuggler, pirate, mercenary, you name it, had led him, toward the end of his life, to a feeling of bored malaise. He had decided that he had done everything he could do, conquered every world he was likely to conquer, bedded all the beautiful women he could want. He had done it all, and had a lot of fun doing it, but what was left? So he had taken his ship out, trying to get enough nerve to do himself in but unable to get over his strict Catholic beliefs he had turned his back on when still a young boy but which haunted him in his old age. Suicide, the one crime for which repentance was impossible . . . Continuing out, out into areas not yet explored or charted, he had found himself wishing that there was some new world, some new experience for him that would give new meaning to his life. Then there had been that odd distress signal, a look at a massive asteroid belt in a huge, sterile system circling a red giant, and, quite suddenly, here he had been on the Well World, the answer to his dream.

Or was it? he now wondered. As a young Ulik he had started again from scratch, learned a new society, new culture, experienced a whole new range of sensuality while accumulating power. But that had been long ago.

Now here he was, once again, at the same point he had been so long ago. There was simply nothing left to do. A velvet prison, Brazil had called it. But there were no Markovian holes to fall through this time, no new Well Worlds to start again.

He thought again of Brazil. If he was as ancient as he claimed to be, he was well over fourteen billion years old. Fourteen *billion* years. The mind couldn't really grasp that. He doubted Brazil's could, really. Never changing, living the same life after a while, life after life. No rebirth, no new experiences. Same form, same old stuff, even limited by the technology of the people with whom he had marooned himself. Entry interrogations—of this new batch, anyway—said that they had tracked him down by research, for even he left records of a sort.

Brazil had hardly been inconspicuous. He seemed to have been involved in every war and movement on Old Earth, always in the headlines, always in the forefront, yet clever enough that, even when his cover occasionally slipped, new legends were spawned. The Flying Dutchman, the Wandering Jew, Gilgamesh.

Brazil was trying to escape terminal boredom and madness, Ortega alone realized. But what the hell do you do when you've done it all and there's nothing left to do? You pilot a freighter between Boredom and Tedium and try and forget who you are, what you are, putting on a kind of mental shutdown.

Brazil said this would be fun. Fun, of all things! And only to Ortega would that make perfect sense.

And that left him with a problem. Should he take on Brazil once again, see if, this time, he was still the master of the dirty trick and underhanded blow, always in control? The temptation was there—it certainly was. It would, as Brazil said, be fun.

But if he, Ortega, won, would there be a victory? If he only knew the answer to that one . . .

# Dillia

ASAM AND MAVRA CHANG LOOKED OUT ON THEIR army. It wasn't huge, by the standards of the history of the universe, but it was immense in terms of the Well World.

"Six weeks," Asam muttered to himself, "all this in six weeks."

She heard him, turned, and smiled. "If we had more time, we'd do even better," she told him. "The Entries are still coming through."

It was, in fact, mostly an Entry army, an army composed of creatures that flew, crawled, slithered, spun, and even oozed. Roughly a hundred and fifty to two hundred from something like eighty hexes—eight thousand alien creatures. To that were added over a thousand Dillians, the best chosen by Asam to avenge Dillian honor, and perhaps a thousand more native Well Worlders who decided, on their own or on orders from their governments, to join this side for the fight.

Such an army had several problems, of course, mostly in terms of communications and logistics. Though simply insuring that the commanders of each racial company had translators and using Com speech where possible eased the former quite a bit.

As for feeding the horde, they would take with them what they could and forage what they could not. They were not an army of conquest but one on the move; still, their sense of destiny made them disregard a lot of feelings about property rights where they were going. Almost half the force were herbivores, like the Dillians, and could get along most anywhere even if the fare was less than appetizing. For the rest, well, they'd taken on some provisions but they would never last—or keep—over the long march. Food worried Mavra most of all, since some of the species were perfectly edible to some of the others.

Another problem was that they were getting too many from the west; redundancies better picked up along the way or left to prepare the way. Many simply hadn't followed instructions, some couldn't. One couldn't adequately brief a billion-plus people.

The premium went to weaponry, and some of it was formidable. Nontech hexes required the crossbow, sword, axe, and pike. The Dillians could hold their own there, with some of the others getting training as they went along. In addition to the Dillians some of the others could handle projectile guns. It took very little training to use a submachine gun effectively, only discipline.

It was the high-tech hexes they feared. Dillia could not supply that sort of armament, and precious little could be bought or stolen by a neophyte army reborn naked into this world. And not much could be arranged for in six weeks, either.

"I'm just amazed that so many of the hexes who voted against us are represented here," Mavra noted. "I would have expected a lot more trouble."

Asam shrugged. "Not that many hexes will actually lay their lives on the line, no matter how they side politically. There's a pretty good backlash of feeling that things would be a lot nicer if we'd only go away, which is what we're trying to do. That'll intensify when a force this size crosses a border. It's easy to rattle the saber if the enemy's five thousand or more kilometers distant."

She nodded hopefully, then said, "But some will fight."

"Some will fight," he agreed. "And the decisive battle they'll try and force will be a nasty one. Don't kid yourself on that. A lot of these people will die before this is done."

That was a sobering thought, and for a while she was silent. Finally she said, "There's word that a deepwater army is forming, too. Did you know that?"

"I expected as much," he replied. "Gypsy said we weren't the only ones—and each hex is getting an equal number of Entries. Remember, Brazil called a lot of his old buddies to him, and there was the crew of your little world. I expect that deepwater force will be necessary, too." He took out an overall map and studied it.

"You think he's really going by sea, then?" she asked. "Up the Josele-Wahaca Avenue?"

"Seems logical," Asam replied. "I'll bet *something* is, anyway. This computer of yours, the one that planned this, seems to have been quite a dirty trickster so far."

She nodded. "And it's a combination. Obie, Brazil, and Gypsy." She paused. "Gypsy . . . I wish I knew more about him. Who he is. *What* he is. He scares me, even though he's on our side. He's like an Obie himself, all that huge computer capacity embodied in one being."

"But your computer mostly did that sort of thing to other people," Asam pointed out. "This Gypsy can only do it to himself."

"So *he* says," she retorted. "I'm not sure I totally trust him."

"Your computer trusted him," he noted.

She nodded. "But if he has equal power to Obie, then Obie could have been fooled. He's too convenient, too good to be true."

"We can't do anything about it," he said philosophically. "When the time comes, we'll know—and then deal with it as best we can. What else can we do?"

She nodded grumpily. As it was, there were too many things in this operation that smelled. Enough to fool Ortega and the Council? She wondered. Who was fooling who?

The army moved. It was fairly easy at first, traveling up through Gedemondas along well-established trails, camping in long lines where possible and posting nocturnals as guardians of the camp. No opposition was expected in Gedemondas, of course, but it worried Asam that, strung out as they were and in cold, high altitudes, they were as vulnerable as they would ever be. Nothing opposed them, though. Gypsy had been correct; they would be unimpeded until Brazil, somewhere, sometime, surfaced.

She had hoped to contact or gather Gedemondans in the passage, but they were out of sight as usual. Occasionally one would be spotted, far off, or they would hear the eerie calls of the great white creatures echoing through mountain passes and around rocky walls, but nothing else. She was more than disappointed; she felt she had gone through that whole damned trip for nothing.

On the western slope of the Gedemondan mountains was a plain, the only flat area in the whole hex. Looking out on it from the high trail, she had the first twinges of memory.

That plain, so empty and peaceful now . . . She remembered a different time, a time when far different armies converged on that plain for a horribly bloody battle so very long ago.

Down on the flat, the sensations were even greater. They had come through just before the major armies had converged, she recalled. And over there they had met their Dillian guide, by that cabin—no, not that cabin, but the cabin's predecessor, perhaps. And there from the north, had come the Yaxa on great, soaring orange wings . . . .

She talked about it a lot with Asam, who had become her closest friend and confidant. He was warm and kind and understanding—and fascinated by her memoirs of a great event that he knew only from the dimness of history books.

Alestol, to the south, with its carnivorous plants exuding poisonous and hypnotic gasses, they were happy to bypass. The Alestolians had massed on the border, it was true, but could not get at the army if it didn't come to Alestol. Although mobile, they were plants, they required occasional rooting in a soil that contained a certain balance of minerals and suspended gasses necessary to their continued existence.

That had left Palim as the focus of intense diplomatic activity, with the council and Mavra's forces playing on the huge, elephantine creatures. Their's was a highly advanced high-tech hex whose inhabitants weighed in at more than a ton each.

But they were gentle giants; they had withdrawn when the warring forces of the Wars of the Well had approached, working out safe passage for one while taking no sides. There were never more than twenty thousand or so Palims in their entire hex—and, therefore, their entire race. They could see no profit in a fight and had voted abstention on the council. They abstained now.

But a hundred and twenty-one of them, all Entries, all former Olympians, joined the force. They were welcome. As herbivores they would place only a slight drain on supplies, but they could carry ten times the weight of any Dillian without even noticing—and just the sight of them was fearsome.

Next was Olborn, about which Mavra Chang still had nightmares. A theocracy whose magic could transform enemies, dissidents, and even casual travelers into donkeylike beasts of burden, they had almost done it to her. For many years she had suffered, half-human, half-donkey, because of them. Her only solace was that the long-ago war had not been kind to them.

And yet, they had voted on the council with the opposition. She had to wonder if her name, after all those centuries, was still cursed in Olborn.

And, true enough, at the border their advance aerial scouts told them that a large armed force of Olbornians was waiting for them. They even brought back photographs of the massed troops, great cats that stood upright and wore some kind of livery that indicated a well-organized army.

"Should be relatively simple," Mavra commented, looking at the photos. "This looks like the way they lost to the Makiem alliance a thousand years ago. We just outflank them and cut them to pieces."

Asam shook his head worriedly. "Uh uh. Think about it. It may be in the dim past for me and most o' the Well World, but that was the most significant event in their history, not to mention the most humiliatin'. I just don't think they'd be dumb enough to do it again. Just a gut feelin', o' course—but there's some dirty work afoot here."

"I don't know. . . ." she responded hesitantly.

"We'll pull up close to the border but we won't cross right off," he said firmly. "I want more recon, day and night, of that area. They're just too much like targets in a shootin' match."

"Those are machine guns they're packing," she pointed out. "And those are gun emplacements. This isn't any pushover—particularly with that swampy area, there, of over fifteen hundred meters. They've cleared it—see? We'll be coming into them, there in the trees, over fifteen hundred meters of open ground that's also soggy, maybe even quagmire."

"You're thinkin' too much in the past," he admonished. "I know a little o' the history here. Hell, woman, that damned war was the most interestin' thing in the history books to me! After them pussy cats got sliced to pieces by the Trelig alliance, well, it blew hell outa their religion. I mean, how can you be the Well World's chosen people and get wiped up like that, like I'd swat a fly with my tail? They turned on the priests, there was a wholesale massacre, and a real revolution. O' course new, strong leaders finally took over. Hard rule was clamped back on, this time by what was left o' the military and the aristocracy. They got tramped on because they didn't truck with other folks, other hexes. Nobody to help 'em out. This is a pragmatic lot now. Bet on it. And they been workin' on their magic, too. I think we got trouble if we do the expected thing here. I want a lot more recon here—and I want a staff meetin' soon after."

"All right, all right," she said, surrendering. "It's your show."

Asam frowned at the photographs. "How many scouts did we send out?" he asked worriedly.

"Fifteen, I think," somebody replied. "All aerial, of course."

He nodded. "And how many got back?"

"Why, all of them," the officer, another Dillian,

responded. "I don't even remember a report of anybody being shot at."

"That's what I thought," he murmured. "Damn! It don't make sense a'tall! Not a bit! Five thousand pussy cats all lined up in neat rows, so's they're easier to attack, and fixed gun emplacements so obvious we could wipe 'em clean with an air attack. And with all that firepower there, do they take shots at us? Try and knock us out o' the air? They do not! They sit there, posin', and smile for the camera. It stinks, I tell you. Stinks wors'n a Susafrit—beggin' yer pardon, there."

One of the commanders, a strange, round creature with short quill-like hairs all over its body, just shrugged. She was used to it by now: to all but her own kind, her race literally stank when it wanted to. It came right out of the pores in the skin.

"Now, then," Asam continued, "let's take a look here again. What would you say the regular, orthodox military move would be here?"

"Use our flying people to drop hell on them," one of the commanders said. "Then, when they scatter to their positions, send forces of one or two thousand on either side and close in on the main one when we get into position. Encircle and that's it." It sounded simple.

"And what's the *last* thing you'd do?" he prodded.

"Attack straight on," another said. "Suicide."

He nodded. "And yet, that's exactly what I intend to do. Go in with a *limited* aerial attack, keepin' most of the force in reserve to cover the flanks. Then we'll send in our biggest, nastiest-looking crowd first, the type that won't get bogged down there. I also want a squad of flyers—those bat fellows will do—to drop a load o' rocks and buckshot on that swamp before dawn. Lots of it—and from a height."

Mavra watched him with growing admiration and fascination. This was his first large-scale battle, yet he sounded like all the generals of past history. Crisp, professional, analytical.

"Buckshot?" somebody asked.

He nodded. "Got to be mines in there. Tell artillery

to bring up the cannon in rows, too. I want a pattern of
fire from just across the border slowly advancin' until
it's covered the whole territory—*before* our people
go in. And emphasize strongly to the troops that they
keep advancin' as long as they don't hear retreat
blown. Understand? Reserves follow the first wave in
sections, wave after wave. Pack 'em in—and move
up the artillery as soon as you can. Expect flank attacks.—And when you get to them trees, here's what
you do. . . ."

Mavra listened with amazement at his detailed instructions. And, after they'd left to convey the message to their troops, she told him, "You're going to kill
a lot of people if you're wrong."

"I'm gonna kill a lot of people if I'm right, too," he
responded gravely. "But this'll be our test, how our
dscipline works, how all our units work together.
And, if I'm right—and I am—I'll be the genius who
won the battle."

Asam had been right about the mines, but he
hardly needed the artillery barrage. The Olbornians
understood a lot more about war this time, of course,
but they themselves were a thousand years removed
from any practical experience. On the theory that the
more mines you had the more enemy you got, they'd
sunk them by the hundreds in that muddy swamp.
When the aerial bombardment of rocks and buckshot
finally hit one, it set off every one near it. The chain
reaction was spectacular in the predawn sky; it
looked as if the entire world were blowing up. The
concussions reverberated for kilometers in all directions, practically deafening all sides and almost
knocking several ghostly aerials out of the sky.

Asam, who had not slept all night, immediately
sent word to the artillerymen to cancel the carpet and
concentrate on widening the area covered. He was
certain now that the mines had been laid in close rows
and that hitting one in a row would set off the entire
row.

He was correct.

Mavra, who had never seen anything like it before,

looked at the exploding, bubbling mass uneasily. "You expect people to charge into *that?*" she asked, aghast.

He nodded. "On the run and laying down fire all the way."

With first light, he signaled for the attack to proceed, and at the same time diurnal aerials took off to either side while more started dropping much more lethal stuff into the trees, mostly inflammables.

The Olbornians, although shell-shocked, knew that the attack was coming and went to their emplacements. They had a good, solid defense line—from the air it could be seen that they had raised bastions, star-pointed redoubts that could cover each other every step of the way. To secure an area, three bastions would have to be taken at the same time while the ones on either side still receiving a withering fire from the ones farther down.

Olbornian artillery waited for the leading wave to get almost to the center of the clearing before they opened up their presighted cannon. Palim, Dillians, Slongornians, Dymeks, Susafrits—they started to go down. Creatures that were crablike aided creatures that were insectival; creatures that were elephantine shielded creatures that were centauroid. And each wave moved quickly to fill in for its fallen comrades.

Asam studied the scene through field glasses and nodded approvingly. "Uh huh. They're holding together, those people of yours."

"They're religious fanatics," she muttered cynically. "They love to die for the cause." Still, she could not deny that, within her, she felt a great deal of admiration for the courage being shown there. And they were all volunteers.

A meter-long creature with a segmented body, dozens of legs, and six pairs of transparent wings came in with a buzz and dropped new photos at Asam's feet. Their thorax-mounted cameras were providing him with the kind of intelligence the Olbornians could only wish for.

"They're breaking," he noted, a satisfied tone in his voice. "By God! They're retreating!"

She smiled at him. "That means we've got them."

He shook his head violently. "Uh uh. They've just realized I caught on to their little game and they're trying to draw us in while they get word to the flanks to change tactics. Whether we win or not will depend on whether there's enough command organization down there to do what I ordered when they reach the trees." He reached over and nodded to his signalman, who was standing with a limelight reflector facing the battle scene.

"Form the columns," he snapped, and the message was sent. "Split ranks and form defensive perimeters."

Not everybody below could be held back by iron discipline, of course. For them, too, it was their first battle, and seeing the enemy falling back was heady stuff to an already emotionally pumped-up force. The ranks behind, though, not having had to face the brunt of the assault, were more easily led, Dillians taking the lead, and a defense line was established across the open area through which more troops poured, some going forward but the bulk peeling off to right and left.

And suddenly the forest erupted with living bodies. Olbornians, yes, but not just Olbornians. The very ground seemed to come alive with hundreds upon hundreds of huge mouths all filled with infinite rows of sharp teeth.

Again the leading forces were taken by surprise and went down; the ones still rushing through the new line, though, formed reserves that peeled off to right and left to support their comrades under attack.

Mavra looked through her field glasses and shook her head. "It's too far away," she sighed. "What *are* they?"

"Well, the ones dropping from the trees are more Olbornians, of course—and I think I see a lot of well-prepared sniper nests up there, too. But they used the forest and the natural color of their allies to disguise the main force."

"Allies?" she echoed, confused.

He nodded. "Giant lizards, with the biggest mouths and biggest bellies you've ever seen. They can lie absolutely motionless for days, but when they want to move, they *move!* I've seen Zhonzhorpians run on two legs at over twenty kilometers per hour—on all fours they can be almost twice as fast and climb a tree or a slick wall right after you." He looked into the glasses again. "Ha! See? They forgot a machine gun isn't a death-ray! It can put up a withering fire, but it can only fell what it hits, and it can't hit everybody!" He turned to the signalman. "Make for all reserves to flank!"

Almost as the signal was transmitted, the remains of their fighting force, some thousand or so soldiers, crossed half a kilometer up and half a kilometer down from the battle and started to close.

Asam sighed and put down his glasses. He looked suddenly very old and very tired. "We got 'em," he sighed. "We won. A lot o' fightin' yet to do, but it's ours."

She looked at him in some confusion. "I still don't understand all this," she told him.

He grabbed for a flask, uncapped it, and took a long pull. It was a lot stronger than ale, but he downed it like it was water.

He coughed slightly, wiped his mouth with his hand, and let the flask, which was on a chain around his waist, drop. He sighed and grinned.

"Allies," he told her. "And who could they get? Not Alestol—they're stuck in their hex. Not Palim, surely. That left Zhonzhorp, to the west. A high-tech hex. It's where those excellent rifles and cannon were manufactured. The Zhonnies voted against us, too—as did most, o' course—and they would also like to see the battle fought on somebody else's territory. Keeps from messin' up the landscape."

The reserves were attacking, closing in now.

"The Olbornians will be comin' back now to try and hit us, but it'll do 'em no good. See? Right now some of our flying folk are givin' it to 'em good, just beyond the trees there. When we combine, there'll be little left in the way of an enemy in our area, and our combined force will push out at the Olbornians. That'll be that. Better part of a day is all."

"I'm *still* confused," she persisted. "Why did you attack the way you did?"

He grinned. "Well, if we'd split up into three main bodies, there would've been maybe two, three thousand tops, to cross that open area. The pussy cats would be down to that number or so after the bombardment, so it'd be fairly even: their turf, our superior racial forms for this kind o' thing. Most of us are harder to kill than them. Then, as the flankers came to the aid of our forward attackers, they'd be hit by the Zhonzhorpians. Again, equal numbers, but their turf, their surprise. Their three forces would be back to back to back, so to speak. If any carried, they could be hustled to some place in trouble. We'd be divided, an enemy force between any two of ours. They'd have held."

She rushed to him, gave him a hug, and kissed him. "Oh, Asam! What *would* I have done without you?"

He looked down at her and smiled. "Found another sucker," he said dryly.

She wasn't sure whether or not he was kidding.

# At the Bahabi-Ambreza Border

"THE MEN ARE GETTNG PRETTY PISSED OFF, SIR,"
the Hakazit general told him sourly. "I mean, it's not
what they signed on for. Hell, I don't believe it myself! Close to nine hundred kilometers and we haven't
killed anybody yet!"

Marquoz shrugged. "What can I do? That whole
Durbis army was set up to take us—force-ray projectors, helicopter gunships, and all—and when we
marched over that hill, everybody decided they'd visit
the seashore for their health. I'll admit it's been a
damn sight easier than I expected—so far. You just
tell 'em that going up the Isthmus isn't going to be any
picnic."

"It better hadn't be," the general huffed. "Otherwise, they'll do us both in and go on a rampage on
general principles."

Marquoz chuckled and turned back to the border. Children, he thought. Like little children always
dreaming and playing at war. The glories of battle
and all that. Inwardly, he was thankful that a force of
fifteen thousand Hakazit troops marching in precision
across a wide swath of countryside had scared the hell
out of the locals. He would need this force later, he
knew, and he wasn't all that certain that, when their
buddies were getting smashed into goo all around
them, the romance might not be over.

He was, he decided, developing a whole religious
faith around the absolutism of genetics, and he
hoped it wasn't a false deity.

Ambreza, he believed, would be another easy mark.
They *wanted* him in Glathriel and would do almost

anything to let him get there. Getting *out* would be the problem.

As with many other races and most of the hexes here, a white flag or cloth meant not to shoot. It was a logical choice. Quite simply, it was easier to see at a distance. He wondered uncomfortably at times, though, about what would happen if he ever met an army whose national flag was white.

Affixing the flag to a staff, he rumbled down the side of a hill to the party below who waited under a similar banner. It was getting to be very routine by now.

The Ambreza were enormous rodents that somewhat resembled overgrown beavers, complete to the buckteeth and large, paddlelike tail. They walked upright, though, on large hind legs, using their tails as added balance, and their look of extreme innocence was deceptive. Once *this* hex had been Glathriel, not Ambreza. A high-tech hex whose "humans" had built a massive and powerful civilization, one that, simply from its own laziness and indolence, outgrew its living space and decided that the lush farmlands of the Ambreza next door were necessary to its continued comforts. Rather than fight a losing battle, the Ambreza had cast about and, as usual when certain impossibilities were needed, found it in the North, among races so strange and alien that you could get them to whip things up for you if you had the right trade goods and they would never even consider that they were making up a weapon, in this case a brutal gas that was harmless to all except Type 41 humans.

In the final preparations, the humans had begun massing on the Ambreza border when, throughout the hex, the canisters of gas were loosed. The Ambreza may have been nontech, but they weren't ignorant. Their own "peace" party in negotiations in Glathriel had triggered the gas releases electronically.

It was colorless, odorless, and quite effective. In some way even the Ambreza didn't understand it worked on the cerebral cortex of the human brain, and, rather slowly, the humans had simply become increasingly less able to think, to reason. The great apes had been the model for the Type 41s, and, mentally at least, great apes they became. The gas didn't dissipate, either; it stayed, and settled into the rocks, the soil, everything, affecting new generations. Most died; the rest became pets of the Ambreza in their expansion into Glathriel.

Brazil had changed all that the last time he was through. Inside the Well he had altered not the gas but, subtly, the Type 41 brains that were affected by it. During Mavra Chang's exile in Glathriel they had been savages, yes, but thinking savages. Marquoz wondered what they were now.

There were five Ambreza, each wearing some sort of medallion that the Hakazit took to be a badge of office or rank. With them were several others, one of whom looked decidedly strange, Marquoz thought uneasily, a huge, looming shape of pure white with only two small black ovals.

He stopped a few meters from the party and stuck his white flag in the dirt. "I am Marquoz of Hakazit," he told them in his most menacing tone.

"I am Thoth, Chamberlain of the Region," one of the Ambreza responded. "My fellow Ambreza are from the central authorities. The others are representatives of the council force invited here, with *this,*" he pointed to the white specter, "their commander, Gunit Sangh of Dahbi."

Marquoz was impressed. He'd heard of Gunit Sangh, although the Dahbi were half a world away. He seemed to recall that Sangh had once tried the same trick the Ambreza had pulled on Glathriel but had been screwed in the attempt.

"I'll get to the point," he said, not acknowledging the others. "We have no wish to harm any citizens or territories, yours included. We only wish to march through the areas under your jurisdiction, Ambreza and Glathriel, as quickly as possible on the way north."

"You are welcome here, friends," Thoth responded, "but Glathriel is a very fragile place. We should not wish large forces to go there. It could upset the ecological balance."

"We must go there to go north, as you well know," the Hakazit parried. "Ginzin is only passable along the northeast coast. Glathriel is necessary. We will do minimal damage."

"Glathriel is not open," the Ambreza maintained.

Marquoz felt his stomach tense slightly. He turned and pointed back up the hill. "As you know, up there is the start of fifteen thousand creatures just like me. Most conventional weapons simply will not harm us. I realize that you have some very sophisticated weaponry that would, particularly the rays, but be aware that we, too, are from a high-tech hex and have our own. We also have seven hundred additional allied troops of various forms, many aerial and a number poisonous. My race is bred as a warrior race. We are not concerned with casualties or arguments. If you refuse us, we will march anyway, using all weaponry within our command to facilitate our course. Should we be opposed we will destroy utterly and without mercy any and all, soldiers and civilians, plants and animals, that are in our path."

"You say 'we,'" Gunit Sangh put in, his voice through the translator sounding still nasty and threatening. "You are not of our world. Those are not your people. I tend to think that, if we overlooked the diplomatic courtesies and simply eliminated you right here and now, that army would have no fight left."

Inwardly, that idea did nothing for his stomach, but he kept his impassive stance and tone. "You're wrong. I have just come from arguing with my generals because the men are upset. They have marched here without killing anyone or anything and that makes them unhappy. They want to fight. Should anything happen to me at this moment, you would lose the only moderating force around. You all would die immediately, of course—and after that Ambreza would be just a memory. Right now two Jorgasnovarians are over principal population centers in Ambreza carrying bombs made from designs I furnished. These are ancient weapons from my old sector of space, fairly easy to make once I discovered that there was uranium in Hakazit. Each bomb is atomic. Each will destroy an entire city and poison the countryside for generations with radioactivity. We can effectively deal with any remaining forces you have here. Make up your mind now. Yes or no. I intend to give the order to march immediately. How they do it is determined by your answer now."

The Ambreza looked shocked. One turned to another and whispered, "Is such a weapon possible?" The other nodded.

Thoth, hearing this, shivered a bit and turned back to Marquoz. "We must have some time to discuss this!" he argued. "Please, a few minutes, at least!"

"You have no time. Yes or no? I want your answer now," he pressed cooly. He actually found himself feeling a bit sorry for the Ambreza; they were so damned politically naïve. That was the hole card for this entire business, he knew. A world with a lot of political and military intrigue in its past would never be taken in so quickly.

"He is bluffing," Gunit Sangh snapped. "We have a solid force here. Let us join with them at this point and make an end to this matter."

Of course, Marquoz conceded to himself, there *were* exceptions.

The Ambreza, however, were done in. After a quick, whispered conference there were nods and Thoth turned to the strange white creature. "Commander, it is *our* hex, you know." He turned to Marquoz. "You may enter for transit," he said hoarsely, gulping a couple of times. "Your march will not be impeded."

Now Gunit Sangh unfolded himself. He was an impressive, vicious-looking creature, with three pairs of sticky tentacles and a face that said here was a thing that ate only living flesh. The tentacles showed sharp reflective shields of cartilage that obviously could cut like knives. The whole creature, close to three meters long, was in its own way as much a killing machine as the Hakazit—and unlike the Hakazit it looked very much in practice, not bluffing at all.

"I can do nothing if the host country forbids it," Sangh spat. "But your untried army will have to face mine yet, off-worlder. You mark my words. *I* am the enemy you will have to face one day soon."

"Any time," Marquoz responded as casually as he could manage. "And, in case you think *I'm* a push-over, well, Colonel Asam sends his regards."

"Asam!" the Dahbi hissed. "Eating the two of you will be the most supreme pleasure of my very long life!" And, with that, to the amazement of both sides, Gunit Sangh seemed to change his color to a more milky white, becoming slightly glowing, less substantial. He folded himself back into his ghostly shape and, without another word, sank into the ground itself as if it were water.

Marquoz felt well satisfied even though the troops would be upset at still no battle. He had faced down the Ambreza and removed another potentially nasty threat, neutralized that big multiracial force, and snubbed the enemy commander all at one time. He was particularly happy to have met Colonel Asam by chance in Zone; otherwise, he would never have known about that story. . . .

He turned, nodded to a subordinate, and green flares were lit and shot into the air. The army started to move. He and his aides stood there and let it march past, looking damned menacing and impressive. The Ambreza and allied forms got out of the way fast; most, he guessed, were heading to nearby communications tents to radio the news.

One of his Hakazit aides inched over to him as they tramped by, masking most other sounds.

"Sir?"

"Yes?"

"Those bombs—superbombs or whatever. Was that for real?"

He drew himself up to full attention. "General, I would no more bluff than I would tell a lie," he huffed, and that closed the matter.

And, of course, it took some time before the aide realized that he had not had an answer at all.

The passage across Ambreza had been swift and easy. Roads were cleared for them; vehicles, in fact, were provided. They avoided the major cities—no use in giving any provocations, he decided—and the Ambreza and allied forces they met along the way mostly stared, gawked, and even snapped pictures occasionally. The cold, crisp weather had the Hakazit breathing steam, and that leant an even more sinister touch to everything. Marquoz liked it. It was good theater.

It was easy to see where Ambreza ended and Glathriel began. It was winter in Ambreza, and the trees were barren and the soil frosted. But there, shimmering slightly, was a lush, green world ahead of them. It was like walking through some sort of invisible curtain from late fall into deepest summer. Glathriel was a tropical hex, and, as they saw, it was one that didn't stop just because an army was passing through.

They were all around, these creatures that looked so much like the dominant race of the Com from which he had come. And why not? These were the prototypes, smaller than the average Com human, but that might have been climate or diet or a combination of things, and darker, too, but very much "human" all the same. Most were naked or wore only clouts or loincloths—that, and collars.

Here were the great plantations from which Ambreza tobacco came, and tropical fruits as well, men, women, children, all ages out in those fields working, working, working, all worked by these human slaves supervised by Ambreza overlords. Occasionally they would stop and gawk at the hordes passing along the road, but not for very long and certainly not without cowering in abject fear and terror.

Over a thousand years, Marquoz guessed, they'd had the aggressiveness bred out of them and the traits needed to do this sort of job emphasized.

There was a commotion ahead, and Marquoz rushed to find the reason for it. To his surprise, he found three very young human women there, seemingly begging or pleading and looking nervously around. They were naked, wore brass collars, and seemed no different from the rest—except they had the nerve to approach the column where nobody could understand them or would even deign to notice them.

"What's the meaning of this?" he thundered.

The women reacted as if they'd suddenly gone mad. "You can hear us!" they cried. "You can understand us! Thank God!"

They nodded. He turned to the leaders of the column. "I want the word passed down the line. Any Glathrielites who approach us are to be taken under our protection and kept awaiting my inspection. Clear?"

Word was passed. Shouldn't overlook any bets or reject any soldiers, no matter how small or flimsy-looking, he decided. Besides, one of 'em might be Gypsy—er, Nathan Brazil. Wouldn't do to leave him behind after going to all this trouble to pick him up, he thought sardonically.

At the night's camp he had them brought to him. They had picked up a few more—perhaps twenty in all—along the way, two males and the rest females. They had come through, of course, as had everybody else, and had awakened in Ambreza. The Well didn't recognize hex-swapping, so Ambreza Entries were deposited in old Ambreza, or Glathriel, while the reverse was true for humans. It made them stand out, of course, and they had been quickly picked up and carted off to Glathriel, where they had been assigned to the fields and had the collars welded on. None could believe the horrible system, and less comprehensible still was the absolute submission of the natives.

His orders had been to reach the northwestern facet of Glathriel and proceed along it to the coast, then turn north into Ginzin and head north until he linked up with Mavra's army moving due west. His communications were good; Jorgasnovarians, who were huge, ugly, flat creatures with gaping mouths and somehow flew like birds, often raced hundreds of kilometers to an accessible Zone Gate for news, then returned. He knew of the battle in Olborn, and the progress beyond it, almost within hours of their happening—and they now were hearing from him.

Ginzin rose before them along the Sea of Turagin now, and still no Brazil. The nasty, hot, volcanic land was inhospitable to most of their kind, but here, right where the land met the sea, it was passable.

He began to wonder if something had slipped.

The going was slow up the coast, and they had particular troubles with their heavy equipment, which helped take his mind off the anxiety some of the time. Still, he had expected Brazil by now—or, rather, a Brazil look-alike he knew well but which would be Brazil as far as everyone else knew. Where was he?

Finally, on the last evening in Ginzin, they camped as best they could, all strung out up and down the beach, and watched the sun slowly set. He sat there, idly watching the play of sunlight on the rolling waves, although the sun was setting behind him and would be gone before it truly set, when he thought he saw something out there. He stared into the gathering gloom, trying to make it out. A ship—there was a ship out there! Waynir was high-tech, and he could see the billowing smoke from belching stacks as the great craft steamed onward to the northwest. It seemed oddly near to shore, though, taking something of a risk; there were reefs and shoals hidden in the shallows here, a product of lava flows from Ginzin reaching the sea and then being covered with coral and other sea creatures. He reached for his field glasses, gogglelike affairs specially built for his strange eyes. They were effective.

He watched as long as the light permitted him, watched as the mystery ship, without cutting steam, lowered a small boat, which headed in toward the beach.

Suspicious of the whole thing, Marquoz notified the guard to put everyone on alert. Here, in a nontech hex, backs to the sea on one side and the volcanic cliffs on the other, would be the perfect place to attack.

They watched and waited warily as the small boat approached. Finally, it came in and two dark figures jumped out and pulled it up on what passed for a beach. The only other member of the boat party waited, then got up and jumped down into the shallow water. He shook hands with the other two—who looked, Marquoz saw, like Type 41 humans—and then as the other two pushed off and jumped in, the passenger made his way up to the waiting force, which visibly relaxed now.

He heard the humans in his own party gasp as they recognized the figure, and for the first time he felt a bit better about this whole thing. He walked down to meet the figure.

"Welcome to the war, ah, Brazil," he called out.

The figure stopped, staring for a moment at the huge, looming creature only half-visible in the darkness, its red eyes blazing. "That you, Marquoz?" he called.

"Yeah, it's me," he replied. "Come ahead. We were beginning to give up on you."

All fires had been extinguished on the sound of the alert, but now they were being restoked. He stepped up to the nearest one, shivered slightly in the slight chill, and nodded in satisfaction.

He was dressed in a pea-green tunic and trousers and wore sandals. His hair was extremely long, down past his shoulders, and he looked slightly weather-beaten and somewhat older than Marquoz remembered—but, then, he'd been here awhile.

Marquoz guessed that the real Brazil probably looked *exactly* like this one, even to the clothing.

"Any problems?" Brazil asked casually.

"Nothing we couldn't handle," Marquoz told him. "You wouldn't like Glathriel. It's pretty unpleasant. Plantation slavery. But, still, we got through without a shot fired, much to the disappointment of some of the boys. I'll give you a rundown later."

Brazil nodded. "Well, we'll have a fight now. If I were the opposition, I'd try and get a force in between ours and Mavra's before we can link up. Might be hairy if we can't make time."

Marquoz stared at him suspiciously. For a moment he found himself wondering, wondering if this was, indeed, Gypsy. The mannerisms, the tone and accent, they were all consistent with Brazil. Could it be . . . ?

And then Brazil reached into his tunic and pulled out a cigarette, reached down for an ember and lit it.

Marquoz felt better.

Brazil made a face as he inhaled. "Local stuff," he muttered grumpily. "Almost all cigar and pipe tobacco. Not really good for cigarettes."

"We all have to make sacrifices in war," Marquoz responded with mock sympathy.

At that moment the humans in the party could not be restrained and started running for the small figure by the fire. He looked up at the commotion, his face a mixture of shock and revulsion.

They prostrated themselves before him and cried out, "Nathan Brazil! Master! We are your servants! Speak and we shall obey!"

He looked at them, a whole range of conflicting emotions passing across his face. Finally he went up to the leading humans.

"Look up at me," he said softly, and they did.

He studied their young faces and forms thoughtfully. Finally he said, almost to himself, "Maybe this god business has some advantages after all. . . ." He looked over at Marquoz. "How many?" he asked.

"Eighteen female, two male," the Hakazit responded.

Brazil nodded. "Maybe this trip won't be such a holy terror after all," he murmured. "Eighteen . . ."

Gypsy, Marquoz thought, was showing through a bit.

# Zone

"BRAZIL'S BEEN SEEN."

The report startled Serge Ortega. Somehow he hadn't quite expected it to be this easy.

"Where?" he asked sharply.

"With the Southern force. Apparently he's been on a ship on the Sea of Turagin all this time. Rowed ashore and joined them just south of the Ginzin border."

Ortega frowned suspiciously. "Are you sure it's him? These are tricky bastards we're dealing with, and he's the trickiest."

"It's him," the messenger assured him. "Some of our people with the force have seen and talked to him and the Entries in the group are acting like God Himself just paid them a call."

The Ulik nodded absently and switched off. Brazil. Visible, easily located, ripe for the plucking, with over three-thousand kilometers left to go to the nearest Avenue. It smelled wrong, somehow. It was too obvious, too blatant, too much a dumb mistake in an operation that had been, so far, beautifully planned and executed. It was as if, with everything going his way, Brazil had suddenly popped up and shouted, "Here I am! Come and get me!"

And he *was* vulnerable. Except for death, he wasn't immune to anything that could happen to anyone else. He suffered pain and torment, and he was wide open to everything from hypno devices to magic.

He punched in a communications code. "Central Command," answered a translator-pitched voice.

"This is Ortega. Now that the information about Brazil has come in, what does Commander Sangh intend?"

The communications officer hesitated. "Sir, I don't think we can give that out right now. Not even to you, sir."

He growled. "I'm coming down there. Something's very wrong here, and I want to make sure there are no slip-ups." He switched off angrily and slithered from behind his great *U*-shaped desk and out the door.

It was still bad in the corridors; there seemed no end to the Entries, and he knew he couldn't protect them much longer. If Brazil were captured, or even if they *thought* they had him, a lot of restraints would suddenly ease around the world.

Central Command was located in the Czillian Embassy, simply because Czill had the best, most sophisticated computers and records and it provided easy access. The machines in the embassy were compatible with the ones in Czill, and information could quickly be traded back and forth by simply having the Czillians take the computer storage modules between home and embassy.

It was crowded, though, with many races, all with forces in the critical area. For one of Ortega's bulk, he had to watch it or get injured by accident by some spiked or poisonous or other lethal creature just trying to keep out of the way.

He spotted Sadir Bakh, the Dahbi second-in-command who was Gunit Sangh's alter ego in Zone. Ortega didn't like the Dahbi much, although with his racial command policies he was dealing here with only half a dozen. Had Brazil gone the other way, Sangh wouldn't have been the commander, but Dahbi would have been in the path of march.

"Bakh! What's the commander going to do about all this? Where the hell is he, anyway?"

The folded Dahbi turned, looking more like a ghost than ever, and sighed. "His Holiness flew to Cebu with the Cebu commander as soon as the Ambreza situation was resolved," he said coolly. "He is there now. We have a mixed force of about twenty thousand ready to go in the area, and another force of almost twelve thousand is currently being ferried across Laibir from Conforte to Suffok, which should be sufficient to cut off that route and the Ellerbanta-Verion Avenue. The enemy is currently split into three parts, the Awbrian part consisting of about six thousand natives and roughly two thousand others. Parmiter is remaining officially neutral, but we believe a large part of it has been bought off by the enemy and will supply the technological weaponry the Awbrian force needs."

"Why doesn't he bomb the damned factories from Cebu?" Ortega growled.

"As the Ambassador must know, Parmiter is *officially* on *our* side. Do we turn probable collaboration into active opposition on a suspicion that *some* Parmiters—they are a rather anarchistic group, you might recall—are doing us harm?"

Ortega nodded glumly. Damn it, the cards were always stacked on the wrong side.

"You're forcing them toward the Yaxa-Harbigor Avenue, then," he noted, looking at the situation map.

"All ours, all armed, all ready and well equipped. It is our feeling that they will go north along the Sea of Storms to avoid as much as possible the high-tech hexes. Once they are north of Boidol, there will be a solid wall of us while they will be in hostile hexes with their backs to the sea at all points. That will effectively isolate the southern and eastern forces from those in Awbri, who will have to break through heavily defended border positions over a long distance to link up. By that time our own forces will be able to move from the Ellerbanta-Verion area to engage them, and that will be that."

He studied it, then decided it was a good, reasonable, rational plan based on current information—and one that seemed absolutely foolproof. That worried him. The other side read maps and had a fair amount of intelligence itself and would know exactly this. The more he looked at it, the more he thought that he was missing *something,* he wasn't sure what. Something wrong. A joker.

He turned to the intelligence chief sitting in front of a computer console. "You have anything out of the ordinary away from the battle lines?" he asked uneasily. "Any reports of any odd occurrences or movements?"

"Nothing much," the chief told him. "We traced that ship Brazil used on Turagin. He owned it—at least, it was bought with a *hell* of a lot of money, about nine times the going price. Bought at least two weeks before he got here and outfitted with a nice crew of multiracial freebooters and cutthroats."

Ortega considered that, too. "Where the hell are they getting the *money* for all this?" he wondered aloud, and not for the first time. There was no common currency on the Well World—many hexes didn't use any—and much of it was in large-scale barter-type trade.

The intelligence chief shrugged. "Gold, diamonds, you name it—they got it. Even a bunch of trade goods, food, manufactured items. We can't trace it, frankly, but I'll tell you this. Whatever they need they ask for, and whatever price is demanded they pay."

"I'd like a general intelligence summary for the past two weeks," he told the intelligence officer. "Somewhere here, I don't know where, there's a joker. Somewhere somebody's laughing at me, and I don't like it."

# Mowrey, in the Ocean of Shadows

"SAIL HO!"

Feet rushed in all directions around the deck of the brigantine, everyone going to their alert post.

It was a large ship, and well put-together. Although it had only a small auxiliary engine for aid in emergencies, becalming, and the like, it was primarily wind-powered and well designed for that purpose.

The crew was the usual racial mix, but it had a disproportionate share of one race, a race never seen before in the memory of the Ocean of Shadows, and one which had no reason for being there now.

A young woman, Type 41 human, ran from the wheelhouse back to the crew's cabin area behind, bare feet padding against the wooden planking. She reached the first door, hesitated a moment, then knocked.

There was a muffled response, and she called out. "Master, there is a ship out there, a big one!"

There was another muffled response, then the sound of someone moving around. After another half-minute or so, the door opened.

"What is it, Lena?" Nathan Brazil asked blearily, rubbing his eyes to get them fully awake.

"A ship! A ship!" she said excitedly, and pointed.

He sighed, went back in for a second and took some water from a bowl, splashing it in his face. "Damn! Just get to sleep and the phone always rings," he grumbled, then rejoined the girl on the deck. Together they walked back to the wheelhouse.

At the wheel was an enormous, jelly like mass, seemingly engulfing the steering mechanism. It was mostly transparent, but veinlike strands ran all through it and in its middle was a pulsating pink mass.

"What have we got, Torry?" he asked the mate.

Two stalks oozed out of the top of the creature; eye-like nodules formed on the end and it put one on him and one on the sea in front of him. "Steamer," the mate replied. "Looks like a regular merchantman, but you never can tell. The glasses are over there." A tendril oozed out of the mass and pointed at a table.

Brazil went over, picked up the binoculars, and peered out. It was still too far to make much of the ship, but they were definitely closing from the looks of the smoke.

"Steady as you go," he instructed. "Looks like we'll pass her, so anything out of the ordinary would just arouse suspicion—and this is a high-tech hex, remember. Just the usual. I'll let Henny do the fronting as usual." He walked over to one of the speaking tubes, blew into it, then called, "Henny, get up here on the double! Company's coming!"

By the time the full lines of the big freighter could be made out, Henny was topside and ready, although bitching more than a little. After a duty tour, she had just settled down in her pool below decks when the call had come.

She was an enormous creature, with rolls of fat hanging not only from her huge, brown body but also from her face, or what there was of it. Two tiny little black eyes peered out of the bulk, and it took some close inspection to find the equally tiny black button nose and see that one of the folds was actually an enormous mouth. Sharp dorsal fins protruded from her back, and she pulled herself along on two monstrous front flippers that turned out to be made of a number of long, prehensile flat fingers—two rows of them, in fact. She was the only creature he had ever seen that had six fingers and six opposing long, flat thumbs. Again he reflected that Henny gave new meaning to the term "ugly," although she insisted that back in Achrin she was considered a real beauty. He had no way of checking the truthfulness of that statement.

She peered out, and he knew that her weak eyes were being augmented by some sort of inborn natural sonar that worked both in air and water.

"Seems routine," she noted.

He nodded. "Routine, maybe, but *any* contacts are a danger at this point. You know that."

"Signals, sir!" Torry called. "I make it as WHAT SHIP AND WHERE BOUND?"

Brazil turned to the woman, still waiting patiently. "Lena, get on the flasher," he ordered, then sat down on the deck of the wheelhouse, an action that would put him out of sight of any curious onlookers on the approaching ship while still leaving him in a command position.

The woman went out and lit the lamp, waiting a moment until it reached sufficient intensity. She looked over at him then, expectantly.

"Make the following signal," he ordered. *"Wind-breaker,* Achrin registry, Betared-bound."

She flipped the signal lever for a little more than a minute, sending out the required pulses, then stopped.

"Add WHO ARE YOU?" he instructed.

That was done quickly, being a standard signal.

*"Queen of Chandur,"* Torry relayed to Brazil. "Makiem-bound." He froze for a moment. "I think it's carrying troops!"

Brazil nodded. "It's to be expected. Some specialist troops and a lot of war matériel. Wish we had something to sink her with, but it's a gnat trying to kill a giant here."

"I might be able to do something," Henny suggested. The Mowrey aren't all that friendly, but they aren't all that mobile, either. I could probably get a message through to our people to hit them, say, in Kzuco."

He shook his head. Uh uh. Too risky. All we need is one word of that and they'll be out to sink us even if they don't suspect I'm here. Let it ride. It really doesn't make much difference anyway."

She turned and looked at him. "Except that what that ship's carrying could kill a few thousand people, perhaps ours."

He shrugged. "Henny, they're asking me to pull the plug on several quadrillion, maybe more." He let it go at that.

"Well, they've got their glasses trained on us," Torry commented. "I'm not really sure I like it, frankly. We got too many of your kind on board. They're bound to report it."

He shrugged again. "So what can they report? Let 'em, Torry. We're pulling the switch in Jucapel anyway. I'll be long gone."

"Yeah, but we won't," Henny responded wryly.

They waited there until the ship passed to starboard and then was lost on the far horizon.

Finally he felt safe enough to get up and stretch. "Don't worry so much," he told them. "They want me, not you. The ship's legitimately in your name, Henny, and the humans aboard are technically the property of the holding company, bought fair and square from the Ambreza. They'll go batty but they won't figure it out. Not now, anyway."

He walked out of the wheelhouse and aft, then went down a ladder to the main deck. Several creatures lay there, sunning themselves. They were great, birdlike creatures distinguished not only by ugly, drooping beaks but also because each had three complete heads, each on a long, spindly neck.

"Either of you up to a long trip?" he asked them.

The center head of one of them rose and looked at him with two yellow eyes. "I guess I can," it said.

He chuckled and shook his head in wonder. "I never can figure out which head to talk to," he said dryly, knowing full well that the creatures had only one brain, that not anywhere near the heads.

"Awbri's due northeast of us right now. Tell Yua to be prepared to move at any moment. Tell her we were spotted by an enemy steamer bound for Makiem, and while I was not spotted, you never know. Tell them, if they can, to get off a message to both the other forces to try to link in Makiem, which seems to be their supply depot. They'll know what to do."

The creature rose up, stretched its great wings, and asked, "What if they try to take you?"

He smiled enigmatically. "If they do, believe me, the others will *know*." He looked over at the other identical three-headed creature. "Besides, I'll still have Rupt, here, for emergencies."

"All right, then, I'm off," said the messenger. "You take care they don't put a bomb on the hull or something."

He laughed. "I've got a fair little protection force of our people under us. You know that. Besides, they wouldn't blow the ship. They could never be sure I was aboard. Now *git!*"

With a rushing of wind from great wings that almost knocked Brazil over, the creature got.

# Makiem

THE BATTLE HAD BEEN UGLY AND TOUGH. THE HA-
kazit had tasted battle now, and removed many of the
doubts Marquoz had about them. They truly enjoyed
themselves all the way, so much so that they had been
a pain to stop even when it was clear that they had
won. He was beginning to worry that they might now
go on killing binges just out of blood lust. It made him
feel safer, but only just, that he was one of them.

The nontech Makiem, who resembled giant frogs,
were vicious fighters and very determined, and they
had been joined by three thousand allies of other races,
including the shockingly electric Agitar on their winged
horses, but it hadn't been nearly enough. Gunit Sangh
had deployed most of his forces far to the north, on
the assumption that they would link up with the Dillian-
led column and head north up the coast. It just hadn't
worked out that way, thanks only partially to Brazil's
message. Now they held Makeim alone, and its key
ports, and waited for the Dillian column to catch up to
them.

The carnage from the battle was grisly enough, but
the troops were now rampaging through the towns and
countryside, looting and burning and destroying what
they didn't like just for the hell of it. He tried to control
it, but found that his powers were somewhat limited. It
was sad, though, to see such destruction unleashed on
a race that was just defending its homeland. About the
only good thing that might come of it, he reflected,
was its warning. Those hexes that had allowed them to
march through had been left virtually untouched, and
much of the supplies they had picked up along the way
had actually been paid for; Makeim, which had resisted,

was paying a terrible price. The news would spread pretty quickly.

He also didn't like the waiting. The more waiting, the worse the rampaging would be, and, of course, the more vulnerable his own force would become. They had held the day here mostly because they had faced mostly green recruits, old-timers, and civilians, all quite disorganized. If they had run into just the main force of the council now massed and organized up in Godidal, they would have been slaughtered. And Sangh must know by now that he had been outguessed. His forces would have to be moved, and they could move just as quickly as Marquoz could with his. He'd rather start first.

As for Gypsy Brazil—as Marquoz had come to think of the man—he had kept far in the background with the human Entries, and they had actually talked very little. It was frustrating, really; he wanted to ask the man so damned many questions, but simply couldn't, not here in this environment, where one slip that he wasn't Brazil might blow the whole bit. It might be easier, later, he hoped, when the two armies had joined.

It took three days for the others to reach him. He could see that they were appalled by the destruction, but it had calmed down now, with most of the froggies taking refuge in the sea and everything that could be looted looted. Mavra and Asam looked well, but not a little nervous at the sight of thousands of battle lizards like himself.

He could only shrug. "They're natural-born killing machines and they've never done it until now. You can't really blame them."

They went over to where the Dillians had pitched their command tent and they relaxed.

"Where's—ah—Brazil?" Mavra wanted to know.

"Oh, he'll be along shortly," Marquoz assured her. "I sent word to his camp. He's been well-protected away from the battle zone, and he hasn't been lonely. He's got eighteen human women who think he's god and who'll do literally anything he asks."

She chuckled but without humor, thinking not only

of the massive destruction around her now but of the costly fight they had had, the many dead and wounded it had left. All that bloodshed . . . and Gypsy was having a ball. She couldn't help but say as much.

"Don't blame him," Marquoz told her. "After all, he's playing a part. He's doing what Brazil would do, and we're treating him just that way. Don't forget that he's painted a target on himself, too."

"That's right," Asam agreed. "All those forces are lookin' for him. Bet he hasn't had a good night's sleep since he joined the force."

She was about to say something else when the object of their conversation entered the tent. He was a small man, made even smaller by the largeness of the others in the tent, and he looked around nervously. "I feel like a shrimp," he remarked. "Gad. This could give you an easy inferiority complex."

They all chuckled at this, and he relaxed, sensing that the ice had been broken.

"Okay, I think we ought to clear this place at dawn," he told them. "The Parmiter are no real threat. A bigger race of pirates you'll never meet, although they're the usual lot. They won't tackle a force our size and there are no heroes among 'em. Playing both sides as usual."

"I remember," Mavra said dryly. "One of the little sons of bitches tried to kidnap or kill me a long time ago, in Glathriel."

Gypsy Brazil let that pass. "Well, we'll be pretty safe from air attacks there, since the Cebu won't want to risk flying into our full laser defenses, which will be operable there."

Asam nodded. "I understand the plan, but I don't like it. A slow march makes us sittin' ducks."

"Which is what we're supposed to be," he reminded them. "My guess is that Sangh will use his force to guard the Yaxa-Harbigor Avenue. It'll be a simple matter for him to shift up to Lamotien and depend on his force plus the Yaxa to keep us out."

"But there's that force just landed to the west," Marquoz pointed out. "They're already on the move."

He nodded. "Yes, and that's the problem. That's

where we either get away with this or we don't. They're
supposed to guard and block the Ellerbanta-Verion
Avenue. If they play it safe and fortify there, we've
got problems. But if they decide to move in for the kill
—sorry about that—and put us in a squeeze, then we
succeed. It all boils down to that. That and a little luck
with Nathan Brazil."

Gypsy-Brazil transferred what little he had to the
Dillians, saying that, Marquoz aside, he felt a little
better and a little safer with them than he did with the
Hakazit.

Most of the time, and particularly when they moved,
they were stiffly correct as befitted his status as Brazil.
The forces felt honored to have him there, to have
been trusted with his welfare. It was a morale-booster
in particular for the Dillian force, who until this were
more or less going through the motions after having
avenged themselves in battle. Now they felt that a
sacred trust had been placed in their hands, and they
were not about to let him down.

But, in the evenings, when they camped and tried to
catch some sleep, he found himself occasionally alone
with Mavra Chang.

At one such time he remarked, "You don't like
Nathan Brazil much, do you, Mavra? I can tell. Every
time you say the name, it sounds more and more like
the vilest cussword you can think of."

She gave him a wan smile. "Why should I like him
much? What's he ever done for me?"

His eyebrows rose. "The way I hear it, he rescued
you from a fate worse than death when your world
turned Com and kept something of a lookout on you."

"Some lookout!" she snorted. "He didn't really have
any affection for me. He did it mostly as a favor, for old
time's sake, to my grandparents. If he really cared, why
give me to Makki Chang?"

He shrugged. "Maybe he didn't know what to do
with you. Figured a woman who'd had nine kids before, all grown, would know how to bring you up
better."

"And when Makki was caught by the cops, leaving

me alone to live in the filth as a beggar and grow up to be a whore—some help then!"

"You didn't turn out so bad," he noted. "It sure as hell toughened you for the life ahead. You became totally independent, fast-thinking, dangerous, in a way—in a good way."

"No real thanks to him, though," she noted. "I did that myself."

"So what was he supposed to do for you? He didn't know you, didn't even know your parents, I think. So he takes you up and raises you himself. Then what? Marry you off to a fat cat? Hell, Mavra, he didn't *owe* you anything. What's the problem?"

She thought about it. What *was* the problem. In Brazil's place, asked to get the child of a couple of children of old friends, she would have done it, of course. But what would *she* have done with the child? Raised her herself? Not likely. It would have cramped her style, changed her life style, restricted her too much. Nor was she really qualified, even now, to raise a child.

"I . . . I don't really hate him," she said almost defensively. "I have, I guess, contradictory feelings about him. I used to feel pretty warmly about him, I guess, but that has just ebbed over the years. I can't explain it."

"And if you can't explain it to yourself, then I can't explain it to you," he told her. "Sooner or later, if you really look inside yourself, you'll figure it out. And, when you do, *if* you do, you might consider that if you had to look for it yourself, it might just be something that he would never have thought of."

She looked at him strangely. "You want to explain that?"

He shook his head. "Not me. But I think your whole life's been a search for something you never realized—and if you realize it, you might find it. Until then, let's change the subject. Any word from Dahir?"

She nodded. "Some. They're pulling back. Free passage. Looks like orders from above, though. They don't want to do it, that's clear, so there may be some trouble, and that makes me nervous. They have magic in Dahir, you know."

He nodded. "I'm well aware of it. It's possible they won't fight, but if old Gunit Sangh is going to pull any fast ones, that'll be the place to do it."

"We'll have you under a pretty solid and constant guard," she assured him. "And we're not as vulnerable as all that. True, we don't have any magic of our own—even if we had some with the training it takes, their magic would only be good in their home hexes, anyway—but we've got some countercharms. I don't think they can get to you."

"Even so," he replied slowly. "Even so . . . I don't feel good about this." He shrugged. "But, hell, when you're a professional target, what can you expect?"

# Zone

**"THERE IT IS!"**

Serge Ortega pounded a piece of paper in his hand and frowned, yet there was some satisfaction in his tone.

The Dahbi raised its head and looked at the sheet. Circled in the intelligence summary was a single item! "Steamer *Queen of Chandur* hailed Achrin-registered brig *Windbreaker*. Mixed crew, Achrin visible on deck, but unusual number of smooth-skinned apelike creatures in crew resembling description of Brazil."

"So?" the Dahbi responded. "Looks pretty routine, despite that crew description."

"Type 41 humans," Ortega noted. "They're agricultural slaves used by the Ambreza. Submissive. Childlike. No government of their own. Just about bought and sold. What the hell are so many of them doing on one ship? And, more important, *who taught them to sail it and why?*"

The Dahbi considered. *"Does* sound suspicious. You've checked with Achrin and Ambreza, of course?"

"Of course," Ortega responded irritably. "The Ambreza *did* have records of a group of thirty sold to a shipping company for use on sailing craft. Said they thought they might be able to handle the sails better and give less trouble than paid crewmembers."

"Sounds logical," the Dahbi noted.

"It's the timing," he replied. "The timing—and the fact that the holding company's hell when you try to find out who it is, even what hex it's in. Achrin's a water hex, so it doesn't have any ship registry to speak of. Interesting, too, that these sightings were in Mowrey. Now, suppose—just suppose!—that somehow they'd managed to have a ringer Brazil."

"A ringer? That does not translate coherently," the Dahbi told him.

"A double. A duplicate. I don't know how, but they used that trick when sneaking him in, remember. Set this double up as a sitting duck, then have us chasing him and fighting big battles for him. And meanwhile, the *real* Brazil, hidden among a bunch of his own kind on a ship, just *sails* up, say, the Josele-Wahaca Avenue. See what I mean?"

"Hmmm . . . I don't know . . ."

"They've played us for suckers and fools all along the line," he reminded the Dahbi. "They've beaten us in battle, they've led us a merry chase, and now they're moving quite differently than we expected and can throw us more curves at any moment. That Awbri force, what's it for? It's just sitting there, not linking up with anybody. Uh uh. I think we'd better overhaul that ship and question that crew. Don't you?"

There was some doubt in the white creature's tone now, but it was tinged with a sense of helplessness. "I seriously doubt that we can do what you suggest right now," he responded slowly. "That is a huge ocean, and, as you must know, most of the species of those hexes are deepwater types except along the coastlines. Most likely, too, if what you say is true, they have covered their tracks by altering the ship or, perhaps, by changing ships. I think the best we can do is ask the Laibirian ambassador here to permit no shipping to pass through his hex—*that* they can do—and force them to land short of their goal."

Ortega whipped out a map and examined it carefully. "Maybe this is all coming clear now. Since they knew that we'd know they had to make for an Avenue, they also knew that, once they started to move in a given direction, there would be only a small number of Avenues open to them. So you take the big forces and push north, generally heading toward Yaxa-Harbigor, with a Brazil double in full view. This nails down our main forces against their main force. More, there will be the temptation to bring Commander Khutir's forces from the west now guarding the Ellerbanta-Verion Avenue over to engage the main force in battle, a decisive battle, in which Sangh's forces and Khutir's forces will have the entire main enemy army, Brazil apparently included, sandwiched between them. What does this do? Leaves the Ellerbanta-Verion Avenue essentially undefended and Brazil, landing by ship, just walks up eight hundred kilometers and he's right on the mark." His tone grew more excited now. "Yes! Of course! And that explains the Awbri force under this Yua sitting tight. If Khutir catches on and stays where he is, her army can do the main fighting, engaging him while Brazil slips through. Or, of course, it can support and protect Brazil if the cat gets out of the bag too early. And, if their plan worked, it could instead be the reserves behind the main force. It's perfect! A work of sheer genius! It's almost insidious!"

"You seem to admire it," the Dahbi noted, puzzled.

He nodded. "I do. A massive piece of misdirection. A magician's sleight-of-hand with standing armies. You appreciate it the more because you look at this mess and you say to yourself, well, we're fighting army versus army, when actually it isn't that way at all. This isn't a war. This whole thing is to get one man into one particular place at one particular time, nothing more. It's good."

"All this presupposes that they somehow *do* have a duplicate of Brazil, and that the real Brazil is on that ship," the Dahbi pointed out. "And that remains to be seen."

"He's there," Ortega said emphatically. "If not on that ship, well, on another ship similar to it. We'll send an alert to all hexes in those areas to be on the lookout. Brazil's disguises are limited in the open country and in alien surroundings. He might have sneaked through without getting noticed before, but not with everybody looking for him.'"

"And Khutir's army, then?"

"Should stay where they're at if they know what's good for 'em," Ortega told him. "And notify Gunit Sangh of the new situation."

"It will be done," the Dahbi assured him. "But I'm not at all certain how His Holiness will take this."

# Yongrem, at the Betared-Clopta Border

THE SMALL LAUNCH CAME ASHORE ON THE WAVES.
A small storm out to sea had whipped them up and
they pounded the surf, making a safe landing somewhat tricky. The coast was rocky here, and a misstep
could mean being smashed against those rocks.

It was just before dawn; light enough to see what
you were doing but not yet the hour when curious folk
might wander down this way. Not that many would,
right in here at the border. The Betareds and the
Cloptans had little love for one another, the reasons
going so far into the past that neither could really give
them anymore, but, like all such feuds, the lack of
rational cause only intensified the feelings.

Never in his memory had Brazil seen so clear-cut
a contrast where hexes met. To his left Betared shivered in the grip of icy cold, the trees were festooned
with icicles, and the snow drifted around them into
wavelike mounds. As if seeing two pictures placed
side by side, to his right was lush, green warmth, a
fairyland of gum trees, palms, and other tropical
growths. The border itself seemed here a physical
thing, shimmering at the juncture with the other, and a
torrent of water poured down a well-eroded path
through the rocks to the sea as warm air met cold.
Only from a third hex would such a sight be visible;
the waves of Yongrem beat with equal force on both
coasts.

There was a tiny thermal barrier between the hexes,
not to keep anyone from crossing through but to provide a small bit of insulation between such different
places. Even so, cloud patterns formed along both

sides and stretched out from the border in both directions. It made the region just at the border dark and fog-shrouded, which was just what they wanted.

His four bodyguards awaited him when the skillful crew managed to get the launch, on the fourth attempt, through the reefs and up onto what served for a beach just on the warmer Cloptan side. He jumped out quickly, waved to the crew, who got quickly back into the water for the even more perilous trip back, and walked up to them.

Two were Punretts, not uncommonly seen neighbors of Clopta, who looked at first glance like giant eight-balls from a mammoth billiard table perched on two huge ribbed, fowllike legs with heads that seemed to be long, flat scissor-shaped bills and little else. The eyes, on two short stalks, actually grew out of the bill near its base and were almost invisible. Just under the bills, hanging down as if part of some garment, were eight flat, droopy segments like leaves of some impossible plant. Brazil realized that these were tentacles.

Two more were Quilst, hardly inconspicuous here despite their own hex's border with both Clopta and Betared. They were almost two and a half meters tall, standing upright on flat-bottomed thick round legs like the trunks of very large trees. Their massive arms looked the same, but ended in fat, massive humanoid hands whose most unusual feature was that the fingers all ended in flat stumps completely covered with a fingernail-like layer. On almost no necks, their immense heads looked to be all mouth, for a giant, rounded snout, with tiny little piglike eyes set back in the head and flanked by two equally small ears that twitched constantly. Incongruously, both wore gunbelts, and the pistols strapped to their sides were of sufficient size to blow holes in small mountains.

The fifth was an Awbrian, looking very uncomfortable on the ground, and very frail when contrasted against the rest of the party.

"Captain Brazil," the Awbrian said nervously. "We are glad to see you. I am Foma of Awbri, and these two Punretts are Squom and Dutrik, the two Quilst Maganong and Sungongong."

He gave each a nod. "All of you are natives?"

"All natives," she confirmed. "I'm afraid I'll have to do a lot of the talking, since neither race communicates in the normal fashion, but they can understand us because of our translators—and they can talk to the Betared and Cloptans, if need be.'"

"Good enough for me," he told her. "I have a heavy coat here, but I'd prefer to stay on this side of the line if possible. Warm weather attracts me more. Guess I'm getting soft from being too little in the open."

"We understand," Foma replied. "It suits us as well. We have an aircar over here which should get us up to the Quilst border in a hurry. From then on we're on foot."

He sighed. "Okay. Suits me. What's the situation right now?"

They walked over to some bushes where a large platform with canopy and control stick seemed to hover a few centimeters off the ground. In fact it *was* floating, for all intents and purposes, since it was supported by thousands of tiny "legs" of invisible energy keeping it aloft like a hovercraft. Although not designed for human comforts, it was, he reflected, more advanced than most local transport he had seen in the Com. They all fit, which was something in and of itself.

"The women of Awbri, freed from oppression after so very long, are massed in your favor," she told him. "We have been joined by some others of many races, all originally from your own land, who are massed with our forces near the border with Agon. You understand that most of Awbri can not be traversed on the ground."

He didn't, really, but nodded anyway.

"There is also an alarm out for you in this area," she told him.

He was startled. "Huh? How'd that happen? Has my, ah, counterpart with the others already made an escape?"

"Nothing like that," she assured him. "It seems that someone in our own forces either stumbled on the truth and talked too much or that the council has hedged its bets and decided to take no chances."

He sighed. "That damned steamer. I knew it. Council, my ass—this is Ortega's doing. He's the only one with the kind of mind to figure it out in advance." He was talking more to himself than to the others. Turning to her, he said, "Well, nothing to do but make the best of it. Khutir's forces are still guarding the Avenue?"

She nodded. "They have made no move as yet, and seem massed mostly in Quilst. That has gained us some friends, like Manganong and Sugongong, here. Although Quilst is officially with the council, the army has not been kind to it and there has been more than a little trouble."

He could understand that. An army of several dozen races, with different physical requirements, would be hell to put up in your back yard and hell for even a tough old bastard like Khutir to control.

"We believe you should ride the border, so to speak," she said. "Up to Lieveru, then into Ellerbanta, where the mountains make it impossible for any army or force to cover all access to the Avenue."

He nodded uneasily, knowing the odds of getting nearly that far. Not, of course, that he intended to do so anyway—but these must not know that. He wished, though, that the others had already made their own break and were out and heading for the home stretch. Everything depended at this point on the continued befuddlement of the council and the traditional thinking of its leadership. If, in fact, Ortega had guessed the plan and managed to convince the others of it, that could upset the timetable. Things could be very dangerous very quickly.

They raced through Clopta at almost a hundred kilometers per hour and were at the Quilst border in just a little under three hours. As far as he could tell they had not been spotted or even seen by anyone. So far so good—but now came the hard part.

Even now those Awbrian forces that had sat still to this point would be on the move, heading straight for the Ellerbanta-Verion Avenue—but they were a long ways away. It *should* draw Khutir south to counter it, past them and to the east of them, while Sangh's forces would be cut off, forced to stand and guard the Yaxa-

Harbigor Avenue from what to all intents and purposes was the real Brazil. It was so close, so close now. . . . Everything had worked so well. Another day, two at best, and things would be well in hand. Another two days . . .

Quilst proved cooler than Clopta, but far less humid, and seemed to be a good compromise. They walked now, still near the border with frozen Betared, but progress was considerably slowed.

For its coolness, Quilst seemed a swampy place, thick with trees and weeds and abounding with enormous mudholes. It certainly didn't look that livable, yet the enormous creatures that were part of his bodyguard came from here.

He was thankful for the presence of the natives; they knew their way around and would keep him from getting into trouble with some unpleasant flora and fauna of which he might be ignorant, as well as keeping him away from population. The two Punretts were less help, but he knew they could swell up to four times their size and in a fight were not merely nasty but tended to eat almost anything that couldn't eat them. You couldn't always pick the best allies in these kinds of situations, you just picked the best you could get.

Out for several hours, they had seen no sign of anybody. That worried him a little; it was too easy. They were walking around one of those large mudholes when suddenly the thing simply erupted. Twenty or more Quilst heads popped up, snorting, then the rest, as if on some kind of elevator platforms.

Manganong and Sugongong snorted angrily, nostrils flaring, and pulled their pistols before suddenly realizing that, in this nontech hex, they were no better than small and fragile clubs.

The two Punretts squawked loudly and swelled up, like balloons attached to a helium nozzle. Crossbows were cocked in the hands of the ambush party, and as the two strange birds swelled, a couple were loosed in their direction.

Suddenly the two circular birds shot into the air, causing the bolts to miss underneath them, and both came down on the heads of the two closest attackers, vicious clawed feet digging into the huge heads and and drawing blood and grunts of pain.

A voice came out of the trees, as the others ducked for cover, loudly yelling, "Nathan Brazil! You and your cohorts will remain where you are! You are under arrest by order of the council."

The two Quilst in the patrol roared at this; the Punretts, if they stayed where they were, would soon kill the huge creatures.

Brazil, who had run for the cover of nearby trees with Foma, turned to her anxiously. He could see that, under the threat of the bows, the two Quilst had already surrendered and were standing meekly, arms up, while the Punretts had loosed their grip and hopped to solid ground. No use in committing suicide.

"Foma!" he hissed. "Get out of here! Tell Yua what's happened. Tell her to draw off that damned army if she has to beat them over the head!"

She looked uncertain. "But they'll get you."

"No they won't," he assured her. "Not me. You tell her to move it. I'll get to her as quickly as possible!"

She stared at him. "I . . . I don't understand."

"Just move out!" he commanded. She slunk off into the woods.

"Nathan Brazil! Come out or we shall shoot your friends forthwith. You cannot escape!" that voice continued. "Betared patrols have been monitoring you for hours. Come out and save lives!"

He sighed, got up, and walked out into the clearing, clearly surprising both his former ineffective body-guards, who eyed his presence with some relief, and the Quilst still standing guard.

"Okay, okay," he called out. "Let's get this over with. No sense in prolonging the agony, damn it!"

From the trees swooped a great butterfly shape, orange wings barely fluttering as it landed on eight tentaclelike feet. Its black skull's head, with two eyes like great red pads, eyed him with the quizzical curiosity of a zookeeper looking over a specimen. Somehow, in this moment, he could only think that he was the object of some sort of racial revenge on every butterfly collector that ever lived.

"I am Jammer," said the Yaxa. "I arrest you in the name of the council. You will accompany me as my prisoner to the nearest Zone Gate. It is useless to resist."

Its segmented body rose in front, and its two forelegs became useful as mittenlike hands. They reached back into a pack, pulling out first a small medical-type bottle and then a syringe designed for its clawlike hands. Brazil sighed. He'd hoped to keep the stall going by just accompanying them to the gate—but they were going to take no chances. *This* he could not allow.

Crossbows were all on him now as the Yaxa approached, needle in hand, until it stood only a meter in front of him, looking down at him.

"So you are Nathan Brazil," it sneered.

He started to chuckle. The chuckle became a laugh, the laugh a roar, until tears almost ran down his face. Before the eyes of the startled Yaxa and Quilst the body shimmered, changed before their eyes. It became taller, different-featured; the skin tone darkened, the entire body build changed. Even the clothes were not the same.

Laughing almost maniacally, the new figure pointed to the Yaxa. "Gotcha!" he managed. And then he did the even more impossible. Gypsy vanished instantly, leaving only the echo of his laughter.

# Lamotien

THE BLACKNESS OF THE ZONE GATE WAS DISTURBED as a shimmering shape took form within it and stepped out. It looked like a small white ape, barely a meter high, but it wasn't.

It was twenty-seven Lamotiens in a small colony.

The creatures on the whole were less than twenty centimeters long, shapeless masses of goo that could control their bodies so thoroughly that they could adapt to almost any environment, grow hair to length and color in an instant, take whatever features or form were necessary. They could also combine, as this one did, into a single larger organism that operated as one, with a common mind. In this way they could duplicate almost any visible organism.

The Lamotien creature didn't give a nod to anyone in the Zone Gate area but scampered quickly off. The Gate, which opened out of a hillside, was flanked by a large number of buildings, each of which was a part of the governmental structure of the hex. Designed for Lamotien, they looked like a haphazard arrangement of building blocks, each no more than a cubic meter, many with tiny windows through which shone the yellow glow of electric lighting.

Gunit Sangh and his headquarters company couldn't fit in any of the buildings, so a large number of tents had been set up in the government square facing the hex. It was not primitive, however; they had electric lights, heating, all the comforts of a high-tech hex.

The simian colony scampered into Sangh's headquarters tent, where the huge Dahbi was relaxing—meditating, he called it—hanging batlike from the ceiling support beam. The Lamotien weren't fazed.

177

Looking up, the creature said, "Commander Sangh! Bad news!" It waited, as there was no reply from the white thing nor any sign of movement. "Commander! A man who looks like Nathan Brazil was apprehended by a combined patrol in Quilst not two hours ago—and it was some sort of ghost or demon creature, not Brazil at all."

The Dahbi seemed to take no notice for a moment more, then, slowly, some movement seemed to ripple through it. Eerily, it flexed slightly and then raised its head, looking down with a horrible visage on the still comparatively tiny creature.

"What is this?" Sangh demanded to know. "What's all this about a ghost or demon?"

"It's true, sir!" the Lamotien responded excitedly. "It seems that, acting on the hunch of your command in Zone, a watch was put out all along the western approaches and they captured someone who looked like Brazil. In fact, the people with the creature were *also* convinced it was Brazil. They verified it under drug interrogation. But when the Yaxa commander of the patrol approached, it laughed terribly, the report says, then changed into someone else entirely and vanished before their eyes!"

Sangh was interested now. "Changed into someone else, you say. Not *something* else, such as you could do?"

The Lamotien looked confused for a moment, more at the nature of the question than anything else. Finally it said, "Well, yes, that's what the report said. The Yaxa flew itself and two of the prisoners to the Quilst Zone Gate and got to Zone."

"But it changed into another Glathrielian form, not any other?" Sangh persisted.

"So they said," the little creatures replied.

"That is interesting," the Dahbi muttered, mostly to himself. He started to move now, and the Lamotien watched, fascinated, as he appeared to glide along the support beam to the side of the tent, then down the tent side to the floor.

"Tell my staff I want a meeting in ten minutes," he told the creature. "Right here. See that they all come."

The little creature bowed slightly, then said, "I will be returning to Zone soon. Any message?"

Gunit Sangh thought a moment, then said, slowly, "Tell them we will attempt to deal with all eventualities, but that they should be prepared to lose."

The Lamotien just stared for a moment. Finally it said, "Lose?"

Sangh nodded somberly. "Where there is one false Brazil there may be twenty, or two hundred," he noted. "We will do our best, but that is all we can do. Tell them, if they have any bright ideas, now is the time to get them to me."

The little Lamotien went out, looking very much in a state of shock.

"The main army is here, in Bache," the field commander told him. "They appear to be massing. We feel they will push into Koorz and try and fight the decisive battle in Yaxa. Lamotien would be almost an impossible position for them, what with the terrible storms and earth movements as well as the Lamotien themselves. They have also avoided fights in high-tech hexes, even going out of their way to do so."

"But they could go to Bahaoid," the Dahbi pointed out. "And thence to Verion. There's almost no force in Bahaoid, and despite its being a high-tech hex, the Bahaoidans are neither very mobile nor very dangerous."

The field commander, a Yaxa, shook her insect's head. "No, I'd be shocked if they tried it, and not a little pleased. Verion looks easy only on a map. It is a tremendously mountainous region, extremely difficult to cross with any force at all, and leaving a small force highly vulnerable to native attack. The Verionites are, shall we say, more savage than we are used to, but they are wormlike creatures that eat rock and can pop up any place and strangle and devour. We're pretty confident of their strategy, since any change favors us even more."

Gunit Sangh nodded, wishing he felt as certain about things as the field commander. "And the Awbrian force?"

"Moving slowly and deliberately towards Ellerbanta and Verion," another reported. "We feel this is mostly a diversion to keep General Khutir's forces pinned down in Quilst."

"You may be right," Sangh responded, "but what's to stop the main force from turning and linking, say, in Quilst, with the others for a drive there?"

"Too much distance," the field commander assured him. "It would take a week to do it. We'd have enough warning to be able to take countermeasures. I might say, though, that Quilst is making a lot of fuss about throwing Khutir out of there. The army has, shall we say, been indelicate, and the Quilst see themselves now as the battleground for a fight between the Awbrians and Khutir."

"They may have a point," the Dahbi noted. "In that case, we'd be in a poor position if the Quilst themselves should turn tables and join with the Awbrians. Order General Khutir to move south to engage the Awbrian force as quickly as possible, preferably out of Quilst. Let Quilst stand guard over the entrance to the enemy and see if we can get some Ellerbantan coverage of their side of the border as a hedge against the unlikely. In the meantime, prepare your own troops to move against the main force while it is still consolidating in Bache. Better a semitech hex friendly to us than a non-tech of little or no use. We've been on the damned defensive the whole way here and we've gotten creamed, played for fools and worse. Let's end this matter, ourselves, with our own forces in a place of our own choosing!"

"It will be done," the others said, a great deal of excitement and anticipation in their voices. Like Sangh, they, too, were sick and tired of the situation and wanted action.

On the way out Sangh asked one of the field commanders to ask the Dahbi's chief aide and fellow creature to step in. This was done, and in another couple of minutes the two Dahbi were alone.

"Your Holiness?" The aide bowed respectfully.

"Sagrah, that matter of which we spoke so long ago

back in our beloved homeland now demands attention," he said cryptically.

"Holiness?"

"We must face reality, Sagrah. We have been out-classed by an enemy who understood us better than we ourselves. We must face the fact that, in all prob-ability, Brazil will reach the Well."

Sagrah wasn't that convinced. "But, Holiness, if the other was a diversion, then the real one must be with their army. If we smash their army we have him, or have him on the run in our territory."

"And if *he* is not the real Brazil?" Sangh shot back. "No, we must do as you say, engage them, fight this out. It can not be helped. But in our own interests —*Dahbi's* interest, Sagrah, since I am the one who led the opposition to him—we must have a hold on him. Go yourself to Zone. Tell our people there to activate our insurance plan—just that. Got it?"

The aide bowed. "Yes, Holiness. 'Activate our insurance plan.' "

"And, Sagrah," the Dahbi leader added, "tell our people to make certain that the Brazil with the main force does not move. I want no sudden disappearances, no funny business. I want that man where one of us can see him at all times. Understand?"

"I hear, Holiness, but I'm not sure I follow all this."

"You don't have to," Gunit Sangh retorted. "But, if you must think on such things, answer this question: why, if you have a duplicate Brazil, go to all the trouble of keeping his existence hidden and secret? Why *sneak* him in so elaborately and so expensively when he's just a diversion? So much so we trapped him mostly by luck? It makes sense only in one way, Sagrah."

The other Dahbi considered the point. "As a diver-sion, he'd have to allow discovery sooner or later," he mused. "That means he was supposed to be discovered sneaking in at a predetermined place and time."

"Very good," Sangh approved. "And since he was discovered early? You see? You make sure of both things, Sagrah. You make sure that the other Brazil remains with the main army, and you activate our insurance plan. We can win this yet, Sagrah. Win it one of two ways. Now go!"

The aide went, leaving Gunit Sangh to ponder the position maps still on the table in front of him. Something had gone wrong with the enemy's intricate plans, of that he felt certain. It was a gut feeling, unsubstantiated by facts, yet it was an absolute conviction with him. Something had gone wrong when that patrol had discovered and unmasked the false Brazil when it did.

The more complex and intricate the planning, the more chances there are for something to go wrong, he reflected. If only he could capitalize on this, he might come out on top yet.

If that *was* the real Brazil with the main force, he was a long, long way from walking up an Avenue and into the Well. A long way.

Maybe forever.

# Bache

It HAD BEEN AN EERIE TRIP THROUGH DAHIR, A LAND that looked at once peaceful and deadly dangerous. The quiet landscape of gentle green forests and large ranch-style farms contrasted with the inhabitants, who looked inscrutable, formidable, and dangerous. They had sat there, atop great horned creatures, not like occasional onlookers or curious parade-watchers, but in highly disciplined ranks, staring with eyes that told nothing of the thoughts behind them.

They were tall and insectival, although not quite insects. Humanoid in shape, they had long, broad feet that ended in sharp claws. On smooth legs leading up to a metallic-looking torso, their slender, exoskeletons were so polished that the creatures looked somewhat like robots in a stylized and idealized picture of such things. They had oval heads, with multiple orifices and mandibles set below oval eyes of faceted gold and above which rose long, quivering tendrils. Their bodies were of many colors, all with a metallic sheen—blues, greens, gold, reds and silver, among others. But their hands looked like mail fists. The seething anger and tension in them was immediately discernible. They didn't like being ordered to stand aside.

Their mounts were mammals, and looked at first glance like classical unicorns, curved horns like conch shells rising out of the center of their horselike heads. But their rear legs were much larger and their hind feet broad and flat, like their rider's. They could sit erect, looking almost like kangaroos, or use their double-jointed hind legs to lope about on all fours, and on close inspection their snouts were narrower, their heads smaller than a horse's.

Of their reputed magic powers nothing could be seen, but the menace of it could almost be felt by the passing forces. They were glad to get through there. It had been decided to use a wide river valley in Bache to regroup and reorganize after the march. Now, so close to their goal and to the major opposition forces, all had to be perfect.

It was late afternoon, but the command tents were already up. Brazil left his own little corner of the field and walked to the main tent shared by Asam and Mavra; Marquoz left his own position to join them. This was to be the last staff meeting of the group, although only Brazil, who had called it, was aware of that fact.

They ate quietly, mostly discussing the eerieness of the Dahir and the tiredness they were feeling, forgetting the rest for a while. Brazil even seemed to become a bit nostalgic.

"You know," he said, "out there, among the stars, trillions of people are going about their normal daily affairs right now. Even back in the Com, as crazy as things were getting, most people are still going about their daily tasks. It's kind of weird, all this. I have never felt at home on the Well World; it's too much of a fantasy land, divorced from reality, from the whole rest of creation, apart and insular."

"I find it refreshing," Marquoz countered. "I kind of like the variety here. Different creatures, different social systems, ways of life. It's a microcosm, yes, but unique, too. You seem to assume that insularity is necessarily bad."

"That's right, son," Asam put in. "After all, this little war is the first in a thousand years, the third in history, and one of the other two was also caused by outsiders coming in. It's really not a bad place at all."

"But you haven't been outside" Brazil noted. "You haven't been anywhere *but* the Well. Tell me, Asam, haven't you ever looked up at that glorious starfield there and wished you could go out there and visit it? Fly from star to star, world to world?"

Asam's expression was thoughtful. Finally he said, "Well, I've been too much of a realist to do much dreaming like that, I'm afraid. Hell, I've still got most of this world to see, and I've seen more of it than most anybody alive. Out there—what do you have? A lot of emptiness and a lot of worlds, like this one, each with one race on it. Big, empty, and everybody always fighting everybody whenever they meet. Nope, I think I like it here."

Brazil looked at Mavra. "You've been both places," he noted. "Last time you were here you did damn near everything to get away. Have you changed your mind?"

She thought it over. "I don't know," she said honestly. "I really don't. Asam has shown me another kind of life, one possible here. And I'm in a form that makes sense here, one that leaves me free, not the crippled beast I was back then." She paused a moment, looking both thoughtful and sad. "But, then, it really doesn't matter, does it? I mean, it's going to be a long, long time before there's space travel in the universe again, isn't there? Unless you like rubbing sticks together and huddling in caves, this will soon be the only game in town.'"

He stared at her. "Maybe," he answered cautiously. "Maybe not. All is relative when you deal with the Well of Souls. And what you say is only true for *this* universe, anyway."

"It's the only universe we've got," she shot back.

He shook his head. "Uh uh. It's only *a* universe, not *the* universe. The energy to start this one came from another. There has to be a complement. Physics requires it. At the center of every black hole, for example, is a singularity. What happens at that point? Does it ever come out? Energy and matter don't cease to exist—they can neither be created nor destroyed. That's the law. Only changed. All that glop has to be *somewhere*—it comes out in the other universe. A white hole. It's the way things work. Just because the Well looks like magic, don't make the mistake of assuming it *is* magic. It's not. It's just simply a technology higher than you can currently comprehend."

Marquoz stared at him. "This doesn't sound like the man I knew, who played the flute for pennies in dives around the fringes of the Com. It doesn't sound like you at all." He looked at Brazil with some suspicion. "Are you really Gypsy?"

He sighed and sat back, seemingly arguing inwardly with himself. Finally he said, so softly it was difficult to hear him, "If I'm not Gypsy, then who or what am I?"

Mavra looked at him in sudden horror. "You're *not* Gypsy!" she gasped. "You really *are* Brazil!" She shook her head in disgust. "All our talks about me, about Brazil . . . How you must have been laughing at me. You son of a bitch!" She whirled around and trotted briskly out of the tent.

The rest were silent for a while, mostly from being unable to think of anything to say. Finally, Marquoz broke the impasse.

"You *are* Brazil, aren't you? That's why you've been avoiding me so much."

He nodded. "Yeah, why not? Cat's out of the bag now. What difference does it make?"

"Quite a lot, if Mavra's reaction means anything'," Asam noted.

He sighed. "Mavra has a problem. She feels deprived, deserted, abandoned at an early age, unloved. That craving for love, for a father, I suppose, turned into bitter hatred of me. Why not? I was the closest to a father figure she ever had. Growing up the way she did, alone, that bitterness formed a shell around her that seldom cracks. If you feel the lack of something, you convince yourself you're better off without it. You take a fierce pride in your aloneness, your loneliness. You turn a liability into a self-perceived asset. That's what she's done. And she's been hurt every time she let that shell drop, even slightly."

"If she needs love, I can give her that," Asam said sincerely.

"It might not be enough," he warned. "She's had so much hurt when she *did* become attached to somebody that she's afraid to do it again. She may be more hung up than you can handle, Asam. Still, I'll give her her own choice. Inside the Well, I can do a lot of things. If she wants to remain here, with you, she can. Her choice."

Marquoz shuffled uncomfortably at all this talk of Mavra. He decided it was better to change the subject to more immediate problems.

"All right, Brazil. Suppose you explain what the hell you're doing here instead of Gypsy—and what we're doing here, too. How the hell do you expect to get in the Well like this?"

Brazil shrugged. "Don't blame me for all this," he responded defensively. "Remember, I didn't even want to be here in the first place. It's that damned computer that came up with everything, right from the start. I got tracked down and hauled to Obie kicking and screaming all the way. It was the computer that convinced the bunch of you to take this course of action, and the computer that charted the course. I'll admit it's a damned crazy machine—Mavra's influence, I suspect. But it *is* a computer, and once all the facts it had were fed into it, it decided that I *must* repair the Well and it decided on this scheme based on all the data it had fed into it."

"Including you," Marquoz noted.

He nodded sourly. "Yeah, that, too. Did him precious little good, though. Did him in, maybe—almost me, too. Well, anyway, Obie was once hooked into the Well, so he knows how it works—how it's programmed, anyway, which is more than *I* do. He decided to run the entire population of Olympus through the big dish to meet his specifications and some others, too, ourselves included. *We* got the treatment—somehow, Obie reconstructed you and Mavra and Yua, for example, to come out as certain specific creatures when put through the Well. Also the rest of the *Nautilus* crew, most of whom were sent ahead here to make the initial preparations. We had to buy the ships, scout the terrain, that sort of thing. The key to the plan turned out to be Gypsy, who, among other things, could somehow make himself into the spitting image of anybody he wanted."

"Who—or what—*is* Gypsy, Brazil?" Marquoz wanted to know. "I thought *I* picked *him* up on a backwater, even though there were always a lot of odd things about him.'"

Brazil slowly shook his head. "I know, I know

to tell you the absolute truth, I haven't the *slightest* idea as to the answer. I'd love to know myself. I think Obie knew, but he didn't tell anyone. At least Gypsy's on our side and is a key to the plan. His power, if that's the best word for it, is the ability to somehow use the Well powers by sheer force of will. I've figured out that much, anyway. Like a little Obie, he can tap the whole thing, but only in regards to himself. He can't zap you or me other places or alter our appearances."

"Like a little Markovian, you mean," Asam put in. "Sounds to me like he's just exactly what they had in mind."

Brazil considered that. "In a way, I guess you're right. He can do just about what any average Markovian could have done, and if he had a full Markovian brain around to tap, to use as an amplifier for that, he could probably do whatever they did."

"He has the whole damned Well of Souls," Marquoz pointed out.

Brazil shook his head. "Uh uh. That isn't the way it works. It's a different kind of machine, run in a different way and for a different purpose."

"Mavra figured, when we learned that it wasn't you that dropped her off on that Markovian planet, that Obie had made a double of Gypsy while Gypsy played you," Asam told him.

"Wouldn't work," he replied. "Oh, Obie could make a construct that looked like Gypsy, but not one that would hold up among friends and associates for any length of time. No, I suspect that when you saw Gypsy you were seeing what Gypsy wanted you to see and hear. I think he has that much power. And when he reached the Markovian planet he had enough reserve force from its own computer brain to maintain the illusion even after he left."

"You're supposed to be a Markovian," Asam noted. "Couldn't you spot another one? If there's one, why not two?"

He shook his head. "No, I don't think that's the answer. It's possible, but highly unlikely. Somehow I have the gut feeling that the answer to Gypsy's mystery is right in front of us, simple, logical, obvious, but we can't see it. It really doesn't matter, except that it'll drive me crazy someday. The fact is that he can do what he can do and Obie used that."

Marquoz looked at the small man strangely. "If Gypsy can do those things, why can't you?"

"Because I'm not a Markovian and I don't have the slightest idea how the system works," he replied quickly. "That doesn't mean I can't fix the problem— I know which buttons to push, so to speak. Except for that I'm really not much different from either of you. I can't see the Markovian energy, can't feel anything special, nor can I use the power. I have power only inside the machine—and, even there, I'm the computer *operator,* not a *designer.* There's a big difference."

"Sounds like you're runnin' yourself down, son," Asam commented. "A whole lot of people have fought and died for you."

"Or something," he responded glumly. "No, there's nothing particularly special about me, Asam. I couldn't even accept responsibility in Mavra's case. I palmed off this inconvenient child on others. She's really got a case against me, I guess."

"Not feelin' a little guilt on that, are you?" the centaur prodded.

Brazil chuckled. "No, Asam, not really. The truth is, if I let guilt get to me, I'd be truly insane. Maybe I am, anyway, but I just can't feel much anymore. I have simply been alive too long. *Much* too long."

"Bitter?" Marquoz asked him.

"Not bitter. Just tired. Very, very tired, Marquoz. You can't believe what it's like to live day after day, year after year, century after century, for uncounted centuries. I'm a foolish, foolish man, Marquoz. I did this to myself. I chose it, freely, without turning a hair or doubting a second. But nobody, *nobody* can imagine how horribly lonely it is. Lonely and dull. Races don't mature overnight; they do it over thousands of years. And you wait, and you watch everybody you cared about grow old and turn to dust, and mankind goes forward maybe a millimeter or less every century or two. Finally you decide you want out, decide you can't take it any more—and you can't get out. You're trapped, absolutely."

"Gypsy told us you might kill yourself once you fixed the Well," Asam said uneasily. "Sounds like he wasn't far off the mark."

Brazil smiled bitterly. "It all depends, Asam. That's the only place I *can* do it, but I can't unless there's somebody to take over the watch, assume the responsibility."

The Dillian suddenly reached down and gripped Brazil tightly in iron fists. "Not Mavra! You won't do that to Mavra!" he growled.

Brazil reached up and peeled the angry centaur's hands from his shoulder. "*I* won't do that to anyone, Asam," he said gently. "I couldn't do it. All I can do is offer choices. That's all anybody in this life gets—choices. I'm the only one in the whole damned universe with no choices, really, at all."

There wasn't much to say to that, so Marquoz brought him back to the original subject. "Well, so what's the plot of this crazy business?"

Brazil looked up at Asam and rubbed his shoulder a little. "Look, Colonel, got one of your cigars? I've been going crazy with these damned cheap bastard cigarettes trying to convince you I was Gypsy."

Asam went over to his pack, rummaged around, found two, threw one to him and stuck the other in his mouth. Marquoz watched them light up mournfully, wanting nothing more than to join them and no longer having the suction in his mouth to manage it.

"I'll just sniff yours," he moped.

Settled down again, Brazil continued the story, explaining things up to this point. "Now, two nights hence, Gypsy's going to deliberately expose himself as me," he told them. "That'll lead them to the correct conclusion that the one they know about is the real one. And I'll still be here—sort of."

Marquoz nodded. "I think I see. Gypsy will use those powers of his to come here instantly. Brazil will make his usual appearances—only you'll be gone.

They'll think they have the correct one and they'll move in for the kill."

He nodded. "And I'll have a day's head start. I plan to leave tomorrow night. A few of those Agitarian Entries we picked up a few days ago aren't what they seem. They're *Nautilus* crew and they've got a couple of those pegasus—pegasi? Eh, who cares? Anyway, I'm about the same size as one of them and they can carry double, anyway. We'll form half the team. A couple of Eflik will take Mavra with us on a conveyance designed for that purpose. Don't look alarmed, Asam, we tried it and it's perfectly safe and the Eflik are more than able to handle the weight if we don't fly more than a couple of hours at a time."

"It's not that I'm thinkin' of," the centaur said darkly.

Brazil sighed. "I *told* you I wouldn't force anything on anybody. Don't look at me like that. I'm not going to do a damned thing. It's up to Mavra all the way. It's her show, really."

"She'd better change the act, then," said a voice behind them. They all whirled around, startled.

Standing there, looking very much his old self, was Gypsy.

"They caught me before I was ready," the newcomer said disgustedly. "Nothing I could do. They were going to drug me."

"Oh, shit," Brazil muttered. "Well, I guess we go now, then. It might still work."

"Why shouldn't it?" Marquoz wanted to know. "So you have to go an extra few hours' flight. That shouldn't be more than an inconvenience."

"It'll be tough on the Eflik," Brazil replied, "but a little more risky for us. We'll have to fly by night, hide by day. Verion will be impossible to cross for the next few days—it's some kind of rutting season there and those worms glow like electric lights. We'll be spotted, and what can be spotted can be reported and maybe shot down. That'll mean a southern route—and Yua's Awbrians aren't far enough along yet to have drawn Khatir's forces away from the Avenue or even provide a good diversion."

"I've helped with that," Gypsy told him. "I stopped off and dropped in on Yua to explain the situation. She's proceeding with all speed. It's riskier than it would be night after next, but the odds are still pretty much with us. I say we go."

Brazil nodded, looking over at Asam. "Get Mavra, will you?"

For a moment the Dillian hesitated, thinking, perhaps, that if she didn't go there was no further threat.

"Not thinking of changing sides now, are you, Asam?" Marquoz prodded the centaur. "If you did, you'd lose her anyway."

The Colonel sighed and went out to find Mavra.

Brazil turned to Gypsy. "You old son of a bitch, you're going to have to explain yourself to me before this is over."

Gypsy grinned. "Maybe. Before it's over," he said playfully. "Hey, Marquoz, about time we got together for this! We're a team again this time!"

"Could be," the Hakazit responded thoughtfully. "Could be . . ."

Brazil shifted uncomfortably. "Wonder what's keeping Asam? Damn it, we've got to get a lot of stuff together before we go, and we have to go as quietly as possible. Gypsy, can you cover for us?"

He nodded. "For a little while, which is all we need. It's a big army, a big, long line. I think I can put in the required Brazil appearances with no trouble and maybe occasionally become Mavra if the question comes up."

"Okay, then. Damn! What's wrong out there? Is Mavra so mad at me she won't even come back? Or did Asam . . . ?" He let the thought trail off.

Suddenly they were all on their feet, nervous and anxious. Brazil looked at Gypsy. "Give yourself some protective coloration," he told the dark man. "We're going to find out what's up."

Gypsy shimmered, changed, became a Hakazit.

"That's a *female* Hakazit," Marquoz noted playfully.

"Got to keep up your reputation," Gypsy came back, and they went out.

They spread out, looking around the flat valley floor. Thousands of creatures of many different races were camped out there, firelights stretching in all directions, but they couldn't see any sign of Asam or Mavra Chang.

Brazil called his humans to him and gave them instructions to comb the area. Gypsy, disguised as a Hakazit, quickly memorized names and faces as Brazil did so.

As more time passed and no word came, Brazil turned to Gypsy and said, "I don't like the feel of this."

"Me neither," Gypsy agreed. "You think maybe we've had it our own way too long and the odds are starting to balance out now?"

"I'm afraid—" Brazil began, but was cut off by a shout from one of his humans. He took off at a run in the indicated direction and Gypsy lumbered along behind him.

Very near the small river was a grove of trees, and it was to these that the runners directed them. Brazil reached the river first and spotted Marquoz, standing there and looking at something in the river mud. Next to the Hakazit stood Asam, looking stricken.

"Right in the middle of the whole goddamn army!" Marquoz snarled. "God! We were so damnably cocky! Those sons of bitches!"

Brazil looked down at the mud. He could see the hoofprints of a Dillian, walking along the river and very near the clump of trees. Part of the bank was torn from its moorings just ahead and there the hoofprints became a tangled, blotched mess. No other prints could be seen anywhere.

"Damn it! How the hell do you snatch a five hundred kilo Dillian out from under the noses of ten thousand friendly troops?" Marquoz fumed.

Asam looked up at Brazil, his face ashen, his expression a mixture of grief and bewilderment.

"She's gone," he rasped in an unbelieving tone. "They've got her."

Gypsy lumbered up behind them, stopped, and instantly realized what must have happened.

"Oh, shit," said both Nathan Brazil and Gypsy in unison.

# Bache, Later That Night

THEY STUDIED, PROBED, INTERVIEWED, AND INVESTI-gated all through the wee hours to no avail. A few Dillians in a camp nearby thought they might have heard a disturbance, some Hakazit close to the trees vaguely recalled seeing some dark shapes in the air, but all really heard and saw very little. Like their leaders, they felt secure inside their own camp and tended to discount any disturbance or commotion as obviously none of their business and certainly not enemy action.

"Why her?" Asam continued to moan. "Why not you, Brazil? You're what they want, not her."

"But they couldn't get to me," he pointed out. "It had to be a small operation, probably only a few creatures, mostly ones also found on our side so they weren't even noticed. Besides, they're skittish now. Suppose they snatched me and I laughed at them, changed into somebody else, then vanished? Then where are they? Uh uh. Now, taking Mavra is a whole different situation. The Dillians idolize her—and, frankly, so do you—so it'll have a demoralizing effect on the troops and their commander. And they know her story—mostly from Ortega if from nowhere else. They know she means something to me—the only family, I guess you'd say, I have. It's possible they know, from capturing some key people or something, that I insisted on her going through the Well with me. Blackmail, a doorstop, I don't know. But it makes sense."

Asam looked angrily down at him. "And you? What will *you* do now?"

Brazil shook his head. "I don't know. I really don't,

Colonel. All I can do right now is get our people to work on this, but time's short. I'll have to decide by tomorrow night, that's certain. I still think I can reach the Well, but it's clear they would take this action only if they were moving on this spot even now. I can't afford to wait or they'll have me cut off." He paused. "And, damn it, it's not right! I don't want the responsibility of turning that machine off. All those people out there . . . All gone, like they'd never been. All the great and small, everybody. I don't know whether I could bring myself to do it."

"Then take someone else," Asam responded.

Brazil looked around. "Who else is qualified? Gypsy? He has to stay here in order for the trick to work. Otherwise I'm an open target. And I'm not sure just what he is, anyway. He might not have any feelings at all about the rest of the universe. Yua? She faithfully expects me to wipe out the universe and create paradise. Marquoz? Somehow, I don't think Marquoz deep down cares a damn about people, except for Gypsy. You? Hell, you don't even know what you're destroying. Only Mavra truly understands the responsibility."

Asam looked sternly down at him. "A lot of good people have fought and died in your name. Don't you have a responsibility to *them?*"

He smiled crookedly and shook his head. "You see? You really don't understand it at all. Civilizations, countless quadrillions of people, their greatness, their thoughts and ideas and achievements . . . they're an abstract to you. Only these few who died here have any meaning for you because they're what you know. The Well World's too limited. There aren't any Michelangelos or Leonardo da Vincis here, no Homer, no Tolstoy or even Mark Twain. No Handel or Beethoven or Stravinsky. Multiplied by all the races in the universe, each with their own stunning creations. You really don't understand what it *is* to erase that."

"I don't understand what you say, it's true," the Dillian responded, "but I think I understand you pretty well. It's not all those funny names and what-

ever they did that really concerns you, I'm thinking.
It's the fact that you haven't got a sucker to take over
so you can die."

Brazil looked at him with ancient eyes, eyes that
showed pain and hurts beyond pain, agony that wisdom nurtures. "If you believe that," he said slowly,
"then you don't understand me at all."

Asam turned and walked back into his tent. It
looked very empty now, and he wasn't sure what he
himself felt about it all beyond the urge to start smash-
ing things. He didn't, though; he reached into his
pack and brought out a very large flask and took a
long, long pull.

Asam never dreamed; at least, he couldn't remember his dreams beyond a couple of extremely vivid
childhood nightmares. Still, he thought he must be
dreaming, there being no other explanation for it.

A rustling sound awakened him—at least he thought
so—but his eyes saw nothing in the darkness at first.
Then, slowly, the room seemed to be filling with a
ghostly kind of white light.

The booze, he thought. It must be the booze. But it
was the booze that clouded his memory, that and the
fatigue he felt, from recognizing at once a sight he
had not seen in a long while but knew well.

Then with a start he *did* realize what it was, and his
hand went to his sword. Guns might do only superficial damage to the damned things, but they could
be sliced the same as anybody else.

"Put the sword away, Colonel. I'm here to talk, not
to fight," said the Dahbi as it oozed the last few centimeters out of the floor and solidified in front of him,
not three meters away.

His hand didn't leave the sword hilt, but while he
tensed he did not yet pull it out.

"What the hell do *you* want?" he croaked.

"What I said. Talk. Nothing more. I have already
harmed you far more than putting a knife in your
heart, as you must be aware. You will never know
how much satisfaction that gave me, nor how it pains
me to have to offer to give her back to you."

He relaxed, but just slightly, a cold chill coming over him. "Sangh. Gunit Sangh himself!" he breathed. "You got guts, I'll give you that."

"There's very little threat, really," the Dahbi replied. "I can swim through the very rock, you know. Besides, I wanted you to know that I personally supervised the little operation earlier this evening. It lends force—and a little justice—to it all, don't you think?"

"You got your bloody nerve," he spat. "Justice!"

"Temper, Colonel, temper!" Gunit Sangh said mockingly. "I have something you want. You have something I want. Obviously what I have can not be far away—there hasn't been time, and you people are, ah, rather bulky, shall we say? But you'll never find her. You might, if you had a few weeks to look, but we're currently marching on you and you are shortly going to be far too busy to do so. Besides, discovery would only mean her death."

"You bastard," Asam seethed. "How do I know you haven't killed her already?"

The Dahbi acted stricken. "My word isn't good enough? Well, perhaps it isn't. But I need her—alive. Dead she's of no use to anyone. Alive, she's a hostage to Brazil and to you."

Asam chuckled sourly. "She's no hostage to Brazil," he told the creature. "That bastard stopped caring for other folks a million years ago. He's as cold as you are, Sangh."

"Sorry to hear that," the Dahbi responded, sounding sincere. "But that just makes things easier in a different way. If he's unpleasant even to you, then what I ask should be all the simpler."

The Dillian eyed the other suspiciously. "What the hell do you mean by that?"

"A trade. Brazil trusts you. I can only assume that he intends to leave your forces before the battle, using your deaths as a diversion—perhaps leaving another simulacrum in his place to fool us. But it won't work. We're going to be looking for that. The odds are he'll never make it to the Avenue, let alone the Well."

"Then what do you need with me?" Asam growled.

"We *might* miss him. The odds are very much against it, but it's possible. He *is* tricky." He paused a moment. "Ah, you *are* sure which is the right Brazil, aren't you?"

"I know who's who," the Colonel told him.

"So, you see, I cover the last possibility. The trade is simple—Mavra Chang for Brazil. Within the next day. Let's say, by this time tomorrow night, at the latest. That will not only accomplish the main objective but also prevent the coming battles. There will be no need to ask people to fight and die, you see?"

Asam frowned. "I don't trust you one bit, Sangh. Since when do you care who lives and who dies except for yourself? I have no guarantees."

"You have several," Gunit Sangh responded. "You get Brazil to a Zone Gate and bring him through. Diplomatic immunity, remember? Even though the council is against you, they will not violate Zone. Take him to your own embassy. We will make the swap right there. Even better, you have couriers from here. Take Brazil, but don't put him through until a courier comes with word that a living Mavra Chang is in my embassy at Zone."

Asam fully relaxed now, thinking about it. Finally he said, "Why are you doing this, Sangh? Why agree to be the commander at all? What the hell are you getting out of this?"

"Consider," the Dahbi replied, "what honors will come to the one who captures Nathan Brazil. The honors, the power, and the influence. Consider the perfect prison, under hundreds of meters of solid granite, the tunnel used to take him down collapsed about him save for a small mechanism to provide food and water. The council will not have Brazil. The Dahbi—I—will have Brazil. An unspoken hostage, so to speak. And I will have the gratitude of all those who did not lose their lives in foolish battles. Consider the effect on Ortega, no longer as feared or as in charge. His place will pass to me, and that fat ancient snake will die at last, his grip on the Well World and the council broken. It's already been suggested that, as an old friend of Brazil's, he can not be trusted in this matter. The possibilities are endless."

Asam shivered slightly, thinking of an unchecked Gunit Sangh in charge, but, oddly, this sinister plan also reassured him. Sangh was being honest with him, partly out of confidence, partly out of the sheer arrogance he exuded. He was saying the stakes were too high to risk a double cross now.

"We will transfer her to Zone after dark tomorrow, as quickly as possible," the Dahbi told him. "We will receive any envoy you like at our embassy there to verify it. Then you will have eight hours to deliver your end of the bargain."

"And after that?" he asked, thinking about it.

"You will be free to return to Dillia together," Sangh told him. "Naturally, this will not settle anything personally between us. That will remain outstanding—as it has. Safe passage for you and the woman, alive, back to Dillia is all I guarantee. After that we have no more bargain."

He sighed. "I'll consider it," he told the creature. "And if I do not come through?"

"Then the woman will be the object of a ritual feast by my embassy personnel and no trace of her will remain," the Dahbi responded coldly.

"You bastard," Asam swore angrily. "You dirty bastard. You and I will settle this personally one day."

"One day," the Dahbi agreed. "But not in the next two days." It turned into its milky white state and slowly oozed into the ground until the last traces of it were gone.

"You bastard," Asam repeated to the dark, but his mind was already whirling. Schemes, plots, ideas, were already hatching. He considered Gypsy—but, no. He couldn't be sure he could trust the strange little man, and something might go wrong, betray them. Sangh was on to the plan anyway, and would still be looking for a Brazil getaway. No, it had to be on the square. He had to choose between Mavra and Brazil, it was that simple. And a simple choice.

# Dahir

THE RANCH WAS BARELY TWENTY KILOMETERS BE-low the border, yet it was isolated enough and far enough for their purposes. Two were Dahbi, the others were Krithians, their huge, beating wings marking time to the call of one to the other. They carried in between them a huge blanket in which lay their heavy burden, unconscious still from the tranquilizers they had shot into her from ambush.

They had been puffing hard when they reached the border, barely able to carry her as far as they did and proud that they had made it with such a burden, but now, in Dahir, they had been aided by the magic of the native priests, and the flying was easy. She seemed to have no weight at all now and they felt renewed strength.

The priests had been riding below them on their hakaks, unicornlike mounts, easily keeping pace and providing what they called the proper energy flow to the flyers. They could also handle a fair degree of trouble should some lucky searcher from the enemy discover them.

Two Dahir stood ready to receive the burden as they landed. They greeted the priests with upraised arms, then turned to the unconscious form now deposited in the area in front of the hukak stables. It was a clear night; the massive, swirling starfield was shining in full glory and seemed to reflect against their bright, shiny exoskeletons as the humanoid insects went to work, first righting her so she was standing on four feet, then assisting the others in dragging her into a large barn. She was still out cold and knew nothing of this.

"Shall we bind her?" the Dahir leader asked the nearest Dahbi. "It would not do for her to get free."

"Bindings can be loosened, or worked free," the white creature responded. "We can not take a chance on such a thing."

"Do we kill her, then?" the gleaming creature wanted to know.

"No. We promised her alive in the exchange. We will have to make good on that promise."

"A simple spell," one of the priests suggested. "It would be absolutely effective—and we have to disguise her when we move her to the Gate tomorrow, anyway."

"Disguise is up to you," the Dahbi told the priests. "That should not be difficult here. But your spells are effective only here. They would be undone by the Gate."

"And could be redone as soon as we were in Zone," the priest pointed out. "Our magic is effective there, at least on a limited basis."

"Too risky," the Dahbi responded. "We can give her no avenue for escape. Also, our master, His Holiness Gunit Sangh, has directed a suitable remedy. Here," the creature pointed, "at the base of the neck, are the primary nerve connections from the brain to the spinal chord. Severed, it will cut off control to the upper torso." With that the creature used its right foreleg with its sharp, knifelike chitin and struck deeply, yet expertly. Some blood gushed out, but not a great deal, and they were on the wound with salve and bandages in a moment.

"And here, at the base of the upper torso, a connector for the other, larger half, almost a second although nonsentient brain directed from the first," the Dahbi noted, and again the vicious blade struck and jerked once inside. It came out covered with dark-red blood, which was again seen to.

"The Dillian is now totally paralyzed," the white creature told them, wiping off its blood-stained foreleg. "The effect is permanent, the damage beyond repair. Note how the arms and legs are frozen in position, a protective biological mechanism when there is nervous damage. They can die if not on their feet, so they freeze when the nerves are cut or damaged to avoid this. The autonomic functions are not affected; they are taken care of by a different set of nervous controls on the other side of the cartilage that routes and supports them. I was careful not to touch those areas."

"They will not go for this," the Dahir priest warned darkly. "They will not trade Brazil for this one in such a condition."

The Dahbi chuckled. "Your magic could freeze her like a statue here. Could not your magic also make her walk?"

The head of the Dahir cocked itself slightly to one side as the priest considered it. "Why, yes, of course."

"And then again in Zone?"

"Ah!" The priest brightened.

"You see? No chance for escape, for without your spells she is frozen helplessly. But the evidence will be otherwise. It will be so reported, the exchange will take place, and the woman will be returned to Dillia."

"Magic has no worth in Dillia," the priest pointed out. "She will arrive a helpless cripple."

"Exactly," responded the Dahbi. "Our bargain was to deliver her alive. Nothing else. We keep our word —to the letter."

"It seems a bit cruel, though," the Dahir commented, not sounding as if he was particularly upset by the idea.

"My master, His Holiness Gunit Sangh, has a claim against the one who loves her," the Dahbi told him. "Killing him would be so very . . . final. And quick. Nor is he easy to kill. This will haunt him and harm him worse than any. His love a hopeless cripple for the rest of her life, and he a betrayer of his cause and his trust, branded so forever even into the histories and legends, and with no prize to show."

The priest nodded admiringly. "It is incredible. Such a settlement of a debt of honor is beyond all save admiration." He looked over at Mavra. "And how much control does she retain?"

"A statue, totally, as if made of stone, from the neck down," the Dahbi assured him. She will be able to control only her eyes, ears, nose, and mouth. All else is forever frozen."

"She can talk, then," the priest noted.

"Only if we let her," responded the Dahbi.

.She awoke before dawn and almost immediately realized what must have happened. Mad, upset, her pride hurt, she had stalked out of the meeting and wandered, eventually, down to the river where she had just walked along, occasionally kicking this or that or just looking at the stars.

They hadn't even made much of concealment. She knew that creatures were in the trees ahead, could see an occasional shape shift or even hear occasional whispers. You just didn't think about risk when surrounded by ten thousand of your own people.

They had used some sort of tranquilizer gun, the kind used on vicious wild animals when you had to get close to them or capture them but not kill. She had no idea what the stuff was, but it was certainly *fast:* she had heard the report, felt the sting, whirled and started to cry out, and then lost first her balance and then consciousness in what must have been, oh, no more than fifteen or twenty seconds.

She tried to move, to see what sort of bindings they had on her now and where and in what she might be, but found she could not. There was a sudden, eerie sense of *déjà vu* about all this. Once before on this strange world she had been captured, paralyzed, and stored in a stable. At that time she had been a sacrifice to the Well by those who had worshiped the thing and had been turned into a malformed monster because of it.

There wasn't much light in the place, although she heard the movements of what appeared to be other large animals, and the aftereffects of the drug, she guessed, were keeping her more or less muddy in the head.

She stood there, unable to do anything, afraid to say anything, for quite some time. Once someone had come, opened a door to one side, and peered in for a moment, but they were out of her peripheral vision and did not come in, but for a very long time now she had just had to stand there stiffly and try and fight through the malaise in her mind.

Now, though, she heard the rustling of something, like feed going through straw, coming close to her. She was surprised, for she would have bet that there were none but animals in the stable up to now. She waited, more curious than apprehensive, to see who it might be—and what. That they would kill her was unlikely; she knew a hostage when she saw one, even if it was her.

The creature stepped out of the shadows and walked almost up to her face. She brightened when she saw it, and the creature put up a shaggy rounded finger to its snout to signify silence.

"We must act quickly," whispered the Gedemondan. "We have very little time and much to do."

"How . . . how long have you been here?" she asked it quietly.

"We have been with you since Gedemondas," the creature told her. "We have kept out of sight and out of mind, as is our wont and our ability. We thought they would try for Brazil, not for you, which is why we couldn't prevent this. The damage to the Well is clouding our perceptions."

"They couldn't be sure it was him," she explained. "So they figure to blackmail him through me. Fat chance on that."

"Nevertheless, you are essential to him," the Gedemondan assured her. "He will not make the repairs without you. And he may not get the opportunity. My brothers and sisters with your force yet tell me that it is not Brazil but one who cares deeply for you who is being blackmailed."

She was puzzled. "Who? Oh—Asam? But—what could *he* do?"

"Deliver Brazil in exchange for you," she was told.

"And we believe he might do so." Briefly the Gedemondan explained to her the sadistic plot he had overheard in the same barn only a few hours earlier.

"But what can we do about it?" she wanted to know. "If what you say is true I . . . I'm paralyzed.

Completely." It shook her to say it, as if voicing it would make it an actuality.

"There are two alternatives," the Gedemondan told her. "The first is to kill you. That would deprive them of a hostage and would, at least, give Brazil a chance to do the right thing."

She considered it. "I think I would rather be dead than . . . like this . . . for so long." She meant it, but it seemed somehow abstract, as if discussing a theoretical problem or someone else, not her. She needed more time to get used to the idea she was a statue, a living lump of immobile flesh.

"There is only one other alternative, and it is a risk and an experiment," the Gedemondan told her.

"Please accept my assurance that they have done an expert job on you. There is no way that your body will move again except under the magic of the Dahir."

She had an uneasy feeling, and seemed to recall little donkeylike creatures in the back of her mind. "What's the alternative?"

"There is a procedure, an odd one, used by a few Well World races, mostly in the North," the white creature explained. "Only in one spot here in the South is it done—and it is as hazardous to the doer as to the subject. It involves the transference of the soul."

She stared at him. "You mean changing bodies?"

The Gedemondan nodded. "Exactly so. The intellect is a thing which may, under certain conditions, be wrenched from the body. We, ourselves, have done this, but always returning to our own physical selves. In your case, of course, that is not possible, nor could we teach it to you in the hours, perhaps minutes, we have left."

"You mean I'd swap bodies? With one of you—or the Dahir, or something like that?" She was fascinated.

"Not exactly," the Gedemondan replied cautiously. "Two souls may occupy the same body only at the price of total madness. An exchange is theoretically possible, but no one has ever done it. Something is lost. The body rejects the newcomer as it rejects the implant of a heart or other organ."

Hope fell. "Then what *are* you talking about?"

"While an exchange is not possible, nor double occupancy, the complex soul of a complex being might be placed inside that of an animal whose own self is so slight as to offer little or no resistance."

"The Wuckl once surgically changed me into a pig," she recalled glumly. "What could be worse than that?"

The Gedemondan nodded. "Very well, then. Understand, of course, several things. First, what soul the animal has remains. It will fight you, but you should win easily, forcing something of a merger. Second, you'll not be able to talk, since you will no longer have a translator—and, if you did, you probably still couldn't use it properly. But, remember this, too: once inside the Well, Brazil can restore you as he pleases, which, we're certain, will be as you please."

"Let's do it, then," she told him firmly.

The Gedemondan nodded, turned, then suddenly said, "Someone's coming!" and vanished. She stared at where the creature had been; it was amazing, in its own way—more so than Gypsy. Now that she knew the creature was there, she could *almost* see it, *almost* hear its breathing and see a little discontinuity. Almost. Gedemondans didn't make themselves invisible; they just made it so that, somehow, one didn't notice they were there.

The door opened and two Dahir came in, looking strange by the light of small kerosene lanterns. They didn't come too far, just looked around.

"I'm *sure* I heard somebody talking," one told the other. They walked on, looking in each stall, occasionally getting a noise from one disturbed animal or another, then reaching her. She played as if still out, eyes closed.

They kept the light on her for some time, then turned. "Well," the other Dahir noted, "there's nothing here now. Probably just the captive mumbling as the drug wears off. You're too nervous, Yoghasta."

"Well, who wouldn't be with those spooks around?" the guard grumbled, and they walked back to the door and went out, closing it behind them.

The Gedemondan was there again, suddenly, and

a shaggy padlike hand went up in a little gesture. Two other Gedemondans moved out of the shadows and stood there, staring at her.

"It will be easier if you are unconscious and if your mind is made receptive to us," the talker said. The padlike palms went to either side of her head. She knew or felt nothing more.

# Bache

"A NEUTRAL COURIER UNDER A DIPLOMATIC FLAG brought this message for you a few minutes ago," Asam said, handing him a small note.

Nathan Brazil stirred from a makeshift folding chair, reached up, took the paper and unfolded it. "They didn't waste much time, did they?" he noted sourly, then read the letter.

Captain Brazil,

As you have no doubt deduced by now, we have captured the Dillian Mavra Chang and transferred her to a place of safety. She is whole and well; the drug used is a simple animal tranquilizer with no lasting effects. She is, understandably, quite upset and her descriptions of us occasionally strain the ability of a translator, but, otherwise, she is in excellent health. We have no quarrel with her and no wish to do her harm. Our armies are moving on you at this moment; friendly eyes are watching you at all times, ready to alert us should you attempt escape, and all nearby Avenues are effectively blocked. You can not hope to win. If you surrender now by simply stepping through the nearest Zone Gate, all this will be ended without further loss of life on anyone's part, including your own. If you choose to ignore this, my only message to you, the woman will die in a most unpleasant and slow manner, and then the battle will be joined. And, please, no crude tricks about sending another double. I assure you that we will put anyone sent to the most severe tests and that a bad result to all concerned would come about if another of your look-alikes

turned into someone else and vanished. I have
heard so much about you I am looking forward very
much to seeing you soon. We have much to talk
about.

I remain, sincerely yours,
Gunit Sangh of Dahbi,
Supreme Commander, Central Theatre,
Forces of the Southern Council.

Brazil balled it up and tossed it into the fire. "Civil
chap, isn't he?" he remarked with a snide smile.

"Like a poisonous spider or hungry snake," Asam
snorted.

"I think we've underestimated him, though, so far,"
Brazil noted, watching the note burn. "Somehow I
thought Serge Ortega would be the big problem, but
this fellow is Ortega without . . . without . . ."

"Conscience?" Asam prompted.

"A sense of honor," Brazil finished. "Conscience
is something Serge has little of, but he's an honorable
man in his own way. He does what he thinks is right
for everybody according to his own lights—whether
it *is* right or not and whether it kills or cures. From
what I've learned of Gunit Sangh, he might possibly
be, at the moment, the most dangerous man alive. I've
run into his kind many times before, among my own
kind."

Asam looked straight at Brazil. "Are you going to
take his offer?"

Brazil smiled humorlessly. "Always it's the easy
way out they offer you," he reflected. "Just do this
that I want and that's all there is to what I want—
*except* . . . There's always an 'except,' you know. No,
I'm not going to turn myself over to him, or Ortega, or
anybody else for that matter. And, don't worry, no
matter what he says, he isn't going to kill her. He'll
figure that it's the only leverage he's got on me if I
get into the Well—and he's right, of course. That may
be where he's made his mistake, though. Once I get
into the Well, get to the little computer governing this
little planet, there's not a damned thing he can do

to her, to me, to anybody, but a hell of a lot I can do to him. I'm starting to build up a whole backlog of folks I'd like to get even with, Asam. I think for the first time I really *do* want to get into the Well."

"Do you think you can?" the centaur asked seriously. "I mean, he says it pretty flat out in the note."

"It's possible," he replied. "More than possible. We'll keep 'em guessing with Gypsy here, of course, so he won't be able to spare his big army coming here to block me, and Gypsy today is down with Yua, not only briefing her but being seen—as me. That'll confuse 'em just enough that Khutir will have to move on her. And I still have a trick or two up my sleeve. Yeah, I think I can get in. I'll leave tonight, in fact, after Gypsy gets back."

Asam said nothing for a moment, then echoed, dryly, "Tonight," and walked back toward his tent to think for a while.

There were staff meetings, commander's briefings, organizational information, deployment, all during much of the afternoon, and that helped Asam a little in his emotional dilemma. What you don't have to think about can't really get to you.

Still, it was always there in the back of his mind, always a dull ache somewhere inside him. He had thought himself in love more than once before, but now he knew that those were hollow things—physical attraction, mostly, or feelings mistaken for love because, not having experienced the real thing, he thought that was what it was. But he loved Mavra Chang. He knew it, deep down to the core of his soul; knew that she meant more to him than his own life, even his own personal honor, which he had cherished most. He hated himself for feeling this way; somehow, in his own mind, he had diminished by falling so totally a victim to such feelings, feelings he had seen in others and regarded only with contempt.

The worst part of it, the most demeaning of all, was the knowledge that Gunit Sangh had identified this vulnerability, placed his slimy foreleg directly on this weak spot in Asam's soul, and applied pressure with such relish.

Briefly, very briefly, he had entertained the hope that Brazil would take the burden from him, call a halt to this madness and resolve the situation. But, no, that way out had been shut. Brazil would try for the Well of Souls tonight, two or three days even by air from this point, and Mavra? Brazil was too confident of Sangh; he, Asam, knew the bastard better. Mavra would be slowly, ritually eaten alive, there was no doubt of that. She herself would see to that rather than be such a hostage, he felt certain; She would convince him that, to Brazil, she was no hostage at all.

Playing on him, too, was a far different feeling, one that his conscious mind would never admit. From the start he had rebelled at Mavra entering the Well with Brazil, just the two of them. Right now, he felt, she loved him, at least in a way. Brazil said she craved love, the father she had never had, and he was at least that to her and perhaps a good deal more. Left the way she was, he knew deep down that the two of them would spend the rest of their lives together on the Well World; good, full, rich lives. But with Brazil, inside the Well, there was that awful nagging fear that she would not come out a Dillian—if, in fact, she came out at all.

He considered Brazil and the cause for which all these creatures from so many hexes were fighting. Why were they fighting? Silly, deluded Entries that even Mavra admitted were products of a cult who believed in a false ending to this; Dillians, out at first for revenge, who had by now had their emotions sated and were trapped in the march; and ones like the Hakazit, who cared nothing for causes but fought because it was fun, a drive built into their massive, hideous genes.

And Brazil himself—some god! A bored, cynical little man who didn't really care about anyone or anything, and who said himself he neither understood the Well's operating principles nor would do anything but leave the universe to go its current stupid way or re-create it in the same image all over again. He was just a man, like so many other men except that one bit of knowledge made him the object of so much misguided devotion. Just a silly little man whose only attribute was that he had lived too damned long . . .

Even further back in Asam's subconscious, where none would ever recognize it, lurked the feeling that Brazil was somehow his rival, that he might offer Mavra what she could not refuse.

He made up his mind for what he considered reasonable, realistic reasons. He made up his mind, then checked the dispensary for what he needed, made a few surreptitious inquiries on dosages and tolerances for Glathrielites, then prepared his means and methods of escape. Like Mavra's kidnapers, he would need aid in the air, which was easy to arrange. He had quite a reputation here; he was the commander of the forces, and they simply wouldn't question what he was doing. The Jorgasnovarians, in particular, had been talked into this by Marquoz and the Hakazit and weren't Entries. They were alien, those flying, tendrilous gumdrops, so much so that they would find it impossible to pick Brazil out of a group of naked Glathrielites. One looked just like another to them, and that was good enough.

Near dusk all was in readiness, and, as luck would have it, Brazil had retired to a small tent to get some sleep in expectation of being awake all night. It was going to be so easy it was unbelievable. He only hoped Sangh understood the time problem and would do nothing rash.

He entered Brazil's tent and closed the flap behind him. The little man lay there, face up, mouth open, snoring slightly. So easy, so vulnerable . . . And yet, he hesitated. Love and honor conflicted, hate and the face of Gunit Sangh seemed to mock him.

His hands trembled as he took the small bottle and filled the syringe with two cc. of the clear fluid. There was no one else about; it would be dark in another hour and his own forces could move in, helped by some convenient guard shifts, night training exercises, and meal schedules he had arranged earlier in

the day. It would work. Silently he approached the
sleeping man, syringe raised.

*"O foolish man!"* boomed a voice behind him.

He whirled, syringe still in hand, and Brazil snorted
and popped awake, then froze as he saw the full ta-
bleau.

There were three of them—huge hairy white creatures so out of place in this atmosphere. Asam knew
what they were in an instant; he had wanted to meet
them almost all his life.

"What the hell?" Brazil wanted to know, sitting up
and rubbing his eyes. "What's all this about, Asam?
And who and what are you three?"

*"He* knows us," said the huge speaker.

"You—you are Gedemondans," Asam croaked, his
voice almost stilled by a combination of shock and
shame at discovery.

Brazil looked gravely at the incriminating syringe
still in Asam's hand. "So you were going to sell me
out," he said sadly. "The great Colonel Asam."

"Sangh . . . came to me. Here. In the middle of the
camp. He can swim right through rock, no place is
really safe from him," the Dillian told them, his tone
wooden, like a man in a dream. "He was prepared to
eat her alive, Brazil. *Eat her alive!"*

"And you were going to trust a bastard like that to
deliver her safe and sound," the little man responded,
shaking his head sadly. "I don't know if we'll ever
learn. Asam, a very long time ago on my own people's
world a man like Gunit Sangh asked us to trust him.
We did, and he swallowed nations whole, one after
another, then summarily executed and tortured millions. It cost more millions of lives to finally defeat
him—and still people turned around and did the same
damned thing with other sons of bitches again and
again. You of all people should know that Sangh
would never keep his word. We discussed it earlier
today. Honor is a foreign word to him—as it seems to
be elastic to you. For jealousy you would betray all
those who have already fought and died in her cause."

"Jealousy? No, Brazil! Love, yes, but not jealousy!"
the Colonel exclaimed heatedly.

"So you know yourself so little," Brazil sighed. "All right, Asam. It's done now."

He nodded. "It's done. I shall, of course, no longer be a burden to you. She is effectively dead now, and I don't want to survive her."

"O foolish man, she lives," the Gedemondan told him.

"But for how long?" he came back.

"She was totally crippled by cruel surgery," the white creature told them. "She would have been a helpless cripple forever, save by Dahir magic. You would have won a living corpse."

The syringe dropped from his hand, and, for the first time in his life, Colonel Asam cried. The Gedemondans stood there impassively, and Brazil sat quietly and waited, waited for him to cry himself out. Finally, after a couple of minutes, he just stood there, head down in shame, silently waiting for his judgment.

Finally Brazil said to the Gedemondans, "I notice you said she would have been a helpless cripple, not that she is."

The Gedemondan nodded. "Two brothers and a sister saw the attack and managed to go along," it told him. "It puzzled the creatures who carried her why she should be so heavy, but they did not see us." There seemed a private amusement at that. "When they could, they contacted her—but it was too late to help her. Our powers are somewhat diminished outside of Gedemondas; we can not influence events nor see them as clearly, and, large as we are, we would have been no match for their force, particularly not in Dahir. The Dahir magic is strong, and beyond our control."

He nodded. "I understand. But you did *something*, huh?"

"They attempted the only thing possible under the circumstances," the Gedemondan told him. "There is a process called transference, for want of a better word. It is something we are aware of, although this was the first time to our knowledge that Gedemondans actually attempted it. It involves removing the es-sence of an individual, the soul, the intellect, whatever you wish to call it, and placing it in the body of an animal."

"Yeah! Sure! I know that process!" Brazil exclaimed, mentally kicking himself for not thinking of it before. "The Murnies once used it on me when my body was destroyed."

"It is so," the Gedemondan agreed. "Those of Murithel are the only practitioners in the South, and then only on very rare occasions. Despite their odd and violent way of life and their unusual superstitions, a few of their wisest have come upon many of the same powers and secrets as we. It was, in fact, through accounts of their actions that we stumbled upon it."

Brazil looked over at Asam. "You see, Colonel? She's alive, she's okay, and out of the hands of the enemy. All they've got is an empty husk."

Asam managed a slight smile. "I'm glad for that," he almost whispered.

"You haven't lost her yet, Colonel," Brazil tried to reassure him. "She's in animal form right now, but inside the Well she can be whatever she wants to be. It's *her* choice, Colonel. It's always been her choice. That much I swear to you."

"Would you care to see her?" the Gedemondan asked. "We have not brought her near the main camp because a large animal in the vicinity of an army with a large number of carnivores would be tempting fate too much, but we can take you to her."

"No," Asam replied. "Not now, anyway. Not after . . . after all this. If she chooses, if she returns, then, perhaps I can face her again. As for me, I will lead this army in battle and I will win the battle. I will live until I can kill Gunit Sangh myself, no matter what the cost." He looked first at the Gedemondans, then at Brazil. "Am I free to go?"

Brazil nodded. "Go on back to your tent, Colonel. It's out of your hands now."

Asam left hurriedly, his feelings too complex to face, his self-loathing beyond imagining.

Brazil sighed and sat back down on his cot, leaned back, and looked at the Gedemondans.

"So what sort of animal did you use?" he asked them.

"We had very little time," the Gedemondan explained, sounding a little apologetic. "We were in a barn in an alien hex full of magic and power and surrounded by enemies. We had, in addition to the time problem, a limited number of animals to choose from—and we still had to get her out and past enemy forces without raising suspicion."

"I understand all that," he told them impatiently. "Damn it, they made me into a stag."

"Our choices were two," the Gedemondan went on. "First were the horned mounts of the Dahir—but that raised a problem. They do not run free, and are used as mounts and draft animals. A wild one would be seen and captured quickly as it has some value. That left the other creature, one that's put out to pasture and allowed to roam free until it is needed. You would call it, in your language, a sort of a cow."

# Lamotien, a Little before Midnight

GUNIT SANGH WAS QUITE LITERALLY CLIMBING THE walls, the ceiling, and oozing in and out through the floor. Others were nervous to even approach his command tent for some time; he had killed the first two messengers who went in there and had issued orders for all sorts of mass executions. None had been carried out, but nobody was willing even to go close enough to tell him this.

Initial rage had come from the first message, which had been from Dahir. It told him that, when the creatures, along with his own agents, had gone to get Mavra Chang and establish the proper spells to get her walking and moving to the Zone Gate, they had met with no success. A cursory examination had been performed and the general diagnosis was that, while autonomic functions still operated, there was, in effect, total brain death insofar as any voluntary motions were concerned. She was, in effect, a vegetable, and even their magic could not work on a body that no longer was able to comprehend an order to send a message over magically relinked nerves.

No one could explain it, but there were tracks outside and around the barn area of no known type. The conclusion: Mavra Chang had been discovered by her friends, somehow, and they, having seen her mutilated state, had done this so that she could give no information or messages.

He had ordered everyone on the ranch immediately executed, but except for the two Dahbi, it was unlikely the order would be carried out. The Dahir were pragmatists, and even the Dahir, not being stupid, would probably be an awfully long time going home or rejoining their forces.

Then had come the second message that Brazil had been spotted with the Awbrian forces moving up from the south. This, together with his routine intelligence asssuring him that Brazil, was, in fact, still with the Dillians and Hakazits not too many hills away in Bache, did nothing to improve his confidence. He felt like his whole beautiful world of dreams was crashing down about him.

Finally, though, he did calm down and came out of the tent. A milling throng of officers of many races had gathered near by, but they all pulled back when he appeared, fully unfolded and extended, a truly awesome sight.

"Fools! I will not hurt you!" he snapped. "We must act and act now or all is surely lost! Make use of the rest of the night to mobilize your entire force. All plans are now in force, all alerts are now proclaimed. We will engage the enemy as soon after first light as is practical. Move!"

They moved, fast and frenzied.

Sangh pointed a foreleg at his intelligence officer. "You! Any further messages? Quit shivering, idiot! I won't eat you! I'm over that—now."

The officer in question, a tiny, weasellike Orarc, continued to shiver, but it responded, "There is a strange, impossible message from your embassy at Zone, sir."

Sangh froze. More bad news would be more than he could stand. "What?"

The Orarc swallowed hard. "According to this— it's unbelievable—but, according to this—"

"Come on! Out with it!"

"Ambassador Ortega is no longer at Zone," the creature told him.

Gunit Sangh froze, stunned. He realized immediately the import of that news—and its total lack of credibility. If Ortega left Zone, then he broke the spell that restrained his aging, and he was already an old man. It was the end of an era that had stretched back to almost two thousand years before the elderly Dahbi himself had been born, the end of a power and personality that had pervaded and colored the only Well

World that Sangh, or anybody else, had ever known.

"It must be a mistake," he responded, dismissing the news. "He was just taking a crap or something." He turned to go back into the tent.

"It's definite, sir," the Orarc insisted. "Some of our own people saw him go through the Zone Gate. No doubles, no duplicates, no other Ulik mistaken for him. There is a new, young Ulik ambassador at Zone and Ortega is definitely gone. Gone home, they said, to die."

Gunit Sangh snorted. "Oh, no. There's something dirtier afoot than that. Ortega would only do that if he were certain not only that he was not going to die but also that the odds favored his plan somehow. I want to know as soon as possible what he did after arriving back in Ulik. I want to know where Serge Ortega is and what he is doing if he survived the trip —and I'm certain he did."

"At once, sir," the intelligence officer responded and turned to go.

Gunit Sangh felt totally calm, but very uneasy. Up to now it was a simple battle of wits. He was losing, yes, but he always had the chance of winning and he always had known the score. Not now. With Ortega suddenly in the game—outside of Zone! incredible!—he had the uneasy feeling that something momentous was going on, some force was coming into play that was beyond understanding or control.

He was suddenly conscious that more than history was being made now; the future itself, and for a long, long time to come. The future was being molded by unseen hands. A changing future, not a static one.

All his life his efforts had gone to maintain the status quo, which he liked very much indeed, and increase his personal role in the leadership of that. But —Ortega gone? Brazil inside the Well?

He spread out the relief maps and tried to occupy his mind with preparations for battle. For the first time in his long life, Gunit Sangh felt afraid.

# Bache, near the Dahir Border

GYPSY PULLED DEEPLY ON A CIGARETTE, THE GLOW lighting up his face in an odd, supernatural effect. The only other light came from the reddish glow that emanated from Marquoz's alien eyes.

Nathan Brazil lit a small torch and studied the scene. "I think it's safe enough right here," he told the others, and they agreed.

The Gedemondans had called Mavra "sort of" a cow, but to Brazil there was very little qualification. Spotted brown and white, she had all the bovine features, and despite being a little shaggy-haired and having two small horns, twisted like the hakak's, into conchlike spirals, she was the same sort of animal as before. He sympathized with her, and by the light of the torch she turned her massive head to study them with eyes that were, he knew, weak, very near-sighted, and color-blind.

She had been less shocked by the transfer than most people would have been; she had been through transformations several times before, not all deliberate or painless. She had waited, then, until they had come at dawn to let the cows out to pasture, and had found it very easy to just go with the herd, let the cow part of her take control, and get out into the hills. From that point she had something of an internal struggle with the cow mind as she tried to assume control and force it away, while doing it as slowly and naturally as possible.

The Gedemondans had met her at a predetermined spot, a small pool used by cows and other livestock out of sight of the ranch house, and had gone with her, breaching the fence when they came to it and continuing down an isolated route to the border.

The Gedemondans, she had noticed, seemed weak and somewhat disoriented and had to stop often. At first she had thought it was just the night's tension catching up to them, but then she realized it was far more than that. Whatever they had done to get her into this body took enormous power and concentration. They all looked much older, somehow, than they had before their efforts on her behalf.

Their condition did not improve in the post-midnight darkness. Even Brazil and the others, who had had no previous experience with Gedemondans and therefore no direct method of comparison, could see the change. Brazil thought back to the Murnies, so long ago, and recalled now that the elders who could do the transference spent half their lives learning the skill that was enough to do them in when used only once or twice. Still, there was an idea in the back of his mind that had started with a tiny glimmer of devious light when he had first heard of Mavra's transference. Though well worth trying, he just wished he felt better asking it, for he now knew the price.

"How many of your people are around?" he asked the Gedemondan communicator.

"Twelve total," the white creature responded, "including myself and the other communicator there."

"And it takes a minimum of three of you to do this transference?"

The Gedemondan nodded. "Yes, three."

He looked over at the weary Gedemondan party, now slumped against the trees. "Would using more of you in such an operation lessen the, ah, impact?"

The communicator saw where he was leading. "No, I don't think so. Which of you are you considering for this?"

His eyebrows rose slightly in surprise. "You mean she could be transferred again? I thought the strain would be too much."

"Actually, it would be somewhat easier," the Gedemondan told him. "She is not a natural part of the body, nor has she been in it long enough to get totally entwined. Part of the problem is identifying and gathering together all of the soul—much easier with a body alien to it than with one of which it is a part."

He nodded, but hesitated, looking again at the tired, worn Gedemondans who had given so much of themselves in the rescue. He didn't like to ask others to go through that.

The communicator understood. "It is all right," he consoled gently. "You see, we believe in what you are doing. It is necessary, it is important. We've kept apart from the rest of the Well World, true, and would still if all were going smoothly. It is not, though. Even at that, we might have been tempted to stay removed from this as we have from all other conflicts, but there is an overriding consideration here that impels us to do anything and everything to make certain you succeed."

Brazil looked up at the creature in puzzlement. "Overriding consideration?"

The Gedemondan nodded. "You see, Captain, we have devoted the entire energy of our race to exploring the ways of the universe, the ways of the Well, and, most important, exploring the innermost part of every sentient being, the soul. We have learned much, but we have also learned that there are things beyond us, bound as we are here on the Well World. An entire world of our own, a huge race that could know and understand struggle, hardships, and the reality of the rest of the universe beyond this tiny artificial bubble—that is the only way to progress, to get to the real truths about ourselves."

"Well, you have one, somewhere," Brazil pointed out.

"We do not," the Gedemondan told him sadly. "There was an error, something, some factor that was overlooked in our preparation here for a real existence out there. We died out—quickly. There does not even seem to have been a second generation."

"How do you know all that?" Brazil asked him. "I mean, even *I* don't know that, and wouldn't without getting deep into the machinery. You couldn't *possibly* know."

"We know," the creature assured him. "Each construct in the universe has its own intricate mathematical codes. We can sense those codes, read them, so to speak. We know the codes are consistent, and we can trace individual races out there from their counterparts on the Well World, even identify a large number of races no longer on the Well World at all, at least in a mathematical sense. And when the race is no longer in existence, there is a gap, a noticeable discontinuity."

Brazil was fascinated. "You mean you can actually *read* the Well's code?"

"To an extent, yes," the Gedemondan admitted. "It is due to that ability that we can use some of the Well's potential ourselves, more or less in the Markovian manner. It's how we can sometimes foretell future trends, spot key people, do such things as the transfer and blind others' minds. You can see the frustration. To be so close to the Markovian abilities and understanding—yet, that close and no closer, for we can not expand, grow, or get into a position where we can look at the situation from the other end, from the universe itself. And that, of course, is why we must help you in any way possible."

Nathan Brazil considered what the creature was saying, then broke into a slight smile. He shook his head slowly and pointed an accusatory finger at the communicator. "You *want* me to start over," he said with a mixture of amazement and amusement. "You want to try it again." So much for altruism, he thought sourly. The same old self-centered elitist bastards were still in charge. He wondered idly how different the society and culture of Gedemondas was from some of the old Com worlds. Still, it made things even easier.

"Look," he explained, "we have two problems here. One is that Mavra is in no current condition to travel and is likely, if she stays this way, to wind up as somebody's barbecue. The second is that Gunit Sangh will be looking for me to make a break now and he'll have patrols and everything he can think of waiting for me. Had things not unraveled when they did, I probably could have done it with few problems. The original plan, as far as it goes, is still sound. The only way in is to fly."

"So you want to get made up as an Agitar, maybe, and then make Mavra your pegasus?" Gypsy guessed. "It's not a bad idea, if she's agreeable."

Mavra's head turned and she gave out a very cow-like "Moo," which was indecipherable.

"Well, that would have been a good idea if we were still following the original script, but I think they're on to that kind of thing now. I don't have the advantages of the Com here, particularly not out here in the middle of nowhere. No costume we could come up with would stand close inspection, and Sangh's no dummy. He'll force down any creature even remotely resembling me, just for insurance. No, let's be a little bit trickier than that. Let's make *both* Mavra and me pegasuses."

"But you won't be able to speak," Marquoz noted. "To everyone else you'll be just dumb animals."

"Then they—we'll—have to have riders," Brazil replied.

"The few such creatures we have were mostly stolen," the Hakazit pointed out. "I'm not sure how much we can trust the Agitar riders."

"Not Agitar," he told them. "A Gedemondan, for sure, since we have to have some method, no matter how basic, to communicate if necessary." He looked at the communicator. "I assume something of that sort is possible?"

The communicator nodded. "By laying of hands, in a basic way," he replied slowly, "the Gedemondan would then become the conduit for both conversations—but it would work, I think. Still, why not two of us?"

"You're useful, but you're not fighters," he told the great creature realistically. "Somebody ought to be along who can shoot a variety of things."

"We are not defenseless, but it *is* true that we can act only in self-defense where a sentient life is concerned," the Gedemondan admitted.

"I think I'm a little too big and heavy for one of those," Marquoz noted ruefully. "Although, truthfully, if there were some way to do it I would love to be there at the end."

Brazil nodded. "All right, then, we'll have to trust one of the Agitar. Pick the best you can and get him and two of the creatures here as quickly as possible."

"I'll do it," Gypsy said, and vanished.

They all stared at the spot where he had just been, and it was Brazil who shook his head in amazement. "How does he *do* that?" he wondered aloud.

"He tells the Well what he wants and it does it for him," the Gedemondan communicator replied.

They all looked at the creature. "You mean it responds to his will?" Brazil pressed.

The communicator nodded. "In effect he is a Markovian," he said flatly.

Brazil shook his head. "No, not that. Markovians on the Well World had no access to the main computer. That would have destroyed the point of the experiment."

"Nevertheless, that is what he does," the creature maintained. "I could feel it, almost see it."

Brazil stared off into the darkness. "Now who the hell could have learned that—and how?" he mused aloud.

The Agitar was an Entry named Prola, a former Olympian with a lot of self-confidence who was honored to be chosen for this mission. As an Agitar male the former Amazon was somewhat uncomfortable, but now saw this as a heaven-sent opportunity.

"I regret I am not very good at riding the beasts, though," Prola said apologetically.

"Don't worry about it," Brazil told the satyrlike creature. "You just hold on and let me do the flying. I hope," he added under his breath.

They gathered around the torchlight one last time and Brazil took out a map and spread it on the ground. "Now, Sangh's almost certainly going to attack this morning. I don't want you to fight. Gypsy, you tell Asam as soon as we're off to pack up everybody and everything he can and start moving *directly* for the Ellerbanta-Verion Avenue. Sangh will be snapping at your heels, but fight only rearguard actions. Marquoz, I think your people could do that effectively. The faster you can go, the less threat from the rear, since the enemy expects you to stand and fight here, not run, and won't have prepared logistically for a chase. If you can, Gypsy, then get down to Yua and tell her the same thing."

"But that will run her right into Khutir's army," the strange, dark man protested. "It'll be a slaughter. Khutir's got her outnumbered and out-experienced."

"But he's going to get word *real* quick that the main force is moving on the Avenue from his flank. I'm betting he'll set up the best defense line he can over the broad front and try and hold until Sangh can come up behind your army. He has to block *both* forces with his army, remember, and that's putting him on the extreme defensive, outnumbered and outgunned."

"While, in the meantime, you'll fly right over his head," Marquoz chuckled. "Not bad. Not bad at all."

"And not as easy as it sounds," Brazil cautioned. "You might yet have to bail us out of enemy hands, but it's the best try we have. If either force can cut through Khutir's lines, well and good. Get to the Avenue, pick the best position, and fight a rearguard action if necessary."

"How . . . how will we know when you've made it?" Gypsy wanted to know.

Brazil chuckled. "Well, the few Gedemondans ought to be able to tell you, but there will be an easier way, particularly if it's dark."

"Huh?"

"If Mavra tells me to, I'll pull the plug," he told them. "And the stars will go out."

Gypsy gulped nervously.

# Bache, near Dawn the Same Day

MAVRA CHANG HAD HAD VERY LITTLE CHANCE TO say anything in all that was now going on, but she had little choice, either, she reflected ruefully. Still, anything beat living out your life as a cow, certainly, and now events had forced her to the Well of Souls whether she wanted to go or not. She would rather have died than be paralyzed her whole life as a Dillian, rather have been a cow than dead, rather a flying horse, of all things, than a cow, and rather anything else but a domesticated animal. That meant going to the Well with Brazil and being there when he worked his magic.

She wasn't really sure, now, how she felt about Brazil, but the news of Asam's betrayal of the cause, dropped in matter-of-fact conversation between Marquoz and Brazil, had almost crushed her. She couldn't understand or imagine such a thing, and to be contemplated in her name and on her behalf made her feel slightly dirty. Another illusion crashed, another something good turning suddenly foul and flawed, hideous. She wondered somehow if she didn't carry some sort of curse with her, something that corrupted or destroyed all those to whom she felt close.

The transfer had been like the last; the animal had been brought up next to her and one Gedemondan had placed its pads on her head, a second on the head of the pegasus, and the third one hand on the head of each of its fellows. Then she had fell into a deep, dreamless sleep.

It was more difficult for her this time, mostly because the brain of the pegasus seemed more complex, more aware than that of the cow's. Its own initial shock and fear she overcame not by ruthless mental pressure as she had the cow's, but more of a gentle reassurance, an offer, somehow, of partnership. After some early resistance and the resurgence of some of the fear confusion brought, the great winged horse seemed to settle down, accept the idea. Once it accepted her, there seemed a moment of dizziness, of double thought and double vision which settled into comfortable accommodation. She was the creature, and the creature was she, yet there was no extinction, no pushing back.

Brazil, too, had this far different experience and it surprised him even more than she. In a sense, his beast won a greater victory, since he was more concerned with what it could do for him than in becoming the pegasus for any length of time.

Yet another surprise was the vision the winged horses had. They saw in brilliant color, far sharper and better resolved than either person had known, and there was additionally an almost incredible sense of depth. With a simple voluntary action, both found they could focus with incredible clarity on an object roughly four or so meters in front of them all the way to infinity. Only close objects were hard to see; the eyes were set a bit too far back along the snout for that sort of resolution, although by closing one eye, a fair two-dimensional picture could be perceived.

In the distance the army was already on the move. The noise could be heard here, to the south, and they could already see in the predawn light large numbers of flying creatures standing guard as the force moved and probing ahead into the northwest.

Prola made some adjustments on Brazil, who, having just gotten over the shock of the transfer and still settling into the new body, was now trying to adjust to the fact that he was a vivid pastel pink while Mavra was light blue. Agitarian pegasuses came in all colors. Although a blow to Brazil's experimental spirit, both winged horses were neutered females.

"Ready for your flight test?" the Agitar asked nervously. He hadn't really had much experience on the beasts and had depended on the horses's good training to do most of the work. Now, with Brazil in there, both were green.

Himself more than a little nervous, Brazil tried not to let it creep over into that part of the body that was still the pegasus. He had flown everything man had ever invented that would fly, and he loved it—but he had never tried it on his own before. He felt the weight on his back now, then the shock of the rider mounting and seating himself in the specially designed saddle, taking the reins, and digging slightly in the sides.

"All right," Prola told him hoarsely. "Let's trot out to the clearing and see if all this is for nothing."

He tried to relax and let the horse do all the work, but managed only partly to succeed. Closing his eyes wouldn't help a bit, but if he could not, then it was hard to relax and let reflex and alien genes take over. He found the wind more obtrusive than he ever remembered it; the creatures obviously could feel the slightest gusts and turbulences and sense what to do about them. He trotted out and around until he stood, facing the wind. Almost before he could think, he felt the gentle prod of the rider, heard the call "Hie!" and he was off, galloping across the plain. He felt the great wings unfold, stretch, adjust themselves to catch the wind, realizing suddenly that much of what was going on organically was similar to his own experiences as an airplane pilot.

And, amazingly, he could *see* the wind! Very opaque, of course, and not obscuring other vision, but there was a different quality to the air moving at different rates that presented clear boundaries to him.

He felt himself lifting up and suppressed his discomfort; the legs continued to kick for a short while, then folded up like some sort of landing gear, into cavities invisible on the ground, which minimized drag and wind resistance. Once up, it was both heady and easy. There was an almost intoxicating feeling to it, to soar and move with the winds and even against them, to whirl and move around freely, without a machine of any sort between him and the elements.

The Agitar gave a few soft kicks and nudges indicating that it was time to go back down. He didn't want to do it, to relinquish this incredible feeling of freedom, but the sun was almost above the horizon now and time was running short.

He had more unease as the ground rushed up at him. The legs came out and were used somewhat as air brakes, but it was mostly the incredibly maneuverable wings that allowed him to slow to a sufficient speed for the landing. The legs pumped in a fast gallop now, and, suddenly, first the forelegs and then the hind legs touched and the wings turned almost sideways, bringing him to an easy stop. Though the heady feeling continued for a while, he was amazed to discover that he had never even breathed hard.

Then it was Mavra's turn, and she showed some of the same hesitation and nervousness that he had felt. He could sense some of the wrong things in her stride and position and prayed that she would relax and have no more problems than he.

He held his breath until she was off the ground and going upward, folding into an amazingly streamlined shape and rising into the sky. Only then did he let out a long sigh and nod his equine head approvingly. She was a pilot and pilots were born to fly.

Finally he allowed the Gedomondan to board and found the extra height and weight a real handicap. It worried him, and for a moment he feared that the combination might prove impossible. The Gedemondan, too, was scared to death at the idea and took a lot of time balancing and rebalancing himself. Brazil thought he probably wished he had helped with the transference at this point.

It took a long, long gallop to get off the ground this time, and he was starting to breathe hard, the wings doing far more beating to carry almost double the Agitarian weight, he was relieved when the Gedemondan, probably more from fright than common sense, leaned forward, resting his head and upper torso on the saddle and the back of Brazil's neck.

It was equally tricky landing, and he almost lost his balance doing it, but he made it, finally, shortly after Mavra had come down. Now he felt more like he had

had some exercise, though, and he realized that he and Mavra would probably have to switch off every hour or two to equalize the burden.

Now they were ready to go on this last leg of the journey. There were a few good-byes, mostly between the Gedemondan and his fellows who would stay behind—wordless in that case, at least as far as could be determined. They steadied themselves and, one after the other, made their way again into the skies. Brazil decided to carry the Gedemondan as long as possible, both to test his endurance and to make sure they could make it the whole way.

Up they climbed, until they were almost a thousand meters in the air, then they circled once, taking a look at the scene to the north, then whirled and headed away to the southwest. Both armies were visible now, no more than a kilometer apart, but both were on the move. He wished he could see Gunit Sangh's face when the troops came over that last rise and found the camp abandoned—but, of course, his aerial scouts were even now reporting that fact to him. He wondered what the Dahbi would make of it, and what he would do to try and counter it all.

They headed south for a while, not only because the land was flatter and they could maintain the lower, easier altitude, but also because it was away from the forces and they were unlikely to be chased even if noticed. From a distance they would more than likely be seen as couriers, hardly worth a chase. About an hour out, when they felt sufficiently removed from the turmoil below, they made slow, cautious turns, first due west for a while, then toward the north.

A number of times they were intercepted by curious creatures, some sentient, others just wild birds and other flying animals curious or upset about these odd-looking shapes invading their skies. Once they feared attack by a giant hawklike bird with nasty talons and beak and a better than three-meter wingspan, but after a lot of screeching and mock attack runs, it had broken off, possibly because they had gone out of its territory, possibly because it decided these newcomers were just too damned big to deal with.

With his experienced eye Brazil estimated their airspeed at roughly forty-five to fifty kilometers per hour. At that rate they would not reach their goal by this route in less than three and a half to four days.

He hoped he was up to it.

After a fitful sleep the first night and some ravenous grass-munching by both of them, they were aloft again. This time Mavra carried the Gedemondan, and Brazil felt a great deal of relief tempered only by sympathy for her greater load. She was taking it well, though, and the Gedemondan, too, was more experienced in the best way to ride. She seemed to be slightly stronger and slightly larger than he, and he didn't resent it a bit.

The second day out passed much like the first, although he had the feeling that perhaps he had been optimistic in the ground they were covering. Highlands were rising below them, forcing them into the upper air. That meant more work to do the same thing, and it meant heavy breathing now.

Suddenly, late in the day, they were challenged. The creatures were enormous elongated disks with popeyes and countless snakelike tentacles rising from the top of their bodies. They had no heads as such, and it was quickly obvious that most of their gray underside was mouth. They showed no means of propulsion and he couldn't even guess what kept them up, let alone allowed them to make such abrupt turns, rises, and falls.

They flanked the two winged horses, nine of the creatures, each two meters across or more and drooling ugliness, and forced them down onto a mesa below. The creatures themselves did not land, but sat, suspended, two meters in the air and looked them over.

"In the name of the council we stop you and challenge you to explain your presence," the lead creature said. It did not have a translator and sounded to them much like cooing and clucking, but the Gedemondan seemed to understand it all perfectly, responding in a similar language.

Brazil and Mavra Chang both stood there, along with the Agitar Prola, unable to do anything at all or

even guess at what was going on. Finally the Gedemondan nodded and the creatures rose up into the sky
and were quickly gone.

"A patrol from Khutir's forces," the white creature
told them. "I had to do some fancy talking to convince
them we were on the level, I'm afraid. You were
fortunate to have brought me; had I not been able to
speak to them in their own Akkokek tongue, we would
have been taken in for interrogation. Let us be off before they have second thoughts."

They took off once more, all three of the others
wondering just what the hell the Gedemondan had
told those things to make them leave them alone.
Brazil made a mental note not to play poker with a
Gedemondan communicator.

Cutting across Quilst they saw little sign of a major
force, which worried them a little. Where was General
Khutir? Had he, in fact, gotten diverted and lured so
far away? Was it going to be this easy?

Other creatures occasionally rose from hidden outposts to check them out, but each time the Gedemondan
was able to either talk them out of doing anything or
give some sort of sign or password that allowed them to
continue. The Gedemondan only chuckled when they
asked about this ability and stated, that, no, he could
not read minds, but he could make weaker minds
conversationally tell him what he needed to know. That
was all they got from him.

The land had gone down again as they flew over
Quilst, a swampy place thick with foliage and vegeta-
tion overlaid with stagnant water and huge muddy
pools. Here and there could be seen the huge creatures
that reminded Brazil of humanoid hippopotamuses
doing this thing or that, but the place was remarkably
devoid of structures or any real signs of industry. It
must be elsewhere, he decided, hidden in the swamps
or under the ground. Certainly there was a clearly
defined network of broad roads and paths connecting
just about every point in the hex with every other.

They passed over the driest spot in the hex, where
the land started to rise again in a series of steppes,
each rough plateau giving rise to the land. Here had

been Khutir's camp and headquarters, it was clear; the scars—and the equipment—were all too visible, and there were still several hundred creatures of various types there, minding the store or helping maintain at least a tripwire guard to the gateway to the Avenue to their north.

They veered to the south of the camp, hoping to avoid notice, and were soon out of the area and to the west of the great Avenue that could almost be seen in the distance.

They had no intention of approaching from the south or from the east, across hostile Verion, but around and through Ellerbanta, keeping well to the west of the Avenue if at all possible.

It was not the best of Avenues to use, and the closer to it they got the more Brazil realized its disadvantages. The land was mountainous, more like Gedemondas than anything else, and while it wasn't particularly cold, the elevation was steadily rising, and with that the problems in continuing to fly.

Mavra realized the problem more quickly than he had. She knew that the winged horses had been unable to function in the upper regions of Gedemondas; they had a definite upper limit, aggravated even more by any significant weight, and there was definitely that.

They had to land more frequently now, and landing spaces were becoming harder and harder to find. They wove above the snow line, where footing was more difficult, and still the mountains rose higher to the north and east of them, the distant ones almost totally obscured by clouds.

They got out the maps of the region and, for the first time, Mavra as well as the others could examine them. She couldn't read the script, but when the relief markings were explained to her it became clear that they could not fly up to the Equatorial Barrier at the Avenue. Not *this* Avenue.

Using the Gedemondan communicator, whose voice served for both Mavra and Brazil as well as himself in these circumstances, she pointed this out somewhat accusingly to Brazil.

"Well, how was *I* to know the upper limits of these

things?" he grumped. "Hell, I don't remember them as real creatures at all. They survived on Earth only as parts of the racial memory, mythological beasties and no more. Still, there's no real choice. We could have gone east, but that would have brought us over Lamotien and Yaxa—and we wouldn't have stood a chance there. To the west the next hex is completely underwater, which is fine if you're the underwater type but not otherwise—and we'd have a hell of a fight through there, anyway. Same farther east—the Avenue's under the Sea of Storms. So this was the only one we could use and we'll just have to live with it."

"But we can't fly much longer or higher," she objected.

He nodded his equine head. "True, we can't. So we have to head to the Avenue. I figure it's over the next range, there, about thirty or forty kilometers at most. It's the only real pass we're gonna get. We'll walk where we have to, fly when we can. Let's do it."

There was no other way to go, but all of them could only think that the Avenue, even two thirds of the way up, would be the last place they should go and the first place to meet any determined opposition. No one had any doubt that, between Gunit Sangh and General Khutir, orders for whatever patrols were stationed there would be firm: Kill *everything* that tried to get up the Avenue. Everything, without exception—and Ellerbanta was a high-tech hex. Anything would work here.

Even the Gedemondan, who felt almost at home in the high, white, and cold environment, shared the apprehension, but there was now no choice.

They came to the Avenue abruptly; a solid mountain wall stood before them, and they decided to make for the top and over in expectation that they would at least sight the Avenue from the summit.

They did more than that. Brazil heaved his large pegasus body over and almost fell into empty space. He looked down, forelegs dangling over the edge, on an almost sheer cliff with a drop of over four kilometers straight down to the Avenue.

He gave a horselike whinny of fear, which brought the others up quickly but cautiously, and together they managed to haul him back from the edge and look out on the sight.

You could hardly see the Avenue at all; clouds, mist, and rock tended to block the view and perspective, but it was there all right, in a couple of tiny clear patches, way, way down. It could be spotted only because it was the one thing nature never seemed to be—straight: A tiny, light-colored straight hairline that was discernible only by the pegasus's exceptional eyes.

But far off to the north, perhaps peeking up beyond the horizon, they could see a black band stretching east to west as far as vision would take them. The Equatorial Barrier, the access to the Well at the Avenues and the very solid and impenetrable wall that kept the alien North from the equally alien South.

"Can you fly in that gap?" the Agitar asked them.

Brazil and Mavra both looked out, saw the wind and the currents, measured the narrowest points of the gap with the unerring sense of the flying horses, and shook their heads practically in unison.

"No way," Brazil told them through the communicator. "The air currents are treacherous through there, the valley too narrow in spots. We're going to have to walk up here as much as possible and try and find a way down there when we can."

Mavra nodded agreement. "I doubt if any flying creatures could do much in that pass."

"But it'll make us sitting ducks for anybody up here," Brazil said gloomily. "And it's curtains if somebody's around who can fly in this altitude."

They started walking.

The journey wasn't easy and involved many roundabout diversions and switchbacks just to keep roughly even with the Avenue itself. They made poor time, and spent a cold, hungry night on the mountain.

In the morning, it was little better. The temperature was far below zero and they were faced with a breathtakingly beautiful but hazardous sight as clouds closed in almost all views below them, even of the slight dips, valleys, and cirques, leaving only the points of the highest peaks popping up into a brilliant, almost blinding sun. Had flying not been prohibited by the lack of oxygen at that extreme altitude, it would still be impossible now. Once up, there would literally be no safe place to land.

The Gedemondan continued to lead the way on foot, the Agitar, bundled in heavy clothing, rode atop Brazil. The white creature seemed less bothered by the conditions and totally unaffected by altitude and cold, and navigated the tricky range with unerring precision.

Still, such precision was not at the expense of overcaution, for anything less would destroy you up here above the clouds, and it was even slower going than before. At midday, Mavra guessed they had made only a couple of kilometers; the black barrier to the north looked no closer and they had made barely the next set of peaks popping up out of the clouds. Brazil was even more pessimistic; he began to wonder if they could make it at all. There was nothing to eat up here, and he was feeling starved as it was. The trouble was, all directions looked the same to him—lousy. There might not, he reflected uneasily, be any way to abort the plan at this point.

Nearing dusk, they were all feeling down, defeated, and more than a little cheated by it all. They linked to talk, but there was very little to say, really. They all were sharing the same dark thoughts.

I've failed, each one seemed to say to itself or to the others; *we've* failed. We've managed to out-think, out-trick, or out-fight every force the Well World has thrown in our way, but now we are dying, victims not of army or plan but of geography.

Darkness fell, and they camped for another lonely, windy, cold night without food and, now, without much hope.

"We tried our best," Brazil tried to console them, although he felt more in need of it than in the mood to give it. "We'll continue to try as long as possible, until we just can't any more."

"I can see only one way out," Mavra told them.

"Tomorrow, early, while we still have strength, we must try and fly down into the canyon."

"How wide is an Avenue?" Prola asked apprehensively.

Brazil thought about it. "Thirty meters, more or less," he replied. "The chasm is a bit wider, of course, but we don't know how far we'd have to glide and what narrow spots we might have to dodge."

"Fully extended," Mavra noted, "my wingspan and yours is roughly eight or nine meters. It doesn't give us very much maneuverability—and with those wicked updrafts and downdrafts, and those clouds . . ."

"It was *your* idea to fly," he came back. "Don't try talking me out of it at this stage. It's the only thing we can do—and I want to do it so little it wouldn't take very much to let me freeze and starve up here."

"Near midday tomorrow, then," she agreed ruefully, "when whatever sun gets down in there is available to us."

They slept fitfully that night, not wanting to think about, let alone face, the day ahead. And when the first of them awoke and looked around, hope was dashed even further. The clouds had risen now; the whole world was a sea of swirling white in every direction.

They nibbled some snow and relaxed, unable to move until the sun or weather patterns burned some of the fog away.

"It's like this a lot near Avenues," Brazil told them. "You get the same reaction when two dissimilar hexes—seasonally, that is—meet at a border, and that's a border out there, of course, a border with a thirty meter strip in between that's subject to wind and weather patterns from both hexes."

They were silent most of the morning, and the mists would not clear. Brazil finally motioned for the Gedemondan to come over and "plug in," as he thought of it.

"Mavra—what have you been thinking about?" he asked gently, trying to get her mind off the situation.

She gave a wry chuckle. "Other places. Other people," she replied. "I wonder how the battle went? I wonder who won? And whether it made a damn bit of difference? I wonder if they bit on that empty shell of a body you left them, or if they're all lined up somewhere, fighting yet. It would be nice to know before I . . ."

"Die?" he completed. "Does that really scare you?"

"Yes, of course, " she replied. "I'm not like you, Brazil. I don't think anyone is. I'd like to see that new universe."

He hesitated a moment, then said, "Well, that tells me something about you I was wondering about." He didn't elaborate, but it settled a nagging reservation he had had. He had wondered, up to this point, whether or not she might not have desired, been happy, in her Dillian existence. Of course, Asam's treachery would have dispelled that, but only for the two of them. It wasn't fair, though, to do to anyone what he intended for her if she could have been happy in some alternate existence.

It wasn't fair anyway, he knew, but she wouldn't believe that until she found it out for herself.

The Gedemondan broke the contact. "The fog is lifting," he noted.

They looked around and saw it was true. The sun was visible now, about a quarter of the way up in the sky, and it was burning through the thin cloudiness that seemed impossible at this altitude.

"I think I see a peak over there!" Prola called excitedly. "And another, there! Yes! I think it's clearing."

The Gedemondan suddenly stiffened and looked around nervously. "I don't think all is well," he whispered. "I sense others near by. I—I allowed my own personal emotions to cloud my senses," he explained apologetically. "Now I can read them. We are being watched!"

They tensed, and the Agitar drew his coppery swordlike tast, which could conduct thousands of volts of electricity from his body. They waited tensely to see who the hell could possibly have penetrated this fog and found them at such a height.

"Helloooo . . . !" boomed a voice from somewhere

just to the left of them, a call that echoed back and forth between the peaks. "Hey! Nate! Where are you?" it called. "Come on—I won! I gotcha dead to rights. You can't move. I took your challenge and I've won, Nate! I've won!"

Brazil gestured with his head to the Gedemondan, who placed a pad on his head allowing speech.

"Over here!" he called wearily. "How the hell did you ever find us?"

A huge figure glided out of the fog and approached them carefully. It carried in two of its six hands a small electronic device.

"This is a high-tech hex, Nate," Serge Ortega told him. "Haven't you ever heard of radar?"

# Above the Borgo Pass

ORTEGA HAD A FAIRLY LARGE FORCE AROUND, AND as they walked with him the size became more apparent. They were also well armed and well equipped with the best in weaponry and detection gear and obviously digging in.

"I must say that it's damned hard to think of you as a pegasus," the Ulik said jokingly. "And a passionate pink one at that! My, my!"

Brazil could only snort at this commentary, since the Gedemondan could only be an effective speech conduit when they were standing still. He and Mavra could only seethe and take it; all hope was now gone.

"The Borgo Pass," Ortega told them. "It's the narrowest point in the whole chasm, barely ten meters clearance on either side of the Avenue and with nice, natural fortifications on both sides. As you saw from the landscape above, anyone who wants to reach the equator has to come up the Avenue itself—and has to get past this spot."

There was a lot of activity around the mostly obscured pass; they could see a portable crane lifting some gun emplacement down into the mist and cloud layer below, supervised by a number of small flying things.

"You might be interested to know how I figured out your plot," the Ulik continued, gloating unashamedly. "To be truthful about it, I deduced it as you went along and the final pieces only fell into place a couple of days ago, but I'd already guessed the rough outline. It was clear from the start, at least after I discovered how you'd evaded our traps in Zone, that yours was a campaign of misdirection. Still, nothing could deny the fact that, sooner or later, you would have to move in force toward one or more of the Avenues, and as soon as the Hakazit moved up the Isthmus I knew from its direction and the direction of the Dillians that you had to be coming to this area. Although your double in the ship gave me some uneasy moments, I admit, I rejected water Avenues as simply too risky. That left Yaxa-Harbigor or here. Now, you had an army for each, as did the council, and a double for each, which drove us crazy. So, which Avenue?" He paused, savoring his moment of triumph.

"I rejected Yaxa-Harbigor not only because the inhabitants around there are incredibly formidable anywhere and damn near absolute in their own neighborhood, but also because that would put Gunit Sangh's army in between, by far the more formidable of the two," he continued. "But a glance at a map showed that, if you turned westward and started the other Awbrian force northward, you'd have a massive double army coming down on a smaller and less equipped council force. Ergo, Ellerbanta, since Verion is inhospitable, nasty, alien, and probably lethal. I'm not sure those fancy charged-up glowworms can be reasoned with. Good thing they're superstitious, though, or we couldn't hold both sides of the pass."

Brazil halted and gestured with his head to the Gedemondan, who understood and made the link.

"All right, Serge, but how did *you* get here?" he wanted to know.

Ortega chuckled. "All in good time, my boy, all in good time. So, anyway, old Gunit Sangh and his crew wouldn't listen to a lot of what I had to say and paid for their mistakes. They got outmaneuvered time and time again. Well, once I knew where you were headed, I decided to take matters into my own hands. Your curious friend Gypsy had told me that I could leave Zone without withering into dust, and I finally had it, completely, up to *here,* with sitting in my private little prison while everybody else had all the fun. Oh, I could have ordered folks over here, but I simply could not deny myself the pleasure of this. You don't know what it's meant to me, Nate, leaving that stinking hole. Seeing stars, breathing clean air, feeling the wind and heat and cold and rain . . . It's almost like being reborn. I may be the only man anywhere who can identify with you, Nate. My little prison, really, isn't that much different than the prison you've been living in all those thousands of years. We were both trapped by our own devices."

"But how did you get here?" Brazil persisted. "I mean, Ulik's almost on the other side of the world from here, even if it *is* at the equator, and that bulk of yours can't fly."

Ortega laughed. "Oh, but it *can*, Nate, although it damned near killed me from being out of practice. I'll show you one in a little while."

"One what?" he wanted to know.

"A trublak," the Ulik replied. "It's a huge, pulpy worm with six pairs of huge, tough, transparent wings, about six meters long. Nasty-looking, but harmless. They are to Ulik pretty much what the horse was to our ancestors—transportation, muscle power, you name it. They're not very bright but easily domesticated. You have these reins, you sit on a saddlelike thing, and you use your own tail as part of the guidance. Took us about five days to get here, but we knew where you were heading before we started, even if you hadn't taken off yet. And no matter what, a good look at the relief maps told me you *had* to come by the Borgo Pass. Just *had* to. It's almost designed that way."

"But how the hell did you know what we were or who we were?" he persisted. "We're pretty well disguised, I think you'll admit."

Ortega shrugged. "Remember, the last time we met you were in the body of a stag. I knew the trick could be done and I knew you knew it. When we got word yesterday that your comatose body had been found in the rubble of battle I pretty well guessed what had happened—and waited here. It had to be a pretty fast ground animal or an airborne one, and I guessed a flyer since you'd want to make speed. What large, flying animal was on the continent and near where your armies had passed? It's easy when you're thinking dirty and playing with a full deck."

Brazil looked around at the frantic activity, slightly puzzled. "What's all this now, Serge?" he wanted to know. "You've won. Looks more like you're still moving in than preparing to move out."

Serge Ortega chuckled even more at some private joke, then called out, "All right, boys! Come on up!"

Out from a point beyond the portable crane came two figures. Two very familiar creatures.

One was a Hakazit, huge and imposing, and the other a tall human with a big grin on his face.

"Hello, Brazil," called Gypsy. "We were wondering if we'd beat you here or not."

"It would seem our timing was perfect," Marquoz noted with satisfaction. "A last reunion before the windup." He turned to Brazil. "I told *you* I wanted to be in on the finish."

The shock of seeing those two was so great that the communications link was broken for a few moments. When he regained it, all Brazil could blurt out was, "What the *hell* is going on here?"

Ortega grinned. "I resigned from the council, Nate. Oh, I've got to admit, up to the last moment I didn't know which way I would jump, didn't even know if I had the nerve to ever leave that place, but, when push came to shove, I really didn't have much choice. *I* couldn't condemn you to the same prison I hated so much. Not me—anybody *but* me, maybe. But I couldn't do that to somebody else, particularly an old buddy like you. I'd done all I could to keep the faith with the council; I'd given them every lead, prodded them this way and that, and even managed to save an awful lot of those Entries from being wiped out. I didn't worry about that after a bunch of the boys decided to ignore me anyway and sent a squad of fifty in to start killing the Entries in the Well Gate. You know what happened? Those amazons of yours got so pissed when the first volleys of arrows flew, they charged that squad and tore it literally to bits! They can take care of themselves pretty good, they can! And since high-tech weapons won't work in

Zone, well, there's nobody with nerve enough to try it now."

Gypsy looked at him, a smile on his face. "And, of course, Saint Serge, personal motives had nothing to do with it at all."

Ortega looked sheepish. "Well, of course, in a very minor way. I've been fighting that bastard Sangh for fifty years, and he's going for broke with this one. If he loses, he *really* loses, this time. He's the greatest threat to the stability of this world that ever was born, and he has to go. Some of the Dahbi aren't that bad. Gruesome, maybe, but a lot of other races are, too. Evil, though? No, that's reserved for Sangh. And his whole pitch has been that if he were in complete charge, he could do anything. Well, he's *been* in complete charge, and he's botched it. If you make the Well, he's botched it totally. He'll not only never be a threat but he'll lose face and standing among his own people, maybe lose his power base. Nobody likes to back a loser, and there'll be a lot of bitterness after all this. The Wars of the Well showed that—people don't like their sons and daughters, friends and neighbors, to be sacrificed at all, but when they get slaughtered in a losing cause, well, that's more than some can stand."

"So you changed sides," Brazil sighed.

Ortega's bushy eyebrows went up. "Why, Nate! I'm *surprised* at you! You know there's never been any side except *my* side. Hell, I've had my cake and eaten it too in this go-round. I've figured you out, outwitted and trapped you, and now I can turn around and stick it good to the ones I have a lot of scores to settle with. It's the time to settle scores again, Nate, I'm dying now and you know it and I know it. There's no way I'm going to die in peace and solitude."

Mavra caught the attention of the Gedemondan, who linked her as well.

"Gypsy, this is Mavra," she began, having to explain it because the Gedemondan was doing all the physical talking. "What happened—after we left? How did Marquoz get here?"

"I'll answer that," the Hakazit told the others.

"What happened was that we really had to pull out too quickly and Sangh's army was on the move. They caught us in Mixtim and there was a bloody battle. In strictly field terms, it was a draw—we might even be said to have won, since a lot more of them died than us. But, strategically, they managed to split our forces and ram through. We couldn't hold, not forever, and the Awbrians were pinned down to the southwest of us, a little too far to help. Gunit Sangh wasn't really fooled by your body, Brazil, any more than Ortega was. It's something he'll keep in reserve to claim a moral victory, maybe, but that's all. He doesn't know you've changed form but he guessed somehow you were making for the Avenue and he's unnerved about what happened to Mavra, here. He took his fastest, most versatile, and nastiest two thousand and punched through the hole, heading straight for here. We couldn't stop him; the balance of his army prevented that. His force is on the Avenue right now, and along about dawn tomorrow he's going to be coming straight up that canyon."

They all turned and looked in the indicated direction, although there wasn't much that could be seen. Finally Mavra asked, "You said he punched through, Marquoz. What about Asam?"

The Hakazit paused a moment before answering. "He's dead, Mavra," he said flatly. "He went out like he'd have wanted to, though. In the midst of the battle, when Sangh's forces bulged and broke the line, he left his command post with two submachine guns, one in each hand, trying to rally the troops to beat back the advance. He almost did it, too. Oh, he was a sight to see, all right! Galloping, cursing, yelling, and screaming as he fired both guns into the troops. His own just had to follow him in, and the carnage they wrought on the enemy was simply fantastic. But Sangh had better field generals than we, and there were simply too many at the breakthrough. He made them pay dearly for him, I'll say that. They were piled up on all sides of him, mowed down like grains of wheat, but no matter how many he cut down, they just kept coming. And when his guns went dry, riddled with wounds himself, he pulled that old sword of his and waded on in, a magnificent madman. There's never been anything like it before on this little world, nor many others, either, I'd say. The Dillians will make him their martyr and legend forever, and even his enemies will sing songs in praise of him."

She said nothing, but there were huge tears in her eyes at hearing this. She hoped it was true, that it wasn't being embellished for her benefit. But, then, she told herself, it was exactly what he would do under the circumstances.

"After the battle," Marquoz continued, "I managed to get together with Gypsy, who'd changed form to avoid being captured, and we tried using Brazil's old body as the final ploy. It *looked* like it worked—they cheered and celebrated, and the fighting stopped pretty well up and down the line. Still, the force that broke through didn't stop and turn around; we figured Sangh wasn't totally buying. We fooled him too many times before. He's going to make sure this time. He's coming all the way up the Avenue."

"I decided to scout up ahead of them and see if I could locate you," Gypsy added. "It wasn't long before I came on Ortega's group settling in here, and I decided to find out what was what. When I learned that he wasn't here to capture you, and that you hadn't been seen, I got back to Marquoz, and with the aid of one of those trublaks he's got, we were able to get him up here to assess the situation."

"You took a chance," Brazil noted. "You couldn't be *sure* of Serge's intentions. He has a history of being devious."

Marquoz only shrugged. "It didn't really matter any more. The end of the game was up here, not back there. I'd done all I could. And, if there *were* any tricks, maybe Gypsy and I could do something about them. It worked out, anyway."

"Yes, it worked out—somehow," Brazil agreed. "It always seems to. It's part of the system. The probabilities, no matter how impossible, always break for me when my survival is at stake." He paused a moment, then continued.

"Serge, how many people you got here? I mean all told, except for us?"

"Sixty-four," he replied. "We had to travel fast and light and I was cashing in I.O.U.s as I went on a target of opportunity basis. Got a lot of good equipment, but not much else. They're all good people, though, Nate, and the position's incredible."

"Sixty-four," Brazil repeated. "Against Gunit Sangh's battle-hardened two thousand."

Ortega grinned. "About even, I think. Oh, I don't think we can hold forever, but we don't have to. First we get you down to the bottom by crane or whatever it takes, get some food in your bellies, then you get the hell out of here. We did a sweep up and down the Avenue this morning—there won't be any nasty surprises. We eliminated them for you." His expression turned serious for a moment. "I had seventy-six when I started. Would have been worse if this high-tech hex didn't abut the Avenue. You get on down there, now. We haven't a lot of time to waste."

Nathan Brazil looked up at the huge Ulik and cursed his inability in this animal body to express what he was feeling inside now. It was odd; until a few minutes ago, he would have sworn such emotions had died within him thousands of years before. Finally he said, "You could come with us, you know, Serge."

"I thought about it," he replied. "Thought about it a lot. But, now, standing here, I wouldn't miss this for the world." He stared hard at Brazil's huge animal's eyes. "I think you understand. You, of all people, should be the one to understand."

Brazil gave an audible, long sigh. "Yeah," he said at last. "I think I do." He looked over at the crane. "Let's get on the road, then."

Serge Ortega nodded. "Good-bye, Nate. For all of it, it was fun, wasn't it?"

"That it was," Brazil responded a little wistfully. "That it was. So long, you old bastard. Give 'em hell."

Ortega grinned. "Haven't I always?"

High, towering cliffs rose from both sides of the

Avenue as it made its way from the swampy low-
lands up to the Equatorial Barrier. Wind whipped
through the pass, creating an eerie, wavering whistle
that also carried the subtle undertones of a crashing
sea, although there was no sea nearby. The Avenue
here was on two levels, a fairly deep center filled with
crystal-blue water that allowed the summer melt to
drain off, creating the Quilst swamp far to the south;
the bank on either side was wide and smooth, although weather-worn and covered with a fine layer of
silt and occasional rocks from the slides. It was quite
a natural-looking valley except that the stream ran
almost dead straight for the length of the border, more
a canal than a river.

The valley ranged from twenty or more kilometers
across to less than fifty here at the Borgo Pass. Large
rock and mudslides had closed it in over the ages to
such an extent that, from a practical standpoint, there
was only two-or-three-meters clearance on the Ellerbanta side, even less on the Verion. The walls of the
canyon, however, were not sheer and never less sheer
than now, at the pass; craggy outcrops every ten or so
meters on both sides of the narrow section made ideal
emplacements and outposts.

Serge Ortega surveyed the scene from almost ground
level with some satisfaction. Things were getting set
up pretty good; as darkness fell there was little left to
do.

Marquoz walked up to him and looked around,
admiringly. "It's damned good organization," he told
the Ulik. "I'm impressed."

Ortega turned and gave an odd half-smile. "I am
always this way," he told the Hakazit. "Even more,
now, at what might be the climactic point of my life."
He settled back on his huge tail and smiled fully now,
eyes looking beyond the other, toward places only he
could see. "Consider the life I lived," he reflected.
"It's been a damned full one, an important one, I
think. Rebel, privateer, smuggler, soldier-of-fortune,
star pilot—you name it, I've done or been it. Then I
came here where, in a very short time, I became a
politician, then ambassador, statesman, and, ah,

world-coordinator. I've romanced thousands, drank, fought, generally had one *hell* of a good time doing it all, too. Now I'm tired and I'm bored. The only thing I haven't done is die."

"You picked a hell of an exit," the Hakazit noted good-naturedly.

"Hah! Think I could end a life like mine rotting away in some retirement home? A nice, peaceful death propped up by some nurses so I could gaze lovingly at the stars? Bullshit on that! No, sir! Never! When I go out it'll be like Asam. They'll make up songs about me for generations. The bards will tell the tales by firelight and my enemies and their children and their children's children shall drink toasts to my glorious memory!"

"And use your memory to scare hundreds of races' children into being good little kiddies," Marquoz cracked. "Hell, man, you've been around so long they won't believe you're dead when they see your body."

Ortega considered it. "That *would* take the cake, wouldn't it, now? Marquoz, I want you to pass the word. When I go, they're to burn my body beyond recognition, beyond any hope of even identifying what sort of creature I was. I want nothing of me left. That'll scare the hell out of the bastards for two generations."

The Hakazit chuckled. "It'll be done," he assured the other. He looked out and down the dark pass. "How soon do you think we'll have company?"

"Advance scouts and patrols any time now," Ortega told him. "No main force until dawn, though. A *fly* couldn't get through this pass at night against those heat-ray generators up there. The cliff face and slides are in our favor, too. They can't get a clear shot at any of them without exposing themselves."

"In fact, I *would* come now," Marquoz came back. "A small force, one traveling light and with skill and silence, with a large part nocturnals and the rest with sniperscopes and computer-guided lasers. I'd do it between midnight and dawn, positioning them just so, knocking out emplacements one by one and quietly. *Then* I'd charge up here with everything I had at dawn."

"I've already considered that possibility," the Ulik replied. "If there's any hint of movement, we can hit floodlights throughout the fifty or so meters in front of us, radar-controlled and tracker types, too. Some of my boys see just fine in the dark, too, and they're up forward, on the watch. We're cross-coding our emplacements, too. Every position fires a slightly changing code to its neighbors every ten minutes. No signal, we light up the place anyway and investigate. There's challenge and reply codes, too, from one point to another. Now, Gunit Sangh probably assumes this, so he'll try it anyway, not to expect anything but just to test out our defenses a little and keep us all awake until dawn when his well-rested troops will make the assault."

Marquoz, who was somewhat nocturnal himself, looked again at the pass. "Hell of a thing, though, asking troops to march up that. If there's another way, he'll take it."

Ortega chuckled. "What are troops to him? He knows the score pretty well, too. Two thousand against sixty-six counting you and the Agitar."

"I know, I know. The terrain is a leveler, but it's not *that* much of a leveler. Not thirty to one. Not when you've got nice, mobile high-tech weapons carried by creatures that can climb sheer cliffs and others that maybe could swim right up that deep current there in the middle."

Ortega shrugged. "The high-tech favors us," he insisted. "They have only what they brought with them and could drag through that gap. No armored vehicles, for example, that could really cause trouble. No aerials, not in this confined space. A full frontal attack through that little gap is what he can do best. He can't even go over and around, as Nate found out."

"But thirty to one . . ." Marquoz said doggedly.

"This is similar to a number of situations in my own people's history," Ortega told him. "My old people's —and Mavra's, and Nate's, too, I think. Not the flabby, engineered idiots of the Com you knew. The ones who started with a flint in caves and carved out an intersellar empire before they'd run their course. The histories were full of stuff like that, although they probably don't teach it any more. Six hundred, it was said, held a pass wider than this for days against an army of more than five thousand. Another group held a fortress with less than two hundred against a well-trained army of thousands for over ten days. We need only two. There are lots of stories like that; our history's full of such things. I suspect the history of any race strong enough to carve civilization out of a hostile world has them."

Marquoz nodded. "There are a few such examples in the history of the Chugach," he admitted. "But, tell me, what happened to those who held that pass after their time limit was reached? What happened to those people in that old fort after the ten days?"

Ortega grinned. "The same thing that happened to the Chugach in your stories, I think."

"I was afraid of that," Marquoz sighed. "So we're all going to die at the end of this?"

"Thirty to one, Marquoz," the snake-man responded. "I think the terrain brings the odds down to, say, five to one. Only a few hundred of them will finally make it through, but they *will* make it. Too late to stop Nate, though, if we do our jobs right. But, tell me, Marquoz, why are *you* here? Why not with them? You could enter the Well with them, get immortality if you wanted it, or anything else you might wish. I think he'd do it for you—it's a different situation than last time. He made you the offer, didn't he?"

"Yes," Marquoz replied. "He made the offer."

"So why here, in a lonely pass on an alien planet? Why here and why now?"

Marquoz sighed and shook his massive head. "I really don't know. Call it stubbornness. Call it foolishness, perhaps, or maybe even a little fear of going with them and what I might find there. Maybe it would just be a shame not to put this body and brain to important use. I really can't give you an answer that satisfies *me,* Ortega. How could I give one that would satisfy you?"

Ortega looked around in the darkness. "Maybe I can help—a little, anyway," he reflected. "I bet if we went around to every one of our people here, all volunteers, remember, we'd get the same sort of feeling I got now. A sense of doing something important, even pivotal. I think that in every age, in every race, a very few find themselves in positions like this. They believe in what they're doing and the rightness of their cause. It's important. It's why they still tell the stories and honor the memory of such people and deeds even though their causes, in some cases their whole worlds, are long dead, their races dust. But you're not stuck in the position, Marquoz. You put yourself directly into it when you could have sat back and made a nice profit."

"But that's exactly what I've been doing my whole life," the Hakazit responded. "I could never really belong to my own Chugach society. I was the outsider, the misfit. My family had wealth, position, and no real responsibilities so I never really *had* to do anything. I studied, I read, I immersed myself in non-Chugach things as well. I wanted to see the universe when the bulk of my race had no desire to see the next town. I was the ultimate hedonist, I suppose—anything I wanted and no price to pay, and I hated it. Just me, me, me—the position most people say they'd like to be in. I can't say I've lost my faith, because I never had any to begin with. The way of the universe was that the people with power oppressed the people without it. And if the people without it suddenly got it, by revolution or reform, they turned around and oppressed still other people or fought among themselves to have it all. Religion was the sham that kept the people down. I never once saw a god do anything for anybody, and most religions of all the races I knew were good excuses for war, mass murder, and holding onto oppressive power. Politics was the same thing by another name. Ideology. The greatest social revolutionaries themselves turned into absolute monarchs as soon as they consolidated their power. Only technology improved anything, and even that was controlled by the power brokers who misused it for their own ends. And what if everybody got rich and nobody had to work? You'd have a bunch of fat, rich, stagnant slobs, that's all."

Ortega grinned at the other's cynicism, the first he had ever encountered that far exceeded his own. "No romances in your life?" he asked.

The other sighed. "No, not really. I never felt much of a physical attraction for anyone else. The Chugach are romantics in a sense, yes; sitting around drinking and telling loud lies about their clans, singing songs and creating artistic dances about them. But, personally, no. I never liked my people much, really. A bunch of fat, rich, lazy slobs themselves. You know, there are stories on many worlds about people lost in the wilderness as babies and raised by animals that come out thinking and acting like animals. There's more to that than to physical form. Externally I was Chugach, yes; internally I was . . . well, something else. Alien."

Ortega's eyebrows rose. "Alien? How?"

Marquoz considered his words. "I once met a couple of Com humans who were males but absolutely convinced that, inside, somehow, they were spiritually female. They were going to have the full treatment, become biologically functioning females. Maybe it was psychological, maybe it was pre-birth hormones, maybe it was anything—but it wasn't really sexual in the usual sense. Those two males were in love with each other, yet both were going to be females. Crazy, huh? I identified with them, though, simply because I was an alien creature in the body of a Chugach. No operation for me, though—it wasn't that simple. I was an alien inside the body of a Chugach, trapped there. I didn't *feel* like a Chugach, didn't *act* like one, didn't even *think* like one. I felt totally alienated among my own people."

"I have to admit it's a new one to me," Ortega admitted. "But I can see how it might be inevitable."

"Not so new. I think all races have their share. Here, on the Well World, with 1,560 races all packed closely together, I've run into a lot of it. I suspect it's a more common ailment than we're led to believe.

People just don't talk about it because there's no point. They're just called mad, given some kind of phobia label, and told they must learn to adjust. And what can you do about it? You can't go to the local doctor and say, 'Make me over into something else.' Consider how many of the humans regarded the Well World with longing. A romantic place, a place where you could be changed into some other creature totally different than you were. And for every one that was repulsed by the idea, there was at least one who fantasized what they wanted to be and were excited by it."

"And that's why you volunteered to spy on the humans and Rhone?"

Marquoz chuckled. "No, I didn't really volunteer —although I might have if I'd ever known about the program. *They* selected *me*. My psychological profile was the type they were looking for: somebody who'd feel as comfortable in an entirely alien culture as they did among their own kind."

Ortega nodded. "Makes sense. And were you any happier in the Com?"

"Happier? Well, I suppose, in a way. I was still an alien creature, of course, but now I was an exotic one. It didn't change my feelings toward my own racial form, but it turned it into something exciting, at least."

It was growing quite dim now, and Ortega looked around. He could see almost nothing in the nearly total darkness, but there was the occasional flash that showed the coded "all's well" from one emplacement to another. And, not far away, he could see a couple of dim figures checking the nets in the river and making certain the mines were active. Nobody would get up that way, either. He turned back to Marquoz and the conversation, a conversation he knew they wouldn't be having under any other circumstances.

"You're not a Chugach any longer," he pointed out. "What did that to to your self-image?"

Marquoz shrugged. "Well, it's not that much of a

change, really. And I had no more choice in it than I had in being a Chugach. Makes no difference."

"But that brings us back to my original question," Ortega noted. "You could have been whatever you wanted if you'd just gone with them."

Marquoz sighed. "You must understand, put the thing in the context of what I've been telling you. You see, this is the first operation I've been involved in that had any *meaning*. It's something like you said for yourself. Found dead in his bed from jaundice, did nothing for anybody, made no difference if he had ever lived at all: that could be the obituary of just about everyone who ever lived, here and anywhere else in the universe. It makes absolutely no difference in the scheme of things whether all but a handful of people live or die. No more than the importance of a single flower, or blade of grass, or vegetable, or bird. It would make no difference if those men who held that ancient pass or that equally ancient fort had, instead, died of disease or old age or in a saloon fight. But it made a difference that they died where they did. It mattered. It justified their whole existence. *And it matters that I am here, now, and make this choice.* It matters to me and to you. It matters to the Well World and to the whole damned universe."

He raised his arms in a grand sweep at the blackness. "Do you really understand what we're doing here?" he went on. "We're going to decide the entire fate of the universe for maybe billions of years. Not Brazil, not Mavra Chang, not really. They're only making the decisions because *we* are allowing them to! Right here, now, tomorrow, and the next day. Tell me, Ortega, isn't that worth dying for? Others may be misfits; they may be born on some grubby little world or in some crazy hex, and they might grow up to be farmers or salesmen or dictators or generals or kings, only then to grow old and die and be replaced by other indistinguishable little grubs that'll do the same damned things. And it won't matter one damned bit. But *we'll* matter, Ortega, and we all sense it. That's why our enemies will sing songs about us and our names and memories will become ageless legends to countless races. Because, in the end, who we are and what we do in the next two days is all that matters, and we're the only ones that are important."

Ortega stared at him, even though all he could really make out were the creature's glowing red eyes. Finally he said, "You know, Marquoz, you're absolutely insane. What bothers me is that I can't really find any way to disagree with you—and you know what that makes me." He reached to the heavy leather belt between his second and third pair of arms and removed a large flask. "I seem to dimly recall from old diplomatic receptions that Hakazits have funny drinking methods but tend to drink the same stuff for the same reason as Uliks. Shall we drink to history?"

Marquoz laughed and took the bottle. "To history, yes! To the history of the future we write in the next two days! To *our* history, which *we* chose and which we determined!" He threw his head back and poured the booze down his throat, then coughed and handed the bottle back to Ortega, who started to work on the remains of it.

"That's good stuff," the Hakazit approved.

"Nothing but the best for the legion the night before," Ortega responded.

A voice nearby said, "Got enough of that left for me? Or would it kill me?"

They jumped slightly, then laughed when they saw it was Gypsy. "Damn it. I keep expecting Gunit Sangh to pop out of the rocks," Ortega grumbled. He threw the flask to the tall man, who caught it and took a pull, then screwed up his face in pleasant surprise.

"*Whew!* Nothing synthetic in *that!*" he approved, then got suddenly serious. "I'm about to go to Yua and tell her the situation. Last I heard she'd taken some of her squad and flown around Khutir's main force on her way here. They surprised the old general good; gave him a sound thrashing. But they're still three days behind."

Marquoz chuckled. "Three days. Couldn't be two."

"Anything you want me to particularly tell her?" Gypsy asked.

"Tell her—" Ortega's voice quivered slightly— "tell her . . . that we'll hold for Brazil. We'll hold until she gets here, damn it all. Tell her a lot of very brave and very foolish people are going to make it all work. And tell her thanks, and godspeed, from old Serge Ortega."

Gypsy nodded understandingly, a sad smile on his own face. "I'll be back in time for the battle, Serge."

The Ulik chuckled and shook his head unbelievingly. "You, too? The number of martyrs we're getting these days must set a new record. My, my!"

"Practicality," Gypsy told him. "You see, when Brazil enters the Well and shuts it down I'll lose my contact with it. I'll no longer be a creature of the universe, only of the Well World from whence I came so long ago. And I was a deepwater creature. I'll be dead from the pressure so fast I won't have time to suffocate."

"You can always return to Oolakash, Doctor, and do it all over again," Ortega suggested. "It hasn't changed all that much, even in a thousand years."

Marquoz looked at them both, puzzled. "Doctor? Oolakash? What the hell is this?"

Gypsy stared at Ortega for a moment. "How long have you known?"

"Well, for a certainty only right at this moment," the Ulik admitted. "I've suspected it almost since the first time we met. You could do the impossible and that wasn't acceptable. The only possible explanation was that you had completely cracked the Markovian puzzle, completely understood just exactly what they did and how they did it. And I could think of only one man who could possibly do that. If you'd been from a race that had done it, well, there'd be more of you. If you were a long-gone Markovian, I think Brazil would have known you, at least when you met. So that left only one man, a man I once knew, the only man I ever knew who understood how the Well worked and whose lifework it was to learn all there was to learn about it—a man who vanished and was presumed dead long ago."

"All right, all right," growled Marquoz. "I think I'm entitled to know what the hell you two are talking about."

"Marquoz," Ortega said lightly, "I'd like you to meet the first man to tame the Markovian energies, the man who built the great computer Obie and whose fault most of this is. Marquoz, Dr. Gilgram Zinder."

The Hakazit looked over at Gypsy, then laughed. "Gypsy? You? Zinder? That's the most ridiculous thing I've ever heard in my whole life."

"That's what threw me," Ortega admitted. "The man who did all that, who finally, first with Obie's aid and then without, managed to be able to talk to the Markovian computers and make them obey his will—and he chooses to go home and become a wandering gypsy and bum?"

Gilgram Zinder chuckled. "Well, not at the start, no. And the human mind isn't up to the training, nor is it perfectly matched for full communication. But I got to the point where I could influence it as regarded myself. Takes a lot of effort, and off the Well World it can cause monster headaches. I really never was able to do much with it beyond myself, and I realized that, without a lot of additional apparatus, I never would be able to get any further, and that needed apparatus would make Obie a toy. It would take something the size of the Well of Souls, and that was not worth thinking about for obvious reasons. So I used the power to wander a while, as Obie and Mavra wandered and explored, over the whole of the universe in various forms until I got bored with it. After all, unlike Obie, I could do little except survive and adapt. So, I went home at last to the Com and found it much improved from my day. It gave me a lot of satisfaction to see that a lot of the worst evils were gone, in part, at least, due to what we accomplished many years before. You understand, I always had lived a very restrictive sort of life. A lonely life. I wasn't handsome, or even distinctive. I had my work, and that's all I had. I had to bribe a woman to bear my child and build my other child myself."

"But your work succeeded beyond your wildest dreams," Ortega pointed out.

"Beyond my— Yes, I suppose it did. I'm now as close to a Markovian as I think it's possible for one of our time to become."

"Perhaps you should have completed your work," the snake-man suggested. "Maybe if you had, we wouldn't be in this situation now."

"Perhaps," he admitted grudgingly. "But, damn it, I gave my entire life to science and they laughed at me, those who didn't try to use the new power for evil ends. And then I had to give my daughter and my race and environment to it, too. And even the good side in that fight, when they were presented with my work, got frightened of it and tried to bury it forever. So I looked at this and I thought, What about me? Where do *I* get anything but royally screwed by the system? Selfless men wind up in neglected graves. I felt like I'd been given a new life, a new chance at all the things I'd missed, and I took it. A new life— a new series of lives. Even the Well World gave you only one start, but I had an infinite number. I was a rich and handsome playboy. Then I tried the other side, as an exotic and beautiful dancer who had to beat off would-be lovers with a stick. I learned to play a variety of instruments and composed music that attracted a serious following. I painted, I sculpted, I wrote a few stories and some poetry. I was on my way to being everything everybody ever wanted to be. The ultimate fantasy was mine: I could be any fantasy I chose, and I was. I enjoyed it all, too. The Gypsy phase was just another one of those, one I particularly enjoyed after teaming up with Marquoz, here—enjoyed it, that is, until the fools dug up my work, misunderstood it, misapplied it, and abused it to their own destruction, the fools."

"Why didn't you step in then?" Ortega wanted to know. "Tell them what they were doing wrong?"

Zinder shrugged. "What could I do? By the time I knew what they were working on it was too late.

Even then I was really blocked. Suppose I *had* suddenly showed up and said, 'Hi! I'm Gil Zinder! I know you think I've been dead a thousand years, but I was only fooling.' Who would have believed me or paid attention to me? I'd never have gotten through the bureaucracy. It's much easier to make a bureaucracy *not* notice you than to notice and take you seriously. I left them the keys to godhood, to the universe, and they took it and destroyed themselves with it. And me—look at what it's cost me! Nikki . . . Obie . . . All that was dear to me."

Marquoz still couldn't quite believe all this. "So *you* killed Nikki Zinder? Your own daughter? Did Obie know?"

"He knew," Zinder assured him. "Although I didn't realize that until I was inside him myself and we could talk. We talked it out at great length, a sort of mutual catharsis. He would have had to do it if I hadn't, and that was the one thing he simply could not do. He could not harm Nikki. I even tried to talk him out of trying to integrate with Brazil, but to no avail."

"Brazil," the Hakazit muttered. "Why did Brazil do that to Obie?"

"Short him out, you mean? For much the same reason that I lose my powers when he turns it off. You see, we have a mathematical matrix here, a set of relationships that says, 'I am the universe and I am this way, according to these laws.' That's the original universe, the Markovian, or naturally formed one. It's quite small, really, compared with ours. The whole thing was barely the size of a small galaxy. Now, the Markovians did it over themselves. They had a second creation, you might say, which, since it originated from the same point as their own for safety's sake, destroyed their planets and incorporated that old universe into ours. And since ours was a much larger explosion, it expanded with ours as well, which is why you find more Markovian worlds out there than around here. But they're the old, dead, original universe. Ours is superimposed on it—they didn't dare wipe theirs out or they'd wipe themselves out as well. This is the matrix imposed by the Well, the mathematical formulae of the Markovian computers, and *that* is what I came to decipher. With it I can adjust the superimposed mathematical building blocks just a tiny bit to suit myself. Obie could do no more than I, but he could do it over a planetary area. The individual Markovians, I believe, could do it even better, since it was matched to their brains specifically. But it is the Well that maintains this mathematically superimposed set. When Brazil turns it off, that set of mathematics will cease to exist. And, when he repairs it and turns it back on, he'll have to instruct it to build a new mathematical model. A new one. It'll be very much like the original, but it will differ in many specifics. It can't be as far-reaching, for example, since he'll have only 1,560 races here to work with. It'll also be formed from the power of his mind, and that will color it ever so slightly. It will be slightly different. *Very* slightly, perhaps one digit in a billion-place equation, but it *will* be different. He can't help it. Obie is part of the old math. So is the universe we knew—the Com, the stars and planets, the races out there."

"I think I understand you," Ortega put in. "Obie was built to cope with this superimposed set of rules, or math, or whatever you want to call it. So is everything we know—except the Well World, which is on a separate, model computer not affected. And Brazil is from the old math, the Markovian math, and Obie simply couldn't cope with him because he was slightly, ever so slightly, off, and that blew Obie's circuits."

Zinder nodded. "A tiny difference, but vital. He just couldn't cope with that difference. The same reason why Brazil can't really change his appearance once he sets it in the Well. He's not a part of the math of the known universe; he reverts always to form. We can't even kill him. There is always a way out provided by circumstance, which is another way of saying that the Well looks out for him. Only inside the Well can he die, since the Well was partly *designed* to change Markovians to the new mathematics."

"Do you think he'll kill himself?" Ortega asked. "I think I understand him now, a little. I've lived too long and I'm ready to go, but I couldn't bring myself to do it. Now I can, and it's a blessing and a relief. You can't believe the lack of a burden I feel. You *can* live too long, Doctor. Particularly when you can't change."

Zinder considered the question. "Will he kill himself? He's said so, many times. He's said that that's the only thing he *wants* to do. I think that's what Mavra Chang is there for—to receive the passing of the torch. She will go inside and be taught the workings of the Well, and it'll be matched to her. Once that happens and he checks her out on it, well, then he can die with a clear conscience. Somebody will be left to guard the truth, and instead of the Wandering Jew the new humans will have the mysterious, immortal woman."

"What a horrible fate," Ortega sighed.

"But it's of her own free will," Zinder pointed out. "When she tells him to turn off the machine, she takes full responsibility for the consequences, all of them. When she emerges, she'll be the only being *anywhere* left based on the present, rather than the new mathematics. She won't be able to be killed, or changed, and she'll be like that until she can turn it over to some wiser future race, if it ever arises, that again discovers the Well equations and does something with them other than destroy itself. If they *do* destroy themselves, some billions of years, perhaps, from now, she'll have the job of starting it all over again and maybe passing the torch herself at that point."

They thought about it, thought about the loneliness, the aimless wandering, without change, without end, the Well not even permitting madness. For a while she would enjoy it, of course, as Brazil must have, as Ortega had in his more limited yet no less oppressive self-exile. But, eventually, she would reach that point when she had lived too long, and she would *know*. "I don't think she realizes the devil's bargain she's making," he said sadly.

Zinder shrugged. "Does anyone? And can we go back and do it all again? Can I undo the damage to the universe? To the Well? No, I think not. Not any more than you can take back any of your crucial decisions." He paused. "I better go now. Yua must be told —and I want to be back by dawn."

Serge Ortega put out his hand and Zinder took it. "Until dawn, then, Gilgram Zinder. We shall meet, together, down there at the canal, eh?"

"At the canal," the other man agreed. "But not Doctor Gilgram Zinder, no, not now. Most of him died in Oolakash about nine hundred years ago. What little of him survived that event died with Nikki on Olympus and the rest with Obie on *Nautilus*. I'm just Gypsy, Ortega. That's the way I want it to be, and so that's who I am. I can be whoever and whatever I want."

"Wait! One more thing!" the Ulik almost shouted. "How will we know if we held long enough? Can you tell me that?"

Gypsy laughed. "If I'm here, you'll know for sure and in a very sudden and messy manner. If not—well, if you can last until night, and if it's clear and you're in position to see a little bit of the sky, you'll see the stars go out."

"But that's impossible!" Ortega protested. "Even if the universe goes out, it would be thousands of years before we'd know!"

"When he pulls that plug," Gypsy told them both, "the universe won't simply cease to be. For all practical purposes it will never have been. There never will have been those stars and dust to radiate that light. There'll be nothing but the dead Markovian universe —and the Well World. Nothing else will exist, will ever have existed, beside that."

It was a sobering thought.

"One last thing," Marquoz put in. "Did you tell Brazil who you were?"

Gypsy chuckled. "Nope. He fished for it, but he wouldn't tell me why a Markovian guardian should be a Jewish rabbi, so fair's fair." And he vanished.

"That's a good point," Ortega noted to nobody in particular. Finally he turned to Marquoz. "Since you're going to be here, you'll take command of the Verion side, I trust?"

Marquoz nodded. "It's all arranged. They're ready to fly me over whenever I'm ready."

For the second time that night Ortega extended his hand in firm comradeship and for the second time it was taken in the same spirit.

"Like with Gypsy," Ortega said. "We'll meet at the canal."

"At the canal," Marquoz agreed. "We'll be only thirty meters apart."

"We'll swim it," Ortega said warmly.

There was a loud explosion downstream, not at all near them, and lights went on farther down. There was some automatic-controlled fire, then everything winked off and there was silence.

"I'd better go," the Hakazit said, the echo of the explosion and shots still sounding up and down the canyon. He turned, then paused and looked back. "You know, wouldn't it be crazy if we won?"

Ortega laughed. "It'd louse up all this for sure."

Marquoz turned back and trudged off in the darkness. Ortega remained, sitting back on his tail and looking out into the darkness, settling down to wait for the dawn and trying, on occasion, to get a look at the obscured stars above.

# The Avenue, at the Equatorial Barrier

SERGE ORTEGA HAD BEEN AS GOOD AS HIS WORD. Although they had passed signs of fighting and occasional dead bodies of hapless patrols, no opposition faced them all the way up the Avenue. A few times they had almost fallen into the water from the unstable rock slides, but that had been the extent of the problem.

Mavra had never seen the Equatorial Barrier except from space, and now that it loomed over her she found it much less a dark wall than it looked from a distance. Partially translucent, it went up as far as the eye could see, a huge dam at the head of the river, which was merely a trickle at this point. She noticed that the area where the Avenue reached the wall was absolutely dry; obviously the only water here would be that which struck and ran down from the enormous barrier.

It looked like a giant nonreflecting shield of glass, not very thick and amazingly shiny and free of any signs of wear. It was only here, at the wall itself, that the true Avenue could be seen—shiny and smooth, like the barrier itself. Where it joined the wall there was no seam, no crack; the two simply merged.

It was near dusk of the second day, but even Brazil could not enter immediately. Using the Gedemondan, now their only companion, he told the other two, "We have to wait for midnight, Well time, or a little more than seven hours after sunset. That means we sit and wait."

Mavra relaxed and looked back up the canyon. "I wonder if they're still alive back there?" she mused aloud.

"Yeah," was all he could say in response. He didn't really want to betray the fact to anyone, least of all Mavra, but he was deeply and sincerely affected by the sacrifice those creatures of many races, some of whom meant a good deal to him by this time, were making. The war was more of a mass thing, an abstract thing, and there were many possibilities in a battle. You could win or lose, you could live or die, but you always had a chance. They hadn't had a chance and they knew it, yet they did it so that he could stand here.

His thoughts went back to Old Earth once again, to Masada in particular. He hadn't been there, hadn't really been very close to the place, but the history of the tremendous sacrifice they had put up, the miraculous amount of time they had held, and, in the end, their total commitment, which ordained death rather than surrender to tyranny, had uplifted him at a time when he had felt desolate and dispirited. If man had such a spirit, there was hope.

There were few such examples of that spirit, he reflected sadly. Few, but always one, always at a time when one would swear greatness was dead, the human spirit dead, and all was lost. This was such a moment now, he reflected. It might be a long, long time before such a thing happened again, but for the first time he found himself believing that it *would* happen again.

He was amazed by the thought, by his capacity to still think it after such a long, long time. Could it be, he found himself wondering, that *his* spirit wasn't dead, either?

He was amazed, too, that there was just the three of them. Just he, Mavra, and the Gedemondan they needed to speak to each other. He had offered it to more, to anybody who wanted to come, in fact. They had chosen to stay at the pass. Maybe they're the smart ones, he thought wistfully. At least they had the choice.

"What will happen when we . . . go in?" Mavra asked him, eying the seemingly solid, impenetrable wall again.

"Well, at midnight the lights will go on for this section," he told her. "Then this section around the Avenue will fade and you'll be able to walk through to it inside. Once in there, neither you nor the Gedemondan will change, but I will. The thing was designed for Markovians, so it'll change me into one. They're pretty ugly and gruesome, worse than most anything you've seen to date. Don't let it bother you, though. It'll still be me in there. After that, we take a ride down into the control room area, I'll make some adjustments to the Well World system to activate it once again and key the Call, then we'll go down and see just how bad the damage is."

"The Call?" she repeated.

He nodded. "The Call. Halving the populations of each hex, preparing the gateways, and impelling those we need to do the things we have to have done when we need them done. You'll see. It's not as complicated as it sounds."

"And what about us?" she asked. "What happens to us?"

"You're going to be a Markovian, Mavra," he told her. "It's necessary for several reasons, not the least of which is that the Well is keyed to the Markovian brain and it really is necessary to be a Markovian to understand what it is and what it's doing. It'll also give you the complete picture of what *you* will tell me to do. That's the worst thing, Mavra. You're going to know exactly what the effect of that repair will be—if it can be fixed. We won't know that until we're inside."

He didn't mention the Gedemondan, of course. He had no idea what he was going to do with the creature, but he would have to be disposed of fairly quickly or he would just get in the way. Obviously, when all was said and done, he deserved some kind of reward, but what he wasn't quite sure yet. Certainly the possibility of a Gedemondan with access to the Well didn't seem that appetizing.

It was quite dark now, and Mavra, gesturing to the Gedemondan, said to both of them, "Look! You can see the stars from here."

The other two looked up, and, sure enough, in the wide gap between the end of the cliffs and the Equatorial Barrier the swirls and spectacular patterns of the Well World sky were clearly visible. It was the most impressive sky of any habitable planet Brazil had known, the great nebulae and massive collection of gasses filling the sky. The Gedemondan did not look long, though; in the well-known psychological quirk of many races and people who were born and lived near stunning beauty, they had simply taken the scene for granted.

Nobody had a watch or any way of telling time now; they would just have to settle back and wait that eternal wait for the light to come on.

"Oh, hell, he decided. Might as well ask the Gedemondan straight out. "Communicator? What do you wish of all this? What shall I do for and with you?"

The Gedemondan didn't hesitate. "For myself, nothing, except to be returned to my people," he told the other. "For my people, I would wish that you examine why the experiment which succeeded here failed out there and make the necessary adjustments so that it at least has an even chance this next time."

Brazil nodded slowly. That sounded fair enough. He wondered about the creature, though, and whether or not it was entirely on the up-and-up. Quite often more than one race would wind up on a given planet once a pattern was established, occasionally by design because they might have something to contribute, occasionally by accident. The process just wasn't all that exact. The insectlike Ivrom, for example, had managed by accident or their own design to get a few breeders into Earth during the last time, and had become the basis for many of the legends of fairies, sprites, and other mischievous spirits. Some of the others, too; once Old Earth had had a colony of Umiau, what it called mermaids, on the theory that perhaps a second race could use the oceans as the main race used the land.

The Rhone—descendants of the original Dillian centaurs—had attained space flight at an early age. An exploratory group had crashed on Old Earth when the humans still thought it a flat land on the back of a giant turtle or somesuch, and they had managed to survive there, even be worshiped by some of the primitive humans as gods or godlike creatures. But they were too wise, too peaceful, for the rough primitivism of Earth; eventually they had been hunted down and finally wiped off the face of the planet. He himself had arranged to destroy their remains and wipe all but legend from the sordid history of what man did to the great centaurs, but when the Rhone, fallen back into bad times, first lost, then regained, space, and again probed the human areas, they had *known,* somehow, of the fate of those earlier explorers. Humans had appeared in their dreams, in their racial nightmares, long before lasting discovery, and it had kept them somewhat distant and apart from humanity even as they entered into a pragmatic partnership with it.

As for the Gedemondans, there were legends, both on the Rhone home world and on Old Earth, of huge humanoid, secretive creatures that lurked in the highest mountains and the most isolated wilderness, somehow avoiding technological man through his whole history except for brief glimpses, legends, half-believed tales. Were some of these, the Yeti, the Sasquatch, and others like them, truly the evolved descendants of some Gedemondans who had somehow gotten shifted to the wrong place? He couldn't help but wonder.

Time dragged for them, on the Avenue, at the Equator. More than once any of the three of them had the feeling that more than seven hours *must* have passed, that somehow they had either missed it, or this entryway wasn't working, or there was some other problem.

The waiting, Mavra decided, was the worst thing of all.

Suddenly the Gedemondan said, "I sense presences near us." He sounded worried.

Brazil and Mavra looked around, back into the darkness, but could see and hear nothing unusual. In both their minds was the fear that, now, at the last moment, the armed force would catch up to them, that Serge Ortega and his group had been unable to hold the Borgo Pass long enough.

The Gedemondan read their apprehension. "No.

Just three. They appear to be to our right. It is very odd. They seem to be inside the solid rock wall, coming toward us fairly fast."

Mavra's head jerked up. "It's the Dahbi!" she warned. "They can do that."

"That's twice I've underestimated that bastard," Brazil grumbled. "While Serge's people hold his army, Sangh goes around them in a way only he can. The force at the pass told him what he needed to know—we were here and on our way. At least he can't take any weapons on that route."

"He doesn't need them," she shot back. "Those forelegs are like swords and the mandibles are like a vise. And we don't have any weapons, either." She looked around. "Or anywhere to go."

"Except in," he sighed. "But we can't count on that."

The Gedemondan turned and stared at a rock wall not fifteen meters from where they stood. Slowly there was a brightening of the rock in three places. They watched in horrified fascination as three ghostly creatures oozed out of the solid rock, seemed to solidify, and stood there, a huge one in front, two slightly smaller in back, like ghastly sheets with two black ovals cut in them for eyes.

Brazil stared at them, fascinated. So those are Dahbi, he thought to himself. He remembered them now, vaguely. More legends and ancestral memory. And the big one in the middle had to be—

"Nathan Brazil, I am Gunit Sangh," said the leader. "I have come to take you back."

Brazil started to move forward to make connection with the Gedemondan so he could reply, but the Gedemondan ignored him and walked to only a few meters from the Dahbi leader.

"You've lost, Sangh," said the Gedemondan in almost perfect imitation of Brazil's accent and mannerisms. "Even if we went back with you now, our own forces are behind yours at the pass. *You* may go through walls, but you can't take me that way."

"I won't have to," Sangh replied confidently. "We shall go back with you as hostage and we shall walk right through that pass to my own forces, which, by that time, will have it secured. Then *we* need only hold it until the balance of my forces moves up to collect us. Your pitiful force in between can't hope to do much more. After all, look at how well your own small force has held the pass against us so far."

Both Mavra's and Brazil's heads came up at this. They had still been holding the pass!

"I stand here in front of the Well," the Gedemondan responded threateningly. "You know the rules, Sangh. I cannot be killed, and I do not wish to be taken."

"I weary of this," Gunit Sangh sighed irritably. "Take him!"

The two smaller Dahbi unfolded, showing their full, grim insectival forms. The effect was startling, particularly on Brazil, who had never seen it before.

The two moved on the Gedemondan, who stood firmly facing them. Sticky forelegs dripping some gruesome liquid reached out for the great white creature, and all along the legs flashed the natural sabers of the Dahbi. The foreleg of the one to the Gedemondan's left touched the creature, who reached over and grabbed it, unexpectedly, in his left hand. There was a brilliant flash of blue-white fire that seemed to envelop the Dahbi, a supernova that flared into momentary monumental brightness, then was gone.

Taking advantage of the stunned shock of the other, the Gedemondan already was turning, his right hand reaching out and taking hold of the other's foreleg before it could withdraw. Again the flare, again, when it suddenly faded, there was no sign of the Dahbi.

Gunit Sangh hadn't lived this long or gotten this far without guts and quick thinking. In a display of courage that rivaled his ferocity, his own foreleg lashed out and took the Gedemondan's head off with one swing.

The headless body spouted blood from the severed neck, which dyed the beautiful white fur, and it lurched forward as if with a will of its own as Sangh, moving with a speed that seemed impossible, retreated back out of the way of the decapitated thing.

The Gedemondan's arms reached out and it took one or two steps forward, then shuddered and toppled to the ground, where it twitched for a few moments, then lay still. Abruptly the stored energy in the body flared up, another brilliant nova, and then it was over. There was nothing left, nothing but the blood and the severed head, staring glassily from the Avenue floor.

Gunit Sangh was shaken, obviously, and a number of different ideas came rapidly through his mind at one and the same time. It was Brazil, but it was now dead, and Brazil couldn't die so it couldn't have been Brazil but if it wasn't, then who *was* Brazil . . . ?

He looked again at the Equatorial Barrier. Just two of the flying horses like the Agitar flew. What . . . ? And why two?

It struck him almost like a physical blow. Mavra Chang's catatonia, Brazil's comatose body, all the powers and magicians' tricks they had pulled.

And then Gunit Sangh laughed, laughed so loud it echoed up and down the canyon. Finally, he looked at the two flying horses and said, "Well, well. The *real* Nathan Brazil, I presume. And who's this with you? Not a genuine flying horse, I wouldn't think. No, could it be that I've also found the mysteriously missing Mavra Chang? Ah! A start of recognition! Yes, yes, indeed it is." And he laughed again. "I've won!" he cried. "All the way to the wire and I've won!"

Behind the two of them a light clicked on.

Sangh saw it and roared with sudden rage. He moved on them, and, almost reflexively, they edged back into the Equatorial Barrier; edged into it and passed through it, inside the Well of Souls before they even realized what happened.

"Not yet!" screamed Gunit Sangh. "Oh, no! Not yet!" and he started for the still-lighted barrier.

Suddenly there was the sound of hoofprints, like a horse charging up the canyon towards the Barrier. Sangh, started, stopped momentarily and turned his massive head to see what it was. He froze.

Glowing slightly like some ghostly, supernatural thing, a Dillian was bearing down on him, a Dillian holding a large, ornate sword in his right hand.

Sangh lashed out with his deadly forelegs but the sword penetrated, slicing through the giant Dahbi like a knife through butter. Sangh screamed in pain and fell, where it started to change, grow more opaque, as it sought its only natural avenue of escape.

The huge centaur laughed horribly, waved its sword, and instead of the weapon there was now a bucket in his hand, a bucket that sloshed with liquid. Sangh's head went up and he screamed, "No!" and then the contents were poured onto the Dahbi, half-sinking in the rock. Where the water struck, the form solidified once more into the brilliant off-white, and the Dahbi leader gave a choking gasp and fell victim to a vicious kick from the forelegs of the centaur that literally severed the Dahbi's body in two at the point where it was half in the rock, half out. It quivered a moment, then went still.

Without a pause, the centaur laughed in triumph and threw the bucket against the far wall, where it hit with a clanging sound, then dropped to the floor of the Avenue. With that, the apparition whirled and galloped back off down the chasm, back into the darkness, and was quickly gone.

Inside the Equatorial Barrier, Mavra stared back at the scene she had just witnessed.

"Speak now, if you wish," came Brazil's voice behind her, definitely his yet somehow oddly changed and magnified. "I can hear your directed thoughts."

"That—that was Asam!" she breathed. "But he's dead! He was killed in the battle. . . . They said . . ." She turned to face Brazil and stopped, gazing in horrid fascination. Brazil was no longer there.

In his place was a great, pulpy mass two and a half meters tall, looking like nothing so much as a great human heart palpitating with almost hypnotic regularity, a combination of blotched pink-and-purple tissue, with countless veins and arteries visible throughout its barren skin both reddish and blue in color. At the irregular top was a ring of cilia, colored an off-white, waving about—thousands of them, like tiny snakes, each about fifty centimeters long. From the midsection of the pulpy, undulating mass came six evenly spaced tentacles, each broad and powerful-looking, covered with thousands of tiny suckers. The tentacles were a sickly blue, the suckers a grainy yellow in color. An ichor seemed to ooze from pores in the central mass, thick and foul-smelling, which did not drip but, rather, formed an irregular filmy coating over the whole body with the excess reabsorbed by the skin.

"No, it wasn't Asam," Nathan Brazil told her, his voice seeming to emanate from somewhere inside that terrible shape. "It was simply justice. The Borgo Pass has held, and that freed an old friend of ours to look in on us from time to time."

She was unable to take her eyes off the terrible thing that now stood with her; but she was able to control her revulsion by strong self-will.

"It was Gypsy," she realized.

"But he looked like Asam to Gunit Sangh," Brazil noted with satisfaction. "It was the way he *should* have died."

"And a good thing, too," she noted. "He almost had us, here, right at the end."

"No he didn't," Brazil told her. "He'd lost as it was. He just didn't notice it. Hard as it is to believe, Mavra, it still isn't time for the Barrier to open up as yet. There was a—malfunction, let's call it. A convenient malfunction, when I was trapped by a deadly enemy. The Well takes care of its own, Mavra, always. Even when you don't want it to. And once inside here, I am invulnerable."

She looked up at him and he could feel her disgust at the shape and form, her revulsion at the horrible smell, like rotting carrion. "*That's* what the Markovians were like?" she managed. "The fabled gods, the utopian masters of creation? Oh, my God!"

He chuckled. "You've seen enough alien forms on this world and in the universe to know that mankind is neither unique nor particularly the model for creation. The Markovians evolved naturally, under a set of conditions far different than man's, far different than most of the races' of our universe. What is horrible to you was very practical to them. By their standards I'm tall, dark, and handsome."

"It would be easier if you didn't stink so much," she told him.

"What can I do?" he replied in a mock hurt tone. "Well, let's get this show on the road. If you got the guts, you'll come to think of this smell as exotic perfume."

"I doubt that," she muttered, but when he started off, using the tentacles as legs, she followed, marveling at the ease and surity of his movements in that form.

"Although the Markovians may look strange, even repulsive, they were our kin in more ways than spiritually," Brazil noted as they went along. "This form breathes an atmosphere compatible with what you're used to. The balance is a little off, but not so much as you'd expect. And the cellular structure, the whole organism, is carbon-based and works pretty much like the other carbon-based organisms we know so well. It eats, sleeps, even goes to the bathroom just like all the common folk, although sleeping's not mandatory at this stage. They outgrew it and acquired the ability for a selective shut down, which did the same thing. At least, they were biologically enough like us to be consistent with what we know of lifeforms everywhere. They don't break any laws."

He stepped onto a walkway on the other side of a meter-tall barrier. When he was certain she followed, he struck the side of the barrier with a tentacle and the walkway started to move. As they were carried along, the light behind them went out and the light in their area and immediately ahead switched on.

"This is the walkway to the Well Access Gate," he told her. "In the early days a shift would come on and off at each Avenue every day. The workers and technicians would come in as we are now and go down to their assigned places. Near the end, when only the project coordinators were left, they limited access to midnight at each Avenue and then only for a short time, mostly to allow the border hexes to get on with their own growth and development. The entrances were later keyed only to the project coordinators, themselves gone native, so that nobody could run back in with second thoughts. The last time I was here I rekeyed them to respond only to me, since it was theoretically possible for somebody to solve the puzzle of the locks."

They moved on in eerie silence, lights suddenly popping on in front of them, out in back of them, as they traveled. The walkway itself glowed radiantly as far as she could see, although no light source was visible. She noticed that the walkway was speeding up and that they were now heading down as well as forward, down into the depths of the planet. Then it opened into a chamber, dimly lit, and below them was a great hexagon outlined in light.

"That's the Well Access Gate," he told her. "One of six, really. It can take you any place you want to go within the Well. We're going to the central control area and monitoring stations. I have to check on things first of all, see if everything will work as planned, and, of course, see just how badly damaged the Well really is by all this. Maybe, just maybe, Obie was wrong and we won't have to do anything really drastic after all."

He stepped off the walkway when it reached the hexagon and walked into its area. She hesitated a moment, then followed him. All light vanished and there was the uncomfortable sensation of falling for a moment, then the whole world was abruptly flooded with bright light, and she was back on solid flooring again.

It was a huge chamber, perhaps a kilometer in diameter, semicircular, the ceiling curving up and over them almost the same distance as it was across the room. Corridors, hundreds of them, led off in all directions. The Gate was in the center of the dome, and Brazil quickly stepped off, Mavra following, nervous that if she remained much longer, the thing could zap her to some remote part of this complex where she would never be found.

Walls, ceiling, even the floor, all appeared to be made of tiny hexagon-shaped crystals of polished white mica that reflected the light and glittered like millions of tiny diamonds.

Brazil stopped and pointed a tentacle back over the Gate. Suspended by force fields, about midway between the Gate and the apex of the dome, was a huge model of the Well World, turning very, very slowly. It had a terminator, and darkness on half its face, and seemed to be made of the same stuff as the walls, although the hexagons on the model were very large and there were dark areas at the poles and a dark band around the equator. The sphere was covered with a thin, transparent shell that also seemed segmented, its clear hexagons matching those below.

"It doesn't look as pretty as the real thing does from space," Mavra commented, "but its impressive all the same."

"You can see the slight difference in reflected light on each hex," he pointed out. "That's Markovian writing. Numbers, really, from 1 to 1,560, in base-6 math, of course. The numbers aren't in any logical order, though, since over a million races, at the outside, were created here and only the last batch, the final 1,560, remain, the leftover prototypes. As soon as one was cleared it would be completely stripped and then rebuilt to the new project and assigned a new number from the cleared hexes in order of new activation. That's how Glathriel can be number 41 and Ambreza, right next to it, 386. It's sloppy, but, what the hell, it wasn't important."

"It's quite impressive and decorative," she commented approvingly.

He chuckled. "Oh, that's not just decoration. That's it. That's the brain that runs the Well World. The working model for the Well of Souls. It's the heart of the whole thing, really, since it's also the main power source to the Well and supplies the basic equations needed to operate properly. In a sense, it's a giant computer program. It draws its power from a singularity that extends all the way into an alternate universe. If the Well's beyond a quick fix, what we'll have to do is disconnect the Well of Souls from that device, which will not affect the Well World but which will have the effect of clearing the programming completely from the Well of Souls itself. Then, when we hook it back up again, it'll get the message as if new data. Since it's a slow, progressive feed, as the program reaches the damaged area it will halt and wait while emergency programs go into effect to repair or replace whatever's needed."

"You can't selectively shut it off, say, to the damaged areas?" she asked hopefully.

"Nope. Oh, it's a good idea, and, I guess, theoretically possible, but we'd need the whole Markovian computer staff here to do it. It would mean completely reprogramming the Well of Souls—that is, writing a new program for it. You can do that with the Well World but not with the big computer, since they never thought it would have to be done twice in the universe, after all."

"So what we're going to do, then, is more or less go back in time, recreating the conditions that existed just before the big computer was activated, then essentially repeat what they did," she said, trying to get it straight.

"Right. And the self-repair and correcting circuits will then go to work on the damage. They were put there because nobody really knew if the Well was 100 percent, whether or not they hadn't made some mistakes, design or construction errors, things like that. So the program is self-correcting; when it hits a section that isn't right, it alters or changes it so that it *is* correct."

"So what do we do first?" she asked him.

He chuckled. "First we go down that corridor there. There's a central control room not far—all those corridors lead to loads of control rooms, one for each race sent out from here—a *lot* more than 1,560, I might add." He led the way, and again she followed.

They came to a hexagonal doorway that irised open, and a light switched on within. Inside was some sort of control room, filled with switches, knobs, levers, buttons, and the like, and what looked like a large black projection screen. Enormous dials and gauges registered she knew not what; there was no way to tell what any of the things did.

A tentacle went out and touched a small panel on a control console, activating what appeared to be a screen but what was a recessed tunnel, oval in shape, stretching back as far as the eye could see, a yellow-white light covered with trillions of tiny black specks. Frantic little bolts of electricity, or something like it, shot between all of them, creating a furious energy storm, a continuous spider's web of moving energy.

"Let's get you squared away first," Brazil muttered. There was suddenly the sound of a great pump or some kind of relay closing, then opening, from deep within the planet and all around her. It sounded almost like the beating heart of some enormous beast.

"I'm just bringing the power up," he told her. "Don't be alarmed. The dials, switches, and such over there are main controls for the mechanisms. Minor stuff like this I can do without any sort of controls, although we'll need some when the power's cut. Okay, that ought to do it."

There was a steady, omnipresent *thump-thump, thump-thump* through the control room.

"Okay, main control room up to full power," he muttered, mostly to himself. "Activate . . . now!"

The world seemed to explode all around her. Vision expanded to almost 360 degrees, hearing, smell, all the senses flared into new intensity such as she had never known before. She could feel and sense the energies all around her, feel the enormous power surges that were suddenly so real they took on an almost physical form, as if she could just reach out and take hold of them, bend them any way she wanted. It was a tremendous, exhilarating, heady feeling, a rush of strength and power beyond belief. She was Superwoman, she was a goddess, she was supreme. . . .

She looked at Brazil with her new senses and saw no longer the ugly, misshapen creature he had become but a shining beacon of almost unbearable light, a towering figure of almost unbearable beauty and strength and power.

She reached out to him not with any part of her body but with her mind, and he seemed to extend the same, a flow of sentient energy, of something, that met hers and merged with it.

And then she recoiled from it, or tried to, for a brief moment. For the first sensations she had received from him had been not of a godlike creature, which he undeniably was, but instead of an incredible, deep, aching loneliness that hurt so terribly it was almost unbearable. Pity overwhelmed her, and she grieved that such greatness should be in such misery and pain. The depth of its misery was fully as terrible as was his godlike greatness and power. It was so great that she feared to reach out again, to make more contact, lest such agony destroy her. She wept for Nathan Brazil then, and in that weeping she finally grasped his essential tragedy.

"Don't be afraid," he said gently, extending himself once again. "I have it more under control now. But you *had* to know. You *had* to understand."

Hesitantly she reached out once again, and this time it was more bearable, suppressed from the direct contact of her mind and his. But it was far too much a part of him to be banished completely; it permeated his very being, the core of his soul, and even its shadow was almost too much.

And now he started to talk. No, not talk, transfer. Transfer data to her, directly, at the speed of his thought, registering the accumulated knowledge of Nathan Brazil on the operation of The Well of Souls, the Markovian physics, the experimental histories, everything about the Markovian society, project, and goals. And she realized what he had done to her, realized now, for the first time, that she, too, was a Markovian, and, in pure knowledge of the Well, his equal. Knowledge, yes, but not in experience, never in experience. For the experience was intertwined with the excruciating agony he suffered, and that he protected her from as best he could.

Finally, it was over, and he withdrew from her. She was never sure how long it had taken; an instant, a million years, it was impossible to say. But now she knew, knew what he faced, knew what she faced, and knew just exactly what to do. She realized, too, that in order to make her a Markovian he had fed her directly into the primary computer, the master computer program itself. She was like him, now, and would be unless she, herself, erased that data from the Markovian master brain.

"I want you to spend a little time here before we proceed," he told her. "I want you to check on the control rooms, read them off, take a look at the Well of Souls and its products. Before the plug is pulled, you must know what you are destroying."

She knew the controls, now, knew how to use them and how to switch them from one point to another. Slowly, together, they examined the universe.

The machinery was incredible, and matched to her new Markovian brain with its seemingly limitless capacity for data and its lightning-fast ability to correlate it, it was easy to survey the known and unknown. Time lost its meaning for her, and she understood that it really had no meaning anyway, not for a Markovian. The very concept was nothing more than a mathematical convenience applicable only to some localized areas for purposes of measurement. It had no effect, and therefore no meaning, to either of them, not now.

She saw races that looked hauntingly familiar, and races that were more terribly alien than anything she had ever known or experienced. She saw ones she know, too: the Dreel who had started all this and humanity, the Rhone, the Chugach, and all the others. There were others, too, an incredible number of others, so many individual sentient beings that numbers became meaningless in that context.

But they were life. They were born and they grew and learned and loved, and when they died they left a legacy to their own children and they to theirs. Legacies of greatness, legacies of decline and doom, things both wonderful and horrible and often both at the same time. What she was seeing was the history and legacy of Markovian man.

But there were areas around the central control room of the human hexes that were mostly destroyed or burned out. Other sections had switched to try and handle, maintain the load, but it was too much of a strain on them and they, too, were burning out, only to increase the load on still others. There was a cancer in the Well of Souls beyond its ability to halt, and it was growing. As it grew, so did the rent in space-time, faster now, ever faster. She realized, idly, that the area of space from whence she came would be gone in a relative moment, and then it would spread even further, ever further.

And, she realized, Obie had been right. As sections maintaining other parts of the universe had to carry the increased load against the soaring tide of nothingness, their increasing burdens made failures occur ever more quickly, in dangerous progression.

The Well could kill or cure the universe, but it could not save itself. Right now almost a sixth of the Well's active control centers were destroyed, burned out, shorted beyond repair. When it reached a third of the Well's capacity, it would be beyond the ability of the Well to maintain the damaged parts; it would go crazy trying, though, and the entire thing would short out, beyond repair. It needed help, and it needed it quickly, or it could not survive. In a sense it was a living organism of its own, she understood, and the cancer was creeping rapidly toward its heart. The final burnout would trigger a protective shutdown by the master program and power source to save itself, but that would be too late, beyond the capacity of the smaller device to repair or replace. There would be *only* the Well World left in the whole universe, it and nothing else, forever.

But she understood Brazil, too. That deep torment in which he lived, a god forever cut off from communion with his own kind, for he was unique in the entire universe, perhaps in all the universes there might be, doomed to walk the Earth and stars as a man who could never die, never change, never find any sort of companionship, yet a man, also, who felt he had a sacred trust.

Moreover, inside here he could feel and see and know those countless numbers of sentient beings whose entire history would be wiped out, who, if repairs were done, would be not even a memory but wiped out as if they had never existed at all, save in the memories of those Entries on the Well World and in her mind and his.

"This isn't the first time this has happened, is it?" she asked him.

"No, it's not," he admitted. "Three times that I know of. Can you understand how terribly hard it is now for me to pull that plug?"

"Three times . . ." she repeated, wonderingly. Three times into the Well of Souls, three times massacring so many, many innocents who had done nothing wrong but live.

"And it was you all three times?" she asked him.

"No," he replied. "Only the last time. I was born on a world now dead and to a people now dead beyond any memory, but it was much like Old Earth. It was a theocratic group, a group that lived its religion and its faith, and suffered for it in the eternal way in which such people are made to suffer by others. I grew up in it and became a cleric myself, a religious teacher and expert, a religious leader, you might say. I was pretty famous for it, among my own people. I had a wife, and seven children, three boys and four girls—Type 41 humans, all, no funny forms.

"Well, another religion grew up near by, and it had a convert-by-force philosophy, and since by that time society was highly technological and advanced in those ways, we were tracked down when that technocratic faith took over our own land, tracked down and made to convert or die. Even though their religion was a variant of our own, they didn't trust us. We were small, clannish, secretive, and we didn't even solicit converts. We were handy. We were weak and fairly affluent, convenient scapegoats for a dictatorial society.

"They came for me and my family one night, when they felt very secure. I was the leader, after all. I had little forewarning, but managed, by sheer luck—good or bad is up to you—to not be at home that night. They took my wife and children, and they put out a call to me: I could betray my people and my faith, or my family would be worse than killed. They would be given brainwipes and then handed over as playthings for the ruling families. There were no guarantees for me if I surrendered, or them, either, but also no way to free them. I got out, went into the desert wilderness, became something of a hermit, although I did channel refugees from my people, the ones who could get out, to various safe havens."

"With that kind of reasoning, I'm surprised you didn't plot revenge," she commented.

He laughed sourly. "Revenge? You can take revenge against a single individual, even against a group, but how do you do it against the majority of the world? Oh, I hated them, all right, but the only real revenge I could take was to keep my people and my faith alive through those terrible times, try and have a historical revenge, you might say, upon them.

"And, one night, while checking out some routes across that desert, I stopped at an oasis up against the side of a cliff and saw something I considered impossible."

"What?" she prompted.

"A centaur, half man, half horse, sneaking down from a cave to drink. Now, understand, this was at a technological stage where I was having to beat helicopter searches, radar, mind probes, and all that, and where colonies had been established on both moons and the nearest planet. Well, he spotted me, and instead of hiding or charging me he called out to me, called my own name! He knew me, even if I had never seen the likes of him before. He told me he was from another, alien civilization far off among the stars, and that that civilization no longer existed. He was the last of his kind. He was the first to tell me of the Markovians, of the Well World, and of the Well of Souls computer. He had quite a setup there, too, I'll tell you, a technological haven carved inside that desert mountain.

"He knew a lot about me, He had monitored me, it seemed, for some time, for reasons of his own, which I didn't then understand. He told me that, through an experimental accident, the entire universe was in danger of total and complete destruction and that he needed help to avert that. He'd chosen me for the task."

"Why you? A religious leader on the run?"

Brazil chuckled. "Well, for one thing he was able to

show me books, alien books, from three or four different civilizations. He had a learning machine that taught me those languages—you're familiar with the type if not the actual device. And, as I read them, books from nonhuman civilizations out among the stars my own people had not yet reached, I realized something almost stunning. I was reading paraphrases or alien adaptations of my own holiest writings, those of my basic religion. Oh, the details were all different, of course, but the basic truths were there, the basic concept of a single, monotheistic God, of the creation and many of the laws. All four had what could be easily translated as the Ten Commandments, almost in the same order, although the stated means of giving them was different. I realized in an instant what he was saying to me by all this."

She didn't follow. "What?"

"That there was something of a universal religion," he replied, "a set of basic beliefs and concepts so close in principles that they simply could not have been evolved independently by so many different races. The centaur himself was a follower of such a similar faith, and it was the similarity with my own, of which I was the supreme surviving authority, that drew him to me. You see?"

She still hesitated. "But . . . you said the repairs had been done *three* times before. How could such a religion pop up this time again?"

"You see the point, then. It couldn't—unless, perhaps, there was at its core a basic truth. Well, with that, I could hardly refuse him anything, and what he wanted was someone to come to the Well, where we are now, and help him pull the plug and start it again. Since it's something of a mental exercise, he wanted someone who shared his own basic philosophical precepts, since some of those, too, would color what went on. Well, of course, that was part of the point. He tricked me, the bastard."

"Huh?"

"He was the sentinel, the heir to the project manager. I don't know if he *was* a project manager or not, or whether, like me, he'd been tricked in the remote past, but what he wanted wasn't an assistant. You see, now that the program is completely stored, it only requires one to direct the reset, although two are maybe a little handier. He put me through, with a lot less preparation than you've had in your life, and then he erased himself from the program. He stuck me with the job and then killed himself!"

She felt some uneasy stirrings, recalling Gypsy's own predictions about Brazil and herself. But instead of voicing them right now she asked, "And what happened after that?"

"Well, I completed the job, closed up shop, and suddenly realized that I knew very little of what was going on, really. So I went home, to Earth, and when the time was right I presented—mostly through trickery, I'm ashamed to admit—my ancient faith to twelve tribes of related people. It was the right decision. Out of that faith grew many of the rest of that world's religions and its codes. I gave 'em the rules. I'll admit that, in the main, they didn't obey those rules any better than the people of my own world had, but they had them and it was, overall, a good thing. The spin-off religions alone were pivotal in our people's history. Islam saved scholarship and the greatness of the ancients from a barbaric world; Christianity kept a cultural darkness from being total and retained a sense of unity that outlasted the bad times and spread to the four corners of the Earth. My new people, unfortunately, suffered the same way as my old had. Persecuted, made scapegoats, they nonetheless kept faith and tradition alive through it all. They came out a hell of a lot better than my last group, too, in the end."

"Brazil?" she began hesitantly. "You say the mental exercise colors the newly created places. Couldn't that be explained by the *last* one to do this having that religion, and putting it, without realizing it, into the collective unconscious of the created races?"

"It could be," he admitted. "I've occasionally thought about it. But it couldn't hurt to believe otherwise, either, could it? Or, perhaps, that's God's way of insuring continuity through all this."

"Somehow I never thought of you as a man of

God," she commented. "And I seem to remember that you told my grandparents you *were* God."

"I have a knack," he told her, "of having people take seriously anything I say if I say it seriously enough myself. And I am a compulsive liar."

"Then how do I know that all that you just told me is true?" she asked playfully. "Maybe *that* was the lie to remove from my thoughts any suspicion you might just be God."

"You'll never really know, will you?" he taunted. "I don't worry about it. People believe what they want to believe, anyway."

"Brazil? Are you going to wipe yourself off the program? Are you going to kill yourself and leave me to take over? Gypsy said as much."

He paused a long while before replying. "That *was* my original intention, if you wanted it," he admitted hesitantly. "Believe me, I want to die. You cannot believe how much I want to die."

"I think I can," she responded kindly. "I felt it at the beginning, remember?"

"You *can't* know, really know," he insisted. "You touched only the surface and have no concept of the depth. No, what I was originally going to do was to tell you all this and then let you decide for yourself whether to take the job, knowing that eventually you'll die a million deaths inside but never die yourself. But now, I'm not so sure. What's another few million years at this stage of the game? I looked into you, Mavra, far more deeply than you have looked into me. You don't have the practice to do it like I do. And the more I looked, the more I realized that you were the best qualified person I knew to take over—the best qualified, but, almost for that reason, I can't do it. I can't condemn you to that loneliness. I just can't do it to someone else, damn it!"

She looked at the strange shining creature with renewed interest and curiosity, almost wonder. "You've never really lost it, have you? Not deep down, you haven't. You're very tired, Nathan, and you've been horribly hurt by all this, but, deep down inside there's still a fire going in that spirit of yours. You still be-

*lieve* in something, in your old ideals. You still believe it's possible for people to reach God, a God you very much believe in even if you're not God himself."

"I'll only tell you this," he responded seriously. "There is something beyond all that we can see, all that we know, something that survives beyond the Well of Souls. Perhaps it's in another parallel universe, perhaps it's all around us but unseen, like the Markovian primal energy. But it's there, Mavra, it's there. Three Gedemondans laid hands on us and our minds went into those of beasts. That's impossible under even these rules, Mavra. *What* got transferred? Whatever it was, it's the only important part of either of us, and it was absolute enough that the Well has twice recognized me as who I am despite both times being in the body of an animal. Can you quantify it, identify it, even here, inside the Well, in Markovian form? Can you see it, see it shining brightly, as I see it in you? What is it? The soul? What's 'soul' but a term for describing that which we can now recognize, and which others throughout time have recognized occasionally but never been able to pin down? What rules do these parts of us obey? Do they die when our bodies die, snuffed out like candles? Ours certainly didn't. Your body is dead, mine probably is. It makes no difference."

"Do you know the answer?" she asked him.

"Of course not, for I have never died," he replied. "And it looks like another long time before I will."

She hesitated before going on. "Nathan, if you want to go, I'll do it. I'll take the responsibility from you. You're free as of this moment. For the first time in your life, Nathan, you're free."

He took that in for a brief moment, then answered, "No, Mavra. I am not free. I'm not free because you were right a moment ago. God help me, I still care!" He paused. "Shall we pull the plug?"

"We must," she responded. "You know it."

"Before we do, I'm going to try something that worked last time," he told her. "It's obvious there are a lot more races than hexes. We might be able to salvage most of them, at least to the same degree that we're doing here. Some won't survive, of course, either because of the damage or because of miscalculation, the laws of physics, or a lot of other things, but there's a chance. It worked last time. It might work again, particularly for those races with some space capabilities."

They went back to the control room and he made a number of adjustments. She didn't realize what he was doing at first, but as she watched she understood.

"We can't do it without souls, Mavra," he reminded her. "We got to have something to work with."

*Slowly, out in space, across the limitless reaches of the universe, the Well Gates came on—came on and, more, started to move. Great, yawning, hexagonal shapes of blackness lifted off their native worlds, lifted off and rose into space. They had but two dimensions, discontinuities in the fabric of reality, for their depth was here, at the other end, at the Well Gate.*

"Timing will be critical," he reminded her. "I'm setting them up as best I can so they'll hit equally, but I can only stall this end for a few seconds at best. When I give you the word, you must pull the plug. Understand?"

She understood now. Understood a great deal. Understood how so many races could have survived this before, understood how a number of races could wind up mixed on the same world. It would be impossible to achieve perfection.

The gates moved into their respective positions. Not all could be used, of course, but there would be enough, enough, if all went right. He would still lose some races, still lose some whole civilizations and ideas forever, but he could save a great many of them.

After a while—who knew or could tell if it was a few minutes, a few centuries?—he said, "All in position. Best I could do. We're going to lose a few thousand civilizations, damn it, but that's better than all of them. I'm moving in, now, moving on the nearest inhabited planet in each region."

On a million different worlds, a million races were startled by the small yawning blackness that descended on their worlds out of the sky, a blackness

that was complete, absolute, and resisted any attempts
to harm it, to blow it up. There was panic, then, only
heightened by what the yawning hexagon did once it
touched their worlds. It started to move, rapidly, almost impossibly fast, too fast to do anything about,
swallowing people wholesale.

"They're in! Holy shit! What a headache I'm getting! Can't hold off the Well Gate much longer. Damn
it! Not enough! Not every race got enough through!
Shit! I'll have to let go. For God's sake, Mavra, pull
the plug now!"

A thought, an impulse, a single exact, deliberate
mathematical command went out. She did it, she, herself, alone. She killed them all—all except the ones on
the Well World and the ones caught in transit.

Across the night side of the Well World, people
would look up at the stars and see a wondrous sight.
The great, brilliant, wondrous starfield that was the
night sky simply flickered, then winked out. There was
only blackness where it had been, a blackness as absolute as anyone had ever seen.

It was reported from one end of the Well World to
the other, told and retold, and the nervous panic began.

Brazil has reached the Well of Souls. The stars have
gone out.

Some died by their own hand, some went mad, but
most simply watched and waited and stared at the horrible empty sky, the lonely, desolate nothingness that
surrounded them and seemed almost to close in on
them.

At both North and South Zone, the Well Gate
ceased to operate. Seals that none had ever known
were there slid automatically into place, suddenly and
abruptly. Many were trapped inside and could only
wait it out. Those who knew quickly threw up additional guards around their hex Zone Gates lest anyone
be lost. For you would not go to Zone through those
gates, not while the Well Gates were shut. They were
being diverted, the Well Gate itself reversed. Anyone
going through a Zone Gate now would never see the
Well World again.

But also, those in the various hexes, North and South, particularly those who ruled, knew they had a deadline, that they had to provide roughly half their populations for that Gate, and that if they did not, the Gates would move and do it for them, indiscriminately. The message was now out, automatically, to all the creatures of the Well World, a message that, until this day, they had believed a meaningless, mythical, or archaic phrase, but a message they all now well understood.

It was Midnight at the Well of Souls.

# The Well of Souls

"I'M SURPRISED THERE'S STILL AIR AND LIGHT IN here," Mavra commented.

"What did you think—that they built this thing in a vacuum?" he retorted. "In order to construct the Well they had to have light and heat and air. It comes with the rest of the planet. But the computer is definitely shut down now, and so are the Well Gates. Nobody in or out. The Zone Gates now take you directly to the Well Gate, one way."

"How many people do you think we trapped in there?"

He laughed. "Mostly Olympians, I'd say, who know what's going on, and maybe some odd guards, patrols, and the like. Maybe even a couple of ambassadors, huh? Scared shitless at the moment, probably."

"Isn't it going to get awfully crowded in there when the others start going through the Zone Gates?" she asked him. "I mean, the Well Gates are big places, but they couldn't possibly hold the huge numbers going through."

"They won't have to," he assured her. "They'll be hung up, like those billions we kidnapped a few minutes ago, waiting until there's an outlet. It's pretty confusing, I admit, but, damn it, the system was set up to populate one world at a time. It was never designed to do what we're doing to it. That's why we'll get *mostly* the population we want on the world we want, but some of the others will get through as well. That's how half the creatures in Old Earth's mythologies got in there to begin with. Don't worry. They're not properly designed for those worlds and eventually they get eliminated, one way or another—at least, I think most of them do. Never *was* sure. Well, we have a long job ahead of us, anyway. Might as well relax and do the best we can."

She looked around at the controls, gauges, even the huge chambers with the countless black-dot relays. There was no energy, no power there. It was gone, except for the system of the Well World, which drew its power and maintained itself by grabbing the energy absorbed by a black hole in some other universe, a very tiny black hole, she noted.

She wondered often about that other universe. Did it have a naturally evolved group of lifeforms? Did it have its own Markovians and its own version of the Well of Souls? There was no way to know, she realized. No way to ever know. Anyone who fell into a black hole here—when there were black holes again —would come out there, of course, but they would hardly be in any physical condition to see what was going on.

It was unfortunate, in a way, that there was no way of knowing. With all this new power and knowledge, the only two mysteries left to her would be parallel universes and Nathan Brazil. But then, she reflected, there *should* be some mysteries left in the world.

"How long will the complete job take?" she asked him.

"Six days," he responded, as if it were obvious. "Well World time, of course, which is the only time we got right now."

She thought back to their past experiences. "Ortega . . . Gypsy . . . Marquoz . . . I wonder if any of them are still alive."

"We'll never know," he told her. "As the experience of the past few months should tell you, it's not good to hang around and be known on the Well World. You have to let 'em go a couple of hundred thousand years so they forget who and what you are, what they are, and all the rest. That way they don't know you when you show up again. Nope, you take yourself out there, in the new universe, and you settle down, and you relax—until you're needed again. And you forget yourself, after a while. The Markovian brain remembers all of it, but that's only here, in the Well. Otherwise you just don't have the capacity, unless they evolve into it or build it. It's a mercy, really, as you'll see."

She thought about it. "You know, there are two of us. We could remain Markovians, this time."

"That's no good," he told her. "Not for us, not for everywhere else. A god gets bored and alienated even more than a human being does. And we can't reproduce, so there would be just the two of us, playing some kind of monster god game or living on some Markovian world dreaming up new exercises for our minds and going batty like they did. Be my guest, if you want, but it's more interesting the other way. It's your choice, though. You can erase yourself, put yourself in any body on any world you want either as a Markovian prototype or, by going through the Well Gate, as one of these mere mortals. Me, I'll stick with our people. They got so many interesting untapped *possibilities.*"

"The ones we send out from here," she said, "will be mostly our people, volunteers or Olympians who know what they're getting into. Those others, though, the ones we kidnapped off those worlds just before the plug was pulled, the ones now hung up in Well World limbo, they're just suddenly going to wake up on a primitive, alien world, cold and mysterious, naked and without any tools or weapons."

"They'll make it," he assured her. "Most of them, anyway. They did it before, they'll do it again. It's a pretty stubborn set of races those Markovians bred. After all this time I find I still like them, for the most part."

"Even the Dahbi?"

"Gunit Sangh was the pure dark side that lives within all of us," he told her. "But he wasn't the Dahbi, just *a* Dahbi. We had our own share of those type. You never met an Adolf Hitler or Dathan Hain. Hardly good examples of our race, but I wouldn't condemn everybody on the basis that we produced a lot of superstinkers." He paused. "You ready for the first step?"

"I'm ready," she told him seriously. "I still don't see how this can be done in six days, though. I admit I never had any formal education, but I *do* know it takes billions of years to do what we're doing."

"Billions of years for *them*," he replied. "Six days for us. Just watch. There's *nothing* out there now. Absolutely *nothing*. Not a single speck. No matter, no energy except the primal energy at total rest. That means, too, there's no space, time, or distance."

"The Markovian worlds with their Gates are still there," she pointed out.

"Well, that's true, but they have no sun, no warmth, nothing. They exist in nothingness, and will until we fix it."

"I know the procedure, thanks to you," she told him, "but I'm still unclear as to exactly what we do."

"You do this," he told her, and reached out for the master control. "Let there be light!" he commanded with a laugh.

Energy flowed once more from the tiny programming unit suspended above the control room entry hall. It flew to the Well of Souls computer and began its reset activation.

Far out in space, billions of light-years from the Well World, a hole was punched. A great black hole from some other universe, the greatest of all black holes that universe had, suddenly found an outlet. A singularity of immense proportions was created, and the accumulated material it had swallowed and continued to swallow, including light itself, burst through from that universe into that of the Well.

Nature reacted as it must; the static universe moved to close the hole, to plug it up quickly, but the Well of Souls now beat into renewed life. It reached out without regard for space or time and seized on the erupting white hole, keeping it open, allowing it to expand and grow. The effect was the greatest explosion possible in physics.

"Whew! A whole hell of a lot farther away than last time," Brazil noted. "Too bad. The Well World will continue to have a black sky. Well, you gotta take the white hole where you find it, and where the fabric is weakest, which is one and the same thing. Won't make any difference to the rest, though, except it might be a little nicer. Won't be much in the way of Markovian Gates in the neighborhood for quite a while. Well, we can relax now. We have to wait for all the usual natural processes to take place. Wow! That's a beauty, though! Look at those energy gauges! Bigger and nastier by far than the last one! We're gonna have a rip-roaring new universe here!"

Little time passed for them inside the Well, for time had hardly any meaning there. The Well World was being kept separate, apart from the rest of the universe as it always had been. The rest of the Markovian universe, too, went along at the old rate and would continue to do so until they slowed everything to match Markovian time.

They checked on the Well, saw that special circuits were already modifying, changing, repairing, even rebuilding damaged sections. They had been in time.

An hour passed. Half a billion years passed. It was all the same thing. The universe expanded. Tremendous gases and other material continued to spin out, swirling as it did so from the forces at the vortex of the big bang.

Twelve hours passed. Six billion years passed. It was all the same thing. Expansion continued. Cooling and congealing continued, even accelerated. Galaxies were forming, and inside those galaxies stars and even planets. The process continued on.

Brazil idly flicked a control. The time rate slowed. By the end of the day it was down to a very small length of time, relatively speaking: barely a few million years an hour.

On the second day he singled out the target worlds and started adjusting the processes by which life would form. The proper conditions were established for life, and on the third day, slowing time even more, he energized those elements, not merely on the planets he was going to use but on all those other worlds as well, worlds which, formed naturally, were good havens for life of one form or another but for which he had no people.

Time slowed more on the fourth day. The amino acids, the crystalline structures, the building blocks of lifeforms North and South on the Well World formed; the carbon-based in the sea while plants now ruled the land, what there was of it.

On the fifth day he slowed the rate still more, with Mavra's assistance, and activated secondary lifeform programming. Animal life appeared, first in the sea, then on the land, all in its proper evolutionary order, all stemming from the single, inevitable first cause.

And they looked at the millions of worlds and saw that they had done it right. It was working—not 100 percent, but more than enough for their needs. They spent most of the time doing this checking, using the Well computer itself to match worlds to lifeforms. A very few couldn't be exactly matched, and that bothered them, Brazil in particular.

"The Gedemondans," he remarked. "That explains the Gedemondans. Once you lay down the physical laws, you have to live by them, obey 'em implicitly. Last time, for some reason, the Gedemondans couldn't be properly matched to a world that formed in this mess. Won't be that problem with them this time, though. I've kept my word on that. They have a world that looks damned near tailor-made. We may have some problems with a few of the others, but we'll do the best we can."

Complex animal life was developing now, the ancestral prototypes of the dominant races of those worlds, flowing logically out of how Brazil and the Well programming had combined those first acids in the initial process, based on the world's material and resources, as well as the biological and climatologic conditions they had to work under. But the Well was very good at predicting how a world would develop, and it made no mistakes. The prototypical new sentient races weren't *exactly* like their counterparts on the Well World, but, overall, they were remarkably close. Natural selection was taking its toll along the main line of dominance, too, leading to the one minor branch that provided what was necessary for sentience, for dominance.

Brazil checked out the Well World. Most hexes had complied with the demands placed on them, but there were a few too disorganized or too primitive to comply, and Brazil now took steps to include them indiscriminately. When their time came, any who fell short of the minimums would find their populations halved by Well fiat.

Some of the Markovians, so long ago—Mavra was now beginning to realize just *how* long ago—had been reluctant, too.

Both of them were prepared by midnight on the fifth day. It was time, they knew, time to insert what was needed to complete the exercise, as Brazil called it.

Every few seconds, between midnight and midnight, another racial group was activated, sent through the Well Gate, out to their predestined planets. Physically, they would never arrive. They would inhabit the bodies prepared for them through billions of years of evolution. These included the millions saved from oblivion by Brazil's actions with the Markovian Gates, who would now be able to carry on their own races, rebuild and grow or die as they themselves decided by their actions.

Because there were still temporal differentials between the Well World and the universe, they were spread at different points, and some would reproduce, grow old, and die, and be thousands, perhaps millions of years different from other races placed on their worlds only minutes later, Well World time.

But for those occasional ones of races not destined for those planets who, accidentally but unavoidably, went along for the ride, there was only an instantaneous trip. But they were incongruities on a primitive world not meant for or designed for them. Most died out quickly, or became half-whispered legends among the generations that followed, but a few would hold on, manage somehow to survive, at least for a time.

At the end of the sixth day, when midnight came, the barriers to the Well Gate were removed, the Zone Gates shifted back to their normal patterns, all was as it was before.

And across the Well World there was heaved a collective sigh of relief.

Temporally, too, they were back on track. Six days had passed for them, almost fourteen for the new universe now being maintained by a repaired, reprogrammed, and revitalized Well.

Nathan Brazil sighed and settled back on his tentacles. Mavra made some final checks and then did the same. It was over.

"Until some new damn fool decides to play around with the Markovian mathematics, anyway," Brazil commented sourly. He reached out to her. "What are your plans now?"

"I need a rest, and I want to think about it," she replied.

And so on the seventh day they did nothing at all.

"Decided yet?" he asked her early in the morning of the next day.

"Yeah. I think so, anyway. Maybe it's a mistake, I don't know. But I have to play along with you, I suppose. Your way, for now. What about you?"

"Oh, this is the fun part, the interesting part," he told her. "Going down there and watching how they develop. It's only after they get there that it starts driving you crazy."

She laughed. "I think it's going to be fascinating."

"Okay," he told her. "Let's get going, then. It's precivilization time in the new world, but by the time we get through all this, it'll be the dawn of so-called civilization. Ugh. You decided pretty much what you're going to be?"

She nodded. "Pretty much the same, I think," she told him. "Matched a little closer to our exit-point culture, of course, but pretty much the same. You?"

"I'm afraid I proved to myself the last time that I couldn't be anybody but what I always was. No matter what, I always seem to come out the same, more or less."

He flickered; the grand Markovian brilliance vanished. Nathan Brazil stood there, much as he had before. There was a slight difference in his color, and his beard was fuller, but it was still undeniably Nathan Brazil.

And, oddly, some of the brilliance still showed through to her Markovian senses the more she stared at him.

She flickered, then stood there, beside him. She was dark, lean, lithe, and yet somehow exotic.

"Still the same old girl, huh?" he cracked. "Not even curious about being a man? Men have it much easier in primitive societies, you know."

She grinned, went over and kissed him, then held up her fingernails. Flexing the muscles slightly, tiny beads of some liquid oozed out from underneath the sharp points. "I can take care of myself," she told him.

He smiled warmly at her and put his arm around her, drawing her close to him. "I just bet you can," he replied sincerely.

# Naughkaland, Earth

THEY WALKED DOWN THE BEACH TOGETHER, THE MAN and the woman, naked and unashamed. Occasionally the woman, slightly smaller than he, would reach down and pick up a shell or pretty colored rock, then laugh and toss it into the ocean. It was a beautiful, brilliant warm day, the kind of day you always wished for.

"It's better than the last one," the man remarked in a tongue totally alien to this bright new world. "Warmer, lusher, richer. I think things might be different, maybe better, this time out."

She laughed, a pleasant, playful laugh. "Always the optimist. Ever the optimist." She threw her arms around him, kissing him long and passionately.

He stood there a moment, looking down into her face and her large, dark eyes. "In time, you may grow to hate me," he warned.

"Or you, me," she shot back, a playful pout on her face. "But not now. Not today. Not with the sun and the sea and the birds calling and a warm wind blowing! Definitely not now!"

The couple continued up the beach, holding hands and letting the warm ocean water wash over their feet.

She stopped, pointed down at the still wet sand. "Look!" she said, wonderingly.

"It's just a sand crab," he told her.

She turned on him, slightly angry. "Are you going to be this grumpy over the next ten thousand years?" she asked irritably.

He laughed. "Hell, no. I'll get worse. But never all the way down, honey. Never all the way down. Because, as short as I am, you made yourself shorter and lighter than I am."

He grinned, and she grinned, and he took her hand and they continued on down the beach.

It *was* a good day, he told himself, and a good place to be alive, if alive he had to be. But he was still Nathan Brazil, forty billion years out, bound for nowhere with a cargo hold empty of anything at all, even clothes on his back.

Still waiting.

Still caring.

But no longer alone.

# ABOUT THE AUTHOR

JACK L. CHALKER was born in Norfolk, Virginia, on December 17, 1944, but was raised and has spent most of his life in Baltimore, Maryland. He learned to read almost from the moment of entering school, and by working odd jobs had amassed a large book collection by the time he was in junior high school, a collection now too large for containment in his quarters. Science fiction, history, and geography all fascinated him early on, interests that continue.

Chalker joined the Washington Science Fiction Association in 1958 and began publishing an amateur SF journal, *Mirage,* in 1960. After high school he decided to be a trial lawyer, but money problems and the lack of a firm caused him to switch to teaching. He holds bachelor degrees in history and English, and an M.L.A. from the Johns Hopkins University. He taught history and geography in the Baltimore public schools between 1966 and 1978, and now makes his living as a freelance writer. Additionally, out of the amateur journals he founded a publishing house, The Mirage Press, Ltd., devoted to nonfiction and bibliographic works on science fiction and fantasy. This company has produced more than twenty books in the last nine years. His hobbies include esoteric audio, travel, working on science-fiction convention committees, and guest lecturing on SF to institutions such as the Smithsonian. He is an active conservationist and National Parks supporter, and he has an intensive love of ferryboats, with the avowed goal of riding every ferry in the world. In fact, in 1978, he was married to Eva Whitley on an ancient ferryboat in midriver. They live in the Catoctin Mountain region of western Maryland.

# The Saga of the Well World

### Jack L. Chalker's series is a futuristic phenomenon!

### Awarded the Edmond Hamilton-Leigh Brackett Memorial Award.

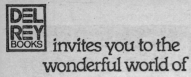